TWICE THE BULLETS, TWICE THE BEAUTIES—FOR ONE LOW PRICE!

WARM FLESH AND HOT LEAD

The man's gun was coming out of its holster, and as the Kansan leveled his weapon, he saw the barrel of the intruder's gun gleam in the moonlight. Guns roared and a series of brief, bright flashes lit the far end of the clearing.

Raquel Mirabal screamed. As Raquel reached the scene of the gunplay, she gasped when she saw the bloody wound on the side of the Kansan's head.

Davy Watson's eyes rolled up in their sockets, and the Kansan pitched backward off the rock, disappearing with a loud splash into the dark icy waters of the lake....

LONG, HARD RIDE

"Shut your trap an' raise your hands, Mister," Hartung growled.

Davy glanced at Marcus, who was in the process of raising his hands, inch by inch.

Hartung scowled at Davy. "The gold. Give it to me."

Marcus's big hand came up as Hartung spoke, and the Kansan saw that there was a derringer concealed in its palm.

"Hartung!" the Kansan whispered, causing the man to turn back to him.

Marcus's derringer flared briefly with a sharp, ringing sound as he fired point-blank into the face of John Hartung.

THE KANSAN

DOUBLE EDITION!

WARM FLESH AND HOT LEAD/
LONG, HARD RIDE

ROBERT E. MILLS

LEISURE BOOKS NEW YORK CITY

To Dave Wasson, my old pardner,
and his trailmate, Susan.

A LEISURE BOOK®

February 1993

Published by

Dorchester Publishing Co., Inc.
276 Fifth Avenue
New York, NY 10001

THE KANSAN

WARM FLESH AND HOT LEAD

PROLOGUE

Shots In The Night

The Kansan breathed a sigh of relief as the thunder of hoofbeats below began to diminish in its intensity. He looked down the slope and saw the pursuing horsemen flash by, ghostly in the cold, eerie light of the moon.

A chill wind rippled through the pines, causing them to sigh and murmur like women moaning in a dream of desire. Overhead, the moon hung low in the bat-black sky, bright and heavy as a platter of hammered Navaho silver. Far below, an owl hooted in the woods, and even farther off, somewhere deep in the belly of night, a wolf howled, its mournful wail ringing up through the tall timber.

Davy Watson hefted the big Walker Colt in his right hand. Then, with an accompanying creak of leather, he thrust the gun back into its holster.

His pursuers had gone, the Kansan told himself as he turned to the young woman who sat in front of him, sharing his saddle.

"We're safe now," he whispered, leaning forward until his lips were brushing her hair, long black hair that was even darker than the sky. "They'll be off on a wild goose chase, darlin'. Now we can git to where I mean to take us."

5

Having said this, the Kansan flicked the reins and emitted two brief, clicking sounds out of the side of his mouth. The big stallion beneath him snorted, shook its mane, and shot up the slope, making its ascent between two rows of sheltering pines.

The woman shivered in the sudden rush of wind that came down through the trees, and the Kansan drew his arms tighter around her supple body. She leaned back against Davy, murmuring his name and telling him that she was very cold.

"Well, you just snuggle up to me, darlin'," he whispered back to the young beauty, his voice husky now, roughened by the surge of desire that had broken inside him like a wave breaking over the rocks of the far-off Monterey Peninsula.

As he drew the young woman still closer to him, Davy Watson caught the scent of her hair. Its fragrance intoxicated the Kansan, purging all thoughts of danger from his mind, and replacing them with perfumed imaginings and visions of desire. He leaned forward in the saddle and pressed his lips to the side of his lovely companion's neck.

She trembled and gasped, and called him her darling in a voice that shook with passion. Then she leaned back, turning her head and offering her full lips to the Kansan. And a moment later, as the stallion made its way up through the pines, their lips met in a long and hungry kiss.

Davy emitted a moan as his darting tongue entered the young beauty's mouth. A bonfire flared in the pit of his groin, and his cock grew as hot and stiff as the barrels of a Gatling gun that had just fired off a hundred rounds.

She gasped again as he caressed her breasts, and called out to God in a voice thick with desire. Then, as she pressed herself against him, squirming as she encountered the imperious stiffness of his erect sex, the young woman in Davy Watson's arms moaned like a timber wolf.

The Kansan turned his lovely young passenger around in the saddle, held her with his left hand, and began to undress her with his right. Then he unbuckled his belt and unbuttoned his pants, after which he grasped the young woman by her midsection. His big hands nearly encircling her trim waist, Davy Watson first lifted her up, and then began to lower the young beauty onto his rigid and burning member. He entered her sopping, musky pussy, and the sudden access of heat and snugness took his breath away.

She called out to the deity once more. The barrel of her vagina gripped the Kansan snugly as she slid down the length of his pole, registering frequent and intense contractions every inch of the way. And when he clutched her firm buttocks and began to move her up and down, in gliding runs along the length of a cock whose moistened shaft now gleamed in the moonlight, the young woman's dark hair lashed from side to side as she shook her head to the cadence of her mounting passion and she cried out into the night, expressing her delight in disconnected phrases.

Up and down Davy Watson stroked, faster and faster, while his stallion continued on its wild course up through the mountain pines, its motion becoming the motion of the lovers. Up and down he stroked, guiding her snug, sweet pussy over his throbbing rod, generating a heat in his midsection which the Kansan imagined capable of igniting the leather of his saddle, sending it up in flames, to flare in the blackness like a torch at a tent meeting.

"Ooooh," Davy murmured, his eyes rolling up in his head as he felt a geyser about to erupt in the pit of his groin. The young beauty moaned back at him and rubbed herself against the Kansan, her sopping, clutching sex plastered against his groin, her straight, jet-black thatch mingling with his dark blond curls.

His pelvis began to jerk as he came, pumping volleys of jism into her.

She, in her turn, bucked wildly, dug her fingers into his hair, threw back her head and gasped as if she were expiring. And when she was finally still, the orgasmic convulsions having subsided, her mouth hung open and her eyes were shut; and her lips, the Kansan discovered, went suddenly cold, as cold as if she had been sucking on a piece of ice. The young woman sighed, shuddered reflexively, and then collapsed in his arms.

A few minutes later, the stallion reached level ground, and Davy Watson tightened his grip on the reins and slowed his mount to a walk. The big horse was breathing heavily, and it blew gusts of air through its nostrils, sending thick jets of vapor out into the chill night.

Still sighing and shuddering, still fused together at the groin, their handsome young bodies silvered by the moonlight, the lovers sat together in the saddle. The stallion snorted and whinnied twice as the Kansan pulled on the reins and drew it to a halt. After long moments spend in nuzzling, caressing, and kissing, the lovers parted, dressed, and dismounted by the shore of a broad mountain lake. There they refreshed themselves, and then the Kansan tended to his lathered stallion.

For over an hour they sat by the edge of the mountain lake, cradled in each other's arms. A rustling in the bushes at the far end of the clearing in which they sat finally interrupted their embrace. Davy gestured for silence. He eased his big Walker Colt out of its holster as he rose to his feet. Then, as he made his way to the far end of the clearing, the Kansan stopped for an instant to turn and gaze at the dark-eyed young beauty who sat waiting for him by the water's edge.

Moving ahead once more, the Kansan held his Colt lightly and wore a smile on his face, for he was sure that the newcomer was none other than his Pawnee blood-brother, who had decoyed his pursuers and arranged to meet Davy by the mountain lake.

He made out a shadowy figure in the moonlight, just emerging from a clump of pines. . . . His blood ran cold when he saw that it was not Soaring Hawk.

The man's gun was coming out of its holster, and as the Kansan leveled his own weapon, he saw the barrel of the intruder's gun gleam in the moonlight. Emitting a grunt of surprise, Davy Watson tightened his finger on the trigger of the Colt.

Blam! Bam! Blam! Bambam!

Guns roared and a series of brief, bright flashes lit the far end of the clearing. Raquel Mirabal screamed as she rose to her feet. Both men fell to the ground. As Raquel reached the scene of the

9

gunplay, she gasped when she saw the bloody wound on the left side of the Kansan's head.

Davy Watson's eyes rolled up in their sockets, and he gave out with a long, plaintive sigh as he rolled down over a big rock. The Walker Colt dropped from his hand, and the Kansan pitched backward off the rock, disappearing with a loud splash into the dark icy waters of the lake.

At the same time that the Kansan disappeared beneath the surface of the water, Bart Braden lurched dizzily to his feet. Clutching the bloody wound in his left shoulder, the Texas ramrod advanced upon a horrified Raquel Mirabal.

"I come fer ya, honey," the big Texan told Don Solomon Mirabal's daughter, smiling like a wolf catching sight of a solitary lamb.

1

The Man Who Shot Davy Watson

The man who shot Davy Watson and then carried off Raquel Mirabal, as she lay in a dead faint beside the body of the young man who had been her very first lover only an hour before, rode south out of Lincoln County, and away from the bloody range war he had precipitated in order that he might possess the beautiful *chicana*, heading back to the relative safety and security of Texas, his home state.

Bart Braden had what he came for, and he had gotten it by gambling everything on one reckless throw of the dice, by rolling a natural seven which cleared the board and gave the Texas ramrod his heart's desire. The stakes in the New Mexican adventure had been very high, and the other players in the deadly game were not so fortunate as he.

Don Solomon Mirabal, Raquel's father, and the most powerful *patrón* among the New Mexico sheepmen, had lost his favorite child, and the lives of many of his devoted *partidarios*, as a consequence of the range war which had been sparked by the invasion of the hated *tejanos*, the hereditary enemies of the New Mexicans.

Bill Fanshaw had lost big, too. The cattle baron,

11

whose empire rivalled those of John Chisum and Charlie Goodnight, had been hoodwinked by Bart Braden into invading the pasturelands of Don Solomon Mirabal when the ramrod had deceived him by witholding word of a proposed settlement with the sheepmen of the New Mexico Territory.

In order to get the jump on his rivals, the Texas cattle baron had sent Braden, his foreman and ramrod, to negotiate the purchase of a strip of grazing land at the edge of the don's territory. This move would have then enabled Fanshaw to drive his Longhorn herds due north, and reach the railheads there long before any of his competitors.

At first the outraged New Mexicans bridled at this, at the thought of giving the hated *tejano* enemy a foothold in the pasturelands which their fathers had fought and died to possess. But compromise eventually prevailed. Profit was the god of the *tejanos*, the sheepmen reasoned, and this singular concession would make Bill Fanshaw their loyal ally, and thus pit his interests against those of his fellow cattle barons. The first loyalty of Fanshaw and his fellow Texans was to the *Yanqui* greenback, and not to each other.

Instead of the luxurious strip the cattle baron had originally requested, the sheepmen offered him one far to the west. . .where the Texans would have to contend with the mountains on one side and the Apaches on the other.

This compromise would be no great loss to the sheepmen, and it shifted to the Texans the problem of dealing with the fierce and marauding Jicarilla and Mimbreño Apache bands. Instead of being truly a concession, this sage move would actually strengthen the dons' control of their lands, which were in constant danger of *tejano* encroachment from the south. Bill Fanshaw, from his southern headquarters in the new settlement of Roswell, would guarantee the security of his new allies' southernmost borders; the other Texan cattle barons were not likely to risk a direct confrontation with a man who had no peers but the giants of the southwestern cattle industry.

Knowing that Fanshaw would still agree to this modification of his offer, preferring such a concession to riskier long-range objectives which might well only be obtained at the cost of a bloody and protracted range war, the New Mexican *ricos* sent as their emissary to the cattle baron none other than Davy Watson. The Kansan and Soaring Hawk, his Pawnee blood-brother, had earlier rescued some sheepherders from lynching by a number of rampaging Texans, and were currently enjoying the gratitude and hospitality of Don Solomon Mirabal.

It was during this time that the Kansan had met the eighteen-year-old Raquel, the don's youngest daughter, a hot-blooded but virginal young beauty on the threshold of womanhood. And Bart Braden had been there, too, having come during the fiesta of *La Conquistadora* to deliver the cattle baron's offer.

It was at that time the Texas ramrod became infatuated with the dark and lovely *chicana*. But Raquel Mirabal's attentions were focussed in the direction of the Kansan, whose square-jawed, blond and blue-eyed good looks, and tales of his perilous and colorful escapades had totally captivated her. But Bart Braden was not in the least dissuaded by the turn of events; he was a man in the grip of an obsession, and had vowed not to rest until the don's young daughter was his.

And possess her he did—at a cost that littered the pasturelands and ajoining *Llano Estacado* with the bodies of men and animals, sheep and cattle, Indians, *chicanos* and whites. Bart Braden had summoned the Angel of Death to New Mexico, and that dark figure swept in on horseback, armed with a Winchester rifle and a Colt revolver.

The New Mexicans had dispatched a *gringo* to deal with *gringos*—but he was one whom they had learned to trust; and if Davy Watson and his companions had only reached Bill Fanshaw, the Angel of Death would not have scoured the New Mexican lands. But the Kansan was intercepted by Braden, who, once he had learned of Davy's mission, clubbed the Kansan unconscious with his gunbutt, took him prisoner, and kept him hidden from Bill Fanshaw.

The cattle baron, deceived by his ramrod into believing that his offer had been rejected out-of-hand, had then led his men on a sweep into the lands of Don Solomon Mirabal. He was determined to force a showdown with the *patrón*, and take as his booty a generous piece of the man's easternmost grazing lands, which would then give him uncontested access to the railheads to the north, thus enabling Fanshaw to market his cattle weeks ahead of his rivals' herds in the eager and clamoring markets of the East.

Bart Braden had come across Davy Watson and his three companions—Soaring Hawk and two of the sons of Don Solomon Mirabal—as they were being subjected to an ordeal by fire in the camp of Pahanca, a Comanche chief. The Comanches had recently run off a great number of Fanshaw cattle, and had traded them off to a pair of *Comancheros*, with whom the Kansan and his companions had unwittingly been traveling.

In the middle of the night, Davy and his friends found themselves encircled by a band of ferocious Comanches. The *Comancheros* then dispensed liquor and firearms to the Indian rustlers, taking the Texas cattle in return and riding off toward the Arizona border. The Kansan and his friends were thus abruptly abandoned by their erstwhile traveling companions and left to the tender mercies of the whooping and screaming Comanches, who became drunker and more savage with every passing minute.

Only a surprise attack by the Texans saved Davy and his companions from being burnt alive in the bonfire around which the wild, drunken Comanches danced. The Texans, having no sympathy for cattle rustlers of any stripe, slaughtered the Indians to a man. After that, having found out about Davy's mission, Braden knocked the Kansan unconscious and ordered him taken back to Fanshaw's headquarters in Roswell—away from the cattle baron, who was at that very moment riding north at the head of a band of armed men to join his ramrod.

Bart Braden had unleashed the whirlwind, and the Texan gave little thought to the consequences of his reckless act. His only concern was with the taking of Raquel Mirabal. And so, armed to the

15

teeth and spoiling for a fight, the Texans thundered off, heading for the great *hacienda* of Don Solomon Mirabal.

Sweeping all before them, Fanshaw's riders traveled over the don's lands with all the fury of a windswept prairie fire. The sheepmen had been caught unawares, and before long the *tejano* enemy had the don's *hacienda* itself under siege.

Under normal conditions the sheepmen could have held out indefinitely. But a new factor had been introduced into the deadly equation: Braden had brought with him a Conestoga wagon filled with dynamite, the new explosive perfected only a few years before by the Swedish chemist Alfred Nobel.

Vowing to destroying the *hacienda* piecemeal, Braden had demonstrated the awesome power of the new explosive and given Don Solomon a last chance to capitulate.

Not while he lived, the stubborn old New Mexican patriarch told the Texans. *On your head be it*, was the judgment of Bill Fanshaw. *But at least evacuate your women and children from the hacienda*, he told the don, not wishing to answer for the blood of innocents.

Mirabal agreed to this, and in a matter of moments the women and children filed out of the embattled building. Here Bart Braden saw his chance, and had Raquel Mirabal sequestered and put under the watchful eye of one of his most trusted hands. The ramrod then returned to Fanshaw's side, where he had been conducting the siege.

The cattle baron knew nothing of his foreman's

16

machinations, and had been shaken to the core by the revelation of the new explosive's incredible power and destructive potential. It was with a heavy heart that he gave Braden permission to resume the storming of the Mirabal *hacienda*.

Great sections of the *hacienda's* stucco walls were blown away, and its red brick roof tiles were sent high into the air, reduced to smithereens as they shot out of sight. And moments later, when the echoes of the earthquake-roar that was the dynamite blast had subsided, the plaza in front of the Mirabal *hacienda* was filled with a ghastly pattering, the thudding sounds of the explosion's debris coming to earth in a bloodchilling rain.

"Give up, Don Solomon!" Bill Fanshaw cried hoarsely, *"For you have no other chance to remain alive!"*

"Even though I die, my family's honor remains alive!" was the essence of what the proud *hidalgo* shot back at the cattle baron.

"There's nothin' fer it but to blow the old fool to Kingdom Come," Fanshaw said with a sad expression and a shake of his leonine head, as he gave Bart Braden permission to resume the siege.

The end was almost at hand, and with it would come the fruition of the ramrod's plans. Once the *hacienda* had been blown apart and the hand-to-hand fighting had begun, he would take Raquel Mirabal and ride off with her, turning his back forever upon his fellow Texans and Bill Fanshaw, the one man whom he had always respected.

That was what Bart Braden had intended to do, but Fortune, which up to that time had been in league with the ramrod, was to have it otherwise.

17

A series of explosions suddenly wrought havoc in the ranks of the Texans, causing great dismay and disorder among them, as well as eliciting cheers from the desperate defenders of the Mirabal *hacienda*. About to depart with Raquel, the ramrod was forced to leave her and hasten to rally the Texans.

The confusion had been caused by none other than Davy Watson and his three companions, who had managed to escape from Roswell and streak northward in hopes of aiding the New Mexicans and saving Raquel Mirabal from Bart Braden. Davy had learned of this from Bill Fanshaw's daughter, who set him free to punish Bart Braden.

Wreaking havoc among the Texans, the Kansan and his Pawnee blood-brother were able to rescue Raquel Mirabal and ride off with her before the invaders had regained the upper hand in the battle.

The cowboys suddenly found themselves leaderless as they came up the dynamited corpse of Bill Fanshaw, and word soon spread that Bart Braden lay buried beneath a fallen wall. And indeed, the ramrod was nowhere to be seen. A short time after that, they were driven from the *hacienda* and sent in full flight back to Roswell, as reinforcements reached the Mirabal spread.

Davy and Soaring Hawk had streaked off into the night, to the foothills in the west. Three Texans streaked after them in hot pursuit, and were decoyed by the wily Pawnee.

Alone with the Latin beauty for the first time, the Kansan made love to her on horseback, after the fashion of the Huns, Cossacks and Comanches. They dismounted to rest by a lake in the high pines,

Raquel Mirabal gazing at the handsome young man beside her with wide, adoring eyes.

Later that night, Davy heard a crackling in the underbrush and went to investigate, certain that it was Soaring Hawk, who was to meet him at the mountain lake. But it was not the Pawnee whom he encountered.

The men fired simultaneously, and both took a bullet. Raquel Mirabal screamed as the Kansan's body rolled down the slope before her and disappeared into the dark, chill waters of the lake. Smiling as he clutched his wounded shoulder, Bart Braden came after Raquel Mirabal.

Davy Watson had luck on his side, and when Soaring Hawk had doubled back to the mountain lake, having eluded his pursuers, the Pawnee brave found the Kansan clinging to some bushes by the edge of the water.

Braden's bullet had creased the side of Davy's skull, and its impact had caused him to lose consciousness. In the darkness of the copse of pines where the sudden shootout had occurred, the Texas ramrod, taking Davy Watson's bullet at the same time that he gunned down the Kansan, left his enemy for dead as he watched the latter's body roll down the grassy slope and pitch into the still, icy waters of the lake.

Soaring Hawk pulled his blood-brother out of the water and tended to him. Apart from a wound that would heal to a livid scar at his hairline, over his left temple, and a headache that he would wake up with for the next week, Davy Watson was unharmed. But his pride had been hurt, and the Kansan vowed not to rest until he had avenged himself upon Bart Braden and rescued Raquel Mirabal.

"Guess we'll jus' take us a l'il ride down Texas-way," he muttered darkly, staring toward the south with flinty eyes and a hard, cold smile.

His face a stoic mask, Soaring Hawk nodded at this. The Pawnee greatly desired to return to his people, as they hunted the ever-dwindling buffalo herds on the prairies of western Kansas and eastern Colorado, but he was by now resigned to the quirks of fate which had so far prevented the two men from returning to their homes and loved ones. The Plains Indian acknowledged the power of destiny in men's affairs, and was duly resigned to the frequent interruptions along the trail that led back to home.

Despite the fact that Bart Braden did not expect anyone to be coming after him so soon, least of all the man he had left for dead, and despite the fact that the Texan's trail was still warm, Davy Watson was not ready to streak off in hot pursuit of Raquel Mirabal's abductor.

The Kansan felt that it was necessary to return to the Mirabal *hacienda*, and inform Raquel's father of what had transpired. Don Solomon had been his host, and Davy felt compelled to reward the sheep-man's kindness and generosity by explaining to the *patrón* that his favorite daughter was alive and well, despite having fallen prey to Bart Braden, the *tejano* enemy.

Upon their return to the Mirabal spread, the blood-brothers saw to their relief that the siege had been lifted, and that the invading Texans, rendered leaderless by the death of Bill Fanshaw and the defection of the obsessed Bart Braden, had been sent flying back to the south in defeat.

Davy was not worried about losing Braden's trail because the circumstance of an *Anglo* and a *Chicana* traveling alone in Texas was rare in the extreme. As long as Braden kept Raquel with him, the tracking of the ramrod would present no great problem for the trail-savvy Kansan and his Pawnee blood-brother.

Upon hearing of Raquel's abduction, the New Mexicans were furious. They volunteered—almost to a man—to ride after Bart Braden. But no, the don told them as he shook his head, a sad and tired smile upon his lips, this was not possible. People of Mexican blood were regarded as second-class citizens in the state of Texas, and a large band of heavily armed Mexican-Americans thundering across the border would be regarded as tantamount to an act of war. The Texans had long memories, and they still harbored hard feelings regarding their treatment in the days prior to the Mexican War. Any force of *chicanos* entering the Lone Star state would cause the *tejanos* to rise up in strength and annihilate it. No, the rescue of Raquel Mirabal by her own people was, for the present, at least, an impossibility.

When Davy Watson informed his listeners that he and Soaring Hawk were off after Bart Braden, the New Mexicans heaved a collective sigh of relief. Don Solomon and his three sons held a high opinion of the valor of the Kansan and *El Indio* (as they called Soaring Hawk), and were profuse in the expression of their gratitude.

The next morning, having thoroughly rested their horses and been generously provisioned, Davy Watson and Soaring Hawk rode off as the dawn began to tinge the eastern sky of the New Mexico Territory with its first, tentative washes of purple, violet and pink. The two men rode off to the south, where the dark sky had only begun to lighten, toward the wild and sprawling land known as the state of Texas.

In 1870, the geography of Western Texas was divided into two sections—the settled territory between the Colorado and the Nueces, and the open, barren wastes that bordered the Rio Grande.

The fertile area, whose flat coastal prairies extended inland for some forty miles, began to rise in gentle swells at that point, running on to the foothills of the Guadalupe range, 150 miles from the Gulf of Mexico.

Rich and broad pastures, characterized by thick, waving grasses, were the predominant feature of this terrain, noted for its abundant grazing in both winter and summer. This was the Texas cattle country; the land that first nurtured the herds which had provided a large portion of the nation's supply of beef after the Civil War.

Advancing westward across the state, the soil grew steadily in fertility, being lavishly distributed in this part of Texas as a black calcareous loam. And where the streams in the other parts of the Lone Star State tended to flow thick and muddy, the waters in Western Texas were as clear as the eye of a sober and upright man. The land was, as many visitors had remarked, as beautiful and luxuriant as any region in the world, bar none.

There were drawbacks, however, which held West Texas back and caused it to fall somewhat short of being a veritable paradise on earth. A relative scarcity of timber inhibited building and fencing, while the dry seasons wrought havoc with the abundant crops; and Indian raids upon the frontier still made settlement in that area a somewhat risky business. In addition to this, counterbalancing the abundant and near-constant summer breeze from the gulf were the northers—furious winter winds that shot down from the upland plains, capable of ravaging great stretches of land in a very short time.

Another problem was that of the Mexicans in the region, of whom there were between twenty and thirty thousand. Relations between the "greasers" and the *gringos* had rarely been amicable, and many Texans of both stripes remembered the vicious fighting prior to and during the Mexican War. The wounds of those years of conflict were far from healed.

The Texans were notorious for their prejudice against non-whites in general, and Mexicans in particular. After the war, those Mexicans who had property and wealth withdrew to Old Mexico, leaving their less fortunate fellows to the mercies of the hated *tejanos*.

They were regarded by the Texans as only a step above Negroes on the social ladder, and were used largely as a supply of cheap labor in the areas of argriculture and stock-raising. Even though, in theory, the Mexican-Americans were considered citizens of Texas, with suffrage equal to that of the whites, in reality they were largely denied access to the state's political machinery.

Another group to figure largely in the way of life of the region were the German immigrants, of whom there were between thirty and forty thousand at the time. In several counties, such as Fayette, Caldwell and Travis, as well as the city of San Antonio, the Germans numbered about one-third of the total population. In Calhoun, Bastrop and Bexar (excluding the aforementioned San Antonio), they constituted one-half of the population. And in Comal, Gillespie and Medina counties, nearly all the inhabitants were German. This predominance had begun to wane as the seventies began, but at the time, the Germans were still a major influence in Western Texas.

German associations required the immigrants to come to these shores in possession of a certain amount of capital ($120 for single men and $240 for married men), thereby excluding a pauper class. The first waves consisted largely of peasants and mechanics, and those who had been able to escape German justice due to their emigration. The hardy, energetic and hard-working Germans adapted well to frontier conditions, and were soon acknowledged by the American residents of West Texas as their pioneering equals.

After the European revolutions of 1848, many farmers and persons of moderate means came to the New World, seeking a better future. Many cultivated men of liberal tendencies came to the American shores then, in hopes of creating a more tolerant society than the repressive and reactionary feudal Europe they had fled.

These new immigrants brought little capital with them and, following the German tendency to invest their money in land, were extremely limited in funds as they began their residence in the new country. But to offset this material lack, the new Germans brought with them rich and diverse intellectual lives and many refinements of taste: the *kultur* of Germany had taken root in the soil of western Texas.

The lifestyle of these new and liberal settlers was often bizarre and incongruous, as European refinement contrasted sharply with their rough backwoods life. As one American author had reported in 1860:

"You are welcomed by a figure in a blue flannel shirt and pendant beard, quoting Tacitus, having in one hand a long pipe, in the other a butcher's knife; Madonnas upon log-walls; coffee in tin cups upon Dresden saucers; barrels for seats, to hear a Beethoven's symphony on the grand piano; 'My wife made these pantaloons, and my stockings grew in the field yonder'; a fowling-piece that cost $300, and a saddle that cost $5; a book-case half-filled with classics, half with sweet potatoes.

"But, as lands are subdued, and capital is amassed, these inconveniences will disappear, and pass in amusing traditions, while the sterling education and high-toned character of the fathers will be unconsciously transmitted to the social benefit of the coming generation.

"The virtues I have ascribed to them as a class are not, however, without the relief of faults, the most prominent among which are a free-thinking and a devotion to reason, carried in their turn, to the verge of bigotry, and expanded to a certain rude licence of manners and habits, consonant with their wild prairies, but hardly with the fitness of things, and, what in practical matters is even worse error, an insane mutual jealousy, and petty bickering that prevents all prolonged and effective còoperation—an old German ail, which the Atlantic has not sufficed to cleanse.''

Germans, Mexicans, Indians pillaging the frontier, and the tetchy-proud, whang leather-tough Texans: such was the volatile human composition of the wild and open land through which Bart Braden rode, taking with him his captive, the dark-haired, sloe-eyed young daughter of the New Mexican *rico*, Don Solomon Mirabal.

Down from the lawless New Mexico Territory the Texas ramrod had ridden, the protesting Raquel Mirabal in tow, her wrists bound before her as she sat in her saddle; down through the Guadalupe Mountains, and into the Lone Star State, skirting its highest point, Guadalupe Peak, en route.

Riding east of the Delaware Mountains, Braden traversed Culberson County and headed south into the Jeff Davis mountain range. Thence eastward, along the course of the Pecos River, through cow-towns like Royalty and Barstow, through river-towns such as Grandfalls and Girvin.

Southward over the Stockton Plateau, and then to the east, over the great open expanse that is the

Edwards Plateau. Farther east, and then southeast, through Telegraph, Medina and Bandera, and into Bexar County, stopping at last in the city of San Antonio.

Riding along an old road that followed a creek bottom, dotted with houses which stood in the shade of live-oaks, trees extremely rare to these parts, Braden and Raquel Mirabal rode the last miles to San Antonio.

In the afternoon the two rode through the clean and quiet streets of one of the small German towns. Braden reined in the horses by the gate of a little cottage whose windows and shutters were edged with a white trim. From within the cottage there came the sounds of people singing. Several voices could be heard, both male and female, sustaining the German song's parts with sweet and well-trained voices.

"Damn, but that there's a purty air," Braden drawled softly, turning his face toward Raquel Mirabal, who sat beside him, her hands no longer bound.

For an instant the beautiful young *chicana's* expression softened, and she nodded slowly. Her eyes lowered, not meeting the bold and intense look of the Texan.

A slight smile came to Braden's lips, only to disappear an instant later. It was the first time that Raquel had responded to him with anything less than anger and contempt.

He sat unmoving in his saddle, staring at her, his strong features set in a mask of impassivity, which was in direct contrast to his searching and hungry eyes. Braden said nothing else as the music soared

27

to a crescendo, the male and female voices rising in heartbreakingly beautiful unison. Raquel's acknowledgement of his statement was enough for him. He regarded it as progress in his strange courtship of Don Solomon's daughter. He sat looking at her, and was content, having absolutely no desire to press his luck. It was progress enough.

At this time, coming up the quiet street, Braden saw a tame doe, wearing a band on its neck to identify it for hunters. It was delicate and graceful, and so tame that it passed within two feet of Raquel's horse. And when she gently leaned over and reached down her hand, the doe paused to lick it. A moment later the young deer left, just as the song was concluding.

"Mebbe we jus' might mosey back hereabouts, one of these days," Bart Braden said under his breath as he flicked his reins, taking one last look at Raquel Mirabal.

Her long black hair glowed softly in the late afternoon light, and her beautiful face reminded the Texan of a carved angel he had once seen in an old Spanish mission on the outskirts of the border town of Del Rio.

Away from the river, and onto the great plain at whose edge San Antonio lies, Braden and Raquel rode. To the west, gentle slopes descended toward the plain; and past that, looking north, the riders saw the gradual rise of land which led to the mountain country.

A thin edging of trees around the city's river provided the only relief on the broad, surrounding landscape of limitless grass and thorny bushes. Mesquite, that short, thin, prickly relative of the locust tree, dotted the prairie, one of the most familiar and ubiquitous elements in the geography of Western Texas. Often the mesquite mixed with other prickly shrubs, such as chapparal, and formed an impenetrable barrier to overland travel for great stretches of ground.

Coming over the western prairie, Braden and Raquel saw the city of San Antonio in the distance, its domes and clustered white houses gleaming gently in the first rays of the sunset. Both of them gazed with interest upon the city's picturesque jumble of buildings, its odd and antiquated foreign aspect.

It had a solemn, Latin air about it, one which contrasted strangely with the rattling life of the Anglos, whose commerce enlivened San Antonio's dusty streets. The streets themselves were crowded with strolling Mexicans, as well as a fair proportion of Germans and Texans.

The display of nationalities was most evident in the shape and style of San Antonio's houses. The American dwellings were set back from the street, and characterized by three-story brick structures, galleries and jalousies, and gardens whose picket fences bordered the walks of the houses.

Trimmer and less four-square were the houses of the Germans, rising gracefully above the old streets, their pink window-blinds contributing a vibrant touch of color to the scene.

All low, and made of adobe or stone, the Mexican dwellings were colored by a wash of either white or blue, and had their single story trimmed sharply by a flat roof.

The eastern entrance to the city had as its most

outstanding feature the square of the Alamo, that bloody landmark in the violent history of Texas. Windowless cabins of mud-daubed stakes, roofed with *tula*, the abundant river grass, were prominent in the area, as were houses of gray, unburnt adobe, whose rooves were better-thatched, and at whose doors there lounged groups of brown-skinned Mexicans.

Upon the far side of the San Antonio river lay the principal part of San Antonio. The river, never varying in height or temperature, flowed beneath the low bridge, sparkling with its limpid and crystalline beauty. It had a rich blue color, and flowed silently and swiftly over a bottom covered with pebbles, and between banks that grew thick with reeds. The bridge and the river combined there to form a place of great beauty and serenity.

The plaza was a strange and anachronous composite. Old and embattled walls, sturdy and Spanish, alternated with American hotels and glass-fronted stores; and from the dome of the stuccoed and forbidding old Spanish cathedral, the call to vespers rang out jaggedly from a cracked bronze bell whose jarring music expressed the plaza's dissonant theme of clashing cultures.

Not far outside the city, along the river, the old Spanish missions were to be found. Ponderous and overbearing, but possessing at the same time a rude grandeur, the missions were enduring monuments to the bravery and ardor of the Spanish *padres* who were among the first Europeans to penetrate the wild and savage country. Foremost among these missions in earliest times had been the Alamo, now a hacked and battered monument to Texan courage.

Aqueducts extended around the city for miles in all directions, revealing to the student of cultures that a larger population had existed when the place was under the Mexican flag. Many of these *acequias* came to be abandoned, but many were still in use, watering extensive garden patches when Bart Braden and Raquel Mirabal rode into San Antonio.

As they made their way into the heart of town, Braden noticed the plump and black-eyed young Mexican girls, conversing animatedly as they strolled the streets that led to the city's main plaza, followed by the erect and dignified figures of the dark and wrinkled matrons who served as their *duennas*.

Mexican men in large sombreros and gaily embroidered short jackets strolled around the plaza, or lounged against brick or adobe walls, smoking cigarillos, singing in Spanish to the music of guitars and laughing raucously from time to time.

Distinct from the Mexicans were the taller Texans, who strolled the plaza with long, loping strides, smoking cigarettes rolled from wheatstraw or chewing tobacco and letting fly great brown gobbets of tobacco juice.

Felt and ten-gallon hats were worn by the *tejanos,* with an occasional Stetson crowning the head of some of the more prosperous-looking citizens. Boot leather creaked and spurs jingled as the Texans exchanged salty observations in their slow drawls, slapping their pants or the leather holsters on their belts as they broke out into loud, sudden guffaws.

Also noticeable in the plaza were the bearded Germans, conspicuous by their starched collars, polished boots and neat suits. Erect and precise, they strolled around as if on a military tour of inspection, greeting one another with elaborate politeness, often doffing their bowlers, derbies and caps as they stopped to click their heels together and bow.

On the plaza, and on the streets leading into it, many of the older Mexican buildings had been remodeled and brought "up-to-date," and were now serving as drinking places, run after the example of New Orleans saloons, the signs on their gaudy fronts simply proclaiming "Exchange."

Outside these saloons and honkytonks the customers loitered, either roughly or exquisitely attired, their dress proclaiming the tone of the establishment before which they stood.

The presence of so many Mexican-Americans made Bart Braden edgy as he rode beside the young *chicana* whom he had abducted from her father's *hacienda*, and the ramrod's right hand was never far from the big Colt .45 that sat loosely in its weathered holster.

All it would take, he reckoned, was one appeal from Raquel Mirabal, one cry of anguish and alarm, followed by the declaration that the *gringo* at her side had recently stolen her away from her people in the New Mexico Territory.

As a number of the Mexicans whom they passed were wearing sidearms, there was a strong probability that Raquel's appeal would not go unheeded. But Raquel did not cry out. Biding her time, she waited for the chance to escape from the infatuated ramrod without being responsible for any further bloodshed, for the sight of the Kansan's shooting had made a deep impression upon the eighteen-year-old girl.

Another reason for her silence was that she had grudgingly begun to respect Bart Braden. The Texan had never forced himself upon her, always treating Raquel with the utmost respect and *cortesia*, almost as if he were a Mexican himself. And formidable as the agile, powerful cowboy was, he would not permit any man to behave toward her with less than total politeness and decorum.

Having recovered from the initial shock of her abduction, the strong-willed and resilient young daughter of Don Solomon Mirabal had determined to avenge herself upon Bart Braden. It would be necessary to lull him into a false sense of confidence first, so she had decided to bide her time. But the Texan would get what was coming to him, she vowed to herself, as sure as mesquite grows in West Texas.

Braden's horse drew to a halt in the street, facing a large and noisy emporium, outside of which were clustered a number of rough-looking types. Raquel's horse stopped beside the Texan's as Braden swung a leg over his saddle horn and leaped to the ground with a display of easy agility. He was beside Raquel's horse a moment later, and reached up to help her out of the saddle.

"Le's go inside, honey," he said softly as his big hands went around her trim waist. Saying nothing, Raquel Mirabal looked past the Texas ramrod as he gently lowered her to the ground.

"By gum, if it ain't ol' Bart Braden, hisself!" a gruff voice called out from behind Braden, just as the latter had put the young *chicana* down. Quick as lightning, the ramrod spun around, his hand poised over his holstered Colt.

A huge bearded man, with eyes as beady and mean as those of a polecat, smiled at Braden, revealing a mouthful of snaggle teeth whose appearance and spacing brought to mind a weathered picket fence. He wore a dusty old slouch hat, a heavy jacket of the type associated with stagecoach drivers and muleskinners, baggy woolen trousers, and thick, low-heeled miners boots which were caked with a heavy coating of mud.

"By God, Bart, don't hoist that piece up at me," the man went on, still smiling his gap-toothed smile, his hot, glittering little eyes now traveling over Raquel Mirabal's shapely form. "It's me, Ford Sweinhardt. Don't you remember me, Bart?" the big bearded man asked in an oily, wheedling voice. "I was with ya when you done rid herd on Jasper Lyons' Longhorns, up Pecos way."

Braden's eyes narrowed as he stared at the man.

" 'Member the time we done rid down into Mexico to git ol' Jasper's cattle back? Well, I'll say we 'bout kicked us some ass that day—'member, Bart? Done tore up them greasers, brought back the herd, an' more'n a hundred Spanish-speakin' cows to boot! 'Twas the next best thing to the Mexican War."

For an instant, Braden's eyes darted nervously over to Raquel Mirabal, who was at his side, taking

34

in the spectacle of the big, bearded man, as were all the men around him. Then, as the ramrod's eyes lit on the speaker once more, a razor's edge smile came to his thin lips.

" 'Member now, Bart?" the man asked eagerly, his gruff voice squeaking as it rose to a higher register.

Braden nodded slowly, his eyes now colder than a norther, the cold sudden wind which sweeps across the upland prairies to the north in the winter months.

"Yeah, I remember you, Sweinhardt," the ramrod said in a voice that expressed absolutely no emotion.

"What brings ya here'bouts, Bart?" the man persisted, not in the least discouraged by Braden's unenthusiastic greeting.

"I come to see Ollie Entwhistle," the ramrod muttered, holding out his arm for Raquel Mirabal to take.

"Well, he's still goin' strong. You can bet yer boots on that. Still serves the biggest steak an' the baddest whiskey in West Texas."

Braden nodded as he and Raquel began to make their way through the crowd of rough men, all of whom cast long and lingering looks at the lovely young *chicana*, once she had walked past them.

"It's real good to see you agin, Bart," the big bearded man said unctuously.

Braden did not respond to this. He thrust open the swinging door before him and nodded to Raquel, his smile softening as he met her eyes.

Music issued from within the honkytonk, along with the sour reek of stale beer and the sharp smell of spilled whiskey on sawdust. A battered old upright piano, stirdent and jangling as its hammers beat out an off-key tune with relentless authority, cut through the babel of the crowd with the violence of a rusty cleaver smashing through beef bones.

"*O, way down yonder in the land of cotton,*" the piano player sang in a raw baritone voice that suitably complemented his instrument, "*old times there are not forgotten. Look away, look away, look a-wa-aaay, Dixieland.*"

A chorus of Rebel yells rose throughout the bar, as a number of former Confederates lifted high their glasses in drunken and sentimental tribute to the Old South, whose memory was still cherished in many parts of the American Southwest.

"Who was that *hombre*?" someone asked outside, after Bart Braden had escorted Raquel Mirabal into Oliver Entwhistle's honkytonk.

"Got the look of a man what means business, I'll say that for him," a man with a high-pitched voice called.

"Oh, that he does," the big bearded man named Sweinhardt growled. "Hardest man I ever did see. Don't fear nothin' that walks, flies or swims. An' he'd draw on the devil hisself, if'n he had a mind to." He nodded and smiled a wry, admiring smile. "Ol' Bart Braden's quick as a panther an' hard as Pittsburgh steel. An' the best damn ramrod an' foreman anybody ever done seen."

" 'Zat so?" remarked a fat, balding man in a checkered flannel shirt, who stood beside Sweinhardt.

"You ain't jus' whistlin' *Dixie*, boy," Sweinhardt told the man. "I done worked with him, up Pecos way, fer over two year." He shook his head. "Most unstoppable sum' bitch I ever did see. Ain't nobody yet ever got on his bad side an' lived to tell about it."

"Who's the l'il *tamale* he brung with him?" someone else asked.

"Dunno," grunted Sweinhardt. "But she's a hot-lookin' piece, ain't she?"

"I'll say she is, bedad!" piped an old man with a stubbly white beard.

"That's the one good thing you can say fer them greasers," Sweinhardt told the men gathered around him, nodding solemnly as he did. "They sure got 'em a passel of fine-lookin' women. I will say that fer 'em."

"Then why's the men so damn ugly?" someone called out in a whiskey tenor.

"All foreigners is ugly," Sweinhardt replied, settling the matter. "Leastwise, the menfolks is."

"Where's Ollie Entwhistle?" Bart Braden called out to the nearest of the four bartenders who worked the long bar that occupied almost the entire left wall of the rectangular room.

"Back in his office, Bart," the man replied, breaking into a smile as he recognized the ramrod.

Braden nodded. "Thanks, Kingston," he said. "Donald McKillop still workin' here?"

The bartender shook his head as he wiped his hands on his stained apron. "Nope. Had hisself a li'l disagreement with ol' Charlie Shuttinger. Charlie pulled a knife on him once't—right here at the bar, an' ol' Donald winged him with that teensie l'il Smith an' Wesson .22 he allus wore

37

tucked in his vest."

Braden smiled at this. "I told him he couldn't bring down nothin' bigger'n a Rio Grande mosquito with that ol' pop-gun," he drawled.

"Well, he pegged Charlie in the arm," the bartender went on. "An' it was enough to make him drop the knife. Then Donald broke a bottle of Old Overholt across't his head, an' slung him out into the street. Dumped him smack in the middle of a big mud puddle."

Braden was grinning, now. "Hell, that ain't no big deal," he told the bartender. "That kinda thing happens in this place all the time."

"Well, that's true enough," the barkeep agreed. "But the onliest thing different there was that Shuttinger was married to the sister of Sheriff Roy Brubaker. An' ol' Roy, he didn't take too kindly to havin' his brother-in-law made a laughin'-stock of in his own bailiwick." The man paused to pick his nose.

"So ol' Roy comes in the next night, bellies up to the bar, orders him a double shot of red-eye, smiles real sweet-like at ol' Donald. . .an' tells him that if'n he's still in San Antone when the sun comes up in the mornin' he's a-gonna tar'n feather him, an' have him rid outta town on a rail."

"Trouble with Roy," Braden drawled, "he ain't got no sense of humor."

"*Humpf*," the bartender growled, taken aback by this thought. "Ain't nobody never cared to find out whether ol' Roy could take a joke or not."

"I did, once't," the ramrod said softly. "Back a few years. He was 'bout to run some tinhorn gambler out of town—when the gent was right in the middle of a big high-stakes poker game with me.''

The bartender's eyes widened. ''You tell ol' Roy to wait?'' he asked in a low voice.

Braden smiled. ''I told ol' Roy that I done had a passel of money invested in that there gentleman, an' wouldn't he be so good as to wait until I had finished conductin' my business.''

The bartender cleared his throat. ''You said *that* to Roy?'' he asked incredulously. ''That man's one mean sum' bitch.''

''That's as may be,'' Bart Braden said softly. ''Ol' Roy, he got all red in the face, an' tol' the tinhorn that he better tighten his spats, an' dust off his Stetson, 'cause he was leavin' on the next stage out.''

''Lord A'mighty,'' the bartender croaked. ''Then what happened?''

''I told Roy I didn't think that was such a good idee,'' Braden drawled. ''Then I told him to hang loose a li'l bit, whilst I finished conductin' my business with the tinhorn.''

The bartender looked around nervously before speaking. ''Ol' Roy, he prob'ly didn't take too kindly to your tellin' him that, now did he?''

There was a wry smile on the ramrod's face. ''No, I reckon he didn't. When I told him that, he got all red in the face an' began to snort like a Mexican bull. 'An' what if I don't choose to hang loose?' he says to me, a-squintin' as if he was seein' me on the far end of a gunsight.''

''Hoo-wee damn!'' exclaimed the bartender. ''What did ya do then, Bart?''

''Oh, I jus' smiled at ol' Roy, real friendly-like,''

the ramrod told him. "An' said that if'n he didn't let me conduct my business with the man, it was a good bet that San Antone was a-gonna have to get itself a new sheriff.' "

"What'd he do then?"

"He made a face like a Comanche who done lost his last horse, pulled out his gold watch, snapped open the lid, squinted at it fer a long time, an' then snapped it shut."

The bartender handed Braden a double shot of rye whiskey.

" 'You got four hours,' " the ramrod went on, "ol' Roy says without lookin' at me. An' then, he turns on his heel an' stomps out of the place."

"*You tol' him that San Antone'd need a new sheriff?*" the bartender asked in awe.

"Yep," Braden replied, smiling his tight, grim smile. "An' Roy's a good ol' boy. He done seen the humor in that."

"I'll say he did," the bartender chuckled. "What's the lady drinkin', Bart?" he asked.

Suddenly, Raquel stepped forward and leaned over the bar, facing the bartender.

"I have been abducted by this man," she told the barkeep, reinforcing her appeal by looking him right in the eye. "This man caused a range war in New Mexico, and took me away by force from my father's *hacienda*."

In response to this, the barkeep grinned sheepishly. "Shucks, I don' know nothin' 'bout that, miss," he mumbled, looking down at his shoes. "But ol' Bart, he's all right with me. 'Scuse me, but I got folks to serve," he said, turning and making his way down the bar.

40

"What do I owe ya, Jim?" a grinning Braden called out, while Raquel stared open-mouthed at the retreating bartender's back.

"Nothin' a-tall, Bart," the man called back over his shoulder. "That there's on the house. It's good to have ya back."

Stunned by the barkeep's response, Raquel Mirabal heaved a forlorn sigh. She was in Bart Braden's land now, she realized, and could expect no help from the *tejanos*, the hereditary enemies of her people.

The full moon sat high in the night sky of Texas, and its beams flooded through the window of a room in the city of San Antonio, edging the big bed, the night table beside it, and the polished boards at the foot of the bed with a cold, silver light.

In the darkest corner of the room a kerosene lamp cast its warmer light with an occasional flicker. Warm and cool, the two illuminations overlapped the center of the room, highlighting the bodies of the naked couple there with a strange and ghostly light.

This light seemed to shift and dance with a rippling brilliance on the broad muscular back of the man in the bed. It shone with the glint of burnished copper as it played over the long, fine hairs on his forearms, glinting again in that fashion as it highlighted his curly brown hair and long, thick sideburns.

Facing the man, lying on her back in the bed, the woman's dark eyes caught the light as she stared up

41

and smiled fiercely between gleaming, clenched teeth. Points of light glimmered in her thick black hair as well, as it fanned out beneath her head and shoulders, shining with the cold and far-off glimmer of distant stars.

Her back arched as she squirmed beneath his touch, and her firm, round breasts jutted up into the air, their thick, dark nipples erect and tender, pointing into the darkness like twin signposts of desire and arousal.

Sweat ran down in rivulets from the hollows of her arms, making irregular traceries as they traveled over her ribcage, the light glimmering on them with the semaphoric radiance of diamonds on a river bed.

The man's hand stroked the inside of the young woman's thigh, the nails of his fingers lightly raking the tender flesh there, causing it to rise in goose bumps. Further and further over her thigh his hand travelled, in a slow, upward course, heading toward the black, fleecy muff and pouting lips above.

"*Ay, ay, ay,*" the young *chicana* moaned as the man's middle finger suddenly parted those engorged nether lips and lightly worked its way up between them. And when he withdrew his finger, having completed his run, he caught the sharp, musky scent of her arousal.

"*Ay, Dios,*" she murmured, her thighs twitching and her pelvis jerking reflexively.

The man leaned over and began to nuzzle her neck, at the same time bringing his hand up to stroke and cup her breast. Then he lowered his head and began to run his tongue in light, flicking

42

movements over her dark areola and nipple.

She sighed like the wind that soughs through the grasses of the *Llano Estacado*, and her body stiffened for an instant, before she broke out into a "Come inside me now, Bart."

Slowly, gently, the man's big hand traveled down over the young woman's body, stroking the quivering flesh beneath its fingers with infinite tenderness and great delicacy. And then, having descended over the gentle slope of her belly, the man's thick fingers entered the matted black tangle of the young *chicana's* pubic hair.

At the same time that his fingers descended, the man's mouth traveled in an upward course, grazing breasts and neck until his lips met and covered hers. The kiss was long and passionate, and the woman began to squirm as his finger stopped its stroking motion and suddenly penetrated her.

She responded with a short, sharp intake of breath, and a twitch of her pelvis. Slowly the man began to work his finger in and out of her sheath, his broad palm making contact with the fleshy cupola that was her mound of Venus.

"Oh, come inside me, *querido*," she whispered intensely, looking up at him with dark and gleaming eyes. "Come inside me now, Bart."

"Oh, honey," Bart Braden groaned as he felt the woman's long, tapering fingers encircle his hot and throbbing rod. Lightly, but firmly, she stroked him, running her hand back and forth over the length of his shaft.

"I want you, Bart," she whispered in that voice of rising wind, sighing with a passion as elemental as the currents that swept over the prairie.

Bart Braden groaned again as he withdrew his finger and raised himself up on his hands and knees, about to move toward her.

"Oh, Bart," the young *chicana* moaned, shifting beneath him and opening her legs as she prepared to take him inside her, still holding his hard, erect sex in her hand.

His forearms came down on both sides of her head, and the Texas ramrod's shadow fell over her face, causing the highlights in her dark eyes to disappear.

Just then the light of the kerosene lamp began to flicker and dance, as the flame burnt down on a wick that was nearly dry. For an instant, Bart Braden's face was bathed in bright light, which revealed a look of intense desire upon his face. His eyes were wide, and glazed with longing, giving the ramrod the look of a man of both great desperation and determination.

His mouth was set in a tight smile and he breathed through his nose in great, rapid blasts. And when the young *chicana* inserted Braden's rod into her wet, musky sheath, the Texan's mouth opened and he caught his breath with a gasp.

He moved his body toward her, and heard a soft, squishing sound as his sex began to glide into her warm and welcoming sheath.

She made a sound deep in her throat and raised her pelvis to meet him. "*Querido*," she murmured huskily as Bart Braden began to penetrate her with long, slow strokes.

They hit a stride and held it for a while, the Texan's tantalizing strokes finally causing the *chicana* to thrust at him more rapidly, urging him on to greater exertions.

"Oh, honey," Braden moaned, after he had intensified his strokes and deepened his penetration for some time. His eyes were shut, and his body began to tremble as the dark and lovely young woman squirmed and moaned beneath him.

"Oh, honey," he said once more, as a railroad flare seemed to ignite somewhere in the back of his brain.

"Ra-quel," he groaned as the crucible in the pit of his groin overflowed, and the molten issue of his passion surged forth out of his jerking body.

"Oh, Raquel!" the ramrod cried out in the night, his anguished voice ringing off the white-washed adobe walls of the bedroom.

Oblivious to the ramrod's cries, the young woman beneath him bucked and thrashed, the force of her own climax tearing incoherent, guttural sounds out of her throat. And when both were satiated, they lay spent and panting in the silver Texas moonlight, the kerosene lamp having gone out a few moment earlier.

After several minutes, Bart Braden got out of bed and put on his clothes. He smiled a tight, grim smile and nodded to the young woman in the bed.

"Goo' night, ho-nee," she whispered back, the traces of a Mexican accent coloring her words. And as the ramrod turned and began to walk toward the door, the dark-haired young woman glanced over at the crumpled wad of greenbacks which sat upon her night table.

A moment later Bart Braden stepped out into the night, the moon over San Antonio silvering his spurs and the handle of his big Colt, and began to walk back toward Oliver Entwhistle's establishment, to where Raquel Mirabal slept a troubled sleep in the locked room which adjoined his.

2
The Kansan Comes To Texas

"Dah-veed, amigo," Anibal Mirabal, Raquel's eldest brother, said to the Kansan as the latter and Soaring Hawk mounted their horses in front of the Mirabal hacienda, deep in the New Mexico Territory. *"Dah-veed,* when you catch up with this *hombre,* Bart Braden, please treat him with all the *cortesia* and consideration that my father, brothers, and I would show the *tejano* gentleman."

"Oh, don't worry, 'bout that, Anibal," the Kansan replied to the New Mexican's irony. "I owe that sum'bitch a bullet," he said, not realizing that he *had* shot Braden in the exchange of bullets by the mountain lake, in whose aftermath the Texan had taken Raquel Mirabal and left him for dead.

"I owe that sum'bitch a bullet right 'twixt the eyes," the Kansan told Anibal Mirabal and his brothers. "And I aim to see the debt paid in full."

"Señor Watson," Don Solomon Mirabal called out in his deep, resonant voice as he stood in the doorway of the *hacienda.* "Promise me that you will exercise all caution in your efforts to get my daughter back from Braden."

Davy looked down at the *patrón's* stern visage and pleading eyes. "That'll be my first concern,

Don Solomon," he told the sheepman reassuringly. "I ain't 'bout to settle Bart Braden's hash while Raquel's still his captive. Ol' Soaring Hawk here—" he nodded in the direction of the young Pawnee brave who sat astride an Indian pony—"an' me intends to make sure Raquel is safe and sound before we start with Braden." The Kansan smiled grimly. "But once't we got her clear, then we're goin' in to finish him off."

"*Vaya con Dios*," the don said as Davy wheeled his horse around.

"You folks take care of yerselves," was the Kansan's reply.

"*Adios, Indio,*" said Jesse Santacruz, the sheepherder whose rescue first embroiled Davy and Soaring Hawk in a range war with the wild and woolly Texans. "*Buena suerte*. Good luck, amigos."

The Pawnee nodded, the resolute set of his features never changing. The Kansan waved his hand.

"Kill him good," Hector Mirabal said, slapping the flank of Davy Watson's passing horse.

"Good as I can," the Kansan called back over his shoulder, as he and Soaring Hawk rode out of the little plaza which faced the *hacienda* of the great New Mexican *rico*, Don Solomon Mirabal.

The *hacienda* itself was an appalling sight, having suffered extensive damage when it was under siege by Bill Fanshaw's Texans. Great sections of the long and rectangular, two-storied building's adobe walls had been blown to pieces when the Texans lobbed sticks of the deadly new explosive, dynamite, at the *hacienda*. The explosions had brought fire in their wake, and its ravages showed in smoke-blackened walls and charred beams and window frames. Anyone with an eye for symbols would have likened the bare and gutted *hacienda*, with its blackened burnt sections standing out against the sunlit dazzle of whitewashed adobe walls, to a death's head. More than anything, the sight of the Mirabal *hacienda* in the glare of the New Mexican sun brought to the Kansan's mind the image of a skull, picked clean by vultures and bleaching in the desert.

It was with this desolate and forbidding vision in mind that the Kansan turned his face to Texas and rode off the Mirabal spread. The expedition was not to be a lighthearted one, considering the fact that Bart Braden, certainly one of the toughest and deadliest men Davy Watson had ever met, would be fighting on his home ground, in the midst of his fellow-Texans. No, it would not be easy.

Even though Bart Braden's trail was cold by the time that Davy Watson and his blood-brother rode southward in pursuit of him, the Kansan had little fear of losing the ramrod's scent. In the state of Texas, the sight of a male *Anglo* traveling in the company of a young, female *chicana* was a curiosity, an extreme rarity in that segregated society. People would remember such a sight; it would not be difficult to pick up the tracks of such an odd couple. Catching up with Braden would not be the hard part of the Kansan's mission; taking Raquel Mirabal and besting the Texas ramrod *would* be, Davy was certain of that.

Heading due south, and riding far to the west of the new settlement of Roswell, which was a stronghold of the *tejano* cattle interests in the New Mexico Territory, Davy and Soaring Hawk followed the banks of the Rio Penasco eastward from the town of Elk, until they reached its junction with the waters of the Pecos River.

Along the Pecos the two men rode, through Lakewood and Carlsbad, past Otis, Loving and Malaga, crossing Delaware Creek in the Red Bluff country, at the point where the Pecos flows through Texas on a southeasterly course.

Past Orta and Menton, and into the town of Pecos, the Kansan and the Pawnee rode, picking up Bart Braden's trail at that point. From there they followed the course of the Pecos to Sheffield, and then into Crockett County, in West Texas, where they headed eastward over the vast expanse of the Edwards Plateau.

Through Segovia and Fredericksburg, and then due south the blood-brothers rode, through Kerr, Bandera and Medina Counties, securely on the Texas ramrod's trail now, crossing over the line into Bexar County, on the last few miles to the city of San Antonio.

"Ain't gonna be long now," Davy told Soaring Hawk, " 'fore we catch sight of our ol' pal, Bart Braden, once't more."

The stoical Pawnee nodded, leaning over in the saddle to loosen his heavy-caliber Sharps rifle in its boot.

"We kill 'im quick," the brave cautioned. "Braden heap dangerous." He shifted uneasily in the saddle, turning to the Kansan as he did. "Too many Texans. Heap dangerous here, I think."

Davy Watson nodded in agreement with this.

"Yep. I think so, too, ol' son. You're right, there—we gotta kill him quick. That's the best way to deal with rattlers and sidewinders."

Raquel Mirabal and Bart Braden spent most of their waking hours together, for the only time that the ramrod let the beautiful daughter of Don Solomon out of his sight was when he locked her in her room at night, on the second story of Oliver Entwhistle's Exchange on San Antonio's bustling main plaza.

The ramrod continued his strange courtship of Don Solomon's lovely daughter. A proud man—proud even for a Texan, Braden was the epitome of humility when it came to Raquel Mirabal. Once he realized that he had the object of his desire securely in his power, deep in the heart of his home state, the ferocity of Bart Braden's obsession abated, and was replaced by a sudden welling of the tenderest feelings that the hardened and cynical cowpoke had ever experienced.

Flowers, compliments, kindnesses, acts of consideration and attentiveness: these were the constant gifts that the Texan lavished upon the dark-eyed and lissome young beauty. And if she had not been his captive, and he her abductor, it could have passed (at least on Braden's end), for the perfect courtship.

For her part, Raquel was astonished by this side of the Texas iron-man's nature. It was a constant revelation, and led her to consider another form of captivity: the one in which men were hostages to their own codes of behavior; the way that they were the prisoners and victims of their own *machismo*. It was an especially hard form of bondage, and an oppression that men—both *latino* and *gringo*—were far from being able to confront, or even acknowledge, for the most part.

She would bide her time, Raquel told herself. And when her moment came, she would avenge herself upon her *tejano* captor, and then escape back to the New Mexico Territory, back to her home and those whom she loved.

All things considered, apart from the small likelihood of being rescued in Texas, Raquel's lot was not a hard one. While she hated Bart Braden for shooting Davy Watson, the first man to awaken her passionate nature, and for taking her away from her land and people, the young *chicana* was at the same time perversely fascinated by the great transformation of the Texan's character.

He had not laid a hand on her, and had always treated her with the greatest respect, never getting drunk and lecherous, after the fashion of most of the *tejanos* she had observed since their entry into the Lone Star State. He had relieved her of the great fear of violation, that specter of rape and abuse which men have visited upon captive women since time immemorial, and one of the deep, primal sources of female anger.

She was his captive—make no mistake about that—but Bart Braden treated Raquel Mirabal with love and respect, denying her nothing but the one thing she wanted most: her freedom.

It was strange and dizzying to contemplate. In two short weeks, the course of Raquel Mirabal's life had been radically altered. In fact, the lives of many people—her father, brothers, family, neighbors, the *tejano* invaders and the unfortunate Davy Watson—had all been deeply affected by Bart Braden's desperate and precipitate act. But the Texan remained unperturbed by the thought of the consequences of his actions. Men in the grip of an overpowering obsession are rarely reflective, or even rational. And he had succeeded; the ramrod had taken what he came after: Raquel Mirabal was his.

But flesh was flesh, and although Bart Braden treated the young *chicana* with the chaste regard of a medieval troubador, his physical needs and the mounting demands of his addictive love drove him to the arms of the women who waited and worked in the *cantina* across the plaza from Oliver Entwhistle's place.

He had been welcomed with warm and willing smiles by most of the bar girls, but he devoted all of his occasional visits to only one among them. Nydia Ramirez was her name; that was all he knew about her, and actually more than he had wanted to know. She was young, and relatively new to the life of a honkytonk girl, but that was of little import to Bart Braden. What mattered most to the Texan was Nydia Ramirez's close resemblance to Raquel Mirabal. And when he made love to her, he made love to a phantom; and when he spent himself in her arms, the name he called out in the darkness was not Nydia's, but that of Raquel Mirabal.

One night, Braden came back early from the *cantina*. Nydia was having her period, and this did not accord with the Texan's idealized image of her;

he did not care to associate blood with Raquel Mirabal. Perhaps this association touched something deep within him, reminding the ramrod of all the blood that had been shed as a result of his obsessive love for Don Solomon's daughter.

Heavy drinking and high-stakes poker were the rule in Entwhistle's Exchange that night, and the denizens of the place were whooping it up mightily as Bart Braden came through the swinging doors, their throats having been well-oiled by increasingly liberal applications of the establishment's spiritous lubricants.

"O-o-oooh, buf'lo gals, ain't ya comin' out tonight, comin' out tonight, comin' out tonight," the piano player sang hoarsely, over the roaring hubbub of the crowd and the discordant clangor of his laboring instrument. *"Buf'lo gals, ain't ya comin' out tonight, to dance by the light of the mo-o-o-ooon?"*

Men were missing the spitoons and splattering their neighbors' boots with the juice of Brown's Mule; men were falling-down-drunk or puking in the streets; men were swearing eternal friendship or glaring about the room in enmity; men were either pining for lost loves or shedding sentimental tears at the memory of their dear, gray-haired, old mothers; some were clustered around the jangling upright, singing raucously, clumsily following the voice of the piano player, baying like spent hounds at the end of a long coon hunt; and others were propped up by the elbows at card tables, seated behind piles of blue and red chips, or scribbling with stubby pencils on crumpled papers, with pale, unshaven faces and doleful countenances, scratching out their markers as they gambled cattle or cabins in a last, desperate attempt to recoup their losses.

The long, polished bar was sticky with the evaporated residue of spilled drinks, the four perspiring bartenders behind it having been far too busy dispensing their wares to stop and apply the bar rag where needed. The air of the big room was thick with the smoke of cheroots, stogies, and cigarillos, a smoke as dense as the atmosphere of a Republican caucus room in the last hour of a deadlocked political convention.

Coming into Entwhistle's Exchange cold sober, the totality of this scene struck Bart Braden as something slightly less elevated than a riot at a county asylum. Shaking his head in disapproval, thrusting drunks right and left out of his path, the ramrod impatiently made his way through the weaving, babbling crowd, heading toward the plush-carpeted stairs which led to his suite of rooms on the honkytonk's upper story.

"*Señor Braden*! *Señor Braden*!" someone screeched in a shrill voice.

The ramrod looked up to the head of the stairs, and saw the old Mexican woman who was one of Entwhistle's chambermaids standing there, wringing her hands and wincing as she called down to him, pale in the face and trembling.

His eyes narrowed as he reached the top of the stairs, towering above her as he studied the old woman's features. Braden saw fear and anguish on her face, and he immediately asked the woman what was troubling her.

"The young *señorita*," she mumbled haltingly,

causing Braden's eyes to suddenly widen.

"What about the young *señorita*?" he asked, urging the frightened woman on.

"Before, she 'ave *fuego*—fire—in room," the woman went on, cringing as she looked up at the big Texan. "So I 'ave to let 'er out—"

"*You let her out*?" Braden said loudly, grabbing the old woman by the upper arms, and shaking her the way a mastiff shakes a rat.

"*Señor Braden—por favor*!" she screamed. "I swear I do to save 'er. But she trick me—is only *fuego* in wastebasket. She push past me, an—"

"Goddammit, you old bitch," the ramrod snarled, shaking the woman again. "You let her go?"

The woman burst into tears as she pleaded for her life, lapsing into Spanish in her confusion. Braden, who spoke sufficient Spanish to understand her, ordered her to tell him where Raquel had gone.

Still sobbing, the woman looked up at the Texan. "*No, no, Señor*," she gasped. "The *senorita* ees steel in room. . .she no go way."

"How come she's still in there?" Braden asked suspiciously, suddenly releasing his grip on the old woman's arms.

The woman gasped and paused to rub her arms and catch her breath. The ramrod's hands were down at his sides, and his fingers fluttered impatiently as he waited for the old Mexican woman to speak.

"Dees man come upstairs—*muy borracho*—him very drunk." Braden's eyes narrowed and his hands became still. "He go after her. The senorita go back an' lock 'erself in room. But thees man, he kick open door, an—''

"Git outta my way!" Braden grunted suddenly thrusting the old woman aside, causing her to fall to the carpeting which covered the upper story's hallway.

Noiselessly, on tip-toe, the ramrod made his way down the hallway, drawing the Colt .45 from its holster as he did.

When he reached the open door to Raquel Mirabal's room, Braden stood to one side of it, his back to the wall. An instant later he leaned to the side and peered cautiously into the room, his finger on the trigger of his pistol.

The sight which greeted the ramrod's eyes caused them to widen in alarm. The first thing he saw was Raquel Mirabal's bed; and the next thing he saw was Raquel's long-limbed body, draped over it.

She was half-naked, her blouse and underthings having been ripped open above the waist. And the big, grimy hand of a man could be seen fondling the young *chicana's* breast. Braden's face went white as he saw the gag in Raquel's mouth and her arms held over her head on the pillow, her two slender wrists pinioned by the big right hand of the bearded man who held her down.

Grunting and writhing furiously, her legs pinned by the man's ham-like left thigh, Raquel was pale and sweating as she struggled vainly to ward off the giant's amorous advances.

"Kitchy-koo, kitchy-koo," the man crooned in his gruff voice as he began to rub his thick beard over Raquel's collar bone, traveling down into the cleft between her full breasts.

He said this softly, and was therefore in a position to hear the hammer of Bart Braden's Colt click back with an ominous finality. And at that sudden, chilling, familiar sound, the big, bearded man sat bolt-upright upon the bed and turned his face to the door of the room.

"*Braden*!" he gasped, the color fading from his face as he spoke in a voice thick with disbelief. "*Braden! You!*"

The man looked up into the huge mouth of the ramrod's .45, then along its dully gleaming barrel, and into two eyes that looked even harder and colder than the metal of the Colt held out before them.

"Should've told me you was comin' by to pay a call, Sweinhardt," Braden said in a voice as cold as death. " 'Cause I'd've come back earlier, so's to welcome you proper-like, *amigo*."

The big bearded man's face was the color of bleached bones, and he sprang to his feet as if the bed had suddenly caught fire beneath him.

"N-n-now, B-b-bart," the man stammered, the pupils of his eyes dilated to the size of lentils as he stared into the cavernous maw of the ramrod's six-gun. "Lemme explain," he blubbered, sniffling loudly after he had said this.

"No need to explain, Sweinhardt," Braden replied softly, smiling a tight, grim smile. "You know what they say, *amigo*: 'One picture's worth a thousand words.' "

"N-no, Bart," the giant stammered rapidly, his knees buckling as he heard the second cock of the ramrod's trigger. "I was drunk, Bart—so he'p me, God. I-I-I didn' know this was yer filly—I swear it.

I didn't know. . .what I was about. I—"

Sweinhardt's voice trailed off into an incoherent falsetto whisper as Bart Braden held his big Colt out at arm's length and leveled it at the man's chest.

"Oh, oh, oh," was all that the bearded giant could manage to say, his jaw dropping to reveal his yellowed, snaggle teeth, his eyes wide as he stared into the .45's gaping maw, the eyes of a partridge cornered by an advancing coyote.

"Thanks a heap fer droppin' by, *amigo*," Braden told the petrified man, his voice the voice of an executioner. "But it's time to go."

"O-o-o-ooo-oooh," Sweinhardt croaked, his voice sounding like a door opening slowly on rusty hinges. "O-o-o-oooh. . ."

Booom!

The big Colt discharged with a thunderous report, its blast ringing deafeningly in the room as it reverberated off the walls.

The .45 slug plowed into the meat and bone of the giant's chest with an audible smack, its impact thrusting him backward, to jacknife over the bed.

Bart Braden stared impassively as Sweinhardt's huge, gross body hit the floor with a thump like the sound of a dropped anvil.

Raquel Mirabal was sitting up now and staring at the body of her fallen assailant, totally oblivious to the fact that her beautiful breasts were exposed to view.

But this did not register with the Texan, who lowered his smoking pistol and began to walk across the room, stopping when he stood above the fallen man.

"What t'hell's goin' on here?" a balding, medium-sized man with bushy eyebrows and a Van Dyke beard called out a moment later, as he came to the doorway of the room, hitching up his pants and struggling to put on his gunbelt.

Braden was staring down at Sweinhardt, his .45 held out at at arm's length, pointing directly at the fallen man's big head.

"Jus' defendin' the young lady's honor," the ramrod murmured as his finger began to tighten on the Colt's trigger.

"Now, hold on there, son," the man counseled from the doorway, reaching out a hand toward Bart Braden.

Ba-boom!

The .45 thundered again, and Sweinhardt's head burst open and flew apart, splattering the floor of the room as if it had been an overripe pumpkin dropped from the roof of a barn.

"Now, why'd you have to go an' do a thing like that for?" the man whined, starting to draw his own pistol from its holster. "I'm Cap'n Paul Myers of the State Po-lice, an' I'm a-goin' to have to take you in."

In reply to this, Braden raised his .45 and fired it at the balding man. The impact of the slug sent the state policeman flying backward out of the doorway and smacking into the railing behind him. The wood of the railing parted with a sharp crack, and the man's body shot down to the building's lower story, to land square on top of a poker table below.

Cries of surprise, pain and consternation rose up from the honkytonk's ground floor, as the falling body knocked a man out of his seat and snapped the legs of the table, sending waves of blue, red and white poker chips cascading to the blotter-green carpeting.

"C'mon, honey," Bart Braden gently told Raquel Mirabal, who looked at him with wide, uncomprehending eyes. "We got to light outta here, now."

"*Dos muertes*," she whispered, acknowledging both dead men, while the Texan raised her from the bed and handed her a jacket.

"*Vamanos, muchacha*," Braden whispered softly as, Colt .45 in hand, he led Raquel Mirabal out of the room and down the plush-carpeted stairs, through the confused and milling crowd below, and out into the cool, dark night of Texas.

"Now, looky here, Albert," an old, white-haired man was saying to an old black man, as Davy Watson and Soaring Hawk dismounted in San Antonio's main plaza. "Why is it," the old white man went on, "that you nigrahs allus seems to prefer certain religious sects. What I mean to say is—" here he paused to clear his throat loudly.

The Kansan pretended to adjust the cinch strap on his saddle while he listened with interest.

"What I mean to say is," the old white Texan went on, "how's it that so many of you people is Baptists, Albert? How come that's so?"

The black man straightened up as he sat on the porch of the building next to the Exchange where Davy and Soaring Hawk were hitching their horses, cocked his head to one side, and squinted at the white-haired man.

"You kin read now, cain't you?" he asked the man.

"Well, shore I can read," the white man replied testily.

"Well, I s'pose you's done read the Bible, hain't you?"

" 'Course I done read the Bible!"

"Den you's probly read 'bout John de Baptis', hain't you?" the black man asked.

"Shore I have," the old white man said impatiently. "What of it?"

"Well," the black man said with a triumphant smile, "you hain't never done read 'bout *no John de Methodis'*, now has you?" The white man shook his head. "You see, I gots de Bible on my side, den," the black man crowed jubilantly.

Davy Watson was chuckling as he entered the Exchange. He and Soaring Hawk passed by the bar and headed for a table, having decided to have dinner before they began their search for Bart Braden.

Making the rounds of San Antonio's many Exchanges could be wearing work, the Kansan thought, recalling his pub-crawling escapades in Virginia City, when he was on the trail of Harvey Yancey, the obscene giant who had abducted the three Mudree sisters. There Davy made the acquaintance of the knowledgeable young reporter Marcus Haverstraw, who guided him on a boozy tour of the many saloons flourishing in the place which had grown up following the discovery of the Comstock Lode.

The epic hangover which had followed as a consequence of the first night's work was enough to convince the Kansan that such a quest ought always to be conducted in a spirit of moderation, and on a full stomach. So it was with this in mind that Davy Watson sat down to a big platter of steak, smothered in onions, and home-fried potatoes, backed up by a huge and frothy schooner of beer. Soaring Hawk ate the same food, but had as his drink, being a man who never touched alcoholic beverages, a tall glass of birch beer. This choice of beverage also skirted the painful and embarassing issue of having to be served at a white man's bar. This was a touchy situation at best, and Davy was greatly relieved when he and his Pawnee blood-brother did not have to drink at the bar of whatever saloon or honkytonk to which their business had brought them.

In the background a painoforte played the *Varsoviana*, and the Kansan had a faraway look in his eyes as he remembered hearing that tune in the *hacienda* of Don Solomon Mirabal, seated at a table and gazing into the dark doe-eyes of the *patrón's* daughter, Raquel.

There were a lot of women in the honkytonk, a place whose sign proclaimed it Wilson's Exchange, and many of them were not bad-looking either, the Kansan realized, feeling a surge of heat in his groin.

"Mebbe we ought to rest up a spell," he said, turning to the Pawnee. Whether Bart Braden had molested Raquel or not, the Kansan reasoned, he would surely have done it by now. There was no longer any point in getting worked up on that score.

Soaring Hawk was eyeing the women, too.

"Yep. Mebbe," he grunted, nodding in agreement with this. The bar girls began to stir as they became aware, with the sixth sense developed in their trade, of the two men's interest, fussing suddenly with their gowns and hair, and flashing bright smiles in the direction of the newcomers.

"Yeah, le's knock off fer a couple of hours, an' then git down to business," Davy Watson told the Pawnee brave, as he raised the last of the beefsteak to his mouth.

"Good," the Indian replied with characteristic brevity.

"Well, dammit all, John," Davy heard one of the Texans at the table behind him say as he sat and smiled back at the bar-girls, "that's the way it is with niggers in Mexico. Them darkies livin' down there actually has an advantage over a white American. The greasers likes 'em better, considerin' us Texas folk a mite too rough fer 'em."

"An' well they should," another chimed in gruffly. "We done kicked their butts enough."

The men at the table all laughed loudly.

"But I swear to God A'mighty, its the truth," the first man went on. "A nigger in Mexico is jus' as good as a white man, an' if'n you don't treat him civil-like, he will have yer butt hauled up to court an' fined by some fat ol' *alcalde*. Can you believe that, boys?"

"Well, that jus' says more 'bout the greasers than it do 'bout the niggers," another man commented. "They ain't none too bright. Why, I done heard this from a nigger hisself—a young buck name of Zachariah, who used to be a slave on my Aunt Eulalie's place in Austin. He done tole me that a colored man, if'n he made up his mind to be industrious, could make him a right comfortable livin' down in Mexico.''

"If'n he was in-dust-tri-ous," the first man crowed scornfully, "he wouldn't be no darkie, now would he?"

The men laughed again.

"Well, what this buck done tole me," the other man continued, "was that wages was low, but they had all they earned fer they own. An' a man's livin' didn't cost him much there. Colored men who was in-dustrious an' savin', young Zachariah said, could make money faster'n the Mexicans they-selves—*because they had more sense*! That's what he done tole me."

"Well," another man grunted, "thar's somethin' to what that boy said, I'll grant you that."

"By gum, Russell," said another, "that's prob'ly the first time in yer life that you ever done agreed with a nigger."

The men laughed raucously.

Davy Watson frowned and shook his head. He was disgusted with many of his fellow citizens, whom he considered to be bigots and shirkers, men unworthy of the great ideals of the Declaration of Independence which was their heritage. The stain of prejudice was a deep and enduring blot upon the American character, and the nation's relationship with its Negro citizens was an especially complex and tormented one.

Even Thomas Jefferson, that great libertarian, Davy reminded himself, while engineering the Declaration of Independence and the Constitution of the United States, had been a slave owner himself.

And the man had begotten several mulatto children by his black slave mistress, Sally Hemming. Jefferson loved that woman, the Kansan told himself, and yet he kept her as a slave. This seemed, to Davy, to embody the great racial contradiction in the American character: noble ideals and a reality of racial injustice; fiery speeches in defense of liberty in the halls of Congress, and lynch mobs in the streets. Why even such a liberal city as New York had recently suffered from racial disturbances. During the draft riots of the Civil War, less than a decade ago, a number of the white citizens of that fair city took it upon themselves to hang a number of their darker brothers from the lamp posts.

And of all the bigoted sum'bitches I've ever come acrosst in my travels, the Kansan told himself, a bitter smile coming to his lips, these Texans has got to be the worst. They spit on the rights of darker folk, an' laugh at the Mexicans for upholdin' them.

He shook his head and sighed. Those poor, brown-faced, priest-ridden heathen actually hold, in earnest, the ideas on this subject put forth in that good ol' joke of our fathers—the Declaration of American Independence.

When, he asked himself, were his countrymen going to get their heads out of their asses, and get down to the business of looking each other right in the eye and respecting themselves for what they were. Then the Kansan recalled the lines he had read in one of his Uncle Ethan's books, a volume published only a decade ago, in the year preceeding the civil war. Its author had remarked the persistent flights to Mexico of Negro slaves in Western Texas, and written:

"Brave negro! say I. He faces all that is terrible to man for the chance of liberty, from hunger to thirst to every nasty form of four-footed and two-footed devil. I fear I should myself suffer the last servile indignities before setting foot in such a net of concentrated torture. I pity the man whose sympathies would not warm to a dog under these odds. How can they be held back from a slave who is driven to assert his claim to manhood?"

To do justice to a great number of his countrymen, Davy recalled that there were many of them—male and female—who were committed to the principles of liberty and justice for all. And their time would come, he told himself. . .for if it did not, then the American nation would surely perish, its life extinguished by the rampant spread of the cancers of racism and social injustice.

The Kansan's spirits were suddenly buoyed, and lifted out of that pool of melancholy in which they had been immersed, when his wandering eye met that of a young woman who stared at him from the head of the stairs which led to the Exchange's upper story.

She was tall and auburn-haired, with cornflower-blue eyes, a long, aquiline nose, full, red lips and a strong jaw. Her emerald green gown swelled at the bosom, and again at her hips. The woman was handsome of feature, Junoesque of figure, and in her early thirties, the Kansan opined. He found himself imagining the way her piled auburn hair would look against the pure white of a clean pillow, fanning out to its full length in radial lines, like the rays of the sun on a bronze plaque. She was definitely the most interesting woman Davy Watson had seen since the day he'd first laid eyes on Raquel Mirabal.

Soaring Hawk had also found a focus for his carnal interests, and the Pawnee was staring across the room, the faintest trace of a smile upon his lips.

"See anythin' you like?" Davy inquired.

"Hunh," the Pawnee grunted, nodding at a blonde in a pale blue gown, who smiled back as he did.

"Me too," the Kansan told him. "That there big gal on the stairs has jus' caught my fancy. Let's get to it, ol' son."

A few minutes later, they were ensconced in a suite of rooms on the upper story of the Exchange, the women of their choice beside them on velvet sofas, making polite conversation and drinking champagne. Soaring Hawk had as his drink a birch beer in a tall glass, garnished with thin slices of Texas lemon and lime.

The big redhead called herself Delia Lee, and the blonde, an emigrant from the state of Rhode Island, was named Mary Louise Pringle. Both were possessed of hearty, fun-loving dispositions, and it was not long before the suite's parlor rang with their laughter. The Kansan laughed with them, and even the normally poker-faced Pawnee was soon smiling broadly, an indication, among his people, of great hilarity.

Delia Lee, upon learning of the customs of Soaring Hawk's tribe, and Plains Indians in general, began to relate the views held by one of her "regulars," a man named Jim Primrose, a former member of the famed Texas Rangers.

He was, the redhead told her listeners, an excellent scout and a very reliable man. Orderly, quiet and disciplined, Primrose was pleasant and open, but at the same time restrained and tactful; certainly not your average frontiersman.

The old Ranger spoke Spanish like a Mexican, and had mastered a number of Indian languages, as well as the signs of several tribes. And although he had the frontiersman's hatred for Indians, Jim Primrose gave them credit for patience, endurance, perceptiveness, and generally respected their abilities as outdoorsmen. And, as a first-hand observer of the red man, Primrose had his pet peeve:

"Why do people who write books," he asked in Delia Lee's anecdote, "always make Indians talk in that hifalutin' way they do? Indians don't talk so, and when folks talk that way to them they don't understand it. They don't like it, neither."

Soaring Hawk nodded solemnly as he met the redhead's eyes.

"I went up with Lieutenant Walpole," she continued, mimicking the old Texas Ranger's drawling speech, "when he tried to make a treaty with the Northern Apaches. He had been talking up in the clouds, all nonsense, for half an hour, and I was trying to translate it just as foolish as he said it."

The redhead paused to knock down her glass of champagne. "An old Indian jumped up and stopped me," she said, continuing Primrose's story while holding out her glass to be refilled.

"What does your chief talk to us in this way

for?'' Delia Lee went on, now switching to the voice and mannerisms of an old Apache chief. "We ain't babies. We are fighting men. If he has got anything to tell us we will hear it. But we didn't come here to be amused; we came to be made drunk, and to get some blankets and tobacco.''

Davy guffawed at this, and the Pawnee broke out into bursts of snorting laughter.

"We ain't babies," Soaring Hawk repeated between snorts, slapping his thigh. "That heap funny. White chief talk to Injun baby, mebbe he get understood.''

"You ain't refilled my glass yet, Mr. Wasson," the statuesque redhead told the Kansan reproachfully, still holding out her empty champagne glass.

"Watson's my handle, Miz Delia," he told her. David Lee Watson.''

"We got similar names," was her reply, "David Lee an' Delia Lee.''

"Just like brother and sister," the Rhode Island blonde said sweetly, with a mischievious glint in her eye.

"Ain't you gon' fill me up, honey?" the redhead asked suggestively, leaning over and exposing her fair and ample bosom to the Kansan.

"I, uh, thought we'd do that inside," Davy told her, his ears reddening as he inclined his head in the direction of the bedroom door.

"Why, I'll jus bet Mr. Watson's heart is already full to overflowing with brotherly love," Mary Louise chimed in again before knocking back her own glass of champagne.

"How long you been on the trail, David Lee?" the redhead whispered in the Kansan's ear, her voice exciting him with its breathy contralto.

"Nigh onto two weeks," he whispered back lustily, suddenly catching the fragrance of her thick, auburn hair.

"You ready to hop back in the saddle, cowboy?" she asked with a wicked smile.

"Sure am," Davy replied. "Been dog's years since I done got the chance to mount such a fine-lookin' filly."

"You've got the look of a hard-ridin' hombre, David Lee," the redhead whispered, coyly lowering her eyes as she did.

"Oh, don't you worry none, Mr. Watson," Mary Louise called out as she plunked herself down on Soaring Hawk's lap. "Ride just as hard as you please. This filly is fully saddle-broke."

They all laughed at this, the Pawnee included. And the couples were still laughing as they retired to their respective bedrooms.

Back in the saddle—Hoo-wee damn! the Kansan thought as the big redhead guided his throbbing rod into her auburn-thatched sex.

He caught his breath as she lowered herself upon him, feeling at every millimeter of penetration the hot, gripping suction of her wet, juicy quim.

Delia Lee squatted over Davy Watson, leaning over and reaching out to rake his hairy chest with long red nails. She began to move from side to side, her hips rotating in churning motions, as she smiled triumphantly down at him, watching the expression on his face through narrowed, cat's eyes.

His own eyes were rolled up in their sockets; he puffed and blew as the redhead's churning hips and gripping, sucking pussy ignited a fire in the pit of his groin.

"Ju-da-a-as Priest," he moaned, writhing beneath the redhead who rode and churned above him.

Slurp, slurp, were the wet hungry sounds that her sex made as she jerked her red-muffed pelvis and quickened her stroke, looking down and running the length of the Kansan's shaft, not stopping until her engorged nether lips were butted against the expanse of his groin, flattened and parted and lost to sight in the thick tangle of his pubic hair.

Then suddenly, up again—as she hooked her groin backward and started on the upswing. And then down again—as the Kansan moaned loudly and shook with delight.

Through narrowed eyes, puffing like a steam kettle on the boil, Davy Watson watched the thick swollen lips of the redhead's sex travel their downward, pouting course over the length of his shaft, which was slick and gleaming with the fluids of her own arousal.

Up and down, in and out. His rod came into view, and then suddenly disappeared within those dark, swollen lips, gripped by the hungry orifice which it had penetrated.

Slurp, slurp. Delia Lee stroked and churned. *Up and down. Slurp, slurp. In and out.* She milked him with her hot and gripping pussy, milked him as surely as a Wisconsin dairymaid milks a prize Guernsey. Faster and faster she stroked, leaning forward now, her forearms resting upon his chest and shoulders.

"Judas Prie-e-eest," he moaned, feeling like a volcano about to erupt. "Great God in Sion," were the Kansan's last words, as Delia Lee's artful movements and eloquent organ ransacked his bodily fluids, causing him to cry out between clenched teeth.

"*Heee-e-e-aaah*!" he cried as a stream of jissum shot out of his over-stimulated organ and bathed her sheath in its milky abundance.

"O-o-oooh, Jesus God!" he yelled, his body beginning to jerk uncontrollably in reaction to the overwhelming orgasm he was at that instant experiencing.

"Oh yes, sweet man!" Delia Lee called out, getting into the spirit of things as she lay over him and writhed, her pelvis butted against his.

"Hoo-ooo, hoo-ooo," she began to whimper in response to the swooping, vertiginous rise of her own orgasm, closing her eyes and clenching her even, white teeth.

The redhead whimpered and the Kansan yodeled, with the bedsprings beneath them providing the ground bass for their amorous duet. In the parlor of the suite the vocalizing could still be heard, carrying as far as the door on the opposite side of the room, beyond which Soaring Hawk and the blonde from Rhode Island made love.

Back in Virginia City, the Pawnee had gone to bed with a redhead and had been fascinated to discover that her pubic hair was much the same color as that of her tresses. And now, upon seeing the fleecy blonde muff of Mary Louise, he crowed with delight.

She was only the second white woman that he had ever lain with, and the brave was still acutely titillated by contrast between the blonde's coloring and that of the Indian women he had known.

Mary Louise, as Desirée the redhead before her, had never slept with an American Indian, and also regarded the encounter with a certain amount of excitement.

She found the Pawnee much gentler with his hands than the general run of white men that she had known. He was, as Indians usually were, much less preoccupied with a woman's breasts than were his white brothers, preferring to caress and fondle her in a great variety of places.

Mary Louise's eyes lit up when the Pawnee leaned over her, put his nostrils close to her bare, warm flesh, and began to snuffle like a hound catching the scent of a possum. This was known to learned scholars in the East as the "olfactory kiss," although Mary Louise was unaware of it. It was an ancient custom that had originally come from Asia, and was still practiced there by many an amorous Asiatic.

Being fondled, caressed and thoroughly snuffled, although never kissed, had aroused the blonde, and her juices were flowing copiously as she sighed and squirmed on the bed, while the Pawnee continued to snuffle his way down to the furry delta between her plump white thighs.

Snuffling and poking with his nose like a pig rooting out truffles, Soaring Hawk conveyed to Mary Louise the impression that he wished her to spread her legs.

Wide-eyed and open mouthed, never having been snuffled in that area before, the blonde wonderingly complied with the brave's wishes.

Still snuffling lightly, and ruffling Mary Louise's fluffy, golden muff with the tip of his nose, Soaring Hawk lowered his head as he came to her two pink lips and the shadowy, musk-scented cleft between them.

Lying on her back, eyes round as saucers, her thighs quivering with anticipation, Mary Louise wondered where the Pawnee would poke his nose next. Would he snuffle between her lips? she asked herself, curious to discover what sensation would attend such an act. Or would he actually try to thrust his nose into her vagina, attempting some strange and exotic form of penetration, wherein the nose is substituted for the organ usually preferred in such instances?

"Oooh," she cried in soft, flute-like tones while his nose skimmed over her mount of Venus. "Ooooh."

He did not penetrate Mary Louise with his prominent, Plains Indian's nose, to her commingled relief and disappointment. But what he did instead surprised the Rhode Island blonde even more, for the "savage" from the plains of Kansas and Colorado suddenly began to indulge in a sexual practice which was more characteristic of Frenchmen and other Europeans of a certain level of sophistication than her fellow countrymen.

"Ooo-oooh," Mary Louise whispered, going wide-eyed at the discovery that the American

75

Indian could be adept at oral sex. "Uum, Mr. Hawk," she murmured arching her pelvis up slightly to meet the Pawnee's pursed, questing lips and the tongue which browsed the downy forestation of her pink and musky coozy.

Soaring Hawk tilted his head sharply to one side, and then pressed his thin lips firmly against the fat, pouting nether lips of the blonde, in the only kiss that he would ever bestow upon her.

"Oh, that feels so-o-o.good, Mr. Hawk," Mary Louise murmured, squirming in response to the Pawnee's vulvic kiss.

Then she emitted a little gasp, as his tongue entered the cleft between those burning and engorged nether lips and traveled upward in a darting, flicking run.

"Ooo-ooo," she hummed contentedly, stretching out her limbs upon the bed, a blissful smile upon her lips as the brave's tongue circled the base of her erect and sensitized clitoris, and then traveled down to her vaginal orifice.

A little while of this, of the Indian's expert and persistent ministrations, and the Rhode Island blonde was moaning and groaning and writhing in the exquisite, tumescent agony that immediately precedes the release of orgasm.

"Oh, Mr. Hawk. Oh."

"Ugh," the Pawnee grunted, his tongue darting over and around her pink, swollen button the way a gila monster's tongue darts flies off a cactus bud.

In a moment more it was she, and not the Indian, who began to whoop. Mary Louise's body stiffened as her climax broke over her in irresistible waves.

"Oh, my land sakes," she whispered minutes later, after it was all over and she had finally recovered enough to open her eyes and speak. "Oh, that was just peachy, Mr. Hawk."

Mary Louise was full of gratitude as she sat up and leaned over the now recumbent Soaring Hawk, planting ardent kisses upon his pectorals and grasping the shaft of his erect cock the way an Iroquois hefts a new tomahawk.

"Oh, Mr. Hawk," the little blonde said between the moist kisses she smacked along the alley that ran along between Soaring Hawk's pectorals. "That was. . .*so* good. . .now let me. . .make you . . .com-for-ta-ble. . . ."

By the time Mary Louise said this, her kisses had travelled down to the Pawnee's groin, and as if to punctuate her statement, she raised her head, parted her full lips and then leaned forward again, taking the head of the Pawnee's lance in her mouth while she worked over its shaft with her right hand, stroking and twirling with all the expertise of a Pawtucket taffy puller.

"Ugh," the Pawnee grunted as the heat of a Comanche bonfire blazed in his groin. And a few moments later he whooped like an Indian on the warpath, firing off a burst of jism into the Rhode Island blonde's warm and ardent mouth.

It was good to come off the trail, the Plains Indian reflected a few minutes later, falling into the deep, dark sleep that follows gratified desire.

3
Bart Braden's Enemies

"Boy, sure feels good t'git yer ashes hauled after a long spell on the trail, don't it, ol' son?" Davy said to his Pawnee blood-brother as the two men sauntered out of the honkytonk which fronted on San Antonio's main plaza.

The Pawnee had a faint smile of contentment upon his face as he nodded to the Kansan.

"Blonde woman blonde all over," he told him, with the air of a scientist who had just verified the results of an important experiment.

"Ol' Delia Lee got herself in the saddle an' took me for one hell of a wild ride," Davy informed Soaring Hawk. "Why, that lady could git a job in the circus jus' 'bout any time she pleased." He shook his head admiringly. "Best damn bareback rider I ever did see."

"Ride like Pawnee after buffalo, huh?" the grinning brave grunted.

"How 'bout you, my brother? You have a good time?"

Soaring Hawk nodded. "Like deer, I browse in grass. Woman moan like catamount in mating time. Then, when that finished, she come round and puff me like peace pipe." He grinned again.

"She smoke 'til pipe empty. Heap good. Heap big medicine."

"Yep," Davy Watson agreed, laughing. "It's medicine like that what'll set ya to rights."

It was then, as the pair made their way down the front steps of the honkytonk, that they noticed the crowd across the plaza, milling in the moonlight, outside of Oliver Entwhistle's Exchange.

"Judas Priest, I wonder what's goin' on over there?" Davy said as they set foot on the boards of the street.

"Must be from shots before. I hear in bedroom. You hear?" Soaring Hawk asked the Kansan.

"Oh, yeah," Davy Watson replied. "I thought that was jus' somebody a-whoopin' it up on a Friday night. You know how wild these Texas boys gits."

"Mebbe somebody shoot somebody," the Pawnee suggested.

"That's a possibility I wouldn't count out," Davy replied, steering the Indian in the direction of Entwhistle's Exchange. "Le's have us a look-see."

"Same old story," the brave told him making a sour face. "White man go to church on Sunday, hear preacher say all men brothers. By Friday, he forget this, get likkered up and shoot brother."

The Kansan nodded and smiled a wry smile. "Judgin' from what you say, I reckon you been around Christian folks a mite."

"Many Christian only Christian on Sunday." Soaring Hawk observed.

"Fella whose book I once read—I fergit his name—said, 'The last Christian died on the cross.' " Davy smiled again. "I know that's a right

79

blasphemous thing to say, but it does make a point."

"Cross is two logs where Jesus hang?" Soaring Hawk volunteered.

"Yep. That's the point of the story."

Not quite getting the point, Soaring Hawk nodded. "I know story of Jesus. What soldiers do to him make me think of Indian torture. Be like Jesus captured by Apache or Comanche, mebbe."

"He was beat an' crucified by Roman soldiers," Davy told the Pawnee.

"Sound like Indian more than white man."

"Nope. They was white men. Eye-talians, from Italy. That's in Europe, where all the white men come from."

At this point they had crossed the plaza, and were on the street outside of Entwhistle's Exchange.

"Hey, mister," Davy said, tapping the shoulder of a tall man in black who wore pipestem pants, a soft, black felt hat and spectacles whose shape and wire frames reminded the Kansan of pictures he had seen of Ben Franklin. "What's been goin' on in this here place?"

"Dunno exactly," the man said as he turned to face Davy, his eyes widening when he caught sight of Soaring Hawk. " 'Pears that one fella—I knew *him*, big man, ugly ol' sum'bitch name of Swein-hardt—was a-messin' 'round with some other fella's gal."

"That's one of the best ways to get shot that I know of," Davy observed.

"Well, he sure 'nuff did," the man in black went on. "Got his head blowed off, as I heerd it."

"Kinda figgers," Davy muttered, reflecting upon the perils of illicit love in the West. "That ain't the kinda thing a man takes lightly hereabouts."

"However," the man continued, "if ever a man needed shootin', it was that Sweinhardt fella. He was rotten through an' through. Warn't above horse thievin', bushwhackin' or a-cheatin' at cards. An' if'n anybody ever had a good word to say 'bout him, I never done heerd of it. Why, I reckon you could say that puttin' ol' Sweinhardt under ground was doin' the municeepality of San Antone a public service." The man frowned and shook his head. "He was one bad *hombre*, an' we's a heap better off without him."

"Who shot this here Sweinhardt?" Davy asked.

"Ain't learned that yet," the man answered. "But that ain't all. After Sweinhardt got his fat ugly head blowed off, some fella who was in the State Po-lice come an' made ready to arrest the *hombre* what done shot him. But he was quick on the trigger, that *hombre*, an' he got the drop on t'other fella. Shot him too. An' at close range, I reckon. Blowed him right through the upstairs railin', an' sent him a-droppin' smack in the middle of a high-stakes poker game. They was poker chips all over the floor from one wall to the other." The man chuckled.

"An' one galoot got hisself knocked out by the fallin' body," he went on. "An another got two front teeth knocked out by the toe of the dead man's boot."

"Who kilt 'im?" Davy heard someone saying in a raw, angry voice, as two men carried the body of a balding man out through the front door of Oliver Entwhistle's Exchange.

"Ain't nobody talkin', John," another voice replied, off to one side. "But I got me one *hombre* who's a-willin' to tell us what he knows."

Davy and Soaring Hawk looked in the direction of the speakers, and then watched as they came together, one of them dragging a third man along roughly, his fist wrapped in the front of the man's flannel shirt.

"Well, who kilt 'im?" the angry-voiced man demanded once more. Davy saw that he was a brawny man with red mutton-chop whiskers and a big, sandy, handlebar mustache.

Cringing as the second man thrust him forward, the third man put his hands up before his face.

"Speak up, man!" the brawny, mustachioed man roared. " 'Cause patience ain't one of my virtues. If'n you don't start a-talkin', like as not I'll be of a mind to make you. An' if'n I have to do that, why, after I'm through with you, you'll wish that you had been taken by Comanches instead."

The third man whimpered and made choking sounds, apparently having lost the power of speech.

As his eyes traveled over the forms of the man called John and his partner, the Kansan saw that both men wore upon their chests the badge of the Texas State Police.

"Quit whinin' like a hound-dawg tied to a back porch," the brawny man ordered, "or I'll blow off yer earlobes, one at a time." He whipped out a huge Smith and Wesson from his holster and pointed it at the cringing, whimpering man's head.

Davy Watson heard this and winced, the state policeman's words bringing to mind his pistol duel on Mount Davidson, high above a sleeping Virginia City, where he had downed the Alabamian procurer, Malcolm Shove—and had his own left earlobe shot off.

Fingering the scar tissue above the absent earlobe, the Kansan watched the drama unfolding before his eyes.

"Seems like ever' body here'bouts knows who done all the shootin', John," the second man informed his partner. "But nary a soul cares to say. So I figger that perticular *hombre* got him a passel of friends, or else ever'body's jus' plain scairt of him. Or mebbe both."

"But this jasper knows, don't he?" the brawny, redhaired man said loudly, his face reddening as he spoke in tones of impatience. The man in the middle covered his face with his hands and continued to whimper, unable to speak.

"He's a buddy of that Sweinhardt fella," the second man said. "So I don't reckon he cares none fer the *hombre* what shot 'im. I'd say he's our best bet to find out who done gunned down ol' Paul."

Click. The cowering man gasped as the brawny state policeman cocked his big Smith and Wesson pistol.

"You got yerself three seconds, mister, to start talkin' or prayin'."

Davy saw the man's knees buckle.

"Better start talkin', *amigo*," the second state policeman advised, grabbing the man by the shoulders to hold him up.

"*One*," the brawny man said in a low, growling

voice, aiming the big gun at the cowering man's head.

"Oooh," the cowering man said in the voice of a baying dog as he fought to regain the power of articulate speech.

"Two."

"Hoo-hoo-woo-oooo," bayed the terrified man in his canine falsetto, still unable to speak.

Davy and Soaring Hawk looked on in great fascination, both of them wondering whether or not the man would get his voice back in time to save his life.

The second state policeman cleared his throat.

"Yiii-i-i-i-iii," the dog-man bayed, tears streaming down his leathery cheeks.

"Don't look like he's gonna come through," the second state policeman said matter-of-factly.

"No, it don't—dadblame it!" the brawny man growled, his thumb going to the hammer of his huge pistol.

Click. The weapon double-cocked loudly, and as it did, the dog-man emitted an eerie, baying wail and fell to his knees on the boards of the sidewalk.

"Three," the brawny man said in a voice as cold as dead men's feet.

"Hoo-oo-ooo, woo-ooo," the kneeling man bayed, still bereft of the power of speech. His tears ran down in torrents, splattering the warped and dusty boards upon which he knelt, and he shook like a man with Saint Vitus' dance.

"Oh, shit," the burly man growled in a voice colored by disappointment. "Ain't nothin' fer it now, but to shoot the sum'bitch."

"Might as well," the second man said in that

matter-of-fact voice of his. "Don't look like he'll ever git his voice back, no-ways."

"Yii-yii-yiii!" wailed the dog-man, fully aware that he was kneeling upon death's threshold. "Yii-yiii-I-I. . ."

"Hold on, John," the second man advised. "I think he's a-comin' 'round."

"I-I-I-I. . ." the dog-man persisted.

"Damn well better," the brawny man grumped, tapping the dog-man on the head with the cannon-sized barrel of his Smith and Wesson.

"I-I-I-I'll t-t-talk," the dog-man stammered, finally able to speak. "D-d-don't shoot m-m-me, mister. Please."

"I won't," the brawny man growled, finally lowering his weapon, "if'n I like what I hear."

"Git up, fella," the second man said quietly, nudging the dog-man with his elbow.

Davy Watson and Soaring Hawk exchanged looks as the man rose unsteadily to his feet.

"All right, mister," the brawny man said, "start talkin'. Who done shot ol' Paul Myers?"

The dog-man looked around nervously as a series of angry mutterings arose from the surrounding crowd.

"Don't you pay them no heed, boy," the brawny man said, glaring from face to face with narrowed and angry eyes. "You's got me to answer to. . .as does anybody else what's got a mind to put in his two cents worth."

Nobody in the crowd chose to challenge the angry state policeman.

"Go on, boy," he told the man who had been a crony of the late and unlamented Sweinhardt.

85

"Let's hear who done the shootin'."

"Fella name of Braden," the dog-man yipped, as a chorus of angry murmurs arose from the crowd. "Bart Braden, I think it were."

"Now, simmer down, folks," the second state policeman cautioned, as the Kansan's jaw dropped and his eyes went wide.

"Bart Braden!" Davy Watson cried out loudly in surprise, suddenly stilling the buzzing hubbub of the crowd.

"What's it to you, *amigo*?" the brawny state policeman growled, impaling the Kansan upon his steely glance.

"Why, I'm after Bart Braden, myself," Davy told the Texan. "Sum'bitch shot me, too."

The crowd began to buzz angrily at this.

"Simmer down!" the second state policeman ordered, whipping out his sidearm and punctuating his command by firing two shots into the air. Immediately following this, the crowd fell silent.

The brawny man looked the Kansan up and down. "Well, if'n you got yerself a score to settle with that fella, then y'all's welcome to ride after 'im with us."

His eyes traveled from Davy to Soaring Hawk. "This here Injun with you, mister?" he asked testily, his eyes narrowing when he saw the scalping knife in the Pawnee's belt.

"Sure is," Davy replied empthatically. "My buddy here's a Pawnee, an' a true friend to the white man."

"Round these parts, an' up north by the Red River," the smaller state policeman told Davy, "we spent us a lotta time fightin' Injuns. How'd you git friendly with this one?''

"This man an' his tribe comes highly spoke of,'' Davy shot back, his face now as devoid of expression as the Pawnee's. He was learning to keep his feelings in check at critical times in his life, times such as this one.

"Me'n him was together with Colonel Forsyth, at the battle of Beecher's Island,'' Davy told the two men, flashing them a grim smile as he recalled the encounter at Arikaree Creek in Eastern Colorado, wherein a force of fifty scouts and traders, under the command of George A. Forsyth, withstood a combined mounted force of nearly one thousand Cheyenne, Arapahos and Kiowas.

The men looked impressed; the Battle of Beecher's Island, as the stand came to be called, was celebrated from Maine to California, having inflamed the popular imagination.

"An' his people scouts fer Major Frank North,'' Davy went on, taking advantage of the impression his words had made.

"Zat so?'' the brawny man rumbled, looking the Pawnee over from head to toe. Frank North was already on his way to becoming a legendary figure for his work with the Pawnees. Under his leadership, they had been able—for the first time, to win several decisive victories over their hereditary enemies, the Cheyennes.

"His name's Soaring Hawk,'' Davy told the two men, "An' he's as good a man as you'll ever be likely to meet. . .which is a thing he'll prove if'n you ever git in a tight spot with him.''

The two Texans exchanged questioning looks.

"My name's Watson,'' the Kansan told them.

"I'm out to git a young lady that Bart Braden done took away from her daddy, up in the New Mexico Territory. An' when I get her back safe-like, I aim to settle that *hombre's* hash—once't an' fer all."

"Well, Mr. Watson," the brawny, mustachioed man said, pausing next to clear his throat. "You'n yer Injun buddy here—"

"Soaring Hawk," Davy interjected.

"Uh, yep. Soaring Hawk," the man went on. "You'n him's welcome to ride along with me'n my friend, here." Saying this, he indicated the smaller man with a jerk of his thumb. The other nodded at Davy and Soaring Hawk. "For we mean to track down this here Bart Braden, an' see that justice gits done."

"You gonna go outta state after him, if'n you got to?" someone asked from the doorway of the Exchange.

The brawny man turned, as did the others and looked the newcomer over. He was a tall bald-headed man, slender except for a "beer belly."

"Now, jus' who might you be, mister?" the brawny man asked, annoyance further roughening his voice.

"I'm Oliver Entwhistle," the man told him, meeting the state policeman's glance. "I own this here place. An' Bart Braden's my friend."

"Well, I hope you done got a chance to say g'bye," the smaller man said sarcastically. " 'Cause I don't spec' y'all gon' see much of him after this."

"You gonna see he gits a fair trial, if'n y'all catch him?" Oliver Entwhistle asked, glaring at the two men.

"We'll take care of ever'thin', mister. Don't fret yerself 'bout it."

"State po-lice cain't never be trusted," the owner of the exchange said angrily, drawing himself up to his full height and staring over the heads of the two men.

"Well, ain't that a crock of shit!" the brawny man retorted angrily, his beefy face going red. "We's Texas Rangers first an' foremost. An' that's how we'll deal with Bart Braden when we git holt of 'im—as Texas Rangers."

"Well, you two is State Po-lice now," Oliver Entwhistle persisted.

The smaller man flicked his badge with his thumbnail. "The State Po-lice is full of scoundrels, shore 'nuf. But that don't mean me'n ol' John here is scoundrels, too. 'Cause we ain't. We's Rangers, through an' through."

"Yeah, but—" Entwhistle began.

"Never mind makin' no argument, mister," the brawny man interrupted, shooting the owner of the honkytonk a hard look. "Braden done gunned down our buddy, an' we aim to run 'im to ground fer that. Now, why don't you jus' mosey back inside, an' wipe down yer bar?"

He said the last sentence in a menacing growl, and his hand was now hovering over the handle of his Smith and Wesson.

Oliver Entwhistle's eyes traveled down to the brawny man's hand. "Y'all ain't man enuf to take Bart Braden," he growled, stepping back and closing the door as he did.

The brawny man spat contemtuously upon Entwhistle's door. Then he turned back to Davy

Watson and Soaring Hawk.

"Well, Mr. Weston," he began.

"Watson," Davy said patiently.

"Uh, yeah. Watson. Like I done said afore, you'n yer friend's welcome to join me'n my partner here."

"We'd be right glad to do that, mister," Davy replied holding out his hand.

"John B. Loudermilk's my name," the brawny man rumbled, pumping the Kansan's hand vigorously. "An' my pal here's T.C. Pritchett."

"Pleased to meet ya," the small man with the pinched and weathered face said quietly, as he offered Davy his hand.

As they shook, the brawny man slowly reached out his hand to Soaring Hawk. The Pawnee met his eye, and after a moment had passed, they shook hands. Then Soaring Hawk and the smaller man shook hands.

"Well," the brawny man said, looking toward the hitching post that stood in front of Oliver Entwhistle's Exchange, "let's go git that sum'bitch."

Realizing that traveling in the company of a lovely young *chicana* presented an unnecessary risk in the western and southern parts of Texas, Bart Braden now made his way eastward through the Lone Star State. Raquel Mirabal rode at his side, casting sidewise glances at her abductor from time to time.

Leaving San Antonio by way of the heights where the neglected Alamo stood, the ramrod headed east, crossing the Guadalupe River at Seguin. From there he went to Lulling and Lockhart, working his way northward to the city of Austin.

Since he had gunned down a state policeman, Braden figured that someone would be coming after him, either a sheriff's posse or a band of the generally corrupt and incompetent Texas State Police. Either prospect did not particularly disturb him, for Raquel had proved to be an excellent rider, and had so far been able to keep up with him under all conditions.

This ability greatly impressed the Texan, and served to increase the intensity of his already supercharged emotions where the young *chicana* was concerned. Courteous, gentle and respectful, both loving and admiring in manner, Bart Braden continued to ply his strange and elaborate courtship. It was a complete turnabout for him: the man who had always stopped at nothing in order to get what he wanted, the man who had been the lover of Bill Fanshaw's daughter, Samantha, and the cattle baron's heir apparent, wooed the daughter of Don Solomon Mirabal with all the patience, delicacy and feeling of a Romantic poet.

While she still considered herself Braden's captive, the Latin beauty gradually became aware of the tender nature of the ramrod's feelings toward her. Raquel had already been much impressed by the way she had been treated—and protected—by the man who had forcibly taken her from the *hacienda* of her father. She was, Raquel had to admit to herself, not unimpressed by the Texan, despite the fact that he represented nearly everything she had been taught to hate and despise.

He was extraordinarily competent—a man who

could do anything that he set his mind to do; and it would be done well, there was no question about that. The Texan had a mind which worked with lightning-like rapidity, a mastery of manual and outdoor skills, the coordination and agility of an athlete, considerable expertise in the use of weapons, iron determination, and a temperament to which fear was a total stranger.

Braden was tall, well-built and handsome, too, the young *chicana* had to admit that. The Texan's thick curly hair, broad sideburns and square jaw gave him a dashing look. All her *amigas* at the convent school of Our Lady of Guadalupe would have remarked that the tall and broadshouldered *tejano* was a fine-looking man. And he walked with the grace of a puma, and had a deep, knowing look in his eye, one which had convinced Raquel that Bart Braden would surely be a most knowledgeable and expert lover.

Indeed, Raquel told herself ruefully, her *tejano* captor was a man of character, ambition, and great ability. Not many men would have presumed to attempt to defy one of the great Texas cattle barons and steal the daughter of a great New Mexican *rico* from right under his nose.

Oh, make no mistake about it, Raquel Mirabal conceded grudgingly, Bart Braden was a bold and fearless man. Few men would have dared ignite a range war merely for the express purpose of abducting a woman.

He was ruthless, as well, Don Solomon's daughter reminded herself, a sudden wave of reproach rising in her heart. He had gunned down her rescuer. Did she not, with her own two eyes, see

Davy Watson's dead body sink beneath the cold waters of that faraway mountain lake? Did not Bart Braden kill the very man who had been her first lover?

Yes, he had, Raquel was forced to admit. That deed, plus the act of abducting her from her father's house, stealing her away from the friends, land and family she loved, had earned the Texan her undying hatred. She would, the young *chicana* reminded herself, get her revenge when the opportunity presented itself. The honor of the Mirabal family would be upheld, make no mistake about that.

What she was forced to admit, having by now spent a considerable amount of time in the company of her *tejano* abductor, was that Bart Braden was a fair man. From what she now knew of him, Raquel was certain that the Texas ramrod was no backshooter or bushwacker. Nor was he a hired killer, *un asesino*.

No, he was a man of honor—that much she would say for him. Hard, determined, even ruthless. Yes, he was that, but he was not a skulking coward; nor was he a man likely to cringe before any opponent, no matter how formidable. In many ways he reminded Raquel of her father.

There had been, she recalled, an exchange of shots during that deadly encounter in the pines by the side of the mountain lake. Each man had fired off several shots. That was proof positive that poor Davy Watson had got a chance to fire back at the man who gunned him down.

At least she could not reproach Braden with cowardice. No, there was honor in the way he had taken her. Raquel thought about the *corridas*, the popular ballads sung by her people, and of the romantic tales of outlaws such as Elfego Baca and Joachim Murietta, the "Robin Hood of the West."

In many of those tales, men had gone against great odds in order to ride off with the women they loved. And that was one more thing that Raquel had to admit: Bart Braden certainly did love her—with a passion that appealed perhaps, more to the eighteen-year-old *chicana* than to an *Angla*, of the same age even though its excesses had bred a series of disastrous consequences.

Pasión. Pasión. Pasión.

The minds of the young girls at the convent school of Our Lady of Guadalupe, at Albuquerque, were consumed by the thought of a passionate love affair. Nearly all of them entertained elaborate fantasies of bold lovers who would come, surmounting all obstacles, and then ride off into the sunset with them. And Raquel Mirabal was no exception.

The circumstances of her abduction and the handsome appearance of her abductor would have driven her former classmates wild with envy, Raquel told herself, now that she had attained a certain perspective on the events which had so radically altered her life.

Ramona Vasquez was betrothed to Julio Santana, a dull and colorless civil servant. Conchita Alvarez would soon wed fat Pepe Guzmán, son of the *patrón*, Don Francisco Guzmán, one of her father's neighbors. Maria Fernandez was being courted by Olivio Ramos, a balding middle-aged merchant. And Raquel Mirabal's best friend, Lucecita Suarez, was being courted by Oscar Aponte, a skinny Albuquerque undertaker.

None among them could match in their wildest imaginings the reality of Raquel Mirabal's daily life. Here she was, having gone from the arms of one bold and handsome man to another. And the second, Bart Braden, that reckless and astonishing man, had killed the first—Davy Watson of Kansas, the man who had touched the lovely *chicana's* heart and made her perform the act of love with him for the first time in her life—and on horseback, no less! *Caramba*! How sad! How beautiful! How exciting!

Who would believe it all? Raquel Mirabal asked herself, as she and Braden caught sight of Austin in the distance. It was all too incredible; that's what everyone would say when they heard her story. But yet, it is a well-known fact that truth is stranger than fiction.

"Won't be long now, 'til we git to Austin, honey," Bart Braden said in his deep and resonant voice, drawing Raquel out of her reverie.

A tiny, reversed Washington was what one celebrated traveler had called Austin, that handsome city on the left bank of the Colorado River. The capital of Texas, Austin's limestone capitol building stood high on a hill, overlooking the general expanse of the city. And from this magnificent cream-colored edifice, a broad avenue ran down to the river, its sides dotted with the major stores and buildings of the municipality.

Buildings of all sorts co-existed in Austin, from

the log cabins of the first inhabitants to the quarried limestone of the municipal buildings and the homes of the well-to-do. Cottages and meaner dwellings were located well back from the main avenue.

The capital of Texas boasted a great number of drinking and gambling places, but not a single bookstore. Churches were rarely to be seen, and Raquel Mirabal shook her head when she considered the question of culture in the Lone Star State. The daughter of the New Mexico *rico* had been schooled in the high culture of Renaissance Spain, having read extensively the works of Cervantes, Calderón, Lope da Vega, and others. She seriously doubted that the vast majority of the *tejanos* could even read at all. . .or do more than make an "X" where their names were required on documents.

"I reckon we can rest here a spell, honey," Bart Braden told Raquel Mirabal as they reined in their horses before a hotel. The ramrod said this confidently, ignorant of the fact that Davy Watson, Soaring Hawk, and two former Texas Rangers were riding out after him.

4

With the Texas Rangers

As Bart Braden had reckoned, the sight of a *gringo* riding in the company of a beautiful young *chicana* was one of the more unusual sights of the southerly part of Texas, and it was not long before the ramrod's pursuers had picked up his trail.

John B. Loudermilk and T.C. Pritchett, the two state policemen who considered themselves Texas Rangers in eclipse, went straight to the Mexicans among the onlookers outside Entwhistle's Exchange, saying that Braden had stolen Raquel from her father's *hacienda*. In this manner, they soon determined which way the fugitive pair had gone. And from the Mexican residents of Alamo Heights, Davy and his companions learned that Braden and Raquel had headed toward the Guadalupe River.

The state policemen were an interesting pair, the Kansan soon discovered, as his trailmates began to tell him about their years of service as Texas Rangers, first to the Republic, and then to the Lone Star State.

Where John B. Loudermilk was big and brawny, T.C. Pritchett was short and sinewy; where the first was loud and garrulous, the second was soft-spoken and taciturn.

The two men, as different as mountain and prairie, were inseparable friends who had served together for many years as Texas Rangers. Paul Myers, the man whom Bart Braden had shot, had also been a close friend of the pair; they had served under him in the Rangers, as well as in the Texas State Police. They rode out in the name of friendship to avenge the killing, vowing not to come off the trail until Bart Braden had been run to earth.

"He's a mighty tough customer," Davy told the two men. "I tangled with him afore."

T.C. Pritchett pursed his lips and let fly an enormous job of tobacco juice, which splattered against a big rock by the side of the trail.

"We's used to dealin' with tough *hombres,* Mr. Watson," he told the Kansan. "Used to come up agin 'em all the time in the Rangers."

"How come you ain't Rangers now," Davy asked, "seein' as how you talks so good about 'em?"

Pritchett shook his head and shifted the huge quid of chewing tobacco to the other side of his mouth. "Ain't no more Texas Rangers, these days," he said tersely.

"How's that?" Davy asked.

"Ol' T.C.'s a man of few words," John B. Loudermilk told the Kansan. "What he means is that the Rangers done got disbanded once't the war twixt the states was over."

" 'At's right," Pritchett muttered.

"Texas was under military control 'til last year, an' the Fed'ral Gov'ment warn't 'bout to let the state organize no bodies of armed men, nohow. So that 'pears to be the end of the Texas Rangers.'' He sniffed and wiped his nose on the sleeve of his buckskin jacket.

"Then ol' F.J. Davis jus' got hisself 'lected Governor of Texas—that carpetbaggin' sum'bitch—an' figgered if'n he was a-gonna stay in office, he done better git him some way to control the people."

"I don't git yer drift," Davy told him.

"Tell 'im 'bout the 'lection, John," prompted the laconic Pritchett.

"Oh," the brawny, mustachioed man said. "Sure 'nuff. S'cuse me. Y'see, the onliest way a carpetbag Ree-publican could ever git elected was by the Fed'ral Gov'ment taking the vote away from them who was Confed'rates, an' friends of Confed'rates, an' givin' that vote to all the nigrahs what done got freed after the war."

Davy had heard of this tactic, which had outraged the defeated Southerners, and was partly responsible for the birth of that mysterious and menacing new organization, the Ku Klux Klan. This mass disenfranchisement was followed by outrageous political corruption, and the scandal of the carpetbaggers.

"The State Po-lice," John B. Loudermilk went on, "was F. J. Davis's way of keepin' hisself in office, 'cause he ain't 'zackly the mos' popular Gov'nor Texas ever done had."

"Not by a longshot," T.C. Pritchett agreed.

"State Po-lice is brand new," the brawny man continued, "but it already looks to be full of scoundrels an' bullies an' backshootin' dogs. Me'n ol' T.C., why we don't hold with such doin's. We didn' know what we was a-gittin' into, an' we ain't so sure that we wants to have our good names associated with a or-ga-nee-za-tion like this here one."

"Cain't be doin' us no good, we figger," Pritchett seconded.

"But someday, they's gonna be Texas Rangers once't more," Loudermilk said emphatically, "an' that's what we's a-hangin' 'round fer."

Pritchett nodded. "It's what we's cut out fer."

"But this here State Po-lice business is a big crock o' shit," the brawny man growled. "Why ever'where we rides, folks is allus a-lookin' at us like we done come to rob 'em blind, or bushwhack 'em first chance we git."

Pritchett seconded this by màking a sour face and nodding.

"Sounds like a passel of rogues an' scoundrels," Davy Watson observed.

"An' that's puttin' it in a good light," John B. Loudermilk told him, scowling like a fighting terrier entering the pit.

"But the Rangers was another pot o' stew," the big redhead sighed. "We done a job o' work in that here outfit, an' some mighty deeds which folks still remembers."

"We was tough customers, Mr. Watson," T.C. Pritchett told Davy. " 'Cause a Texas Ranger could ride like a Mexican, trail like a Injun, shoot like a Tennessean, an' fight like a devil."

"As ol' Cap'n L.H. McNelly (who was skinny as a rail, had the con-sump-tion, an' never done weighed more than 135 pounds, soakin' wet)

100

said," added John B. Loudermilk, " 'Courage is a man who keeps on a-comin' on.' "

"What he done meant," Pritchett explained, "was that you might be able to slow down an *hombre* like that, but they's no way in hell you're gon' whip 'im. For the man what keeps on a-comin' on is gonna git there hisself, or damn shore make it possible fer the next *hombre* to git there."

"They's a pome 'bout the Texas Rangers," Loudermilk told Davy and Soaring Hawk. "It goes like this:

" *'The stars have gleamed with a pitying light*
On the scene of many a hopeless fight,
On a prairie patch or a haunted wood
Where a little bunch of Rangers stood.

They fought grim odds and knew no fear,
They kept their honor high and clear,
And, facing arrows, guns, and knives,
Gave Texas all they had—their lives.' "

"Beautiful pome, ain't it?" asked Pritchett. "Fella name of W.A. Phelson done writ it."

"Them's fine words," the Kansan agreed.

" 'Member ol' Rip Ford?" Pritchett said to Loudermilk. "Back in '58, when we done taught the Comanch' a lesson they never fergot."

"Tell 'em 'bout it, T.C.," the big man urged.

"Shucks, John," Pritchett said, shifting uncomfortably in his saddle and looking down at the trail, his face flushing to a deep, beet-red color. "You tell 'em."

"Ho, ho," the big man laughed as he gazed

warmly, at his buddy. "Sometimes I fergit that ol' T.C. aint' much fer talkin' 'round strangers." He shook his head. "Why, when we's on the trail on our own, he chatters like a blackbird. Cain't hardly shut 'im up. It's me who's the quiet one, then."

"Go on an' tell 'em, John," Pritchett mumbled, still blushing furiously.

"Right," his mustachioed partner said, turning in his saddle to face Davy Watson and Soaring Hawk. " 'Twas back in '58, like I done said, an' ol' Rip Ford—Major John S. Ford, properly speakin'—got the order from Governor Hardin R. Runnels to pertect the frontier."

He paused to clear his throat, hawk up a gob of phlegm, and spit it out on the side of the trail, after which he resumed his story.

"Ol' Hardin Runnels got hisself elected only a few months afore, an' he was determined to make his mark. An' jus' 'bout the best way to do that were to straighten things out somewhat on the Texas frontiers.

" 'I impress upon you the necessity of action an' energy,' " Loudermilk said in an exaggerated manner, as he impersonated the former governor of Texas. " 'Follow any and all trails of hostile or suspected Indians you may discover, and if possible, overtake an' chastise them, if unfriendly.' "

Pritchett, no longer red in the face, began to chuckle loudly.

"That's what he done writ," Loudermilk informed his listeners, chuckling now himself. "He was a fancy-talkin' man."

"I reckon," Davy agreed, smiling. Beside him

rode Soaring Hawk, who wore his usual Pawnee deadpan and seemed unaffected by the performance.

"So ol' Rip Ford, he done went on a campaign up north, in April of '58, with four detachments of Texas Rangers and their allies, the friendly Tonkaways, Anadarkos, an' Shawnees from the Brazos Reserve. Me'n ol' T.C. was there with 'im, an' we left the Red River an' lit out fer a branch of the Washita, where we was well out of Texas, an' deep in Comanche territory."

The Kansan's eyes narrowed as he remembered the close call that he'd had with Pahanca's Comanches in the southern part of the New Mexico Territory. They were a wild and dangerous bunch, without equal as fighters on horseback, and even the dreaded Apaches steered clear of them.

" 'Bout the tenth of May," John B. Loudermilk went on, "our Injun scouts come across't a buffalo carcass what had a couple of Comanche arrows still in it. An' the day after that, they done seen a passel of Injuns runnin' an' killin' some other buffalo. They tole by the tracks of the ponies where the Injuns done set up camp."

He paused to hawk up another mouthful of phlegm and spit it out.

"Next mornin', we done hit the camp—all 215 of us," the brawny ex-Ranger went on. "The Tonks demolished five lodges by the time we rid in an' took 'em some prisoners an' a heap of Comanche ponies. Two of the devils escaped and took off fer the Canadian River. Well, we tore ass after them bucks—all of us, Rangers an' Injuns—an' run three mile after 'em, when what d'ya suppose we done seen?''

"More Injuns, I 'spect," was Davy's response.

"You bet yer boots, more Injuns," John B. Loudermilk replied emphatically. "We done topped this ol' hill, an' seed a mess o' tepees on the far side of the Canadian. Turns out it was the main Comanche camp."

"Tha's right," Pritchett mumbled after letting fly a jet of saliva and Brown's Mule.

"But them sum'bitches was warned by the ol' boys we took off after," the big man continued. "An' when we come down towards 'em, they come toward us at the same time, led by a tough ol' buzzard name of Iron Jacket, who the Comanches figgered to be downright bullet-proof."

Davy recalled the great massed charge of a thousand mounted Indians at the Battle of Beecher's Island, which was led by the notorious Roman Nose, a chief who had also enjoyed a reputation for invulnerability. . .until that charge, the Kansan recalled, when one or more of George A. Forsyth's brave and gallant little band—among them, Eli Zigler, Sigmund Shlesinger and other renowned scouts—brought the Cheyenne down, never to rise again.

"Man ain't been born yet what's bullet-proof," Davy told the two Texans.

"Well," Loudermilk went on, "the Comanch' made themselves a big noise 'bout ol' Iron Jacket bein' that way. He had him this purty ol' shingled an' glitterin' coat of mail—he done got it from a Spanish fella, I fergit how—an' he sure 'nuff looked bullet-proof, covered from crotch to chin with all that overlappin' steel plate he wore."

T.C. Pritchett spoke up while the other Ranger paused to wipe his nose on his sleeve once more.

"Danged if'n we didn't think t'would take a blacksmith to bring 'im down."

Davy and John B. Loudermilk laughed loudly at this comment. Soaring Hawk's expression was as stony and inscrutable as ever while he stared at the small Texan.

"So on they come," Loudermilk resumed, "led by ol' Iron Jacket, who looked like a runaway boiler off'n some Mississippi paddleboat. An' they were all kinds of Comanch' behind 'im, a-whoopin' an' a-screechin' like the devil on a tear."

The Kansan nodded. "Comanches is mighty hellacious Injuns."

"That's fer shit-sure," the Texan agreed. "Well, anyway, ol' Iron Jacket, he rid towards us like a bat out of hell, bringin' that horde of caterwaulin' Comanch' with 'im.

"All of a sudden fiye or six rifles fired from our side, an' ol' Iron Jacket's horse goes down, a-throwin' the rest of the Comanch' into turmoil an' confusion."

"His horse certainly warn't bullet-proof," chuckled T.C. Pritchett.

"No, sir, nor was that ol' chief," his partner told Davy and Soaring Hawk excitedly. "Rifle balls was a-plunkin' an' a-clangin' as they struck that there coat of plate mail—from where I was it sounded like someone peein' on a tin roof—an' Iron Jacket spun around, teetered this way an' that fer a spell, an' then hit the ground, soundin' as if a mess o' boiler plates had fell off'n a Conestoga wagon."

"He wasn't bullet-proof no more," Pritchett mumbled gleefully.

Loudermilk continued his narrative. "Jim Pockmark, the Anadarko captain, an ol' Doss, one of our Shawnee guides, done claimed the honor of puttin' Iron Jacket away. They was a bunch of holes in the ol' boy's boiler plate, so any number of fellas might've done it.

"The charge broke, an' the battle done fanned out at that point, 'til it covered a circuit more than six mile long by three mile wide. From time to time the Comanch' would try to rally an' make a stand, but we was jus' too much fer 'em."

"Men cussin', women screamin', Injuns hollerin', children a-cryin'," Pritchett added. "If'n you was to die an' go down to hell, I shorely doubt you'd hear anythin' wuss'n that."

"At that point, the Comanch' sent in another chief—never did find out who the fella was," Loudermilk informed his listeners. "An' he led a charge on our flank, where the friendly Injuns was gathered, but ol' Chul-le-que, the Shawnee cap'n, shot the devil off'n his pony. Shortly after that, we druv the rest of 'em off—them that was still alive—which warn't a whole hell of a lot."

"Guess that took care of 'em, huh?" Davy Watson asked.

"T'warn't over yet," T.C. Pritchett said, after sending a gob of tobacco juice whizzing past his horse's ear. "Tell 'em, John."

"We done chased them other Injuns until our horses couldn't take no more—why, they was lathered up like they was 'bout to get a shave. Then we rid back to the Injun camp an' began to divvy up the spoils."

He wiped his nose on his buckskin sleeve. "But that warn't all," Loudermilk said, sniffling as he withdrew his sleeve. "Turns out there must've been another Comanch' camp 'bout three or four mile up the Canadian, an' them sum'bitches got roused by all the commotion we done whipped up kickin' ass, an' made as if they was a-gonna charge us."

"They was up on this ol' hill," Pritchett told Davy and Soaring Hawk, "a-hootin' an' a-hollerin' like a wolf pack catchin' sight of a flock o' sheep."

"Oh, they was a-yippin' an' a-yappin' to beat the band," John B. Loudermilk seconded, "an' screechin' all sorts of Injun abuse at the force of Tonkaways, Anadarkos an' Shawnees who come with us from the Brazos Reserve."

"Comanch' is wild sons o' bitches," T.C. Pritchett added gleefully. "An' they don't care none fer Reserve Injuns—does they best to wipe 'em out whenever they can."

"But them ol' boys from Brazos warn't no pushovers their own selves," the brawny ex-Ranger said, picking up the thread of the narrative without missing a stitch. "An' they tol' young Lieutenant Shapley P. Ross, who was a-leadin' the Reserve Injuns, to tell ol' Rip Ford that they was a-gonna draw out them Comanch' an' that us Rangers ought to stay in line an' git ready to back 'em up, if the need should arise."

"Them Comanches is sure full of fight," Davy said, his voice accompanied by the creak of leather as he shifted in his saddle.

"Oh, they's a bunch o' shitkickers, all right," the smaller of the two state policemen replied, his shyness disappearing in his excitement.

"So," his brawny, mustachioed partner went on, "the Comanch' began to come down from that there hill. An' as they come, they tried to draw out the Reserve Injuns, a-hopin' to git them so angry an' excited that they'd lose they heads an' jus' go after them, without no thought of strategy nor safety."

"You should've seen it," Pritchett piped up. "Them Comanch' was a pourin' over the hill, callin' the other Injuns every kind of cussword they could think of, makin' faces like the booger man, shakin' they fists an' lances, a-tryin' to git our Injuns all worked up."

"I seed this here book, once't," John B. Loudermilk reflected, " 'bout knights in armor a-chargin' an' a-knockin' each other off they horses. An' y'know somethin?" he asked rhetorically. "Them Injuns mixin' it up shore reminded me of them there knights of old."

"Yep. I seen pitchers like that," the Kansan told the ex-Ranger, recalling his Uncle Ethan's library.

"I reckon that's what it was like," Loudermilk confirmed. "They was shields an' lances, bows and' fancy headgear, horses a-prancin', an' feathers flappin' in the breeze like pennants at some courtly tournament of old.

"Durn battle looked like knights mixin' it up, too. If t'warn't fer the occasional crack of a rifle, a body'd think he was on some ol' battlefield in the days of yore." He sighed.

"All that mixin' it up was nice an' showy, but it

didn't count fer a hell of a lot. Them boys stabbed an' jabbed, cussed an' whooped, an' fired off arrows fer 'bout half an hour, without neither side doin' a whole lot of damage to the other.''

"Then it was time to send in the Texas Rangers," T.C. Pritchett said. "But the Comanch' done backed off, and' quit the field."

"But we took off after 'em," Loudermilk said in turn. "An' the fightin' got kinda general between us an' the Reserve Injuns agin' that mess of Commanch'. We whupped 'em ever' time met 'em. This went on 'till it was nigh on to two o'clock.

Now, you got to 'member we-all been goin' at it since seven that mornin'. So by the time we druv off that last pack of Comanch', we was all plumb tuckered out—men an' horses together.''

Pritchett spoke again. "Why, then we done heard that ol' Buffalo Hump was only twelve miles away with *another* big bunch of red devils—uh, s'cuse me," he said suddenly, going red in the face as he looked at Soaring Hawk. "They, uh, was more *hostiles* there 'bouts," he went on, now staring at the toes of his boots. "But we was all jus' too wore down to light out after 'em."

"But we done got what ol' Rip Ford sent us after," the brawny man added, beaming proudly at the Kansan and Soaring Hawk. "Ol' Rip, he figgered we done mixed it up with more'n three hunnerd Comanch' that day. An' the Rangers done kilt seventy-six of 'em. An' we captured more'n three hundred horses—"

"That got their goat," T.C. Pritchett chuckled. "Comanch'd druther stop a bullet then have to travel on foot. Why, them big-headed, barrel-chested, bandy-legged little fellas might be the slickest horse riders you ever done seen, but they ain't worth a hoot in hell on foot, I'll tell you that much!"

"Yep," his partner went on. "We done even took us eighteen prisoners, women an' children mainly. An' do you fellas know somethin'? All what the Texas Rangers lost was two men. Now, how 'bout that?" he crowed.

"That there's the gospel truth he's a-tellin' you boys," T.C. Pritchett affirmed.

"An' you know what ol' Rip Ford done said?" John B. Loudermilk asked in his rhetorical fashion. "He done praised young Shapley P. Ross to the skies fer leadin' them Reserve Injuns so good, an' then he done paid tribute to Pitts, Burleson, Nelson an' Tankersley—the men what led his four Ranger detachments."

He took off his ten-gallon hat and scratched his head. "Now, what was it he said? . . . Oh, yeah," he recalled, putting back his hat. "Ol' Rip said," he paused to clear his throat.

" 'They behaved under fire,' " he continued in a ringing, magisterial voice, " 'in a gallant and soldier-like manner, and I think they have fully vindicated their right to be recognized as Texas Rangers of the old stamp!' "

"Yep, that's jus' what we was—Texas Rangers of the ol' stamp," T.C. Pritchett said loudly, his voice trembling with emotion. "An' by Gawd, we will be agin', one day."

"You can bet yer boots an' saddles on that," John B. Loudermilk agreed. Then he broke into a wide, boyish grin. "Know what ol' Cap'n Nelson done said 'bout the Rangers?" he asked, pausing to wipe his nose on his fringed sleeve once more.

"He said in his report," the big man with the sandy handlebar mustache went on, " 'The only distinction in the ardor of the entire command was the relative speed of their horses.' "

"Guess that took care of the Comanches for a spell," the Kansan opined.

"Oh, I reckon it did that," Loudermilk agreed. "They done had enuff of us fer some time to come. We taught 'em a lesson, jus' like we done taught one to the Mexicans afore 'em."

"Shore 'nuff," seconded T.C. Pritchett. "Tell 'em 'bout the Mexican War, John. Tell 'em what the Texas Rangers done to ol' Santy Anna an' his boys."

"I'll tell 'em 'bout that over biscuits an' beans," the brawny man told his partner. "For if'n I don't git some food inside me, I swear I'll topple out'n my saddle. Ain't nobody else hungry?" he asked.

They were all hungry; each man nodded his head by way of reply.

"Well, then," John B. Loudermilk said, pulling on the reins and leading his horse off the trail and over to a clump of brush, "git out the skillet an' the coffee pot, an' once't we's filled our bellies, I'll tell ya 'bout the great deeds the Texas Rangers done in the Mexican War."

"Rangers has allus been tough *hombres*," John B. Loudermilk told Davy Watson and Soaring Hawk, as he spooned the last of his pinto beans out

111

of the battered and dented tin plate he held with his big left hand.

"Guardin' frontiers big as the ones we had in the early days of the Republic calls fer a breed of men what can ride like the wind, scout like an Injun, an fight like a bear what almost lost its balls in a steel trap."

The Kansan smiled as he stretched his arms; then he yawned and leaned back against his saddle, basking in the warmth of the campfire.

Soaring Hawk sat beside him, cleaning his Sharps rifle as he listened and stared inscrutably at the former Texas Ranger.

Somewhere to the north, in the distant hills, a coyote howled at the moon with the voice of a lost soul. The fire flared for a moment, as it consumed dry mesquite, chaparral, and sticks, sputtering and crackling as it cast a bright light on the four men who sat around it. Not far from the campfire, four tethered horses stirred, neighed softly, and switched their tails.

"Rangers got tough from fightin' Injuns an' Mexicans," Loudermilk said as he set his plate down by his side.

"Lots of Injuns," T.C. Pritchett volunteered from across the fire. "Cherokee, Tonkaway, Karankaway, Waco, Tawakoni, an' Comanch'."

"Delaware an' Shawnee was friendly, as was the Tonks later on," added Loudermilk. "But the Comanch' was the baddest Injuns you ever did see. They could ride like devils an' fight like bobcats."

"We done met the Chiricahua Apaches, an' they wasn't no angels their own selves," Davy told him.

The brawny man and his small, sinewy partner

both nodded. "They's tough boys, all right," Loudermilk conceded. "But they wasn't as wild as the Comanch'. Why, we still got our hands full with them suckers. Nowadays, they's into cattle rustlin' in a big way."

"Me'n ol' Soaring Hawk learned about that at first hand," the Kansan informed the two men. Then he told them of their capture by Pahanca's Comanches, and their subsequent rescue by Bart Braden.

"You mean the same *hombre* we's about to ride down?" Loudermilk asked incredulously.

Davy nodded. "Those was Bill Fanshaw's cows they run off. An' Bart Braden was Fanshaw's ramrod."

Pritchett stared across the campfire at the Kansan, a puzzled look on his face. "So he done saved your life?"

"I reckon," Davy growled, suddenly looking down as he began to poke among the embers with a stick. "But the sum'bitch gunned me down, later on. An' I sure wouldn't have run into no Comanches in the first place, if'n I hadn't been after him fer runnin' off with that gal, Raquel Mirabal."

"That do make a difference," Pritchett agreed.

"Uh, what was you sayin', Mr. Loudermilk?" Davy asked suddenly, looking up from the embers.

"Oh yeah," rumbled the brawny man with the sandy handlebar mustache. "I was talkin' 'bout how the Rangers got seasoned by fightin' Injuns an' Mexicans. Them Mexicans allus treated us tricky-like. Fust they invited American colonists down into Texas—tha's when ol' Moses Austin an'

113

his boy, Stephen, done come here. An' then, five years later, they tried to kick us out.''

"They tried all sorts of lowdown tricks," added Pritchett.

"They come in an' invaded us a couple of times," Loudermilk told his listeners. "An' they even had them a plot cookin' to raise all the Injuns against us at once't, so that they would jine together an' overrun us Texans. Them Mexes was allus renegin' on their word, an conductin' a heap of treacherous business behind our backs.''

"We done fought the Mexicans fer years," Pritchett said. "An' even defeated ol' Santy Anna at San Jacinto." He sighed. "But they was a heap of Mexicans, an' jus' a handful of Texans.''

"We was plumb lucky that they was havin' a passel of trouble at home in them days," Loudermilk told them. "Or I reckon we'd all be speakin' Spanish right now. They had them two political parties—Centralists and Federalists—what was allus fightin' amongst themselves. And the Frenchies was givin' 'em a hard time, as well. Lucky fer us.''

Pritchett nodded in vigorous agreement.

"Howsomever," Loudermilk went on, "things was still up an' down. We done sent out a ex-pee-dition to Santa Fe once't, hopin' to open up trade, an' we got our butts kicked good fer our pains." He smiled wryly and scratched the stubble on his chin. "We wanted to take the place over by nego-tiation, but the ex-pee-dition warn't well-planned. The Mexes caught our boys an' put 'em in the cala-boose. Hell, they even shot a bunch. The survivors were let go later, an' finally made their way back to

Texas.''

"Then the Mexicans come an' captured San Antone," T.C. Pritchett informed Davy and Soaring Hawk. "But they done withdrew to the Rio Grande after two days."

"Later on, they sent this ol' boy—General Woll was his name," Loudermilk added, "fer a second surprise attack on San Antone."

Pritchett chuckled as he recollected those turbulent days. "Me'n ol' John here warn't no more than sixteen or seventeen at the time. We was jus' boys."

"We mighta been boys, by Gad, but we rid with the Texas Rangers!" his partner said proudly.

"Yep," agreed the other. "An' ol' Jack Hays was leadin' us. He was one of the finest men ever to enter the service."

"An' ol' Matthew Caldwell," Loudermilk said loudly. "He was allus the fust to raise the war-whoop, an' the fust to mix it up with the enemy."

"Damn straight he was, John!"

"Well, us Texans ree-tali-ated by sendin' our own ex-pee-dition down into Mexico. Onliest problem was that it was full of wild boys and adventurers who wouldn't take no discipline. An' ol' General Somervell jus' had to give it up, 'cause he didn't have him no way of keepin' so many wild galoots in order. So he done headed back up into Texas, takin' 'bout seven hundred-fifty men with him. The remainin' three hundred decided to stay in Mexico an' kick 'em some ass.

"They come to be known as the Mier ex-pee-dition. That was 'cause they started out by attackin' a town by that name. But the Mexican troops arrived in strength, an' the Texas boys had to surrender after a desperate fight, seein' as how they got confused when their leader, William S. Fisher, got hisself wounded. So they surrendered, once't it was agreed they was to be treated as prisoners of war, an' kept near the northern border.''

Loudermilk scowed. "But the Mexicans marched 'em over to Matamoros, an' then down to Monterey. It was allus that way," he said bitterly. "You could never trust them greasers no futher than you could toss a Longhorn steer.''

"Mexican promises is worth less than Confederate money," commented T.C. Pritchett.

"That's right," said John B. Loudermilk, wiping his nose on the fringed sleeve of his buckskin jacket. "But the boys met up with some other Texans down there, fellas who had been captured at San Antone, an' they all made to escape.''

The two Texans exchanged mournful looks.

"They went through the desert, 'twixt Saltillo an' the Rio Grande, an' had the devil's own time of it. They was lost in the desert, without food nor drink, hunted like wolves, an' friend to no man. Purty soon, they was eatin' grasshoppers an' lizards, an' burrowin' in the dry dirt for water, with their tongues all black an' swole. They chucked away their guns to lighten the load. An' some of them got so crazy from thirst that they tried to drink they own pee.''

Pritchett shook his head tiredly as Loudermilk went on with his grim narrative.

"Five of 'em died in the desert. Four made it to

Texas. Three was never heard of again. An' all the rest was caught an' sent back to Salado in chains.

"Ol' Santy Anna wanted to have all the Texans shot, but the American an' British ambassadors raised such a ruckus that he only shot eighteen of 'em. The rest was jailed in Mexico City an' Perote prison, where they was treated real bad."

"Real bad," echoed T.C. Pritchett. "Fellas like Big Foot Wallace an' Samuel H. Walker."

"They was finally released, in dribs an' drabs. But there was a lot of hard feelin' 'bout how the Mexicans treated 'em. An' when they come back to Mexico City, at the head of ol' Zachary Taylor's army, them boys done settled more'n a few scores."

"You best believe *that*," Pritchett told Davy and Soaring Hawk.

"They done got even some," allowed Loudermilk.

"Shoot," said Pritchett in a wistful voice, going red in the face as he looked around the campfire. "Them was the days."

"You bet yer boots," agreed his partner. "An' they'll be back again, T.C." He turned to Davy and Soaring Hawk. "Why, we rid with the finest: Colonel Jack Hays, Matthew Caldwell, Big Foot Wallace, William N. Eastland, Samuel H. Walker, and the McCulloch boys—Ben an' Henry."

Pritchett was aroused, now. "Lord, what a sight it was to see Jack Hays mounted on his big ol' bay horse. An' he warn't much more'n a youngster, his own self. No more'n twenty-four or twenty-five. With dark, flashin' eyes, a full head of jet black hair, an' a face plumb full of character. Now, there

117

was a man," he said proudly.

"Did you know," Loudermilk said, pointing to the Kansan's holster, "that yer firearm there was named after a Texas Ranger?"

Davy shook his head as he looked down at the big Walker Colt.

"Shore was," the other continued. "Back in '36, some of the Rangers had got holt of young Samuel Colt's fust revolvers. But they was too dainty, an' nigh onto impossible fer a body to reload on horseback—an' that's what the Texas Rangers needed more'n anything."

"Why, afore the repeatin' revolver was invented, the Rangers had to use single-shot pistols," Pritchett informed Davy and Soaring Hawk. " 'Twarn't like it is nowadays. An' when we done fired all our guns at the enemy, we had to hop down off'n our horses an' charge 'em on foot." He shook his head. "We wasn't no match fer the Injuns, then. Them sum'bitches could send off nine arrows on horseback by the time we reloaded."

"That's the truth," rumbled John B. Loudermilk. "So finally, ol' Sam Walker was sent up to New York, to buy some arms fer the Republic of Texas." He paused to throw some brush and wood on the dying fire.

"Now, ol' Sam was a Injun an' Mexican fighter second to none," he went on, "an' he done tole young Samuel Colt that his new pistols was the best he'd ever come across't, but that they was a mite too light an' flimsy fer reg'lar use on the frontier."

"Y' see, what he needed," interjected Pritchett, "was a pistol what could be loaded in the saddle, whilst an *hombre* was ridin' hell-bent-fer-leather. There warn't no way you could do that with the one he had, 'cause the barrel had to be taken off so's you could replace the empty cylinder with a full one. That meant the rider had to holt onto three parts—tyin' up one hand, whilst he held the rest of the pistol in t'other." He leaned over and spat a gob of tobacco juice into the fire.

"Well now, this made sense to Samuel Colt, an' so he took Sam Walker back with him to his factory in Paterson, New Jersey. An' when ol' Sam finally come back to Texas, he was totin' a batch of new Colts. They was named after him—called the Walker revolver." The wiry Texan squinted as he peered across the campfire at Davy Watson's holster.

"It was a mite differnt from yours, Mister Watson. The fust Walker Colt had a lever rammer attached to the underside of the barrel, which seated the bullets in the chamber without never havin' to remove the cylinder. An' it had more weight an' a perfect balance, so's you could use it as a club to knock out some ornery galoot who warn't wuff shootin'."

Pritchett chuckled. "We bought a few of 'em then, in 1839. But that didn't save young Colt from goin' out of business in 1842."

"Went bankrupt," rumbled Loudermilk.

"When the Mexican War come, we sent ol' Sam Walker back to New York City, for to buy one thousand of the sixshooters from Colt—two fer each Texas Ranger. But Colt didn't hang onto any models, an' Sam didn't bring his with him. Then Colt advertised in the newspapers, but still nothin' turned up. So he designed a new gun fer us—they call it the 'Old Army Type' now. We didn't get 'em in the beginnin', but they did come to Vera Cruz, where we done landed afore marchin' on Mexico City.''

"By Gad, them was the days!" exclaimed John B. Loudermilk, slapping his knee with a meaty hand. "Once't we entered the Union, an American army was headin' by land an' sea to meet the enemy at the Rio Grande, which we claimed as the border with Mexico instead of the Nueces. Well, the U.S. gov'ment was ready to back up its words with action, by gum! 'Cause ol' Zachary Taylor done come down with his boys to kick ass.''

"Ol' Rough 'n Ready," T.C. Pritchett murmured fondly.

"Hot damn!" rumbled Loudermilk, a faraway look in his eyes. "That was the chance't that all us Texans had been waitin' fer—the chance't to fight Mexico on equal terms." He rubbed his big, callused hands together and grinned. "We was waitin' a long time fer that little shindig to break out. Why, they was even a song writ to celebrate the occasion." The former Ranger began to sing in a rich, rough baritone.

> *"Then mount and away! Give the fleet steed the rein—*
> *The Ranger's at home on the prairies again;*
> *Spur! spur in the chase, dash on to the fight,*
> *Cry vengeance for Texas! and God speed the right."*

"*Eeee-yaaa-a-a-a!*" an excited Pritchett cried at the song's end.

Wide-eyed and caught up in the fervent

memories of the Texans, the Kansan nodded. Even Soaring Hawk leaned forward, watching the two former Rangers with eyes that glittered in the light of the campfire.

"The fustest Rangers to render service to ol' Zachary Taylor was Samuel Walker an' his scouts. Them boys did what the reg'lar U.S. Cavalry couldn't. They went way behind the enemy lines an' sniffed out his whereabouts, then ridin' back like lightnin' to tell ol' Rough 'n Ready—in spite of the fact that the roads was crawlin' with Mexican soldiers."

"Yep," agreed Pritchett. "Fellas without our kind of experience never could've did it."

"What the Rangers done, time an' again, was to git where nobody else could—nor dared," John B. Loudermilk told the Kansan and his Pawnee blood-brother. "Them boys was all ol' Injun an' Mexican fighters from the git-go—cept'n maybe fer some of the East Texas Rangers—an' the best of 'em was in Ben McCulloch's company."

"Yep," Pritchett agreed once more. "Me'n John rid with Ben until the company was disbanded, once't Monterey got took. Then a bunch of the boys went home to look after their families, 'cause the Injuns was a threat on the frontier at that partic'lar time. But me'n John was young an' free, so we jined up with Jack Hays hisself."

"An' we done whipped us some Mexican ass," Loudermilk rumbled warmly. "Both with Jack Hays an' ol' Ben McCulloch."

"Ol' Ben McCulloch," sighed Pritchett. "Why, when we was with him, we was the best-mounted, best-armed, best-equipped an' appointed corps in the rangin' service."

"An' they was a heap of Rangers in Mexico in them days," added Loudermilk. "When it come to danger, Ben McCulloch was the coolest man I ever did see. Why, his face was a mask that would make a Injun's look like a kid making faces through a window pane. An' when a 'mergency come up, it didn't confuse ol' Ben a-tall. Hell now, it jus' quickened his brain. That boy didn't know the meanin' of fear."

"Damned if'n he didn't," seconded Pritchett.

"Ben was a bold 'un," Loudermilk told them. "He'd allus struck like a shot—out of the blue—takin' *ranchos* an' villages in his way as he scouted the routes to Monterey. We done traveled more'n two hundred-fifty mile in ten days, trackin' all over enemy territory. We saved the Army a heap of trouble when Ben tole ol' Rough 'n Ready that the direct route to Monterey warn't worth a shit."

"So we went roun'-abouts," said Pritchett, picking up the thread of the story from his partner. "The Texans was fustest, bringing ol' Zachary Taylor with 'em. The Mexicans was all walled up in Monterey, gawkin' out at us an' lobbin' the occasional shot at the troopers. A lot of the soldiers left the ranks an' walked toward the city, hopin' to catch sight of some Mexican soldiers. An' the Texas Rangers rode all around the walls of Monterey on their horses, doin' the tricks they used to do in the old days, when they was in contests with Mexicans an' Comanches."

"Next day," Loudermilk said, "we went down the Marin Road, an' into the chaparral, ol' Ben

McCulloch's boys at the head of the army. We even went under the guns hidden on Independence Hill. We also run smack into a heap of dismounted Mexican cavalry, but we got out an' retired in good order.

"The next mornin', we moved out with Gen'l Worth's boys. An' when we come 'round the *hacienda* of San Jeronimo, we come face to face with a bunch of mounted lancers who was backed up by a lot of infantry. Gen'l Worth gave the order to dismount, but Ben McCulloch didn't receive it. So we met the Mexicans head on an' tore a piece out'n their hides, whilst we cleaned up the Saltillo Road.

"Next, Gen'l Worth decided to take Federation Hill. On one end, facin' us, was a battery of cannon; on t'other, Fort Soldado, which overlooked the city. He sent four artillery companies, which he turned into infantry, up the hill, along with six companies of Texas Rangers—all on foot. The enemy was thick as flies above us, but we soon knocked out the battery. Then we was all tearassin' to the fort, to see who'd get in it fust."

"By jingo, that was a sight!" crowed Pritchett. "All of them boys flyin' over this here ridge—infantry, artillery, the Loo'siana volunteers, an' the Rangers, of course, whoopin' an' hollerin' like Comanches."

"Gad, it was a sight," seconded his partner. "An' a storm was brewin', to boot. Why, the black clouds was so low that the opposin' sides on the heights of Independence an' Federation Hill was firin' cannonballs at each other over the tops of 'em. Soon the storm broke, stoppin' the artillery fire as chain lightnin' struck all over the place an' rain come down in buckets.

"Next day, we went to take Independence Hill. It was three o'clock in the mornin' when we-all went up, but the damn thing was so hard to climb that we was only halfway up by dawn. The Mexicans figgered nobody could git up from the Saltillo Road, an' so they didn't even bother to guard it. Some *did* discover us, as we neared the top, an' they fired off some shots. But none of our boys opened fire 'til we was but twenty yards from the top. Fer a while it was hot an' heavy, but then we done took the hill.

"The final obstacle in our way was the Bishop's Palace. Suddenly, whilst we come up to it, the Mexicans sent up a slew of reinforcements from Monterey, as if they meant to push us off the hill. Quick-like, the Rangers was divided into two companies—Jack Hays on the right, an' Sam Walker on the left. Behind the Rangers was five companies of soldiers. An' in the very front was the Loosiana boys, led by Blanchard." He sniffled and wiped his nose on his sleeve once more.

"Then the Mexicans began to form their ranks afore the palace, with battalions of infantry holdin' rifles what had bayonets fixed to 'em, an' smart-lookin' squadrons of light cavalry with fluttery banners and lances, an' heavy cavalry with fancy helmets an' big swords. Lord, but they was a sight!

"So they began to move toward us, with a rattlin' of swords an' a whinnyin' of horses an' a blowin' of bugles. They made straight fer Blanchard's men, who began to retreat.

"Then we stood up in our cover an' let 'em have it," Loudermilk growled. "Blastin' 'em on the flanks an' in front like a thunderstorm. Then us an' the reg'lar troops all charged at once't, sending the entire Mexican garrison tearin' down the hill like bats out of hell.

"Soon after that, we swept into Monterey, comin' in by two streets what ran parallel. The Mexicans had pulled way back, as far as their Cemetery Plaza, an' it was there that we fust met some stubborn re-sistance."

"Damn straight," muttered Pritchett.

"Had to take them suckers street by street, an' house by house," John B. Loudermilk informed the Kansan and the Pawnee. "They finally had enough after we blowed up an' took their big post office buildin'. After that, the Mexicans wanted to parley." He smiled. "We done whupped 'em good."

"Damn good," seconded Pritchett.

"What happened once't we was in Monterey warn't allus so purty," Loudermilk said. "Y'see, some of the Rangers who had been prisoners thereabouts recognized the fellas what had abused 'em so bad, an' done settled their hash on the spot. It drove the army boys crazy, but there warn't no holdin' the Rangers back."

"They settled a heap of hash, by golly," Pritchett said. "Fer some time after we took Monterey, the soldiers was findin' dead bodies all over the place. 'Cause whenever a Ranger'd spot some varmint who'd tortured an' humiliated him in the old days, why he'd light out after the him, an' shoot that fella down on the spot. An' the next

125

mornin', the soldiers'd find the body."

"Army writ 'em up as suicides," Loudermilk told Davy and Soaring Hawk.

"After ol' Rough 'n Ready broke the back of Santy Anna's army at Buena Vista, they was *guerillas* fightin' all over the place, from Vera Cruz to Mexico City."

T.C. Pritchett giggled. "Them boys *really* drove the Army crazy. So they sent ol' Sam Walker out to fix things up."

Loudermilk began to recite: " 'So *guerillas, robadores,* take warning. . .for the renowned Captain Samuel H. Walker takes no prisoners.' That's what one gent writ."

"He began to clean up right good on the line from Vera Cruz to Mexico City," Pritchett added, growing suddenly grave. "But on the afternoon of October ninth, him an' his boys run smack into Santy Anna an' his full command. The fight was hard an' desperate, an' by the end of it, ol Sam Walker lay dead on the ground, havin' took bullets in the head an' chest.

"That was around the time we-all got our new weapons. All in all, each of us had a rifle, two one-shot pistols, an' a brace of Samuel Colt's new sixshooters. An' we also carried knives, hempen ropes, rawhide riatas an' hair lariats."

"An' by Gad, we was a wild-ass lookin' bunch!" exclaimed Loudermilk, "wearin' long, bushy beards an' long-tailed blue coats, an' bob-tailed black ones, ol' raggedy panama hats, black leather caps an' felt slouch hats. Our horses was all shapes an' sizes an' kinds, from Texas ponies to Kentucky thoroughbreds.

"We was led by Colonel Jack Hays hisself, an' he was jus' the boy to keep the roads open. Once't when we was attacked in a mountain pass by a big force of Mexicans, we emptied all our guns an' then began to fall back, whilst ol' Jack hisself covered our retreat. But purty soon, we got to Mexico City." He cleared his throat, and then spat into the campfire.

"Know what one fella writ about us?" he asked rhetorically. The brawny man began to mimic the speech of an educated Easterner. " 'Hays's Rangers have come, their appearance never to be forgotten. The Mexicans are terribly afraid of them. Today they brought in several prisoners. This is one of the seven wonders. . .for they generally shoot them on the spot where captured.' "

"We shook 'em up when we come into Mexico City, all right," said Pritchett, chuckling as he unrolled his blanket. "They used to crowd the streets when we'd ride by, jus' to get a look at *Los Diablos Tejanos*."

Loudermilk was chuckling now. "That's what they called us: The Texas Devils." He scowled suddenly. "But when we come there, many Americans was bein' killed. So we done give 'em a eye fer a eye, an' a tooth fer a tooth. They also called us *los tejanos sangrientes*—the bloody Texans.

"I'll give you this, we didn't let nobody fool with us. Once't, as we was ridin' by, some sneak thief stole a Ranger's handkerchief. The man what owned it called fer the fella to stop, but the sucker jus' kept on goin'. So the Ranger took out his Colt and put a bullet in 'im. Then he went over to the dead man, picked up his handkerchief, an' went off like nothin' ever happened." He shook his head. "Nope, they didn't fool much with the Texas boys."

"Damn, I guess not," muttered the Kansan, shaking his head.

"Once't, when we hit Tehuacan after ridin' all night, we jus' missed ol' Santy Anna hisself. The buzzard must've been warned by spies."

"His apartments was deserted," Pritchett told Davy and Soaring Hawk. "But the table was set fer breakfast, an' candles was still burnin' on it. A crystal inkstand had been knocked over, and the ink was still wet. We jus' missed that sucker."

"Well, we did get a whole lot of goodies he left behind," Loudermilk added. "Santy Anna had a coat what weighed a full fifteen pounds, 'cause it was covered with gold an' decorations. We found lots of Miz Santy Anna's tiny dresses. An' a gold bullion sash, too.

"But the best of all was a cane—made of polished iron, topped by a pedestal of gold tipped with steel. Above that was a eagle chock-full of diamonds, emeralds, sapphires an' rubies—with a diamond in his beak the size of a crab apple."

"It was right purty," Pritchett mumbled as he stifled a yawn.

"We give it to Jack Hayes," Loudermilk told his companions. "But Major William H. Polk seen it, an' hankered to give it to his brother. So Jack give it to him, an' told him to tell President Polk that it was from the Texans."

Davy and Soaring Hawk exchanged wide-eyed looks.

"But we did git to see that ol' sum'bitch, Santy Anna," John B. Loudermilk told them. "When he was leavin' the country, he had stopped at Jalapa. Well, us Rangers got wind of it, an' decided to go there an' gun 'im down when he arrived.

"We was set to kill 'im, for Santy Anna done waged a inhuman an' unchristian war against the people of Texas. Many of us had lost relatives an' friends at the Alamo, Goliad, San Antone, an suchlike places. All we wanted to do was pay the butcher back fer what he done to our people." He shook his head and scowled. "That ain't unreasonable, is it?

"But ol' Rip Ford, Jack Hays, an' some other officers come up to us at Jalapa, an' appealed to our better natures. But he was a cold-blooded murderer, we said, still fixin' to gun him down like a mad dog. They admitted this was so, but added that the world had already condemned Santy Anna fer his butchery of prisoners, an' that his reputation as a soldier was forever stained." Loudermilk smiled a bitter smile.

"Then they asked if'n we-all would dishonor ourselves by killin' him. But we said he was not a prisoner of war. But they said it was the same—he was travelin' under a safe-conduct, an' so killin' him would be somethin' the world would look upon as a as-sass-i-nation. 'You would dishonor Texas!' they said."

Pritchett interrupted with a long, loud yawn. Then the wiry little man stretched out his arms as he lay down, using his saddle for a pillow.

"Well, that done it," Loudermilk resumed. "We wasn't 'bout to dishonor Texas fer nothin'. But we-all did watch ol' Santy Anna come by in his

129

big, open carriage. All us Texas Rangers stood on both sides of the road, an' looked that coyote square in the eye when he passed.''

The Kansan nodded, fully aware that the two former Texas Rangers had lived in the bosom of history.

"His wife was in the carriage—she was a purty l'il thing who smiled an' nodded as if she was goin' to a state ceremony—an' his daughter, too—she kinda looked like him, poor child. An' I swear that sum'bitch went white in the face when he fust seen us, all of his ol' enemies from Texas. He musta had the thought more'n once't that all of us had purty good cause to fill his carcass full of lead. Ain't that right, T.C.?''

The other man said nothing.

"Howsomever, that dog held hisself erect like a soldier ought—I'll say that much fer him. An' all the Texans jus' stared at him whilst his carriage rolled by, all of 'em cold-eyed an' silent as the grave.''

"Judas Priest, he musta shit his pants," Davy exclaimed.

Loudermilk smiled at this. "Soon after that, the war ended. Then we finally went back to Texas.'' He yawned and stretched his arms out in the air. "Ah, them was the days, wasn't they, T.C.? T.C.?''

Loudermilk turned to his partner, who lay stretched out on the ground with his hat pulled down over his eyes. The only reply he got from the smaller man was a snore.

In an Austin hotel called the Lone Star, Bart

Braden sat alone at a table in the dining room and drank sourmash bourbon, taking his whiskey in a shot glass. Another shot glass sat on the table, by the empty chair across from the ramrod.

Outside, the moon went behind a bank of clouds, and the dark night made itself felt within, its encroaching gloom suddenly contracting the flickering light of the dining room's kerosene lamps. This oppressive change in ambiance caused the people in the room to hunch their shoulders, narrow their eyes, and regard their neighbors with suspicion.

All except Bart Braden. The Texan sprawled comfortably in his chair, a half-smile on his thin lips as he held the glass of bourbon up to the light and turned it slowly, watching the star-like refractions made by the cut-glass.

The ramrod was pleased with the way things had been going for him. Unaware that Davy Watson, Soaring Hawk, and the two former Texas Rangers were on his trail, he had decided to take his ease in the capital for a day or two. He and Raquel Mirabal had earlier enjoyed a long, leisurely dinner, and the young *chicana* was now asleep in her room, with the door unlocked. . .which was something that Bart Braden had never permitted before.

Since the pair had entered the state of Texas, the ramrod had locked Raquel in her room at night. This he had done as much to keep intruders out as to keep his lovely prisoner in. But she had confronted Braden about this only two hours earlier, when he had escorted her back to the room which adjoined his.

"You are going to go out and lock the door

now?" Raquel had asked.

the Texan nodded. "Yep. Like I been doin' all along, honey."

"I want you to leave the door unlocked, so that I may open or close it as I choose," Raquel told Bart Braden.

"Well, if'n I do," he drawled, "what's to stop you from slippin' out on me?"

"I give you my word I will not escape from this room tonight, *Señor* Braden."

As he stared at her, the Texan pushed back his hat and began to scratch his head.

Her dark eyes met his. "Don't lock the door. It makes me feel trapped."

"You'll gimme your word?"

"I am a Mirabal," Raquel said with quiet pride. "And my honor is precious to me. My word is my bond."

The ramrod continued to gaze deeply into her eyes for a long time after she had spoken. "Your word's good enough fer me," he told Don Solomon's daughter.

"*Muchas gracias, Señor Braden*," she said, nodding to him as he stood in the doorway of the room.

"You *could* call me Bart," he told her quietly.

"Good night, *Señor* Braden," were Raquel's last words, before she closed the door on Bart Braden.

Notwithstanding that rebuff, the ramrod considered that he had made great progress. In spite of herself, the young *chicana* was coming around. Braden was as determined as ever to possess Raquel Mirabal. . .but it would be with her consent, and no other way. He had patience; he could wait. He was in his home state, and time, so he thought, was on his side.

Chink. The shrill sound of glass making contact with glass cut through the hubbub of the dining room, followed by a soft, gurgling rush, as Braden poured himself a brimming shot of bourbon. He reached out, picked up the glass, and raised it slowly to his lips, taking pains not to spill any of the liquor.

Then, as the ramrod knocked back the shot in one swig, a man came over to his table. The stranger was tall and lean, with a sallow complexion and dark, deep-set eyes. The trigger of his Colt had been filed down, and he wore his holster low, and tied to his thigh with a rawhide thong. And when Bart Braden looked up, he saw that the man had the eyes of a hangman and a smile as cold as the heart of a glacier.

"Mr. Braden?" the man asked in a voice that sounded like sandpaper in a bass register.

The ramrod nodded, straightening up in his seat as he noted that the man's voice was fully as cold and bleak as his smile.

"What can I do fer ya?" Bart Braden asked softly.

"My name's Dan Cain," the stranger rasped. "An' I got me a matter of some importance to discuss with ya, Mister Braden." He gestured toward the empty chair. "Mind if I sit down?"

Braden gave the lanky, cold-eyed man the once-over. "Be my guest, Mister Cain," he replied, smiling his straight-razor smile as he reached for the bottle of bourbon. "Care to wet yer whistle?"

"Don't mind if'n I do," he said hoarsely, taking off his broad-brimmed leather hat as he sat down in the creaking chair.

"Here's mud in yer eye," Braden said, raising his glass aloft, still staring at the stranger.

"Bottoms up," the man replied, just before he knocked back his bourbon.

"Arthur Planken told me you was lookin' fer me," Braden drawled, his eyes on the stranger's face. "How'd you know I was in town?"

The man sniffled, pulled out a soiled, crusty handkerchief, and blew his nose in it. Bart Braden poured another round of drinks as he waited patiently for the man to reply.

"Jim Hawkins done tole us," the cold-eyed man told the ramrod as he wiped his nose with the soiled handkerchief. "An' once't ol' Captain Haggerty heerd you was in these parts, he sent me a-ridin' *pronto* to see ya."

Even though his features remained devoid of any expression, Bart Braden's eyes widened at the mention of the name Captain Haggerty.

The man in question, Captain Daniel Patrick Haggerty, was a former officer in the Confederate Army, attached to Baylor's command during the brief period at the opening of the Civil War when the Confederacy had held Texas. Ruthless in enforcing Baylor's own brutal policy toward the Indians of Texas, Captain Haggerty was equally ruthless toward the Union soldiers who became Baylor's prisoners of war. Few of the prisoners in his care survived, but those who lived to tell the tale of the many atrocities committed on the captain's orders caused the Union Army to put a price on the man's head and thereafter try him *in absentia* and subsequently sentence Haggerty to death by hanging.

When the tide of battle turned, and Texas fell to

the Union forces, causing Baylor to beat a hasty retreat, Haggerty and several of his followers—all desperadoes of similar temperament—rode across the Rio Grande, and into the sanctuary of the wild Mexican borderlands. There they mingled with their brother fugitives—renegade Indians, Mexican *bandidos* and revolutionaries, runaway slaves, and deserters from both the Union and Confederate armies. In that no man's land there were outlaws of every stripe: *Anglo* and *chicano*, black and Indian.

Haggerty was now one of the chief cattle rustlers in the southern and eastern parts of Texas. More than a dozen men rode behind him, and the captain often hired out this private army. His allegiance went invariably to the highest bidder. Nor was the man above hiring out his "lads" (as he called them) for various other services of a criminal nature, such as robbery, extortion, and even assassination.

Throughout Texas, New Mexico, Arizona, and northern Mexico, he was known as "Horrible Haggerty," and his men were known by the name of "Haggerty's Hellions." All of the captain's retainers were fugitives of one sort or another, including the remaining Confederate deserters who had originally gone south with him; and those few among them who had not yet killed a man were only waiting for their chance to do so.

To a man, these desperadoes feared and respected Haggerty, for the genial, beefy, red-faced Irishman had put more than a dozen men under six feet of earth. . .and did so each time with a smile on his face. A renegade Catholic, Daniel Patrick Haggerty feared neither man nor God, and firmly believed that the only reward a man enjoyed was in

135

this life, consisting of whatever he could grasp with his own two hands, obtained by way of his own native cunning and ferocity.

Few men in the West were more cunning or ferocious than the sly Captain Haggerty, and few men dared go up against him. He killed without mercy or compunction. The Texas State Police had proved ineffectual in their attempts to bring the outlaw chief to justice, and since the Texas Rangers were no longer in existence, Haggerty felt free to scour the Lone Star State.

"Cap'n'd like to talk with ya, Braden," the tall, sallow man named Dan Cain went on, interrupting the ramrod's thoughts.

"To the captain," Braden said, hoisting his glass aloft and smiling a smile as sharp as the edge of a scalping knife.

"I'll drink to that," Cain replied, hoisting his own bourbon.

"Now, jus' what does the captain want with me, Mister Cain?" Braden asked. "Me'n him ain't 'zactly what you'd call close friends. He done run off some of ol' Bill Fanshaw's cows once't, an' I followed 'im clear into Mexico, an' brought most of 'em back. The captain rode off leavin' five of his boys dead on the ground. An' I caint swear to it, but I think I winged ol' Captain Haggerty, too." Recalling this, the ramrod began to chuckle.

"Yep. You shore 'nuf did," Cain told him, grinning as he scratched the salt-and-pepper stubble on his chin. "You done trimmed off a hunk of the fat what hangs over the captain's belt. Didn't do 'im any real damage, but he was a-cussin' ya fer days—ever' time he done went to stuff his shirt in his pants."

136

"I was shootin' a mite low that day," Braden drawled. "Lucky thing fer ol' Haggerty, else't I would've put a bullet through his big fat heart."

The outlaw nodded. "We all has days like that, I reckon."

"What's Haggerty want, Cain?" Braden asked once more.

The man squinted at him and leaned across the table, speaking in a low, hoarse voice.

"Don't y'all know what's a-goin' on these days, Braden?" he asked, looking suspiciously around the room.

"I don't catch yer meanin'," the ramrod answered.

"Bill Fanshaw's dead."

"I figgered that, Cain. What else is new?"

"That fella you done shot in San Antone—"

"Sweinhardt?" the ramrod asked contemptuously. "Sum'bitch needed shootin'."

Cain shook his head. "Uh-uh. T'other one. 'Pears he was State Po-lice."

"That ain't no big deal," Braden said, yawning and stretching his arms out in the air. "State Police don't worry me none."

"It's more'n that, Braden," Cain told him. "Turns out he was a ol' Texas Ranger."

Braden shot him a hard look. "So?" he asked, his eyes suddenly narrowing.

" 'Pears that two of his buddies is a-comin' after ya. They was Rangers with him; now they's State Po-lice. They's a-ridin' to git you, Braden. An' they got two more *hombres* with 'em."

The ramrod's eyes widened. "Two more, huh? Who might these fellas be?"

Cain leaned back in his creaking chair. "Don't

rightly know. They got the look of strangers. Heerd they come down from New Mexico. One of 'em's a Injun. Dunno what tribe. Ain't one of our'n.''

"Well, I'll be hornswoggled," Braden whispered, causing the pale, gaunt man to lean in toward him even farther.

"What is it, Braden?"

"Fella with the Injun," Braden said, "he 'bout six-foot tall, with dark blond hair an' blue eyes?"

Cain nodded. "That's him. Says you done shot 'im, an' he owes ya a bullet."

It was the ramrod's turn to nod. "Yep. I reckon so. But it looks like that sum'bitch was even luckier than ol' Haggerty. We had us a li'l shootout up New Mexico way. That fella done winged me in the shoulder, an I left him fer dead." Braden frowned and shook his head at the thought of his rival for the affections of Raquel Mirabal. "How d'ya like them apples?" he muttered harshly. "Guess I'm gon' have to go out an' kill that sum'bitch all over again."

"Once't the word of the shootin' of that ol' Ranger gits here in Austin," Cain told him, "they's gonna be a heap of folks out a-lookin' fer ya, Braden. 'Specially since you got that filly with ya."

Braden's smile disappeared when Cain mentioned Raquel Mirabal.

"Yer a fugitive from the law, yer own self," Cain went on, an evil smirk on his face. "An' so the Cap'n sent me to ask if you could see yer way to lettin' bygones be bygones. He wants ya to throw in with 'im, Braden. Cap'n Haggerty, he got a lot of respect fer a man like you, an' he tole me to tell ya that as sure as God made little green apples, he'll make it well worth yer while."

Chink. Gurgle. Braden poured two more shots of sourmash bourbon. He was suddenly and painfully aware that his fortunes had taken a sharp turn for the worse, and had begun to weigh the advantages and disadvantages of an alliance with the notorious Captain Haggerty.

"To yer future, Braden," Cain rasped as he hoisted his shot glass.

The ramrod shot him a hard look as he knocked back his drink.

"Well, what's it gon' be?" the outlaw asked, as Bart Braden suddenly rose to his feet.

"Lemme sleep on it," Braden told him. "Where can I find you, Cain?"

"I'm over to Cogswell's place," the pale, gaunt man said as he stood up and held out his hand to Braden.

The ramrod shook his hand. "I'll let ya know in the mornin'," he told the cold-eyed outlaw.

"I'll be waitin'," Cain said as Braden turned and walked off.

The moon had come out again, and its cold light silvered the streets of Austin. The ramrod frowned as he walked in the moonlight, uncomfortably aware that he must make an important decision by morning.

When he finally went to bed, Bart Braden was glum and agitated. It would have cheered the Texan considerably had he known that, by morning, he would once again have the Kansan in his gunsight.

5
Braden and Raquel

Davy Watson, Soaring Hawk, T.C. Pritchett and John B. Loudermilk rode into Austin about an hour after the sun had come up. They took their horses to a livery stable, left them there, and then set out on foot through the dusty streets of the Texan capital, in search of breakfast.

"Pretty place, ain't it?" the Kansan said as he looked at the creamy limestone of the Capitol building glowing softly in the early light. Rolling hills surrounded Austin, and wooded slopes led out to the prairie beyond. Past the Governor's mansion, Davy saw a small church with a fetching German turret; and as he turned his head, he saw a stone church which was considerably larger than the first.

"Austin's s'posed to be bang in the center of the state," T.C. Pritchett informed him.

"Aw, who gives a shit about that, T.C.?" the small, wiry ex-Ranger's partner remonstrated.

"Well, John, not many folks knows that," the shy Pritchett mumbled, going red in the face.

"I surely hope not," Loudermilk growled back.

"Why'd they put it in the center of the state?" asked Davy Watson, his curiosity aroused by now.

" 'Cause they's a bunch of addled ninnies," the brawny ex-Ranger muttered darkly. "Who in the Sam Hill gives a damn 'bout why the capital has been plunked down in the 'zact middle of the damn state?"

T.C. Pritchett looked at Davy, and rolled his eyes heavenward.

"They does dumb things like that," Loudermilk continued, " 'cause they wants the credit of bein' the first state to plunk its capital smack dab in the middle." He scowled and shook his head. "Folks in this country goes hog-wild 'bout breakin' records. An' it don't matter a-tall what the record is. It don't have to be important, nor count fer much. Just so long's the old record has been broke." He shook his head again. "Dumbest dang thing I ever heerd of in my whole life."

"There," Soaring Hawk said loudly, causing the three men with him to turn and look where he was pointing.

Hoffmeister's Restaurant, a sign proclaimed above windows distinguished by both their sparkle and the clean white curtains behind them. Outside the place, the boards of the street were still damp from having been recently scrubbed.

Davy sniffed and made out the inviting aroma of homefried potatoes and sizzling bacon. He sniffed again, and picked up the dark, heady scent of freshly brewed coffee.

"Go eat there," the Pawnee urged, nodding toward the place.

John D. Loudermilk sniffed loudly. "Damn!" he exclaimed. "If'n I ever meet up with a lady what cooks stuff that smells jus' half as good as that, by

Gad, I'll marry 'er on the spot."

"Anythin' smells that good caint be bad, John," T.C. Pritchett told his friend.

"How 'bout you, Mister Watson?" Loudermilk asked, turning to the Kansan.

Davy nodded as he spoke. "Why don't we jus' mosey in there, an' take a chance on the place?"

The brawny, mustachioed man nodded in agreement. "Yep. Let's go, fellas. Why, I'm so damn hungry, I could eat a Mexican—sombrero, spurs an' all."

They went up to the door, found the place open, and trooped in. Within ten minutes' time, they were all eating a hearty breakfast of bacon, scrambled eggs, flapjacks, corn pone, home-fried potatoes and coffee.

Hoffmeister was a beefy, bald-headed old German who had been in Texas for more than twenty years. The meal was served by his nephew, a tall, blond young man whose name was Seibert Thurnhofer.

"How long you been here, Zeeburt?" John B. Loudermilk asked the young German.

"Here I am now almost ten months," Siebert replied as he came to the table bearing a second pot of Hoffmeister's delicious coffee.

"Are ya glad ya came to Texas?" Loudermilk asked, continuing his friendly interrogation.

"*Ach, ja!*" Siebert exclaimed. "It iss better a t'ousand time to be in ziss country here."

"Surely things ain't as comfortable here as they was in the Ol' Country?" Davy Watson asked.

"*Was ist dies* com-for-r-r-table?" a puzzled Siebert called out to his uncle, who was already cleaning the grill where he had just been cooking.

"*Gemütlich*," was the old man's reply.

"*Ach, gemütlich*." Siebert nodded. "*Gemütlich*." He turned back to Davy. "No. Here is none zo com-for-r-r-table as in Germany. But I like here be-causs I am free."

"You mean you wasn't free back home?" Loudermilk asked Siebert.

The young German shook his head. "There gives no freedom in Germany. The Kaiser rules by the soldier. Zey was to have me in the army, but I come here. I run from zem and come wit Uncle Ludi."

"What d'ya do fer fun, hereabouts?" John B. Loudermilk asked.

"Here it iss hard for the young man to have the fun. Here the *Amerikanisches* gentlemen do not know of the pleasure. When they come for to be *miteinander*. . . ." He looked to his uncle.

"Togedder," Ludwig Hoffmeister told his nephew.

"Togedder," Siebert Thurnhofer repeated. "When ze Texas menfolk comes togedder, all zey do is to drink viskey, play ze cards, and shpit in ze fire."

Davy Watson began to laugh.

"Or zey make ze great row an' punch in ze face each other," Siebert went on. "Or shoot to pieces ze vindows. Ze pleasure here iss not ze pleasure ze gentlemen hass in *Europa*."

"No, it sure as hell ain't, I reckon," the Kansan agreed when he had finally stopped laughing. The two Texans beside him stared at Davy Watson with poker faces.

"He jus' don't unnerstan' local customs," John

B. Loudermilk told Davy, after Siebert had gone back into the kitchen. "From what he done described, I'd say them Texas boys was a-havin' themselves a high ol' time."

T.C. Pritchett nodded as he wiped his chin with a linen napkin. "Them Germans don't know how to have a good time," he said, the expression on his face now as grave as Soaring Hawk's.

"What was you laughin' at before, Mister Watson?" John B. Loudermilk asked as Davy Watson plunked a silver dollar down on the polished table top.

"Oh, jus' somethin' that occurred to me when ol' Zeeburt was talkin'. T'warn't nothin' you boys could catch holt of."

Still poker-faced, the two Texans nodded.

The sun was shining brightly when the Kansan stepped outside Hoffmeister's Restaurant. . .and into Bart Braden's gunsight.

It so happened that Hoffmeister's Restaurant was situated diagonally across the street from the Lone Star Hotel, the place where Bart Braden and Raquel Mirabal were staying. And as the Kansan walked out into the street, it was by a curious coincidence that the Texas ramrod was at one of the windows which faced the restaurant.

He immediately recognized Davy Watson and Soaring Hawk, who followed the Kansan out onto the street. An instant later, Braden had raised the window and was in the process of lining Davy up in his gunsight.

Braden had entered the room only a few

moments earlier, bearing Raquel's breakfast on a tray, as was his custom each morning. After having put the tray down on a night table, the ramrod paused to arrange the flowers which sat on the table in a China vase, flowers he had personally sent up to the beautiful *chicana*.

Having rearranged the flowers to his satisfaction, Braden looked up and gazed idly out the window, his eye suddenly caught by a mangy stray dog that sauntered down the middle of the street.

The dog made its way past Hoffmeister's just as Davy Watson opened the restaurant's front door and came out onto the street. Braden's eyes narrowed as this happened, his glance traveling from the dog to the open door.

"Hey," he murmured in a low voice as he recognized the Kansan. The sound of an opening window was followed by the creak of leather which accompanied the drawing of the ramrod's gun.

"Well, well, well," Bart Braden muttered, his gunsight coming to rest on a line with Davy Watson's chest. "Ain't it a small world," the ramrod told himself, his finger tightening on the trigger of his gun.

"Bart," Raquel Mirabal whispered behind him. "He's not dead—Dah-veed is not dead!"

Braden shook his head, his eyes never leaving the Kansan's form. His eyebrows went up, and a deep crease appeared in his forehead. *It was the first time that she had called him by his name*!

"He's not dead," the young *chicana* whispered. "You didn't kill him!"

Braden shook his head again, his eyes and gunsight glued to Davy Watson. "I reckon not," he whispered back. "Watson's a lucky fella. . . .But his luck done run out." The Texan's finger tightened on the trigger once more.

"No, Bart," Raquel Mirabal whispered urgently. "Don't kill him—please!"

Unseen by Don Solomon's daughter, the Texan scowled. He continued to squeeze the trigger as he moved his gunhand slightly to cover Davy Watson, when the latter stepped off the boards of the sidewalk and into the street.

"He tried to kill me, Raquel," the ramrod said in a husky voice. "An' we done shot it out, fair 'n square. But now he's a-comin' after me at the head of a posse. That's what I done learned last night. So he's fair game, now."

"Please, Bart," she pleaded, "no more killing. There's been more than enough of that already."

There was no emotion in his voice when he replied. "What if I don't shoot hin, Raquel? What then?"

"Bart, I. . ." she began.

"What you gon' do then—ride off with that saddle tramp?" he interrupted, his voice colored by tones of intense bitterness. "I know you was sweet on him, Raquel. That why you want me to spare him?"

"But you *didn't* kill him, Bart," she whispered urgently. "I didn't know that."

"So what?" he said coldly.

"That changes things, Bart," she told the ramrod.

For several moments after she said this, there was silence in the room. Finally, Braden spoke.

146

"What d'ya mean, 'this changes things'?" he asked in a quiet voice.

"Between you and me," she told him. "That's what's changed."

His back still to Raquel Mirabal, the Texan closed his eyes and bit his lip.

"Don't shoot him, Bart," she pleaded again.

"No, I won't, honey," he said with a sigh, lowering his gun as he did.

"Thank you, Bart."

Again there was a long silence, broken only by the creak of leather as the ramrod holstered his gun.

"You fixin' to go to him?" Bart Braden asked in a voice that was barely audible in the room.

Raquel Mirabal stared at the Texan's broad back.

"No," she whispered. "Let *Señor* Watson and *El Indio* ride off. It is enough that you have spared their lives."

Braden's big hands hung by his sides; he began to clench and unclench his fists.

He cleared his throat before he spoke again. "Well, I guess that's the end of the trail fer us."

Raquel's eyes widened. "What do you mean?"

"Yer free to go back yer daddy," he croaked. "I ain't gonna hold you agin yer will no more."

"You would let me go free?" the lovely young woman asked incredulously.

Still looking out the window at the man who had once taken Raquel Mirabal away from him, Bart Braden nodded his head.

"But this changes things, Bart."

Finally the ramrod turned to face her, just as

Davy Watson and his three companions began to walk down the street. A horsefly came in through the open window, and buzzed loudly as its wings rubbed against the glass of the windowpane.

"How does it change things, Raquel?"

"Now I see that you are a man of honor, that you are not a *pistolero*. . .and not a killer."

"I could take Watson in a fair fight any time," Braden told her quietly.

"You are a very brave *caballero, Señor* Braden," Raquel told him, a half-smile upon her lips.

"What you gon' do now?" he asked in a husky voice.

"That depends upon you, *Señor* Braden," she told him, a mischievous gleam coming into her eye.

"I don't catch yer meanin'," he said. "What do ya want me to do?"

She began to move toward him. "I want you to get to know me better. . .Bart."

"Take off yer badge, T.C.," John B. Loudermilk told his partner. "If'n folks knows us fer State Po-lice, ain't nobody gon' tell us a damn thing."

"Reckon you got yerself a point there, John," Pritchett replied, reaching up and unpinning his badge.

"State Police is kinda unpopular, hah?" Davy asked.

"You ain't a-shittin'," the big, brawny man told him. "Ever'body hates or fears 'em. Ain't nobody in the whole damn state what likes 'em."

" 'Cept'n other like-minded varmints an' outlaws," Pritchett added.

"Oh, they ain't all crooked," Loudermilk explained. "They's some good 'uns—honest men like me an' ol' T.C. here. But fer all the good it does, they might as well be crooks. 'Cause the scoundrels is in charge—right up to Governor Davis, the man who done organized the State Police to keep him an' his carpetbag administration in office."

"Reckon that there scalawag's 'bout the biggest scoundrel of 'em all," Pritchett told Davy.

"Ain't a-tall like you said the Rangers was," the Kansan observed.

"Hell, no!" Loudermilk bellowed. "By Gad, there ain't never been nothin' on the face of this earth like the Texas Rangers—nor will there be, I 'spect."

"Y'know somethin', John," T.C. Pritchett told his partner. "We's honest fellas, ain't we now?"

"Damn right we are," the brawny ex-Ranger answered loudly.

"Well, then, I think we's jus' a mite too good fer the State Po-lice." He stared at the badge in his hand for a moment, and then casually tossed it over his shoulder.

"Ain't he somethin'?" John B. Loudermilk said proudly. "Ol' T.C.'s a great one fer doin' the right thing." He unpinned his own badge. "An' I'm right behind ya, as usual, ol' buddy." Then he proceeded to bend the badge double in his thick fingers before throwing it away.

"Le's go an' telegraph headquarters that we

149

done ree-signed," Pritchett told his partner.

"An' then," Davy Watson added, "we can finish trackin' down that sum'bitch, Bart Braden."

Bright and warm, the morning sun streamed through the window of the hotel room, and this time, as Bart Braden made love in a sunlit bed, it was not to some phantom of his imagination. No, this time the Texas ramrod had achieved the fulfillment of his desire: Raquel Mirabal lay naked and willing in his arms, making husky cat-sounds deep in her throat as she urged the man she had once hated on to greater heights of passion and endeavor.

Raquel was making love for what was only the second time in her life, but she took to it as a duck takes to water. And Bart Braden, a man possessed of a fair degree of bedroom expertise, had never been gentler or more adept in his life.

The young *chicana's* head tossed from side to side, her jet-black hair lashing the white pillow, and she closed her eyes and began to moan through clenched teeth.

Bart Braden's hands were caressing her full, firm breasts. His fingers were active, too, as he rolled her thick, erect nipples between thumb and forefinger from time to time, or traced a series of teasing, concentric circles around her large, dark areolae with his fingernails, causing the flesh on her breasts to rise in goose bumps.

"*Ay,*" she moaned. "*Ay, querido.*" Suddenly she arched her back, gasped and shuddered. Then, as she relaxed her muscles, Raquel reached down her hands and tangled her long, tapered fingers in the ramrod's curly brown hair.

Bart Braden's face was buried in Raquel's thick muff, and his tongue darted between her nether lips, running up and down their slick pink insides, pausing every now and then to circle and lick the bulb of her clitoris. This elicited a gasp from the New Mexican beauty and caused her to move her pelvis toward him, thrusting her black, silky pelt into his face.

"Oh, Bart," Don Solomon Mirabal's daughter moaned as she writhed beneath the *tejano* enemy of her people. "I feel as if I'm going to explode."

The Texan's only reply was an ardent, rumbling grunt, as he raked the smooth insides of her long, trim thighs with his fingernails and then riffled their sweat-gleaming hollows with his thumbs. After that, he drew his big thumbs down along the outside of the *chicana's* dark, swollen lips.

"*Ay, Dios*," Raquel moaned as she writhed and thrashed on the bright, sunlit bed, calling her Hispanic God at the onset of ecstasy.

"Oh, Bart. It's rising in me like the Gila River in a flash flood," she moaned, her eyes rolling up in their sockets. "I'm going to—ooooh!"

As she came, Raquel Mirabal lost the power of articulate speech. Her words were suddenly transformed into feline moans and the deep guttural sounds of the puma that ranges the foothills of the Guadalupe Mountains.

Bart Braden's ardent lips and darting tongue had done their work in much the same manner that a flash flood erodes the red-clay soil of northwestern Texas. The Texan's expert and persistent kissing, sucking, licking and nibbling had flooded the *chicana's* nervous system and eroded her consciousness with its resultant orgasmic rush, bringing Raquel, in her dark ecstasy, almost to the brink of oblivion.

"*Dios mio!*" the lovely eighteen-year-old groaned, her tense body suddenly jerking as it began to relax. Her full-lipped mouth hung open, and when Braden came up to kiss it, he found those lips cold with the coldness that succeeds the dissipation of the heat of passion. A red flush had broken out on her cheeks and upon the skin above her breast bone, and she moved her head back and forth slowly upon the white pillow, her eyes closed, sighing like the soft summer breeze which comes down to the prairie from the mountains.

She lay still for a long time, savoring the after-taste of the pleasure which had come to her as a result of her second coupling with a man. And as Bart Braden's big, rough hand began to caress her hair and cheek with a tenderness worthy of the gallant and devoted heroes of medieval European literature, the raven-haired young beauty smiled.

Things had changed for Raquel, there was no doubt about that. Bart Braden was no longer seen by her as a cold-blooded murderer; he was not the *asesino tejano* that she had first taken him for. By this time, her romantic schoolgirl's imagination had made of the rough cowpoke a champion equal in stature to the legendary heroes of the Old World, to Charlemagne's Roland, to the Black Prince, or even El Cid himself, Roderigo Diaz de Bivar, the great knight who gave his life to liberate Valencia from the Moors.

When she opened her eyes again, the first thing that Raquel Mirabal saw was the handsome and square-jawed face of her champion. As he smiled down at her, the corners of his eyes crinkled, and he displayed two rows of white, even teeth.

Raquel's heart opened, and two small tears formed in the corners of her eyes as she smiled back at her Texan lover.

"You all right, honey?" Braden asked with concern when he saw her tears.

"*Si*," she whispered, reaching out her hand and grazing his thin lips with fingers whose touch was as light as the brush of butterfly wings. "Everything is fine, Bart. *Gracias, mi amor. Muchas gracias.*"

There was a strange new warmth in the ramrod's eyes as he gazed down at his love.

"I aim to please you, honey," he whispered back. "More'n anything else."

She stroked his thick sideburns and smiled up at him. "You please me very much," she told him in a husky voice. "And now it is my turn to please you."

Her hand traveled down to stroke the ramrod's hairy chest.

"I hope that I shall please you," Raquel went on. "You must teach me how to please you, Bart, darling."

As she said this, her hand traveled down the Texan's chest, her long fingernails lightly raking his flesh and leaving swaths of goose bumps in their wake.

"You please me plenty all ready, Raquel," Braden told her, in a voice infused with desire and tenderness.

Her hand had descended into the hollow beneath his ribs, and was still heading south.

"I want to please you even more, Bart," she told him, her gaze meeting his as her hand traveled down his belly.

"Ain't nothin' could please me more'n givin' you pleasure, honey," the ramrod told her, his voice now charged with emotion.

"But there is more, *mi corazón*," she whispered, her voice rising like a hot wind from the Mexican interior. "There is more."

Braden emitted an audible gasp as the young *chicana's* long, tapering fingers wrapped themselves around the shaft of his sex, the sudden access of warmth and pressure taking the Texan's breath away.

As she felt the ramrod's cock stiffen in her hand, Raquel Mirabal smiled a bright smile at her lover.

"*Pasión*," she murmured, after licking her full lips. "*Mi pasión es para ti, querido Bartolomeo.*"

"*Pasión*, hah?" the ramrod grunted, smiling a wry smile as he raised his body, feeling the brush of Raquel's thighs beneath him as she parted her legs.

"*Si mi corazón,*" she whispered intensely, guiding his stiff, swollen organ into the dark and scented grotto of delight between her long, trim thighs,

"*Ay-y-y-y,*" she gasped as the Texan entered her with a squish. And Bart Braden gasped too, as he felt the tight, intimate grip of the beautiful eighteen-year-old's warm, wet pussy.

"Oh, Bart," Raquel whispered intensely, as her lover began to stroke, slowly and deeply, causing the young *chicana's* pelvis to twitch in anticipation and the muscles in her abdomen to contract.

Braden was smiling through clenched teeth as he slid his throbbing cock deeper into the hot, welcoming sheath of his beloved, the woman for whom he had started a range war and surmounted all obstacles in the path of his desire, his dark angel of passion.

"*Te quiero mucho*," he grunted, declaring his desire in Raquel's native tongue.

Her eyes were glazed and she writhed beneath him, as heat and pressure spread in her groin with the swiftness of a forest fire.

"I want you, too, Bart," she whispered back, just before the welcome, brain-searing blackness and the tidal wave breaking in her groin swamped her consciousness. "I want you very much."

The Texan emitted a sharp, sudden wail, sounding as if he had just been stabbed in the back. His body was seized by a succession of violent tremors, and he called out in the bright, sunlit bedroom with the voice of a man drowning in some vast, dark ocean.

"Oh, yes, Bart. Yesss," Raquel hissed as the serpent of desire uncoiled in her groin and began to thrash about wildly, lashing her on to a sudden and unexpected climax, the Texan's orgasm having greatly excited the young beauty.

They came together then, their groins butted at the crescendo of their passion, Raquel's straight black thatch interwoven with the dark brown pubic curls of her lover. The *chicana's* contralto wails complemented the baritone groans of the Texan.

After the tidal wave of their shared passion had

crested and ebbed, the handsome pair fell into a sleep as deep and dark as the bottom of the far-off Atlantic Ocean, an ocean which neither of the lovers had ever seen. And while they were steeped in the dreamless blackness that follows upon total satiety, the morning sun continued to shine through the window of the hotel room, its light gilding the recumbent forms of Bart Braden and Raquel Mirabal.

6
Captain Haggerty's Hellions

Captain Daniel Patrick Haggerty shifted his two hundred and eighty pounds in the saddle, squinted as he looked off into the sunlit distance, and scratched the copper-colored stubble on his chin, the sound made by his nails running over those bristles resembling the crackle of a distant brush fire.

"Jesus, Mary an' Joseph," the big Irishman swore. "Now, where d'ya suppose that Braden fella could be?"

Beside him, on his left, a tall man with a bald head and a black patch over his left eye replied in a bass voice. He was Eli Satterthwaite, a long-time desperado, and an ex-Texas Ranger, one who had been drummed out of the service after being convicted of rustling and extortion.

"It ain't five o'clock yet, Cap'n," Satterthwaite reminded Haggerty. "If Bart Braden said he'll be here, he'll be here."

The captain reached down his left hand and patted the roll of fat that overflowed the upper edge of his gunbelt, touching the place where Bart Braden had shot him years before.

"D'ya suppose the lad will bring the Mexican

157

wench with him?'' he asked.

This time he was answered by the man on his right, a short, stocky fellow with a bowl haircut and buck teeth. Richard Lingeman was the man's name, and he had been an officer in the Confederate Army, serving under Haggerty during the Civil War. He had fled to Mexico along with his chief, rather than risk a court martial and subsequent firing squad for the many atrocities he had committed on the Irishman's orders.

"If'n he brings the gal, it might be a good thing fer us, Cap'n,'' Lingeman told Haggerty. "I hear tell she's a purty li'l tamale.''

"Heh, heh, heh,'' chuckled the graybeard behind him. The man sat tall on a black stallion; he must have been at least in his middle sixties, but appeared to be as physically powerful as any of the twelve other bully-boys who rode with Captain Haggerty. He tended to the band's wounds, and his name was Doc Doucette.

"If you dast touch that there little tamale, ol' Bart Braden'll blow yer clinkers off,'' the old man boomed in a resonant bass voice. "Heh, heh, heh. Ain't you heerd what he done to ol' Ford Sweinhardt in San Antone?''

"Sweinhardt warn't no sickly little fella, neither,'' chimed in the man beside Doc Doucette. He was a small, skinny, weasel-faced man known as Squint Ryerback. The "daddy" of all cattle rustlers in West Texas, he had spent the last few decades preying on the Longhorn herds there, and in the New Mexico Territory as well.

Richard Lingeman smiled and displayed his maloccluded teeth. " 'Twarn't me Bart Braden done shot," he said with a leer, rolling his eyes in the direction of the tubby, red-faced Captain Haggerty.

Eyes widened to the size of small saucers, and jaws dropped to the end of their hinges when the desperado made this remark.

The beefy Irishman shook his head as he turned to Lingeman. "Bedad, it's a forward fella y'are, Dickie," he exclaimed loudly, in reply to the other's thinly veiled reference to his shooting by Bart Braden. But as he said this, Haggerty was smiling paternally at the outlaw.

Lingeman had the distinction of being the captain's favorite, as well as his right-hand man. Had anyone else in the band of ruffians made such a remark, it was dollars to doughnuts that he would be crying out in pain and writhing in the dust a moment later, with two slugs from the Irishman's sevenshooter in his belly.

The captain's smile was taken as permission to laugh, and the remaining eleven outlaws all began to snicker or guffaw at Lingeman's wit.

"Well, well, well," Captain Haggerty said genially as he surveyed his band of cutthroats. "So yez are all amused by Dickie's bright remark, are yez? Well, in that case, Dickie me lad, if Mister Bart Braden ever gets it in his head to quarrel with Haggerty's Hellions, I'll leave it up to you to teach that boy-o some respect."

The bully-boys began to snicker. Lingeman went red in the face as he glared at his fellow outlaws, shooting nasty looks at them, looks that were as hot as a flaming arrow.

"Well," the desperado mumbled, sniffling and

patting his dusty holster, "if'n Bart Braden needs a lesson, then I'm just the *hombre* what can teach it to him."

"Deeckie ees no virgin when it come to takin' care of bad *hombres*," a potbellied Mexican named Eufemio Salcedo told the others. "I seen him make *muchas muertes*, many dead men, *amigos*."

Wanted on both sides of the Rio Grande, Salcedo and the man beside him, his brother, Fernando, were notorious cutthroats and expert rustlers who had joined forces with Haggerty years earlier. Their intimate knowledge of the territory south of the Rio Grande was invaluable to the outlaw band.

Lean and handsome where his brother was squat and ugly, Fernando Salcedo nodded empthatically, seconding Eufemio's words.

"*Ach du lieber*!" bellowed a huge, bearded German named Oberst. "Bart Braten iss not zo easy to zhoot. Maybe Tickie zhoult go after him ven he iss azleep."

The desperadoes laughed loudly at this.

Linegeman's eyes narrowed as he took the big German's measure. Oberst was no great shakes with a sidearm, he knew that, but the giant had killed more than half a dozen men with his bare hands.

"You ain't so damn funny—y'know that, Oberst?" Lingeman growled, the fingers of his gun-hand twitching by his holster.

"Ah, now, where's yer sense of humor, Dickie-boy?" Captain Haggerty called out loudly, clapping Lingeman on the back as he did.

"An' youse guys t'ought dat Joymans had no sense of humor, huh?" a burly man with a waxed mustache and thinning brown hair chimed in. His name was Michael Shaughnessy, and he was a tough who hailed from the ferocious New York City slum neighborhood known as Hell's Kitchen. He was a professional assassin, and was used whenever Haggerty had a score to settle.

"Ah say, where's yoah sense o' humor, Richud?" asked a lean and solemn-faced man with black muttonchop whiskers. His name was Arthur Danforth. He was a Virginian by birth, and an outlaw of necessity, having fled prosecution for the crimes he had perpetrated as one of the ranking officers in the notorious Confederate prison at Andersonville, Georgia.

"Ah, c'mon, Dickie-boy. Give us a smile," coaxed Daniel Patrick Haggerty.

"It vas chust a choke," the massive German rumbled, holding out his two carpet-beater hands. He sat astride a big brown gelding, but his huge frame made it look more like an Indian pony.

"G-g-g-give ol' F-f-fritz yer h-hand," stammered a small man with blond, Bill Cody hair, and an Adam's apple the size of a goose egg. He was physically unprepossessing, but was a crack shot whose deadly skill with rifle and pistol had earned him the name, Dead-Eye Dan Bates.

Behind Dead-Eye Dan was another horseman, a huge Indian, who nodded in agreement with the little man's words. His name was Puma, and he was a Jicarilla Apache, one whose viciousness and double-dealing practices had caused his own people to banish him from their campfires.

"Ah, go on, lad," Haggerty urged his favorite. "Give ol' Fritzie yer hand."

"All right," Lingeman grunted, scowling as he slowly extended his hand to the German. "But it warn't funny."

As his huge hand encircled Lingeman's, the German sneered. "You got to learn to take a choke, Tickie," he rumbled.

Feeling the sudden pressure on his gun-hand, Lingeman tried to jerk it back, glaring angrily at the giant as he did. But his hand remained imprisoned within Oberst's massive paw.

"Tut, tut, tut, Fritzie, me bucko," Captain Haggerty cautioned. "None o' yer little parlor games now." He turned in the saddle and looked around at the assortment of desperadoes behind him.

"I want yez all to remember that we're just one big family. Why, just t'ink of me as yer beloved father, boys, as yer dear ol' da'."

The German exploded into laughter at this, and let go of Lingeman's hand. In another moment, he was joined by the other bully-boys. Even Lingeman had to laugh, his discolored buck-teeth jutting out of his mouth as he did.

"Now, that's better, me lads," Haggerty said cheerfully, beaming at his family of cutthroats, bushwhackers and rustlers. "Oi want yez all to get on loike kissin' cousins."

"Cap'n, they's a cloud of dust up ahead," Squint Ryerback called out, pointing westward.

"Man and woman ride with Dan Cain," Puma the Apache told his leader, naming the last remaining member of Haggerty's Hellions, the man whom the captain had sent to palaver with Bart Braden.

"Now, ain't that gratifoiyin'," the beefy Irishman said sweetly. "It looks as if Mister Braden has seen fit to jine us."

"Heh, heh, heh," chuckled old Doc Doucette, as he turned to Richard Lingeman. "This ought to be good, boys. This ought to be good."

The other bully-boys smiled and nodded their heads. All except Richard Lingeman, who narrowed his eyes and began to scowl darkly at the approaching riders, at the tall, broad-shouldered cowboy who rode beside Raquel Mirabal and the desperado known as Dan Cain.

"So he went over to Haggerty, by Gad!" swore John B. Loudermilk, banging his meaty fist down on the bar of the Lone Star Hotel. "Well, how d'ya like them apples, boys?"

"Reckon we-all got our work cut out fer us, John," T.C. Pritchett dead-panned.

"Well, they's sure 'nuff gon' be a heap of fightin' " Loudermilk agreed. "They's 'bout fifteen guns in that gang, countin' that fat ol' scoundrel, Haggerty."

"An' Braden's worth four or five ord'nary men," the Kansan acknowledged grudgingly.

"Bee-jabers!" exclaimed the barkeep, a thin, balding man named Joe Smith. He had overheard Bart Braden's conversation with Dan Cain, and had relayed the information to Pritchett and Loudermilk, both long-time friends of his.

"Yep. 'At's a passel of guns, all right,"

Loudermilk admitted after he had wiped his nose on the sleeve of his fringed buckskin jacket.

"You don't look discouraged any, John," Joe Smith said as he leaned over and began to wipe the bar.

"Not a-tall, Joe," the brawny man replied. "Them's Texas Ranger odds. Me'n ol' T.C. here's used to goin' up agin' that many guns."

Pritchett nodded. "Ain't nothin' new fer us, Joe."

"What about you fellas?" the barkeep asked, looking from Soaring Hawk to the Kansan.

"Ain't nothin' new to us, neither," Davy Watson told the man, recalling the Battle of Beecher's Island and his life-and-death showdown with the Landry Gang in Hell's Canyon.

"Just mean more to kill," Soaring Hawk assured Joe Smith, as the barkeep handed him a second glass of sarsaparilla.

"Well," Smith said to the four men who stood on the other side of the bar, "I 'spect y'all got yer work cut out fer ya."

"'Member, this here's special," John B. Loudermilk rumbled. "We's got two good reasons to light out after 'em, Joe. First, that Braden fella done gunned down ol' Paul Myers. An' second, we been after that fat sucker, Haggerty, ever since sixty-five."

"This gives us a chance to settle both scores, Joe," T.C. Pritchett told the barkeep.

"Well, y'all take care," Joe smith called out as the four men walked out of the bar and dining room of the Lone Star Hotel.

"Don't you worry none 'bout us, Joseph," John

B. Loudermilk called back over his shoulder. "It's Bart Braden an' that nest of vipers what's got to watch out."

Outside the Lone Star Hotel, the four men mounted their horses and proceeded to ride out of Austin, heading in an easterly direction.

Through the agency of a Mexican named Juan Bedoya, a long-time paid informant of theirs, the two ex-Rangers had learned of Braden and Raquel's departure in the company of Dan Cain, only a few hours earlier.

By the time that the sun was past high noon, the four riders had picked up Braden's trail, and were gaining on him with every passing mile. And by the time that they sat down to supper around a roaring campfire, the Kansan had calculated that they would overtake the fugitives sometime in the latter part of the coming morning.

Captain Daniel Patrick Haggerty's pig-eyes glittered as he stared at the young, raven-haired beauty who rode toward him, flanked by the Texas ramrod, Bart Braden, and the thin, cadaverous-looking desperado, Dan Cain.

The men who surrounded the tubby, red-faced Irishman all stared at the young *chicana* with burning eyes. Although Bart Braden was the eagerly awaited visitor, Haggerty's Hellions had immediately, and to a man, turned their attention to the proud daughter of Don Solomon Mirabal.

Riding at her left hand, the pale outlaw with the black pencil-mustache had a faint, self-satisfied grin on his face. He had brought a new recruit for

Captain Haggerty, a man who had never before been on the wrong side of the law, but who was at the same time one of the toughest and deadliest men in all Texas.

This the desperado considered to be a feather in his cap, for the major gainful employment of Haggerty's Hellions—extortion, thievery and murder notwithstanding—was cattle rustling. And who knew the great Longhorn herds of Texas and New Mexico better than Bart Braden, the top hand who had been for many years foreman and trail boss for Bill Fanshaw, the cattle baron who had lost his life in the recent attack upon the spread of Don Solomon Mirabal?

Captain Haggerty was overjoyed. Having Bart Braden as an ally, the Irishman reckoned, would give him access to the pick of the herds of such renowed cattle barons as John Chisum and Charlie Goodnight, to say nothing of the late Bill Fanshaw's Longhorns, which were grazing peacefully to the north, just begging to be led away, like so many sheep. And make no mistake about it, Daniel Patrick Haggerty firmly believed that he was the shepherd to lead that particular flock to greener pastures.

For his part, Bart Braden appraised Captain Haggerty and his Hellions with a cold eye. Here he was, the ramrod told himself, riding with Raquel Mirabal, the woman he loved, into a den of thieves and murderers. They were fourteen mean and vicious *hombres*—including Haggerty, the cruelest and most cold-blooded of them all. Ordinarily, Braden would not have trusted them any farther than he could have heaved a brahma bull; but as things stood now, the ramrod considered them to be a necessary evil—for the present.

The shooting of a Texas state policeman had made him the object of a statewide manhunt, or so Braden thought once he had learned that the two men who rode with Davy Watson and Soaring Hawk were brother-officers of the dead man. He knew nothing of the fact that the state policemen were riding out after him for personal reasons, or that they had once served as Texas Rangers under the man he had killed.

The presence of state policemen on his trail so soon after the incident in San Antonio led the ramrod to believe that the State Police were indeed scouring the lower half of the Lone Star State for him. Normally this would not have particularly disturbed him, since Braden was a man who could take care of himself in any situation, but this time there was a further consideration and a greater responsibility.

While Bart Braden gave little thought to his own safety, he gave much thought to that of Raquel Mirabal. He had to get her out of Texas, and as soon as possible. And the safest way to achieve this goal, the ramrod had decided, was to form a temporary alliance with Captain Haggerty. But there would be a price for Raquel's safety, he knew that; the devil would have to be given his due. Braden did not know exactly what he was going to do as he rode up to Haggerty and his Hellions; and although he looked confident and determined, the Texan was far from clear as to the best way to get Raquel Mirabal out of Texas.

As for Raquel herself, while aware that she was

in an increasingly dangerous situation, the eighteen-year-old was at the same time thrilled beyond her wildest imaginings.

Her school friends would never believe what was happening to her—not in a thousand years! And if they should, why, each of them would turn green with envy, for Raquel Mirabal's daily life had become the veritable embodiment of the deepest romantic fantasies of the *muchachas* of the convent school of Our Lady of Guadalupe.

In one stroke, through the agency of her abductor, Bart Braden, Raquel Mirabal had found love, romance and adventure. It was a young girl's dream. And now that the Texan had proved himself an honorable man, Don Solomon's daughter gave herself freely to him, immersing herself in a stream of extravagant characters and colorful adventures. And because she felt so secure under the protection of her formidable lover, the young *chicana* consequently ignored the grim reality of her situation.

"Well, well, well, if it ain't Himself," Captain Haggerty called out in a cheerful voice as Braden drew near. "If this ain't a pleasant surproise."

Braden wore a poker-face as he nodded slightly and murmured, "Haggerty," by way of acknowledgement.

"Oh, an' such a lovely lady," the captain cooed. "Prettier flower never grew in the state of Texas. Captain Daniel Patrick Haggerty at yer service, Miss." He took off his dusty hat with a flourish, and bowed as low in the saddle as his great belly would permit.

Enchanted and embarassed at the same time by

the Irishman's gallantry, Raquel Mirabal lowered her eyes and nodded in acknowledgment of the compliment.

Braden's glance traveled over the band of ruffians who sat to horse behind Captain Haggerty. To a man, they looked mean, low-down and dangerous. Not the traveling companions he would have chosen under normal conditions, Haggerty's Hellions were just what he needed to get Raquel and himself out of Texas in one piece.

"We rode out here to meet yez," Haggerty told Braden and Raquel with a smile. "Our camp's back a few moiles, in a noice outta-the-way place. Why don't yez come there, an' break bread with me an' my lads?"

Bart Braden nodded. His eyes were cold and his thin lips were set in a grim, dangerous smile, an expression which had come upon his face when he saw the way that Haggerty's Hellions were eyeing Raquel Mirabal. This annoyed the ramrod, but it did not worry him overmuch. From his earlier talk with Dan Cain, he had gathered that Haggerty and his men had knowledge of the circumstances which had led to the shooting of Ford Sweinhardt, and he felt sure that none of the desperadoes would have the stomach to go up against him, even for a prize such as the beautiful young *chicana*.

They rode off in a northeasterly direction, Braden and Raquel riding with Captain Haggerty, and the rest of the desperadoes following close behind them. Before long, the riders came to a creek, which they followed as it began to meander through several large clusters of boulders. There, in the midst of that natural fortification, they came upon the outlaw camp.

A fire was burning there, and a kettle was simmering above it, tended by a bald-headed Negro mute named Jimmy Blount. He had been Haggerty's manservant since the days before the War between the States, and the Irishman jokingly referred to him as his son.

"Oh, I hope it's somethin' tasty an' fillin' ye've cooked up fer yer auld da'," the captain wheezed as he climbed down from his horse.

Jimmy Blount nodded eagerly, and grunted in reply. His skin was blue-black in color, and when he smiled, his teeth appeared whiter than the keys of a new pianoforte.

The contents of the kettle proved to be an Irish stew, and it was tasty indeed, the riders found out, once they had tended to their mounts and seated themselves around the campfire.

In addition to the stew, Jimmy Blount had baked sourdough biscuits. There was even dessert, in the form of dried fruit. The meal was washed down with steaming cups of the bitter black coffee of the trail.

"I doubt that God in his heaven ever doined any better," Haggerty said, mopping up the last of his gravy with the remains of a sourdough biscuit. "An' if, as I personally t'ink, there ain't nobody up there," he went on, cocking an eye at the heavens, "then we've had the best of it, ain't we?" He sighed and made a declamatory gesture with his hands. "Ah, well, it's eat, drink an' be merry, for on the morrow we shall die."

B-w-w-woarp! Oberst, the German, rent the air with an ear-splitting belch.

"Ah, man, ye've got no respect for foine sentiments," Captain Haggerty complained. "Here I am, expressin' deep an' elevated feelin's, an' what d'you do, Fritzie? You belch loike a hog at a trough. Now, appolly-joize to the young lady, won't ya?"

"*Ach, entschuldigen sie, fraülein,*" the giant rumbled in a *basso profundo* as he blushed and bowed to Raquel Mirabal.

"Well, now," Haggerty said, rubbing his pudgy hands together and turning to face Bart Braden. "I t'ink it's toime that we was talkin' about what we moight do fer each other, Mister Braden."

The ramrod met his eye and nodded.

"I'm sure you know what would fill my auld heart wi' cheer," the captain told him. "Gettin' my hands on a few t'ousand head of Texas Longhorn—that's what I'd loike most in all the world, Mister Braden." He had a sly smile on his red, puffy face. "Now, what would you be loikin' most?" he asked the ramrod.

Braden put his hand on Raquel Mirabal's knee. "I want to get this lady an' me outta Texas in one piece," he told the beefy Irishman.

"An' ya want me'n my lads to make sure you get out safe, hah?"

Braden nodded again.

"Well," Haggerty grunted, straightening up and rubbing his hands togerther, "an' what would ya be t'inkin' of doin' fer us in return?"

"How 'bout gittin' you all the Longhorns you can herd south?" was the ramrod's reply.

"Ah, now yer playin' a chune that's sure to set the loikes of Paddy Haggerty an' his boys to jiggin'," the captian told Bart Braden, smiling an avaricious smile as he did.

"I'll see that you git yer fill of Bill Fanshaw's Longhorns," Braden said to Haggerty. "An' I'll show ya the safest way to git 'em out'n the New Mexico Territory."

"Oh, yer just the one to warm an' auld fella's heart," Captain Haggerty cried out in an ecstasy of greed.

"But first, I want yer help in gittin' Miss Mirabal to Loosiana," Braden went on. "We'll drop her off in Shreveport—jus' across the state line. An' then I'll ride back with you an' yer boys, an' lead y'all to the pick of Bill Fanshaw's herds."

Haggerty scratched the stubble on his jowls and sighed. "Now, I'd loike to do that, Mister Braden, really I would. But I'm afraid that I can't."

The ramrod shot him a hard look. "Why the hell not?" he asked.

"Because," the Irishman replied reasonably, "I need the young lady around fer reasons of security. . .to guarantee that you do the job proper-loike, so to speak."

"You sayin' you don't trust me, Haggerty?" the Texan growled.

"Now, now, Mister Braden, I wouldn't say that. It's not the sort of thing you should take personal-loike. Remember, if ya will, that fer a fella loike meself to survive in a line of work such as this one, it ain't a good idee to trust anybody. D'ya see what I mean, now? So let's just consider what I said a condition of our little business transaction, shall we?"

"What about about her?" Braden asked

roughly.

The captain beamed at him. "Oh, ya have no need a-tall to worry about the young lady, I can assure you of that. She'll be safe an' snug while we're out on our little round-up. I promise ya there won't be the sloightest danger to her."

Braden's eyes narrowed as he stared at Captain Haggerty. "Damn well better not be," he growled testily. " 'Cause if so much as a hair on her head is mussed when we git back, Haggerty, I'm gon' hold you personally responsible."

"Why, she'll be as safe an' comfy as if she was in some grand ol' hotel in New York or London," the beefy, red-faced Irishman said, smiling beatifically as he looked from Raquel to Braden. "We'll just roide over to Hodgson, a town not far from here, where a good friend of mine will put up Miss, ah—" Here he stopped to look inquiringly at Raquel.

"Mirabal," she replied, suddenly embarrassed by the outlaw's attentions.

"Miss Mirabal," Haggerty resumed. "Why, my auld pal, Monte Tittiger, an' his woife, Ethel, will see to it that Miss Mirabal gets the best of treatment whoile we're away. An then, when we've concluded our business, Mister Braden, you can drop boi Tittiger's place fer the young lady. An' me an' my lads will be more than deeloighted to escort yez into the fair state of Louisiana."

This was not what Bart Braden had intended to settle for when he first rode into the outlaw camp; but he had shot Haggerty once, and could therefore see the man's point in wishing to retain Raquel Mirabal as a hostage.

The Irishman was no fool, the Texan acknowledged ruefully. And if, as he thought, there was a manhunt on for him, then sticking with the outlaw band until he and his love were out of the state would certainly be the wisest course to follow. Haggerty commanded a small army, and the State Police had proved totally ineffectual in bringing the outlaw and his followers to justice.

It would have been a different story in the days of the Texas Rangers, Braden reminded himself. But there just didn't seem to be any men of that caliber in the ranks of the State Police. . . .

"Well, me friend," the captain said cheerfully, "now, what'll it be? Will ya t'row in wit' us for this one grand round-up? Will ya lead Paddy Haggerty an' his children to the Promised Land? Will ya lead us to Bill Fanshaw's Longhorns?" He smiled sadly at the ramrod. " 'Tis certain that poor Fanshaw—God rest his soul—" here he paused and crossed himself—"will be needin' 'em no longer."

"Oh, yeah," chuckled Richard Lingeman. "All that beef'd jus' bar-be-cue in hell."

When he heard this last remark, Bart Braden stiffened. Then, with trembling hand he tilted back his hat and slowly turned to face the buck-toothed desperado. The ramrod was smiling that dangerous, straight-razor smile of his, and he regarded Lingeman with eyes that were colder than a tombstone in Alaska.

"Bill Fanshaw was my friend, mister," he said quietly, still smiling his grim smile at Richard Lingeman. "An' if I hear you make another stupid remark about him, I'm gonna knock all them snaggle teeth of your'n right down yer throat."

Lingeman's eyes went wide and his jaw dropped at this. Then, after having gasped several times and taken several deep breaths, the outraged bully-boy glared at Bart Braden and growled his reply to the ramrod's threat.

"You mus' be gittin' ready to jine Bill Fanshaw in hell yer own self, Braden," Haggerty's favorite told the Texan in the heat of anger. " 'Cause you done talked that shit of your'n to the wrong *hombre*, this time."

Watching this encounter breathlessly; Raquel Mirabal saw the steely glint in her lover's eye and suddenly became afraid.

Braden rose slowly to his feet. "Think you're the right man to take me, Bucktooth?" Braden asked in a quiet voice that was as hard as the head of a bullet.

"Now, now, me lads," Captain Haggerty called out, an edge of anxiety to his cheerful and conciliatory tone of voice.

"Keep out of this, Cap'n!" roared a furious Lingeman. "You heerd what he done called me. Nobody calls me that—an' lives!"

"Ah, Dickie-boy," the captain pleaded, "sure, an' the man didn't mean nothin' by it." He turned to Bart Braden, and shot him an imploring look. "Tell 'im you didn't mean nothin' by it, Braden. Now, go ahead, won't ya?"

By this time, Lingeman had jumped to his feet, and all the desperadoes near him backed away, intending not to get caught in the line of fire, should a gunfight occur.

The Texan's eyes glinted like sunlight on a gun

barrel, and his smile was as bleak as a hangman's heart.

"Tell 'im you was only joshin', Braden," Captain Haggerty pleaded, aware that someone would soon be lying dead upon the ground if he could not placate the two hard and violent men who faced each other across the campfire.

Dan Cain, who was near Bart Braden, gently pulled Raquel Mirabal with him as he stepped out of the line of fire.

The ramrod saw this out of the corner of his eye, and nodded to Cain. His cold eyes never left Richard Lingeman, who now stood rocking slowly back and forth, looking ghastly and sinister in the firelight, the fingers of his gun-hand fluttering nervously above his holster, like bumblebees hovering over a daisy.

"Now, for God's sake, man," Captain Haggerty implored the ramrod, "tell auld Dickie ya didn't mean nothin' by what ya said just now." The beads of sweat that streaked the Irishman's face glimmered like diamonds in the dancing light of the outlaw campfire.

As he listened to Haggerty, Braden watched Lingeman with the cold and predatory eyes of a hawk. "What I meant to say," he began, "was that ol' Dickie here. . ." Suddenly he paused, causing all the outlaws to lean toward him and cock their ears in his direction, anxiously awaiting the Texan's next words.

Lingeman's face was red as a beet, as he angrily gaped at Braden, and his eyes looked as if they were about to pop right out of his head.

"Ol' Dickie here," Braden drawled, resuming

after an uncommonly long pause, "is jus' 'bout the ugliest fucker I ever done set eyes on. . .north or south of the Rio Grande."

That did it. Lingeman emitted a scream of rage. His hand darted down to the sixgun at his side.

BLAMBLAM!!

Two shots rang out loudly in the Texas night, splitting the air with their belling roars.

Richard Lingeman shot backward, blown off his feet, and fell down on his back in the dust, his chest and heart blown apart by the two big slugs from Bart Braden's Colt .45.

"Oh, Jesus God—ye've killed him!" screeched Captain Haggerty, wringing his hands as he regarded the bloody bundle of meat and rags that had been Richard Lingeman.

Braden's gun was still smoking when he holstered it. "He made his play an' lost, Haggerty," the ramrod quietly told the devastated Irishman. "Sum'bitch asked fer it."

"Ah, fer the love of Christ," the captain wailed in a voice that quavered and broke, "ye had no cause to kill poor little Dickie over some stupid remark he made."

"I told you before," Bart Braden said quietly, "Bill Fanshaw was my friend."

Raquel Mirabal's wide eyes were gleaming as she looked up at her champion. He had Spanish pride, that one. He had not hesitated to defend his honor against these *bandidos*, Haggerty's *Yanqui* and *Mexicano* scum. Don Solomon's daughter was deeply moved by her lover's bravery, and she tacitly approved of the shooting of Richard Lingeman.

When Captain Haggerty finally turned from Lingeman's body and looked at Bart Braden, it seemed to the ramrod that the outlaw chief was on the verge of tears.

"How could ya do such a t'ing, Braden?" he said in a small, choked voice. "I was very fond of that lad. He was my friend." The big, fat man sniffled. Then he turned and walked away, out of the light of the campfire.

"They was, uh—real good buddies," Dan Cain told Bart Braden, with a leer that was in sharp contrast to the grief expressed by his leader. He was, as Braden found out later that night, first in line to succeed the late Richard Lingeman as Captain Haggerty's right-hand man.

The Texan nodded. "Yep, it's a damn shame, Cain. But if they was such good buddies, then that boy should've listened to ol' Haggerty."

As he turned to the lovely eighteen-year-old, Braden heard the sounds of muffled sobbing out in the darkness, just beyond the light of the campfire.

It was not the best way to begin his brief partnership with Captain Haggerty, the Texan reflected somberly as he drew Raquel close to him, seeking in the touch of her flesh the warmth that had suddenly gone out of his.

The ramrod knew that the Irishman never forgot, nor did he ever forgive a slight or an insult. He realized that he would have to be on his guard every moment of the day and night, from here on out. And as he smiled down at Raquel Mirabal, the Texan cursed himself inwardly, cursed himself for ever bringing the woman he loved to this nest of vipers.

"So they're a-gone to Hodgson, by Gad!" exclaimed John B. Loudermilk, smacking his fist into his palm. "So that's where them suckers go each time they disappears in these parts."

"They done give us the slip more'n once't in East Texas," T.C. Pritchett told Davy Watson and Soaring Hawk. "We never could rightly figger out where they'd gone to."

"It was like the ground done swallyed 'em up," Loudermilk added. " 'Twas the damnedest thing."

"Y'mean somebody's been puttin' 'em up in that town—Hodgson—all along?" the Kansan asked.

The two Texans nodded.

"Sure as a bear shits in the woods," rumbled Loudermilk. "An' now I know jus' who that someone is."

"Monte Tittiger, that's who," Pritchett added.

"Yep," agreed his partner. "Sum'bitch's the onliest one what's got the space to hide more'n a dozen horses. Couldn't be nobody else."

"How's that?" asked Davy Watson.

"Tittiger owns most of Hodgson," T.C. Pritchett explained. "Gen'ral store, saloon, hotel—"

"An' livery stable!" crowed John B. Loudermilk.

"Why, whenever Haggerty an' his Hellions come to town, ol' Tittiger must tuck their horses in his stable, an' board them owlhoots right in his damn hotel."

Pritchett nodded. "We never did trust that varmint nohow, did we, John?"

The burly ex-Ranger shook his head. "We sure as hell didn't. An' now we know why."

"We gonna go in after 'em tonight?" the Kansan asked, darting an anxious look at Soaring Hawk.

Pritchett shook his head. "We might mosey up there later on, an' size up the sit-chee-ayshun."

"But we ain't gonna do nothin' right away," Loudermilk added. "We gonna wait 'til sun-up. . .so's we can wish them boys a proper good mornin'."

"Where shall we go, Bart?" Raquel Mirabal asked her lover, snuggling up to him in the bed they shared in their room in Monte Tittiger's hotel in the East Texas town of Hodgson.

"I reckon we'll jus' sashay over to New Orleans, once't I done got ol' Haggerty his cows. An' then, I thought mebbe we might take ship to Californee."

"California," Raquel murmured excitedly, resting her head upon the Texan's chest. California was a place of romance and adventure to Don Solomon's daughter, a beautiful and abundant land whose Spanish names and heritage made her feel somehow as if she belonged there. And she *would* feel at home in California, the young *chicana* reminded herself, because so many of her people were there.

"Yes, I would like to go to California, Bart," she told her lover. "No one would know us there."

"Yep," Braden murmured, nuzzling her neck.

"I figger we could get us a right good start there, honey."

"You must be very careful," she told him, suddenly turning over and raising herself up on her elbows in order to face him. "I think these *hombres* are very dangerous."

"Yer right about that, Raquel," the ramrod agreed. "Meaner an' nastier varmints never trod the face of the earth."

"I don't trust *Capitan* Haggerty."

"Shows you got good sense. Why, he'd think nothin' of shootin' his own mother in the back, if'n there was somethin' to be got from it."

"And *you* shot his best friend," Raquel said accusingly.

The ramrod sighed. "That's a fact, honey. But you can be sure I ain't never gonna turn my back on Haggerty. Not never."

"I can't wait until we get out of Texas," Raquel murmured, her hand travelling down over his chest and belly.

"You ain't got long to wait," the ramrod told his love. "We jus' gon' pick us up a few cows, first."

"Oh, Bart," Raquel whispered in a voice which registered both surprise and delight. "You're already hard."

Braden twined his fingers in her thick, black hair. "Tha's jus' my way of payin' attention," he whispered back as Raquel's long, tapered fingers closed around his erect sex.

"You must show me more, *querido*," she whispered intensely.

"You like what we do, huh?" he asked as she

181

gripped him with both hands.

"Oh, yes," the young *chicana* answered in a voice that shook. Then she licked her full lips and began to lower her head. "*Oh, yes!*"

Braden's eyes widened suddenly, and he lifted his head off the pillow. And when he looked down, the ramrod was surprised to see his innocent young lover kneeling over him, her head poised above his groin.

She turned and shot him a hot, excited look. "I want to please you, Bart," Raquel whispered in a throaty voice. "I want to. . .kiss you." She stopped speaking and looked down to where she gripped his engorged sex in both her hands.

Staring in fascination at the beautiful and naked eighteen-year-old who hovered above him, watching her as carefully as a quail watches a goshawk, Bart Braden swallowed and then cleared his throat softly.

"I want to kiss you, Bart," Raquel repeated in a voice that shook with passion. "You have to. . .tell me. . .what to do." She cast him an imploring sidelong glance.

"Uh, well, Raquel," the ramrod began, shifting uncomfortably in the bed and looking straight up at the ceiling as he let his head drop back on the pillow, "you, uh, kinda got to go somewhat easy." He cleared his throat again. "It's like you, uh, don't gotta squeeze so hard, honey."

A flush began to suffuse the Texan's face as he said this, and he continued to stare fixedly at the ceiling.

"Oh," Raquel said in a small, alarmed voice, suddenly releasing her grip on his rod with the speed of a cowhand who had unwittingly picked up a rattlesnake instead of a branding-iron.

"But what else you was doin'," the ramrod went on, closing his eyes as he spoke, "was fine, honey. Right nice."

An instant later, he felt her fingers encircle his sex once more, lightly this time, followed by a resumption of the rubbing and stroking she had begun earlier.

After stroking his pole for some time, staring down at his groin with rapt attention all the while, Raquel finally spoke. "I want to. . .kiss you, Bart," she told Braden with gentle persistence.

"Uh-huh," he grunted, his face now the color of a slab of raw beefsteak. The Texan cleared his throat again. His eyes, opened once more, remained turned to the ceiling. "Main thing you got to remember," he mumbled, "is not to do no bitin'." For an instant he glanced down at his groin, and then quickly returned his gaze to the ceiling of Tittiger's Hotel. "That's very important, honey."

"I see," she whispered back, staring down at the prize in her hand like a little girl who has just been handed a kitten. "What else do I do, Bart?"

"Oh, well. . ." He cleared his throat for a long time. "You, uh, kinda take it in yer mouth, an'—"

"*All of it*?" she asked in alarm.

Braden's face was redder than ever. He closed his eyes. "Well, the top part, mainly," he mumbled.

"The *what*?" she asked, not fully catching his drift.

"The, uh, top part. The head."

"Oh. Is that what they call it?"

"Uh-huh. That's right, honey."

"Is that all I take in?"

"Well, if'n you feel you can take in some more—without gaggin' or nothin' like that, then I guess y'all can go ahead an'—you know." He opened his eyes, and then covered them with his forearm.

"What do I do then, Bart?" Raquel asked eagerly as she continued to rub and stroke him.

Again Braden cleared his throat. Then he heaved a deep sigh. "You, uh, sorta lick an'. . .suck." He cleared his throat once more. "You know," he said lamely, "stuff like that."

"Lick and suck," she repeated in a voice that registered a degree of puzzlement.

"Uh, yep," the ramrod went on. "Sorta like a deer at a salt lick. Or a kid a-pullin' on a lollipop."

"Oh, like *that*," she whispered, suddenly understanding what she had to do.

The ramrod sighed, his tense muscles finally relaxing. "Yep. That's right, honey."

As he closed his eyes once more, Bart Braden heard Raquel murmur something in Spanish, something he did not catch, the intonation of the words reminding the Texan of a prayer.

The young *chicana* thrust her hands down as far as they would go along his shaft, pressing into his groin and causing his *glans penis* to stand out well beyond her fingers. After that, she ran her tongue lightly and tentatively over his *glans*, and followed that by drawing back slightly as she moistened her full lips.

Then Raquel slowly lowered her head, parting

her gleaming lips and slowly taking the head of Bart Braden's sex in her mouth. Next, she began to do something that she had never been taught in the convent-school of Our Lady of Guadalupe.

Braden groaned, making a sound like a pole-axed steer dropping to the sawdust of a slaughterhouse floor.

As Raquel Mirabal pulled and sucked and licked like a two-year-old enjoying its first lollipop, she hummed happily.

The ramrod was breathing heavily now, snorting great blasts of air through flaring nostrils as the beautiful and passionate eighteen-year-old worked him over.

Her fingers traveled up and down over the shaft of his cock in light, spiralling runs. And her tongue started tremors in the pit of his groin, tremors which reached up his spine and penetrated his brain with waves that impinged upon his consciousness, causing the Texan to suddenly recall the image of an Oklahoma oil well about to blow.

As for Raquel, she was thoroughly caught up in the excitement of forbidden games, the convent-schoolgirl in her utterly fascinated by the dark joys of the flesh.

"Oh, God!" Braden moaned, his body suddenly stiffening as he was swept along by the irresistible tide of orgasm. *Sweet Jee-sus!*"

Then the oil well blew, and Bart Braden grunted as a gusher of jism shot up through his ureter tube and streamed out into the ardent mouth of his beloved.

Raquel Mirabal's eyes went wide as her lover suddenly came in her mouth.

"*Ooooh—don't stop, gal!*" he cried out in anguish as Raquel suddenly froze with surprise. This was an aspect of "kissing" that the Texan had neglected to discuss with her.

"*Uuunh,*" she grunted, recovering her wits almost immediately, and ministering once more to her writhing lover, after swallowing the first installment of his copious emission with a gulp.

The gusher flowed for some time, and the adaptable Raquel did her honey proud. And after she did, the grateful ramrod proceeded to initiate the eighteen-year-old further into the delights of oral sex, as he performed cunnilingus on her once more.

"Oh, Bart," Raquel Mirabal sighed as they lay together in the sweet aftermath of a night of energetic lovemaking. "It was wonderful. . .like nothing I have ever done before."

"You did right good, honey," the Texan murmured sleepily, planting a tender kiss on the nape of Raquel's neck and inhaling at the same time the delicate fragrance of her hair. And as he began to drift off to sleep, Bart Braden recalled Captain Haggerty's words:

"*Eat, drink and be merry, for tomorrow we shall die.*"

7

The End of the Trail

"I got to git that gal outta there afore ya start pumpin' lead into Tittiger's Hotel," the Kansan told the two former Texas Rangers.

"Aw, shoot," grumbled John B. Loudermilk. "That's gon' take the teeth out'n our surprise attack."

T.C. Pritchett nodded in agreement with this.

"Boys, I promised her daddy I'd bring 'er back in one piece afore I left New Mexico an' rid out after Bart Braden." He looked from Loudermilk to Pritchett, staring deeply into each man's eyes. "Gents, I give my word."

Loudermilk puffed up his cheeks and blew a whistling stream of air out between compressed lips. He raised his big hands in a gesture of helplessness and turned to his partner.

Pritchett sighed. "He done give his word to her daddy, John." There was a look of resignation upon his face.

The brawny man with the handlebar mustache sighed back. "Reckon we got to honor that, all right," he rumbled.

There was a relieved look on Davy Watson's face as he looked at his Pawnee blood-brother.

The four men were in the town of Hodgson, standing in the shadow of the livery stable owned by Captain Haggerty's old friend, Monte Tittiger, as they watched the hotel across the street.

The two ex-Rangers had chosen the stable as their vantage point because, with the outlaw gang's horses under their control, they would virtually have Haggerty and his bunch bottled up in Hodgson. Their original plan had been to encircle Tittiger's Hotel, and call for the immediate surrender of the desperadoes. And if no surrender was forthcoming, the Texans had decided to put the place to the torch, and shoot the outlaws as they fled the burning building.

"You gonna shoot them down jus' like that?" the Kansan asked, jarred by the cold-blooded scheme.

Both men nodded.

"These is the worstest scoundrels an' murderers in the whole state of Texas," Loudermilk explained patiently. "They'd only be dancin' at the end of a rope sooner or later, you can bet yer boots on that. An' thisaway, we's jus' makin' sure they don't escape."

"That's how we dealt with real bad 'uns in the Rangers," Pritchett told Davy and Soaring Hawk. "Jus' savin' the state time an' expense."

Davy Watson shook his head in disbelief.

"This ain't no instance of stringin' up some poor, innocent men," Pritchett went on. "Ain't no question but that all them boys in there is guilty—each an' every one, mind you—of the worstest crimes on the books. An' don't fergit, Bart Braden's a murderer, his own self."

"Shoot," Loudermilk growled. "That includes ol' Monte Tittiger an' his wife. Why, they's been accessories to the crimes of Haggerty's Hellions fer years now, I figger, 'cause they been shelterin' them boys—an' God knows what else."

Pritchett looked somber as he nodded a second time.

The Kansan had to admit it was basically the best way to deal with such a great number of desperadoes. After all, he and his companions were outnumbered four-to-one by the Haggerty bunch. But the presence of Raquel Mirabal in the hotel complicated things.

"Well, how d'ya propose to git that li'l filly out'n the hotel without wakin' up Haggerty an' all his friends?" asked Loudermilk.

"An' since Braden done ab-ducted her in the first place," added Pritchett, "it's fer damn sure he won't be far away from that gal."

Nodding at this, Davy Watson frowned as he recalled his midnight shootout with the Texas ramrod. Bart Braden was an extremely dangerous man, one who should never be underestimated.

"How you goin' git that gal out?" John B. Loudermilk asked once more. "Without ruinin' our little surprise?"

"It ain't gonna be easy," opined T.C. Pritchett.

The Kansan smiled at them grimly and then shook his head. "It ain't gonna be all that hard, neither," he told them.

Tap. Tap. Tap. . . .Tap. Tap. Tap.
A light-but-persistent knocking on the door

awakened Bart Braden. The ramrod was up on his feet in an instant, drawing on his trousers as he whispered, "Who is it?" and cast an anxious glance at the sleeping Raquel Mirabal.

"It's Monte Tittiger, Mr. Braden," a hoarse voice whispered back from the other side of the door.

"What d'ya want?" the Texan whispered as he drew his Colt .45 out of its holster at the foot of the bed, where his gunbelt was hung on a bedpost.

"Cap'n Haggerty wants to talk with ya, private-like."

By this time Braden was standing to one side of the door, with his gun held up at chest level. Recognizing the landlord's voice, the ramrod began to relax.

"Cap'n sent me up to ask ya to meet him down-stairs," Tittiger went on beyond the door. "In the bar."

Braden darted a glance at the bed, and was relieved to discover that his beloved was still asleep.

"Hold on," he said, reaching for his flannel shirt with the hand that held the Colt .45, while he turned the doorknob with his free hand.

When the Texan opened the door, he was not prepared for the sight which greeted his eyes. There before him was Monte Tittiger, indeed, but with the barrel of a gun pointed up under his fat chin. And behind Tittiger, one hand on the Walker Colt and the other around the landlord's neck, stood the Kansan.

The only sound in the hall at that moment was Bart Braden's sharp intake of breath as he recognized the man who was hunting him. And before the ramrod could raise his own Colt, Soaring Hawk thrust the barrel of his Sharps rifle under the Texan's nose.

"Make one wrong move, Braden," the Kansan told his enemy, "an' Soaring Hawk here'll blow yer head apart like a overripe punkin what's been trod on by a plowhorse." His eyes were hard as Vermont granite, and his smile was as bright and sharp as a new Bowie knife.

"Well, I'll be hog-tied," Braden whispered in astonishment. "Watson—it's you."

"Goddamn right it's me, Braden," the Kansan replied in a steely whisper as he held out his hand. "I'm here to finish our business."

The ramrod bit his lip and darted a quick look over his shoulder at the still-sleeping Raquel Mirabal. Then, as he handed Davy Watson his Colt .45, Braden sighed and shook his head.

Davy took the gun, and then hit the ramrod in the chest with his forearm, thrusting him roughly back into the room. Then the Kansan entered, taking with him the sweating and red-faced Monte Tittiger. Soaring Hawk followed them, and quietly shut the door behind him.

"Git over by that wall," Davy told Braden, gesturing to his left with the Walker Colt. He thrust Tittiger roughly toward the wall. Soaring Hawk stepped forward and leveled his Sharps at the two men, motioning for them to raise their hands.

"Raquel," the Kansan called out in a firm, quiet voice. "Raquel, git up. We come to take ya home."

191

She fluttered her eyelids, stared at Davy Watson blankly for a moment, and then sat up with a start.

"*Dah-veed*!" she cried. "It's you!"

He raised a finger to his mouth, signaling for silence. "Git yer things on," he told her. "We're takin' you outta here."

Then Davy turned to Bart Braden. "Reckon you'll have to come, too. So don't try nothin', Braden. Y'hear?"

The Texan nodded. "I ain't 'bout to put Raquel in any danger."

"Well, now, I reckon it'll depend more upon you than upon me," the Kansan told Braden, as Raquel Mirabal donned her underthings beneath the cover of a bedsheet. And when he suddenly realized that the naked young *chicana* must have been sharing a bed with the ramrod, Davy Watson scowled.

"I ain't gon' give you no grief, Watson," Braden told him. "Not while Raquel's around."

"You damn well better not," the Kansan growled. " 'Cause I'm just itchin' to put a couple of bullets in you, Braden. But instead of that, I'm a-handin' you over to some fellas from the State Police. Seems they're right anxious to make yer acquaintance."

He smiled his Bowie knife smile. "Them boys is gonna be right glad to see you."

"*Dah-veed*!" Raquel Mirabal whispered urgently. "You can't—"

"Hush up, Raquel," Bart Braden told her, shaking his head as he turned to the young *chicana*. "The man got me fair 'n square."

Davy shot her a troubled look. "Hurry up now,

Raquel. We ain't got no time to waste."

In another minute they were all out in the hall, tip-toeing along the carpet, on their way to the stairs which led down to the ground floor of Tittiger's Hotel.

"My wife's upstairs," Tittiger whispered anxiously, turning to the Kansan. "What about her?"

Davy waved him out the door. "She'll just have to stay put fer now," he told Tittiger. "Le's go.'

Then they were out on the street, heading toward the livery stable, with Tittiger in the lead, Raquel and Braden next in line, while Davy Watson and his Pawnee blood-brother walked several paces behind the ramrod, slightly off to each side of the prisoners.

They were halfway across the wide, dusty, main street of Hodgson now. From the rear of the little file, Davy could see John B. Loudermilk peering around the corner of the livery stable. The ex-Texas Ranger was nodding in admiration as he regarded the captors of Bart Braden.

Well, the worst is over, the Kansan told himself, smiling a wry smile as he shepherded Raquel, Braden and Monte Tittiger across the quiet street in the first light of dawn. *Now that we got Raquel back an' turned Bart Braden over to the State Police, all's we got left to do is deal with a dozen or so bad hombres that's a-sleepin' in Tittiger's Hotel.*

For an instant the Kansan thought about Monte Tittiger's wife. He wasn't especially looking forward to her being in the hotel when Loudermilk and Pritchett called for the surrender of Haggerty and his Hellions.

Bam! Bam!

Suddenly two shots rang out, echoing loudly in the quiet street. They came from behind, from the direction of the hotel. Davy Watson crouched down and spun around, and as he did, the Kansan saw Bart Braden lurch forward and fall to the ground.

Bam!

Another rifle shot rang out, and the slug whined over Davy's head as he raised his Walker Colt and began to scan the front of Tittiger's Hotel. An instant later, he spotted the assailant: Captain Haggerty, his huge bulk thrust across the sill of an open window, was working the lever of a Winchester rifle as he sent another cartridge into its firing chamber.

Boom!

By the time that the Kansan had taken aim at the outlaw chief, Soaring Hawk had already fired his heavy-caliber Sharps rifle. The shot was a near-miss, blowing the window frame to smithereens just to the right of Captain Haggerty's head. The fat desperado cried out as a shower of splinters scored his face, and he ducked back inside the room.

At this point, Davy heard the sound of windows being raised. On both sides of the spot where Haggerty had opened fire, men with drawn pistols were leaning out of windows and beginning to bang away at the group in the street.

Bam! Bam! Davy's big Walker Colt bucked as he sent two shots at the gunman directly across from him. Then, without waiting to see whether or

194

not his shots had found their mark, he spun around, still crouching, and came up behind the prisoners.

Raquel was kneeling beside Bart Braden, cradling his head in her lap. To his chagrin, as the Kansan ducked down beside her, he noticed tears streaming down the New Mexican beauty's cheeks.

"Git over there, Raquel," Davy ordered, pointing to the livery stable where John B. Loudermilk was firing at the hotel with a carbine.

Whi-i-ing! A bullet whined, and then spanged just behind Raquel Mirabal, sending a jet of dust into the air as it plowed into the ground.

Davy's eyes widened as he watched the young *chicana* shake her head stubbornly. Out of the corner of his eye, he could see Monte Tittiger rush by, his back prodded by the barrel of Soaring Hawk's rifle.

"Hah! Got that sum'bitch!" John B. Loudermilk cried exultantly as he lowered his rifle, smiling grimly at the hotel window where Arthur Danforth, the Virginian outlaw, dropped his pistol out the window and followed it a moment later, pitching down to the street.

Bam! Blam!

The shooting continued as Davy Watson squatted down beside the fallen Bart Braden and looked Raquel Mirabal in the eye.

"Judas Priest, you're stuck on this galoot!" he exclaimed in amazement as he looked down at the Texas ramrod.

Bwi-i-ing! Another bullet spinged in the dust, not more than a foot away from Raquel Mirabal. And as the Kansan stared down at the bloodstained front of Braden's flannel shirt, he heard the answering roar of Soaring Hawk's Sharps.

The sound of shattering glass filled the air. Braden grimaced in pain as he tried to speak.

"Git Raquel outta here, Watson," he said.

"I won't go unless we take him along," Don Solomon's daughter told Davy in a firm voice.

The Kansan nodded, realizing that taking Braden with him would be the best way to ensure Raquel's cooperation. He leaned over, grabbed hold of the lapels of Braden's denim jacket, and pulled him to a sitting position.

At the same time, in back of Tittiger's Hotel, a door creaked open and two armed men rushed out into the daylight.

Blam! Blam!

Two shots rang out, and the last of the men to leave the hotel was flung against the wall. He cried out loudly, clutched his right side with both hands, and sank to his knees in the dust.

"*Fernando!*" Eufemio Salcedo cried when he turned and saw his dying younger brother. Then the pot-bellied desperado spun around and leveled his gun at the copse of cottonwood trees which faced the back of the hotel at a distance of more than a hundred feet.

Salcedo fired off two answering shots before the second volley from the cottonwoods cut him down.

In the copse of trees, his rifle resting on a sturdy limb, T.C. Pritchett looked up and nodded, smiling in grim satisfaction.

By this time a third figure had appeared at the door. Michael Shaughnessy, the ruffian from Hell's Kitchen, pegged three wild shots at the ex-Ranger, cursed loudly, ducked back in the hotel, and slammed the door shut.

"*Get him! Shoot the bastard dead*!" Captain Hagerty roared, foaming at the mouth as he leaned out the shattered window and began blasting away at Bart Braden, whom the Kansan had just slung over his back.

"Skeedaddle, Raquel!" Davy called out, tottering for a moment under the ramrod's weight as he straightened up.

From a series of windows adjacent to Captain Haggerty's, the Hellions began to pour their fire out onto the street.

Bam! Bam! Whi-i-ing! Blam! Boom!

"*Die, ya filthy, murtherin' bastard*!" Haggerty roared in a paroxysm of insane rage, still banging away at the man he hated above all other men. "A loife fer a loife! Now I'll avenge me poor Dickie!"

The Kansan sighed with relief as he saw Raquel Mirabal disappear around the corner of the livery stable, where John B. Loudermilk continued to pepper the outlaws with his carbine. And as he lurched around the corner himself, Davy heard the reassuring boom of Soaring Hawk's Sharps, as the Pawnee covered him from one of the building's front windows.

Raquel Mirabal cried out in anguish as Davy Watson staggered into the stable and dumped Bart Braden onto a pile of hay.

"Oh, he's hurt badly!" she gasped, kneeling at the ramrod's side.

The Kansan scowled and shook his head as he made his way to a window. And as he did, Davy stepped over the recumbent form of Monte

Tittiger.

"What happened to him?" he called out to Soaring Hawk as he knelt beside the window.

"Nothing," the Plains Indian called back. "Too busy to guard him, so I hit on head with rifle."

"Cap'n! Cap'n!" Squint Ryerback yelled in alarm, "The damn hotel's on fire!"

"Oh, Jay-sus!" the beefy, red-faced Irishman moaned. "What? *This* hotel?"

Across the street, the Kansan's eyes went wide as he saw flames leap up from both sides of Tittiger's Hotel, with accompanying clouds of smoke which began to billow up past the windows of the wood frame building's second story.

"Good work, T.C., ol' hoss!" John B. Loudermilk roared exultantly. "Whoopee! We gon' smoke out them varmints now!"

"Fire an' brimstone!" Doc Doucette called out as he ducked into Captain Haggerty's room. "It's spreadin' like blazes, Cap'n—on account of that damn wind what's a-comin up from the east!"

"Holy Mary, Mother of God!" the Irishman swore, turning to the powerful graybearded old man. "Now, where's the Salcedo boys? Did they get over across the street?"

Doucette shook his head. "Nope. Some jasper was layin' fer 'em in the cottonwoods. Done plugged 'em both."

"Jay-sus Chroist!" the outlaw chief screamed in a voice shrill with rage and frustration. "It's that bloody fookin' Braden! He put the jinx on me, by God!"

Just then Eli Satterthwaite, the big, bald-headed

198

man with the patch over his eye, bolted into the room.

"The buildin's goin' up like kindling!" he called out in a voice that shook. "They got us trapped like rats in here. What we gonna do, Cap'n?"

The Irishman's face was redder than ever, and his jowls danced to the pulse of his anger. "Get me Tittiger's woifes!" he ordered, turning to Michael Shaughnessy.

"Right y'are, Cap'n," the New York City ruffian grunted as he rose to his feet.

A moment later he cried out in a high-pitched, whimpering voice and collapsed on the floor, a bullet from the Kansan's Walker Colt in his right temple.

"*Dead-Oiye!*" Haggerty screamed. "*Dead-Oiye, where are ya?*" The fat desperado slammed the butt of his rifle down on the floorboards. "Them bastards over there is after pickin' us off one-by-one. Git over here, an' give 'em what for!"

The scrawny little man with the oversized Adam's apple and the Bill Cody hair scurried into the room on all fours, a sharpshooter's Henry rifle in his left hand.

"I-I-I was tryin' to get the sum'bitch what f-f-fired the house in my sights, Cap'n," Dead-Eye Dan Bates explained. But he hung too c-c-close to the buildin'."

"How'd the place go up so fast?" asked Doc Doucette.

"M-musta done s-s-soaked it with k-k-kerosene whilst we was all asleep," speculated Bates. Then he crawled to the window, giving the body of Michael Shaughnessy a wide berth.

"Git over here an' pop off a couple of them divils across the way," Haggerty told him impatiently.

"I-I'll do m'level best, sir," said the scrawny desperado.

"Who's coverin' the back of the bloody house?" Captain Haggerty asked in sudden alarm.

"Fritzie an' Puma's watchin' it, Cap'n," Bates said out of the side of his mouth as he scanned the front of the livery stable.

"Who else is left?" Haggerty asked.

"Dan Cain an' Jimmy Blount, far's I can tell, Cap'n," was Squint Ryerback's reply.

"I'll go get Monte's ol' lady," Doc Doucette boomed as he began to crawl out of the room.

Just then, Dead-Eye Dan Bates fired off a brace of shots.

Blam! Blam!

"*Ooooof!*" grunted John B. Loudermilk, his carbine flying into the air as one of the slugs from Bates' rifle shattered his left forearm. The brawny ex-Ranger ducked behind the livery stable wall, sagging against it as he drew his sixgun.

Back in the burning hotel, the sharpshooter had moved his rifle, and was in the process of lining the Kansan up in his sights.

"Here comes Number Two, Cap'n," Bates whispered, exhaling gently as his finger tightened on the trigger.

Boom!

Thunder broke across the street as Soaring Hawk's Sharps rifle detonated. And with a sound much like that of a melon smashing under the blow of a blacksmith's hammer, the sharpshooter's head burst apart under the impact of the slug from the Pawnee's weapon, spattering the room and its occupants with bits of brain and bone and flesh.

"Yahoo!" Davy Watson yelled. "You got that sum'bitch, my brother!"

The back door of the hotel creaked open once more, and Jimmy Blount, the captain's mute manservant, jumped out and began to dash for the shelter of a buckboard that stood no more than twenty feet away from the building.

Blam! Blam! Bam! Bambam!

Two shots rang out from the cottonwoods, followed an instant later by three more from the opposite direction. And as Jimmy Blount clutched at his gut and fell to the ground, T.C. Pritchett uttered a strangled cry and threw up his rifle. A bullet had caught him in the eye, entering his brain. By the time that the ex-Texas Ranger hit the ground, he was dead.

"That takes care of you, *amigo*," Dan Cain muttered as he drew back from the window and lowered his smoking pistol. "Now we can get outta here."

"Mister Watson," John B. Loudermilk called out in pain and sadness a few moments later. "I think they done got ol' T.C. I don't hear his rifle no more. We got to keep the back of the hotel covered, or them varmints'll all break loose. Now, I'm shot, an' losin' lots of blood, so you or yer buddy'll have to go over there."

"All right," Davy Watson called out. "Cover me, you two."

Fortunately for the Kansan, great sheets of flame leapt up before the front of the hotel as he made his perilous sprint across the wide street. This, in combination with the heavy covering fire laid down by Soaring Hawk and Loudermilk, enabled him to skirt the building and reach the cottonwoods unobserved.

"Bedad, I've got a woman here," Captain Haggerty roared out the window when the flames had momentarily subsided. "An' I'm goin' to use her to shield me when Oi come out of this place, so give way."

"That don't cut no ice with us, Haggerty!" the brawny ex-Ranger roared back. "That ol' slut is as guilty as you are, an' I ain't got no qualms 'bout lettin' her have one 'twixt the eyes, neither. Yer a dead man, anyway, so whyn't you jus' let 'er go, an' come out a-fightin' like a man?"

"Oh, Captain—don't let 'em shoot me!" blubbered Monte Tittiger's wife, a tall hatchet-faced blonde.

"Cap'n, the back is clear!" Dan Cain called out as he dashed into the room. "The stairs is startin' to burn, an' if'n we don't shag ass outta here right away, we'll roast like wieners."

Boom! The Sharps rifle cracked across the street, and Dan Cain suddenly shot back through the open door, the latest victim of the hawk-eyed Plains Indian.

"Down, lads!" the captain cried. "Oh, bejaysus," he moaned, gnawing on a knuckle. "Whoever's got that big gun is an even truer shot than poor ol' Dead-Oiye."

Haggerty turned back to the window, taking care not to expose himself, and cupped his hands over his mouth.

"All right, whoever y'are," he yelled. "We're

comin' out with our hands up. Give me an' my lads a minute to get downstairs, an' we'll send Monte Tittiger's auld lady out ahead of us."

"Come ahead—but come out with yer hands held high," John B. Loudermilk yelled back in a voice shot through with weakness and pain.

"Now, lads," Haggerty whispered to his men. "Collect the others that's still aloive, an' we'll go stormin' out the back door, trippin' loike the hammers of hell." He waved them out impatiently. "Go on, we ain't got much toime."

"What about woman?" he was asked by Puma the Apache, once he had crawled out of the room. The big Indian was holding Monte Tittiger's wife, who by this time was pale with fear.

"Bring the auld bag along," Haggerty growled as he lumbered toward the stairs, covering his face as a sheet of flame leapt up before him. "It can't hurt to have her wit' us."

Several seconds later the back door of the hotel flew open, and the surviving outlaws burst out and headed for the safety of the cottonwoods. . .unaware that the Kansan was there, waiting for them.

The first one out was Squint Ryerback, who made for the trees as if the devil himself were on his heels. Next came the giant German, followed closely by Eli Satterthwaite and Doc Doucette. After them came Puma, dragging Tittiger's whimpering spouse with him. And last, but certainly not least, his jowls trembling as he ran, came Captain Daniel Patrick Haggerty.

The Kansan lined the foremost outlaw up in his gunsight and waited patiently. As he aimed T.C. Pritchett's Winchester, the Kansan steadied himself against the very same limb which the fallen ex-Texas Ranger had used. The man's corpse lay at Davy Watson's feet.

Squint Ryerback was now only twenty-five feet away.

Blam!

The Winchester cracked, and the little man shot backward, rolling over in the grass to land in a heap, his scrawny neck bent at an impossible angle.

Thirty feet behind him, the three big men skidded and floundered as they clumsily attempted to stop dead in their tracks.

Blam! Blam!

Eli Satterthwaite screamed and spun around, his pistol flying through the air. The bald man with the black eyepatch clawed at his throat, as he sank to his knees and uttered wet, gurgling sounds.

Old Doc Doucette dropped to the ground and began to fire back at the unseen rifleman in the cottonwoods. Fritz Oberst looked from the trees to the burning building, and then back to the trees. Firing a brace of shots, the giant lumbered off, heading for the shelter of the buckboard that stood behind the hotel.

Blam!

The Kansan's slug caught the German in the small of the back, causing him to straighten up and stop dead in his tracks. Then he turned stiffly and began to fire in Davy's direction.

Davy fired off one more shot before he ducked behind the tree. Oberst and Doucette had finally located the Kansan, and were now making it hot for him.

In the meantime, Haggerty and Puma, who continued to drag Mrs. Tittiger with him, sought shelter behind the buckboard.

Boom!

There was a sudden, thunderous roar, and the Apache was knocked off his feet, never to rist again, dragging the screeching, terrified woman down to the ground with him.

Captain Haggerty dove for the ground and rolled over until he collided with Monte Tittiger's wife. Then, just in time to avoid taking Soaring Hawk's second bullet, the fat desperado thrust the woman in front of him.

Bang!

Splinters flew through the air as a slug blew apart a branch not six inches above the Kansan's head. Oberst was on his knees in the grass now, bracing his gun in both hands as he took careful aim at Davy Watson, who swore and did his best to reload the Winchester before he got shot.

Boom!

The German giant shot forward and flopped on his face without uttering a sound. Soaring Hawk's shot had blown the top of the man's head off.

The Plains Indian, once he had been stalemated by Captain Haggerty, ducked back around the house, intending to deal with the other surviving desperadoes. Then he saw Oberst about to shoot his blood-brother, and quickly dispatched the German.

"I give up," boomed Doc Doucette, flinging his pistol up into air and rising stiffly with his hands held above his head. "Don't shoot an old man."

"You just come forward 'bout ten paces, Pop,

an' then stay put,'' Davy ordered the big old man. Then he turned back to the burning building and was surprised to see Soaring Hawk facing Captain Haggerty, as the latter held Tittiger's wife in front of him as a shield and aimed his gun at the Pawnee.

Haggerty had rushed around the corner just as the Pawnee was about to reload his Sharps. Soaring Hawk tossed the gun aside and went for the scalping knife in his belt, but the Irishman shot him before he could draw it.

Bam! Bam!

Captain Haggerty fired two shots at the Pawnee, one of which knocked him to the ground. And then the outlaw chief moved in for the kill, thrusting Tittiger's wife aside as he started forward and drew a bead on the fallen Indian.

''Judas Priest!'' Davy Watson exclaimed as the billowing smoke suddenly hid the captain and Soaring Hawk from view. It was impossible to aim at anything now, and certainly too far away for him to run there in time to save his blood-brother. The only thing the Kansan could do was to wait and pray.

''Now, ya red bastard!'' Captain Daniel Patrick Haggerty cried out in exultation as he aimed his gun at the fallen Pawnee, who lay unconscious on the ground before him.

Crack! Crack!

Two short, sharp bursts rang out in the smoky air. Captain Haggerty dropped his gun, howled like a banshee, and began to claw at his back. His eyes were already glazing when he looked around and saw Monte Tittiger.

The captain's former accomplice held a smoking

Derringer in his hand. "How dare you treat my wife that way!" Tittiger said to Haggerty, just as the latter gurgled and fell on his face in the grass.

As the smoke cleared, Davy Watson saw Monte Tittiger chuck his Derringer onto the grass, turn toward him, and raise his hands in the air.

"I'm unarmed, mister," Tittiger called out as his wife ran to his side. "An' you don't have to worry 'bout Captain Haggerty no more."

"Jus' keep 'em up, an stay where you are," the Kansan called out to the man who had shot the Irish desperado. Then he took one last look at the corpse of T.C. Pritchett and stepped out of the shelter of the cottonwoods.

"Git over with them two people," Davy told Doc Doucette, once he had made sure that the old man was not carrying any concealed weapons. And after searching Tittiger and his wife, Davy knelt down beside he body of his Pawnee blood-brother.

To his relief, the Kansan discovered that Soaring Hawk's wound was not a fatal one. Captain Haggerty's bullet had caught the Plains Indian in the upper part of his right thigh, sending him to the ground. And when he fell, Soaring Hawk had banged his head against a rock.

When he had bound the now-conscious Pawnee's wound, Davy left him propped up in the buckboard, with a pistol trained on the prisoners. And as he started toward the livery stable, the Kansan wondered why John B. Loudermilk had not joined him.

Tittiger's Hotel was blazing away like a Fourth of July bonfire, and as Davy Watson made his way across the street, its bright and flickering light illuminated the front of the livery stable.

He saw a pair of boots sticking out from behind the wall as he rounded the corner of the building, boots he recognized as belonging to John B. Loudermilk. And when he turned the corner, the Kansan saw the ex-Texas Ranger sitting slumped against the wall of the livery stable, a pool of blood around him, his head on his chest, and his hat lying on the ground.

Apparently the shot that Loudermilk had taken from the rifle of Dead-Eye Dan Bates had not only shattered his forearm, but opened an artery as well. The brawny state policeman had bled to death.

When he went inside the building, Raquel Mirabal raised her head from Bart Braden's chest and shot Davy Watson a stricken look. The Kansan realized that the ramrod, the man who had stolen Raquel from her home and caused so much death and devastation, was dead, too.

"I loved him," Raquel said in a small voice. "*Ay, Dios*," she wailed, brushing the dead Texan's cheek with trembling fingers. "*Bart, mi corazón*!"

The Kansan bent over, took the stunned *chicana's* arm, and helped her to her feet.

"C'mon, Raquel," he whispered. "I'm gon' take you home to yer daddy."

Then I'm gon' home to Kansas, he told himself as he led her out of the livery stable. *An' this time, I ain't lettin' nothin' stop me.*

THE KANSAN

LONG, HARD RIDE

ONE

The Homeward Trail

Well, here's to home, the Kansan told himself as he raised aloft a hooker of rye whiskey in a honkytonk in the Texas panhandle town of Amarillo.

It was the fifteenth of April, 1870, and Davy Watson stood at a long hardwood bar in a place called Behson's Exchange and knocked back his drink, secure in the knowledge that he would be home in less than two weeks. And nothing on earth would stop him this time, the Kansan had resolved; nothing would interfere with his finally returning to his loved ones, to his family, and to Deanna MacPartland, the woman who waited for him.

She *was* waiting for him. Davy felt certain of that, even though he had not heard from her once during the two years of his odyssey throughout the American West and Northwest. He was positive that Deanna would still be waiting where he had left her, in the town of Hawkins Fork, in Anderson County, Kansas. He had written a number of times, but circumstances never permitted him to stay in one place long enough to receive Deanna's reply. But Davy knew in his heart that she still waited for him. He was willing to bet his life on it.

5

She would be there when he finally came off the long, hard trail that he had set out upon in order to avenge the cold-blooded murder of his father at the hands of desperado Ace Landry.

He could see her now, in his mind's eye, as he had entered her bedroom for the first time, the flickering light of the kerosene lamp causing the shadows to weave and dance behind the blue-eyed, blonde-haired little beauty who was the first woman with whom he had ever lain.

He could see everything: her red lips parting in a welcoming smile to reveal two rows of white, even teeth; the singing curves of her lissome body; the full swell and pink, erect nipples of her firm young breasts; the curly, golden fleece that was the forestation above the the grotto of delight between her trim, alabaster thighs. . . .

"Hoo-wee," Davy Watson groaned, slouching forward to lean over the bar in a sudden fit of embarrassment as he realized that his lover's nostalgia had resulted in an erection. He motioned for the barkeep to refill his glass and then rested his elbows on the surface of the bar.

A moment later he picked up his fresh hooker of rye, as the barkeep made a cursory pass with his rag before walking off to serve a dusty and clamorous crowd of trailhands at the other end of the bar. The light from the cut-glass lamp above his head glimmered like stars on the prairie when the Kansan squinted and peered at it through his shot glass. Wreaths of smoke drifted by and occasionally obscured the light, as the denizens of the noisy honkytonk puffed on cigars, cheroots, and wheatstraw cigarettes, giving the place the look

6

of a Kansas City convention hall.

He knocked back his whiskey and once more thought of Deanna MacPartland, his blonde angel of passion.

"Uuuhh," he groaned, feeling his flagpole hard-on strain against the crotch of his trousers. Suddenly a husky whisper behind him caused the Kansan to turn his head.

"Is that a second pistol you're totin', cowboy, or are you just feelin' rambunctious?"

His ears burning like a Comanche bonfire, Davy Watson slouched even further over the bar and looked around.

He saw a small brunette standing just behind him, to his left, her hands on her hips and a wide grin on her pretty face. She had heavily-lidded brown eyes, which enticed and invited, eyes of the type referred to as "bedroom eyes." Her mouth was a big, red cupid's bow, and was topped by a charmingly impudent *retroussé* nose. The woman's face was a perfect oval, and her pale skin looked as smooth as silk.

Davy cleared his throat and lowered his eyes. "Was you, uh . . . addressin' me, Miss?" he mumbled as the pert brunette continued to grin at him mischievously. He had taken notice of her earlier, when he'd first entered the place, and decided that she was the one among all the girls in the honkytonk who interested him the most.

"Cowboy," she said in her soft, husky voice, "I can spot a stiff pecker a hundred feet away. An' I just came over to find out what's on your mind."

Damn, he swore to himself. *This li'l gal's better at spottin' a hard-on than a yard dog sniffin' out a*

7

soup bone.

He cleared his throat again. Davy's ears still burnt furiously as he regarded the little brunette. In his heart the Kansan was totally faithful to Deanna MacPartland, but his angel of passion was still hundreds of miles distant.

"You, uh, musta read my mind, Miss," he muttered, raising his eyes to meet hers and smiling as he did.

"Not exactly, cowboy," she replied, drawing closer to him. "But let's just say I noticed a sudden change in your profile."

He laughed at this, and motioned to the bartender.

"Lemme buy you a drink," he said. "My name's Watson. Davy Watson."

"Wasson," she repeated. "Y'know, I once knew a gent by that name. Fella from Florida. I think his name was Lee Wasson."

"Mine's *Wat*-son," he corrected gently.

"Oh, *Watson,*" she said. "You kinda mumbled."

"Guess I did, Miss," Davy admitted, turning back to the bar in his embarrassment.

"And you're blushing," the little brunette cooed. "Isn't that sweet?"

"Give the lady a drink," he told the barkeep, blushing even more than before.

"Whyn't you have him send two bottles of champagne back to my room, Mister Watson?" she asked, brushing his cheek with cool fingers. "Then we can be comfortable . . . and get to know each other better."

"Uh, yep," he grunted, turning away from the

8

grinning bartender. "That sounds like a real good idea."

She gave him a wink and a warm smile.

"My name's Jenny Willoughby, Mr. Watson. If you're in shape now, whyn't you escort me back to my room."

"I'd, uh, like to do just that," he told her, straightening up and throwing three silver dollars on the bar. Then he turned and offered her his arm. Embarrassment had long since wilted his erection, and the Kansan was able to leave the bar with ease.

"Send up two champagnes, Josh," Jenny Willoughby called out over her shoulder to the barkeep.

As they walked across the floor, heading toward the private rooms at the rear of the honkytonk, Davy listened to the voice of the man who played the pianoforte. He was a lean, dried-up looking little fellow whose deep, rich voice rang out in the crowded room.

"Write me a letter, send it by mail," the man sang. *"And back it in care of the Barbourville jail."*

The Kansan's eyes narrowed. Where had he heard that song before?

"Down in the val-ley, val-ley so lo-o-ow. Hear the wind blow, boys. Hear the wind blow. . . ."

Now he remembered. The song had been sung by the man who'd gunned down his father. Davy Watson had heard it when he and his companions stalked Ace Landry and his gang among the rocks and cliffs of Hells Canyon, in the wilds of the Idaho Territory.

How long ago it all seemed to him now, and how many miles away! The Kansan had practically come full-circle in his travels, and the end of the trail was almost in sight. In less than two weeks he would be back at the Watson farm by Pottawatomie Creek, in Anderson County.

He had left his home state a boy, and was now returning to it a man. Davy Watson had traveled far and wide. He had ridden as far north as Hells Canyon in Idaho, by the banks of the raging Snake River; as far west as the wild and fabulous metropolis of San Franciso; as far south as the dusty old towns of West Texas and the dry lands of the Mexican border.

He had seen the untamed heart of the wilderness in Idaho, traveled across the plains of Kansas and Colorado in the company of his Pawnee blood-brother, Soaring Hawk, watching the last of the great buffalo herds ride off in clouds of dust; ridden beneath the red Apache sun of the Arizona Territory, in the company of Geronimo and Cochise; survived an avalanche in the Donner Pass, that bleak and fearsome gateway to the Plain of California; laughed and whooped in wonder, as he viewed the mighty, rolling expanse of the Pacific Ocean, the first of its kind that he had ever seen; walked among the rubble of diggings and smelled the sulphurous reek of the Burning Moscow Mine in the silver-laden fields of the Comstock Lode high above Virginia City, on the trail of adventure which had led him over thousands of miles in the past two years.

The Kansan had seen the wonders of the great North American continent, and had met a number

10

of its most extraordinary inhabitants, as well.

There was Big Nose Vachon, that lusty mountain of a man, and Jack Poole, too, the Indian scout who had befriended Davy and Soaring Hawk and fought beside them at the Battle of Beecher's Island. Both were dead now, having perished in the great showdown in Hells Canyon, where the four companions had wiped out the entire Ace Landry Gang.

Then the Kansan remembered Marcus Haverstraw, the Virginia City newspaperman who had been his guide in the town that silver had made, as well as in San Francisco, where they delivered the three Mudree sisters from white slavery. Davy smiled fondly at the recollection of the volatile reporter and wondered what his friend was doing at present.

He recalled the great Apache, Cochise, and the fierce little man who had come to call Soaring Hawk his brother—the war chief, Geronimo. He also remembered White Wolf, the prophetic medicine man of the Pawnees, and Pahanca, the chief of the Comanche band that had almost roasted Davy and his blood-brother in their bonfire during a drunken revel.

John B. Loudermilk and T.C. Pritchett: those names suddenly came to mind, the names of the two former Texas Rangers who had been the companions of his most recent adventure, losing their own lives as they went up against the deadly band of outlaws known as Haggerty's Hellions.

Davy thought of Bart Braden, the Texas ramrod who had started a range war for the sake of Raquel Mirabal, and abducted the Mexican beauty from the hacienda of her sheepman father, Don Solomon Mirabal. Braden was the man who had gunned down the Kansan, and set him off on a quest for vengeance that led from the New Mexico Territory to the interior of the Lone Star State.

There had been bad *hombres* aplenty, the Kansan recalled as he and Jenny Willoughby entered a private room at the rear of Joe Behson's honky-tonk. *Rascals, cutthroats and scoundrels.*

Captain Haggerty's name, as well as Bart Braden's, had triggered this association. The fat, redheaded Irishman had been a former officer in the Army of the Confederacy; he was a genial man who spoke in a soft, honeyed voice and killed without mercy, striking with the speed of a rattle-snake.

Jock Forbes was a major in the United States Cavalry, the commander of a fort in the Arizona Territory. And he fancied himself a great soldier, cast in the mold of that dashing and reckless officer whom he idolized, George Armstrong Custer. He had determined to advance himself by wiping out the Chiricahua Apaches—man, woman, and child. But Cochise had been cleverer than he, and Jock Forbes's bones lay bleaching in the sun, picked clean by vultures, in a desolate place known as Eagle Pass.

The obscene giant, Harvey Yancey, and his ally, the San Francisco gambler, Bertram Brown, had almost killed Davy Watson and Soaring Hawk. But the Pawnee and his white blood-brother had lived to see the dangerous pair in hell first.

Ace Landry was fathered by a rattlesnake and nursed by a Gila monster. The lapsed Mormon had

12

been the most cold-blooded killer that the Kansan had ever come across; it was only by a great stretch of imagination that the desperado could even be called human. But the murder of Davy's father had been fully avenged when the dying mountain man, Big Nose Vachon, took the outlaw in a deathgrip and dove into the icy, churning waters of the Snake River, never to surface alive.

Bart Braden was a man whom the Kansan had always regarded with mixed feelings, even though the man had shot him. The Texan had not been an outlaw until he ran off with Raquel Mirabal and provoked a deadly war between the Texas cattlemen and the sheepherders of the New Mexico Territory. He had been one of the hardest and most dangerous men that Davy Watson had ever encountered; but at the same time, the Kansan admired the man's guts, skill, and fearlessness. But by now, Bart Braden's corpse must be mouldering in an obscure grave in the small Texas town where Captain Haggerty had shot the ramrod in the back. Davy had left his body there, as he took Raquel Mirabal to the authorities and arranged for her return to New Mexico.

And what about the women? Davy Watson asked himself, as his glance traveled over the contours of the well-made honkytonk girl's body. God Almighty, there had certainly been a number of them along the way, since he had hit the vengeance trail two years ago in Kansas. And while he loved no one but Deanna MacPartland, Davy had been involved with a number of remarkable women in the course of his travels.

The image of the young Pawnee woman, Bright

Water, flashed in his mind's eye like a picture projected by a magic lantern. He had met her in the camp of Soaring Hawk's people, and the tall, dark-eyed Indian had been his second lover. Davy remembered the night they had spent making love by firelight in a Pawnee teepee, neither speaking the other's language, but able to communicate their feelings and desires all the same, through pantomimed gestures, passionate glances, and ardent embraces.

The raven hair of the Pawnee then reminded him of the jet-black tresses of the young *chicana*, Raquel Mirabal. The Kansan had been the New Mexican convent-girl's first lover, and he took her virginity on horseback, after the fashion of Huns, Russian Cossacks and Comanche Indians.

Faith, Hope and Charity Mudree were sisters, three full-bodied little women with hot, gypsy eyes and passionate natures, who had all piled into Davy Watson's bed at the same time for a tipsy, giggling orgy which nearly sent the convalescing Kansan into relapse. *That* had certainly been a rewarding experience, he told himself, sighing nostalgically as he and the little brunette named Jenny Willoughby entered the private room.

Who else? He nodded. Consuela Delgado. The grave, quiet Mexican widow who had been his lover in the new settlement of Phoenix, in the Arizona Territory. Her passion ran deep and silent as a subterranean river, but once its force had been tapped, it blew like a geyser.

Della Casson was the woman whom the Kansan recalled most fondly. Tall, black, and beautiful, the New Orleans courtesan had the grace of a

14

panther and the eyes of an African gazelle. They had met in the wild Barbary Coast section of San Francisco, where Della saved Davy Watson's life, interposing her own body between the Kansan's and the Derringer of her lover, Bertram Brown.

She had been wounded in the shoulder, but not fatally, despite a great loss of blood. And when she said goodbye to Davy Watson, there were tears in the black enchantress's eyes, for she had grown to love the Kansan. And for his part, if his heart had not been with Deanna MacPartland, he probably would have given it to Della Casson.

Now, there was a beautiful woman, Davy thought, wondering where she might be at that very moment, wondering whether or not he would ever see her again.

"Would you like a glass of champagne, Mister Watson?" Jenny Willoughby asked, summoning Davy up from the depths of the sea of memory.

"Yes'm, I would," he told her. "An' you can call me Davy, Jenny."

The little brunette gave him a big smile. "Davy it is," she said cheerfully, as she poured two glasses of champagne.

Outside, the crowd buzzed merrily, and the *thud* of glasses hitting the bar and the *chink* of poker chips being stacked rose above the deeper sounds made by the drinkers.

The Kansan was in high spirits as he took the glass of champagne from Jenny Willoughby. He was feeling fit as a Kentucky fiddle, which was a pleasant and distinct change from the previous aftermaths of his adventures on the homeward trail.

15

In the showdown with the Landry Gang at Hells Canyon, Davy had been shot in the side, and had nearly died from the consequent loss of blood. In fact he would have, had not his Pawnee blood-brother cauterized the wound with his scalping knife.

After that, he sustained several wounds in the course of his pursuit of Harvey Yancey, the desperado who had adbucted the three Mudree sisters. Malcolm Shove, an Alabama gambler and procurer, had shot off the Kansan's left earlobe in a pistol duel on the slopes of Mount Davidson, high above Virginia City. Shove himself was less fortunate, as Davy Watson's slug had torn through his heart, killing him instantly. And in San Francisco, the naked Kansan was slashed across both forearms with a broken bottle as he attempted to defend himself against the gambler, Bertram Brown, who was about to take his life. Only the timely intervention of Marcus Haverstraw had saved Davy.

In the desolate wilderness of the Arizona Territory, Davy had been taken prisoner and given fifty lashes by order of the post commander, Major Jock Forbes. He carried the scars on his back, as a reminder of the nightmarish episode in his travels which had begun when Soaring Hawk freed Geronimo from the jailhouse in Phoenix.

Then, in the lawless New Mexico Territory, he and Soaring Hawk had come within inches of being roasted in a roaring bonfire by a wild band of drunken Comanche Indians. Luckily, they were rescued by Bart Braden, the man who later shot the Kansan and left him for dead.

It was only from his most recent adventure that Davy Watson had emerged unscathed. Throughout his pursuit of Braden across the vast state of Texas, the Kansan remained unharmed. And not even in the great shootout with Captain Haggerty and the Hellions, which cost Davy's two former Texas Ranger companions their lives, was he so much as scratched.

In the past he had spent days and weeks in pain, recovering from his wounds. The Kansan thanked Almighty God that he had come through in one piece this time. He had never felt better.

"Well, here's to the purty gals of Texas," he said, smiling at Jenny Willoughby as he raised his champagne glass.

"That's real sweet of you, honey," she replied, smiling back at him. "But I'm from Arkansas."

"Well then," he went on, not at all taken aback by this revelation, "to all the purty gals what's come *to* Texas."

"I'll drink to that," Jenny said, raising her own glass. "And here's to handsome men," she smiled at him warmly, "wherever they're from."

They drank, and Davy refilled the glasses. Jenny picked up hers, stood up, and began to walk over to the Kansan.

"Mind if I sit beside you?" the little brunette asked softly.

"Hell no," he told her. "Make yerself to home. That'll just make it easier fer us to git acquainted." He moved to one side of the horsehair sofa and patted the cushion he had just vacated. "I'd be right pleased to have your company, Jenny."

17

"Aren't you the gentleman," she cooed happily, sitting down and snuggling up to the Kansan. And in fact he was a very polite man and had a way with women, a way of showing tenderness and concern, which almost invariably touched their hearts. It was this very quality of humanity which had saved Davy Watson's life in San Francisco, when Della Casson had prevented her lover, Bertram Brown, from shooting the Kansan as he lay sleeping beside her.

Jenny warmed to Davy immediately, and before long they were standing beside the bed at the far end of the room.

"You kiss real good," she told him as they held each other, swaying gently, the kerosene lamp behind them casting long shadows on the bed.

He leaned over to nuzzle her neck and caught the sweet scent of lavender.

"Funniest thing I ever heard 'bout kissin'," she whispered, pausing to gasp and shudder as his tongue grazed the tender skin on her neck just below the earlobe, "was what some ol' colored man said once."

She reached down her hand and brushed the bulge in the Kansan's trousers. Then, gently but firmly, she gripped his stiff cock through his pants.

"This here ol' colored man was sittin' on a barrel behind a general store in Fayetteville, Arkansas, where I come from," Jenny went on in her breathy whisper. "He was talkin' to a friend of his, another ol' colored man. I was just comin' 'round the corner of the house when I heard what that ol' man said. I declare, it stopped me dead in my tracks."

"What'd he say?" Davy asked, unbuttoning the top of the little brunette's blouse.

"All of a sudden, as I was 'bout to turn the corner of the house, that ol' colored man cleared his throat an' said to his friend, 'Lord A'mighty, I don' know *how* them white folks kisses. They ain't got no lips.' "

Davy began to laugh.

"Now, don't y'all go gettin' too jolly," Jenny told the Kansan, releasing her grip on his rod and pressing her groin against his. " 'Cause laughter an' passion mixes like oil an' water. An' I surely don't want you laughin' yourself out of a hard-on."

"You're a right funny gal," Davy told her. "Does that kind of thing happen often?"

"Not if I can help it," she replied, opening the buttons of his fly, and going down to her knees.

At the same time, the Kansan unbuckled his gunbelt and let it slide down his legs to the floor. A second after that, Jenny had opened his belt and unbuttoned the top of his pants.

"There's a time to be jolly, an' a time to be serious," she told him, looking up at the tall Kansan as she pulled down his pants. "An' this is where we get down to business. Carnal pleasures is serious business."

He chuckled. "So we'll git jolly later on, huh?"

"That's right, honey. Later on," she murmured, pulling down the pants of his long underwear and taking his stiff rod in her hand.

"Oooh," he gasped, as she took him into her mouth. Then she began to gently stroke the shaft of his cock at the same time that her tongue fluttered around its head in the manner of a moth brushing its wings against a screen door.

Davy reached down and gently entwined his long, thick fingers in the little brunette's tresses. Her hair was fine and silky to the touch, reminding the Kansan of the pale blue ribbon that Deanna MacPartland wore in her blonde hair.

Jenny continued to stroke, suck, and lick with considerable expertise. With her free hand, she cupped the Kansan's balls, or raked his thighs and buttocks with her long fingernails.

"Oh, you're right good at that, Jenny," the Kansan murmured, squirming as he felt a mounting pressure in the pit of his groin.

"Uuu-uum," she groaned back, obviously enjoying her work.

Lick. Stroke. Flutter. Suck. Stroke. Gradually, almost imperceptibly, Jenny began to increase the tempo and intensity of her ministrations. Davy Watson was now breathing between clenched teeth; droplets of perspiration beaded his upper lip, and his eyes had begun to glaze.

An image of Della Casson appeared as he suddenly closed his eyes, calling to mind the time that the black courtesan had made love to him in much the same fashion as the little brunette from Arkansas.

"Judas Priest!" the Kansan groaned, his body tensing in a small shudder. "I feel like an overstoked boiler on a Mississippi steamboat."

"Hu-uuuunh," grunted Jenny Willoughby, her head bobbing up and down like a woodpecker working over a wormy pine tree.

"Oooooph," grunted the Kansan, his entire consciousness now focused on the pit of his groin.

"Uunh, uunh," she grunted in response, her head now moving with the speed of a shuttle on the looms of the great New England textile mills.

The next sound Davy uttered was a deep *"Whoo-ooof!"* as he proceeded to pump a load of jissum into the girl's hot and ardent mouth.

Lights flashed inside his head, tracing thin, fiery paths across the darkness behind his shut eyelids. A welling feeling of release immediately filled the vacuum left by his jettisoned fluids. For a moment, a fleeting instant, he felt a perfect inner peace, a tranquility which descended upon him like God's own grace.

Jenny Willoughby removed the Kansan's cock from her mouth, swallowed, wiped her lips with the back of her hand, and then got to her feet. As she looked up at Davy Watson, the Arkansas brunette saw that he was breathing heavily and smiling warmly at her.

"That was right fine," he told her. "Yer a credit to the profession, Jenny."

"I take pride in my work, Davy," she replied. "Let's get in bed, now."

"There's gonna be more?" he asked, surprise coloring his voice.

"Well, you're a young fella," she whispered back. "An' I'm sure you got a lot more pep in you. An' you're right sweet—good-lookin', too . . . which kind of gits me excited." She looked up at him and smiled as he stepped out of the bottoms of his longjohns.

Then Jenny took him by the hand and led him to

21

bed. "This is sort of a busman's holiday for me, honey," she said. "So let's enjoy ourselves without no further delay."

Once he had opened the last button, the Kansan reached inside Jenny's shirt with both hands, and was both pleased and surprised to discover that she was not wearing any undergarments.

"Uuum," the Arkansas brunette murmured as his deft, gentle hands traveled up from her narrow waist to the smooth flesh on her back. "You got a nice touch, honey," she said, raising her head to smile at him.

Davy leaned toward her; they kissed, and the Kansan caught his breath as Jenny Willoughby's tongue grazed his lips. Then he pressed his lips firmly against hers, and thrust his tongue deep into the sweet hollow of her mouth.

At the same time, he put his arms about her waist and began to unbutton Jenny's skirt. A moment later, the garment fell to the floor and, when their kiss had ended, the Arkansas brunette stepped back and stood before him, clothed only in her bright, mischievous smile.

"Ain't you the purty li'l thing," Davy Watson murmured appreciatively.

She was, indeed, standing before him in her rose-and-alabaster nakedness. Her long brown hair trailed down over her shoulders, the deep brown tresses contrasting markedly with her fair skin. Long, brown hair peeped out from her underarms, and her muff was as thick as the coat of a brown bear in mid-winter.

Her breasts were high and rounded, twin apples of delight, almost perfectly formed in the manner known to the French as *beauté du diable*—the devil's beauty.

She had a fleshy mount of Venus, which swelled above her sex like a hillock above a cavern. Her thick brown pubic hair ran down over her swollen outer lips like ivy on a trellis. Her thighs were smooth and unblemished, with still more of her long pubic hair trailing down into their hollows.

"Oh, you're back in form, Davy," Jenny cooed. "How nice!"

He stepped forward and drew her to him, clasping her firm, pert buttocks as he did. Jenny, in her turn, took the Kansan's erect cock in her warm little hand and began to stroke it gently and slowly.

They kissed again, lips pressed firmly together, their tongues grazing and darting with a life all their own, as if they were salamanders engaged in a courting dance. Jenny stood on tiptoe, placed Davy's rod between her thighs and began to move up and down the length of his shaft, each stroke parting the thick, furry outer lips of her pussy.

"Ooooh, you're steamin' me up, cowboy," she told him in a husky voice.

"Well, you're kind of excitin' yerself," the Kansan told her, reaching up with his right hand to fondle her breast while he pressed the broad palm of his left to the small of her arching back.

"Yesss, yessss," she hissed, beginning to writhe and squirm, rubbing her pelvis against his. "Oh, yesss. Touch my breasts, Davy."

Davy lowered his head, his tongue grazing the side of her neck as he did, working a rapid, flicking trail down to the cleft between her breasts. Then he moved his head slightly to the side, his butterfly

23

tongue tracing a fluttery path over to a delicate pink areola and long, erect nipple.

"Oh, yes, Davy. Oh, lick it. Suck it," Jenny moaned, beginning to tremble all over as the Kansan's tongue traced a series of concentric circles around her small areola and the fibrillate bull's-eye of her nipple.

Her pelvis was now glued to his, and she gasped loudly when Davy slowly took her long, stiff nipple into his mouth, tonguing and sucking it with gentle persistence. And soon her trembling became a series of convulsive shudders. Moaning softly, Jenny curled her fingers in the Kansan's hair and drew his head toward her. Then she bit him gently on the side of the neck.

"Let's get on the bed, Davy," she groaned. "My calf muscles are beginning to knot up."

He took his mouth from her breast, suddenly aware that Jenny had been standing on tiptoe all the while. Then he stepped back slowly, looking down in excitement as he watched the shaft and head of his cock gradually emerge from between her thick nether lips. And when he had disengaged himself, the Kansan picked the little brunette up in his arms and carried her over to the bed.

He held her in one arm while he drew back the counterpane. Jenny had her arms around his neck and was whispering obscene, exciting things in his ear.

When he looked down at her, after depositing Jenny on the clean, white sheets, Davy saw that the perfect oval of the little brunette's face was dark and swollen with passion. And after exchanging a few torrid kisses with the excited young woman, he ran his hands and mouth down her body, pausing to work over her sensitive breasts on the way to her pouting, furry pussy.

"Oh, oh, oh!" Jenny Willoughby exclaimed, her body suddenly stiffening like a corpse in *rigor mortis.*

Davy was about to take his mouth from her breast when the girl wrapped both arms around his neck and proceeded to hug him to her bosom.

"Oh, suck it—suck it, Davy!" she gasped, her body beginning to jerk convulsively as the tidal wave of orgasm broke inside her.

Hoo-wee! the Kansan exclaimed in his thoughts, as he continued to suck her warm, firm breast. *This here's one hot li'l filly—one who can git pleasured just by havin' a gent suck on them sweet titties of hers!*

"Oh, my Lord," Jenny Willoughby murmured, her body suddenly relaxing as a red flush spread over her face, neck and breastbone. "There I go again," she sighed, a smile of bliss on her face.

She looked up at him with a smile on her face. And after planting an affectionate kiss on her breast, Davy drew back to look at her.

"Oh, you're so sweet," she cooed, stroking his cheek with a soft little hand. "That was truly wonderful."

"I reckon you're right lucky, Jenny," the Kansan told the smiling little brunette. "Bein' able to have yer pleasure so easy-like."

"It's a gift from God," she told him. "I'm very grateful to Him. Each time it happens, I offer up a silent prayer of thanksgiving."

He was curious. "Does it happen every time?"

25

Jenny shook her head. "Oh, no," she whispered back. "Only with fellas I like. Otherwise it's just the ol' jackrabbit game, where the men get the pleasure an' I get the money."

He nodded. "So that's how it works."

She gave him a sweet smile. "Oh, yes. I'm only sensitive with people I like." She put her arms around his neck and drew him to her. "An' I like you a whole lot." Saying this, she kissed him.

"Now, you lie down," she said, scooting out from under the Kansan and rolling him over on his back. Then she leaned over and blazed a trail of criss-cross kisses down the side of his neck, pausing at intervals to bite or nuzzle him gently.

He groaned in a deep voice as he stretched out and relaxed on the bed.

Jenny's mouth now traveled south of the Kansan's collarbone, and her darting, agile tongue made its way through the hairy tangle that covered his chest.

"Lord, you got the movin'est tongue," he whispered, bucking slightly as she hit a ticklish spot. "Ooo-ooo," he moaned, squirming as she circled his nipple and raised a crop of goose flesh on his chest.

After several moments of this, her tongue darted into the deep alley between his pectorals and worked its teasing, skipping course down to his belly. Having made several runs up and down his ribcage, Jenny briefly circled Davy's navel, and then proceeded further south. She took his cock and held it lightly in one hand, running her tongue up the underside of its shaft, circling its head, and then suddenly culminating the movement by taking it into her mouth.

"Ooo-ooo," Davy groaned again, as he entered the expert embrace of her mouth. His cock was stiff and pulsing, and the Kansan was ready for action once more, feeling hotter than the barrel of a Sharps rifle at the end of a buffalo hunt.

Jenny did this several times, and then continued on her way southward. She licked and tickled his balls, causing Davy to buck again, and then ran her tongue down his scrotum in light, flicking traces until she came to his perineum. Here she made him grunt and groan like a dropped grizzly, as her incredibly dexterous tongue whisked back and forth over that highly sensitive erogenous zone.

After that, she ran her tongue over the hollows and insides of his thighs, even further inflaming the Kansan. Then she ran down even farther, her quick, tantalizing licks grazing the tender insides of his knees and calves, and then traveling further down.

After that, Jenny's tongue skimmed over his ankles, his instep—which tickled Davy and made him laugh out loud—and came to rest at his toes.

Having his toes sucked was a relatively new experience for the Kansan, and he discovered that it aroused him mightily. Again Jenny Willoughby's accomplished tongue came into play, as she licked the insides and undersides of Davy's toes, eliciting groans of pleasure from the young cowboy beneath her.

By this time the Kansan's erection reminded him of the flagpole in front of the governor's mansion in Topeka. He had never imagined that his feet could be so sensitive, and this revelation led him to wonder about other little-explored parts of his body. And further, he asked himself whether areas not now sensitive could, with patience and expertise, be made so.

"Well, that's the ol' up an' down," Jenny told him as she raised her head. "How'd it feel, honey?"

"Oh, just great," he replied, still breathing heavily.

"What can I do fer you now?" she asked in a soft voice.

"You know what I'd kinda like fer you to do, right now?" he whispered, grinning at her.

She shook her head. "Uh-uh. What?"

"I'd like you to come up here, an' sit on my face."

Jenny laughed softly, her eyes wide with surprise. "Why sure," she whispered back. "That'd be right nice, Davy."

He had been fascinated and aroused by her hairiness, and licked his lips in anticipation as Jenny moved up on his body, rubbing her thick muff and the fat lips of her pussy against his chest as she did.

As her knees came to rest upon his shoulders, Jenny looked down at the Kansan and flashed him a big, warm smile. And then she began to inch her pelvis toward his head, her thick, bushy muff covering his chin like a tumbleweed coming to rest at the base of a rock, her swollen nether lips beginning to part in the vertical smile of passion.

The rich perfume of her arousal filled his nostrils as Jenny Willoughby lowered herself onto Davy Watson's waiting mouth. Her muff hove into view

28

above him, causing the Kansan to think of thunderclouds rolling over the prairie. He puckered up and made ready to kiss those pouting lips which came toward him out of the dark cloud.

Jenny Willoughby moaned softly, and then emitted a surprised little gasp as Davy's tongue suddenly parted her throbbing, swollen lips and skimmed up their moist, pink insides. Placing his big hands on her soft thighs, the Kansan began to work on the girl in earnest, gently controlling the pressure and angle of his ministrations by moving his head or lightly pulling her toward him.

Up and down his tongue went in its ardent course, pausing at times to probe her vaginal vestibule and skim her perineum on the downward stroke, or to circle and lick the roseate bud of her clitoris on the upward. A few minutes of this sort of intense attention had Jenny Willoughby moaning like a catamount at the height of the mating season and squirming like a she-wolf waiting to be mounted.

As for the Kansan, the heady odor of her juices, the intimate response of that pulsating nether mouth, and the warm, firm clasp of her satin thighs on the sides of his head all combined to create in him a delirious and intense ardor which resembled an early stage of drunkenness. He was, Davy realized, intoxicated with the pleasures of the flesh.

"Hoo-wee-ooo!" Jenny cried suddenly, with the sound of a coyote baying at the full moon, her pelvis twitching reflexively as she experienced a body-wracking orgasm.

Then, once the powerful spasm has passed, Davy

Watson planted a farewell kiss on those lips which had already begun to detumesce, and allowed the spent little brunette to roll off him.

Jenny was down, but not out, and after several minutes spent in silence, with open mouth and closed eyes, she was up again, smiling her bright, mischievous smile at the Kansan.

"Over you go," she told him, motioning for Davy to roll over on his stomach. And once he had done so, she proceeded to massage his back in a brisk and expert fashion.

"Boy, that feels right good," he told her. "Where'd you learn how to do that?"

"Picked it up from a Swedish gent," she grunted, applying pressure to his sacroilliac with both hands. "Fella name of Nils Lagerstrom. He was one of them Swedish massagers."

"He taught you right good," the Kansan sighed. "Right good."

"Here's somethin' he didn't teach me," Jenny told him. She grazed the small of his back with her long fingernails, and then raked upward with a backhand swipe, raising goosebumps on the tender skin of his scrotum.

"Now, ma'am," he told her, "if'n I had me some Swedish massager a-doin' that to me, why, I'd regard that there fella a mite suspiciously."

Jenny Willoughby laughed at this. Then she ran her hand under Davy's body, caressing his balls and finally taking hold of his erect cock.

"Uuum, I guess you must be burnin' to get back in the saddle, cowboy?" she murmured, stroking his pole.

"I could do with another ride. That's fer damn sure."

"You ever done it doggie-style?" she asked.

"You mean like in 'git along li'l dogie?' "

Jenny shook her head. "Nope. *Dog*-gie. Like the dogs in the street. You seen 'em doin' it, haven't you?"

"Uh-huh."

"Well, le's do it that way, Davy. All right?"

"Do I have to bark much?" he asked.

Jenny burst into laughter. She gave his cock a gentle squeeze. "You're a pretty funny fella, yourself," she told the Kansan.

"Well, you jus' missed one hell of a time, ol' son," Davy Watson said, entering the hotel room he shared with Soaring Hawk. "That li'l gal I met was like a one-man band. Why, she had more ways of doin' things in bed than Injuns has got kinds of smoke signals."

The Pawnee sat up on the floor (for he never slept in the white man's beds) and cocked an eye at Davy Watson.

"She make smoke signal in bed?" he asked.

"Well, not exactly," the Kansan replied to the deadpan, tongue-in-cheek brave. "But she sure could puff one hell of a peace pipe."

His blood-brother nodded. "She wish you well. Make big medicine."

"Heap big medicine, my brother," Davy said wearily as he sat down on the side of the bed and began to pull off his boots. "We made big medicine fer a couple of hours."

"When get peace pipe cleaned," the Plains Indian commented solemnly, "always feel better."

The Kansan nodded. "They don't clean pipe no

better'n that gal from Arkansas.''

"Sleep now," Soaring Hawk told him. "We leave when sun comes up."

"Yup," Davy agreed, his boots thudding as they hit the boards of the floor. "We're on the ol' homeward trail fer sure this time, my brother. Make no mistake about it."

The Pawnee nodded, his face an inscrutable mask, which looked as if it had been carved out of stone.

"It won't be long afore we're home," Davy Watson went on. "Then you can hunt them ol' buffalo to yer heart's content."

Soaring Hawk stared at him. "I have dream before you come here. I dream that buffalo all gone by time we get back. And I dream my tribe all old and weak. No more warrior. No more young woman. No more papoose."

"Aw, it's just a dream," Davy grunted as he crawled between the sheets.

"Someday soon, be real," the Indian said flatly. "White man kill too many buffalo. Too many, too soon. Not let herds grow. Someday this dream be true."

"Aw, yer goin' on about nothin'," the Kansan murmured, anxious to reassure his friend. "Why, I'll bet there's gonna be buffalo runnin' over the plains a hundred years from now. White man ain't so stupid he's gonna kill off *all* of the buffalos on the Great Plains." He lowered his head onto the pillow.

"White man not stupid," was Soaring Hawk's reply. "White man greedy. Not care what happen after him. Long as he make money. White man pray to Jesus and Great Father, but for him real

32

god is Yankee greenback.''

Davy Watson's only reply was a snore that could have held its own with a buzz-saw.

Stoic as ever, Soaring Hawk nodded slowly and lay back down on the floor. The Pawnee was asleep almost before his head made contact with the boards.

The Kansan slept a troubled sleep that night, his repose disturbed by a crazy-quilt patchwork of dreams and nightmares. It was as if the collected sense impressions of the past two years had suddenly welled up in the depths of his mind, like some great, dark tide, and overran the dam of memory, swamping his mind with its seething torrent of images.

He saw the towering vastness of Hells Canyon, and the fierce, swirling waters of the Snake River, which ran through it. He heard gunshots ring out in that awesome place, echoing and re-echoing along the steep canyon walls until they sounded like explosions at the center of the earth.

He felt the sting of the lash on his back, and whimpered in his sleep with every whirring stroke. He shrank from the lapping, fiery tongues of flame which leapt from a huge bonfire tended by a horde of drunken, painted, and murderous Comanches. He felt the earth shake, and watched tile and masonry sail high into the air, as the powerful new explosive, dynamite, tore apart the *hacienda* of his friend, Don Solomon Mirabal.

Davy watched in horror, seated on a horse in Eagle Pass, in the Chiricahua Mountains of the Arizona Territory, looking up helplessly as Cochise's Apaches sent a hail of lead and a rain of boulders down upon the heads of the panicked troopers of the U.S. Cavalry. Men and horses screamed in pain and fright, and the floor of the pass was littered with the bodies of soldiers and animals.

A brief respite from these fearful visions brought the Kansan to a bedroom on the second floor of Mrs. Lucretia Eaton's bawdy house in Hawkins Fork, Kansas, the place where he had first laid eyes on Deanna MacPartland. He was in that room with her once more, standing mute and awestruck in his union suit, as his blonde angel of passion undressed by the dancing light of a kerosene lamp. And then she was undressed and coming toward Davy with open arms.

The next thing he saw was the gaping maw of a Colt .45, and behind it the handsome, sneering face of Bart Braden, the Texas ramrod. The Kansan went for his gun, but his muscles would not respond, and he moved with agonizing slowness, as if he were fighting his way out of quicksand.

Blam! Blam!

The mouth of the huge Colt spat flame, as Bart Braden fired pointblank into Davy Watson's face.

The Kansan screamed and sat bolt upright in bed, rivulets of cold sweat streaming down over his face.

"You have dream?" Soaring Hawk asked from the floor.

"You ain't just whistlin' Dixie," Davy croaked. "I had me a heap of 'em. An' most of the damn things was the kind I wouldn't even wish on an enemy."

"No matter. Soon we be home. Go sleep."

"You're right there, ol' hoss," Davy said, yawning as he lay down again. "Soon we'll be home."

TWO

Buffalo, Pawnees and Bright Water

Since they had reached the Great Plains, Davy
noticed a great change in his Pawnee blood-
brother. Soaring Hawk sat taller in the saddle and
had a glint in his eye that the Kansan had not been
aware of for some time. The Plains Indian had
suddenly become alert in a way which suggested
that all his senses were attuned to the new en-
vironment, that he was one with nature.

Davy Watson nodded his head as he glanced at
Soaring Hawk. It was only natural, he concluded,
that his companion should be affected this way, for
the Pawnee was now in his element: he had been
born and bred on the plains of western Kansas and
eastern Colorado. The brave knew all the creatures
that inhabited the plains—creatures that ran on the
ground, flew in the air, or burrowed beneath the
surface of the soil. And he had learned the lore of
the plains, the habits and behavior of all living
things there, and how to hunt and trap those whose
flesh, feathers or skin were necessary to the
survival and well-being of his people.

Foremost among these was the buffalo, that
great behemoth of the plains, whom the Indians
considered a special gift to Man from the Great
Spirit, the Father of All Things.

The Pawnee Nation was divided into two distinct segments, hunters and tillers of the soil. Agriculture was the mainstay of a good number of tribes, who remained peaceful and sedentary in their ways, content to live the quiet life of the farmer. But the remainder of the Pawnees clung to the old ways, to the warlike and nomadic existence of the Plains Indian, hunting and fighting and following the seasonal movements of the buffalo.

Numbering in the millions in earlier days, the buffalo had traveled over the plains in great, thundering herds, their advancing mass recalling to distant observers the shape of a giant thundercloud. Up to the middle of the nineteenth century, the buffalo had seemed as numerous as the fishes in the sea. But that had all changed by the time that the Seventies had rolled around.

Now the mighty herds were fast dwindling, and it seemed as if the buffalo were being stampeded into a deadly course whose end would mean the extinction of the species. The white man was the agent of destruction in this case, for he butchered the buffalo for sport and commerce. Men like William F. Cody, Tom Nixon, and Bill Tilghman, crack shots and former Indian scouts, made names for themselves as they daily brought down great numbers of the beasts. And even worse, a veritable legion of buffalo hunters scoured the plains, butchering their prey and leaving the skinned carcasses to rot beneath the sun, slaughtering the animals without so much as a thought to replenishing and maintaining the breed.

This wanton slaughter upset the Plains Indians and posed a grave threat to their way of life. Often, the response of the enraged Indians was to go on the warpath and slaughter the buffalo butchers. This course of action promptly drew its own outraged response from the commercial interests involved, which then resulted in punitive expeditions against the Indians by the United States Cavalry.

Ever since that fateful day when young Samuel Colt's first repeating weapons had been introduced into service, the tide of battle had begun to turn against the American Indian. In the days before Colt's revolutionary development, the Plains Indians had clearly held the upper hand as far as the balance of power was concerned. Some tribes, like the Comanches, were so proficient with the bow and arrow—while riding on horseback!—that they could fire off nine arrows in the time it took their white adversaries to reload a single-shot pistol or rifle. But that had all changed by the late Sixties.

Repeating Colts and Winchesters had given the white man an awesome advantage in the area of firepower, and in any pitched battles the Indian was almost certain to come out second best. Only those tribes, such as the Apaches, who had mastered the hit-and-run tactics of guerrilla warfare were able to oppose the U.S. Army with any degree of success.

As was the custom with American business and government, the threat of halting the slaughter of the buffalo aroused infinitely greater concern than the issue of further slaughter of the American Indian. Business, with its mercantile definitions of progress and the pursuit of happiness, had always let the question of profits influence its consideration of the question of the lives of the indigenous inhabitants of the North American continent. And besides, the vast majority of the white population regarded these people as utter savages, and somewhat less than fully human—perhaps a cut above domestic animals, but certainly no higher in the scheme of things than Negroes or Mexicans.

Thus had a new provocation arisen, and with it a new way to fleece the American Indian. The jackals and vultures gathered in Washington to exert their political influence; these predatory men saw a chance to eliminate the savages who were threatening their commerce . . . and turn a neat profit in the bargain.

Not only would the Indians be punished with the might of the U.S. Army (admittedly not an overly formidable force in the post-war years), but then the men who were already profiting from the wholesale extermination of the buffalo, along with their allies in Washington, would have first crack at the lands of the Indians, many of which had become increasingly valuable properties as the United States continued to expand in the final third of the nineteenth century. The buffalo herds would surely vanish—and with them, the American Indian.

Davy Watson had thought about this dilemma often as he and his Pawnee blood-brother came to the final stages of their long journey home. He had first become aware of it in his conversations with his late friend, the Indian scout, Jack Poole.

Poole had been with the Kansan and Soaring

Hawk when they had come upon the crews of the Union Pacific Railroad, laying track supplied by "Hell on Wheels," that fearsome contraption developed by Jack Casement to provide material and support for his "iron men," in their race to link up with the Southern Pacific in Promontory, Utah. This demonic and impressive sight had saddened the scout and impelled him to discourse upon the impending death of the Old West.

As a cowhand and Indian scout, Poole had traveled throughout the West for the greater part of his life, and he had taken note of the many changes in it from the end of the thirties to the end of the sixties. The signs of civilization would soon be everywhere, now that the railroad was about to connect the American nation from coast to coast.

The buffalo were being exterminated ruthlessly in the name of profits, with no heed paid to the fact that, if the wanton slaughter continued much longer, they would soon be extinct. The American Indian was being crowded and swindled out of lands which had become his by right of treaty with the government of the United States, and forced into barren and inhospitable regions. Clerks, pencil-pushers, and tax-collectors would soon be thronging in on the railroad's iron wheels, destined to displace many of the wild and woolly free spirits who had originally settled the West.

The signs of change were everywhere upon the face of the land, the Kansan realized, and before too long there would be a new West. He thanked the Lord that he had been privileged to have known the old one before it changed under the inexorable march of progress. Change was good for some folks, he told himself, and not so good for others. And the price of progress in the West would be paid by its victims, the pioneers and the Indians.

The Kansan sighed as he shifted in his saddle and stared out across the sweeping plains of eastern Colorado. Then he glanced at Soaring Hawk, and wondered how his friend's people had fared during the brave's long absence.

He noticed that the Pawnee was unusually restless. Soaring Hawk sniffed at the air like a dog on a coon hunt, and he leaned forward across the neck of his small, swift pony and scanned the distant horizon with his eagle's eyes.

"What'cha lookin' for?" Davy asked, once the brave had straightened up on the back of his mount.

The Pawnee made no reply, but reined in his pony and then jumped to the ground. An instant later, he was down on his hands and knees, leaning forward as he put his ear to the ground. He remained in this position for some time.

"Buffalo," the Pawnee told the Kansan when he finally got to his feet. "Big herd come from east. Come our way, by and by."

Davy Watson smiled at his friend. "You ain't seen no buffalo fer some time now, have ya, ol' son? I bet that's gonna be a welcome sight."

His face a stoic mask, the brave nodded. "I see buffalo many time," he told a surprised Kansan. "When I sleep. Come to me in dream. Spirits, too. People who die. Tell me things. Tell me what to do."

The Pawnees set great store by what their ancestral spirits told them, and they received advice and wisdom through the medium of dreams. Soaring Hawk had often gone to bed with a problem and awakened the next morning with its solution, revealed to him, he maintained, by the spirits of his tribe.

Davy thought it was eerie, the way the Indians put their trust in spirits. But yet, he felt there was something to it. After all, at the beginning of his odyssey throughout the West, the medicine man of Soaring Hawk's tribe had foretold that Ace Landry, the man who had gunned down the Kansan's father, would himself be killed. And sure enough, the desperado had met his end at the showdown in Hells Canyon.

The Indians lived so close to nature, the Kansan recollected, that many of its deepest secrets were revealed to them. And if he, as a Christian white man, could believe in the Holy Spirit, it didn't seem all that farfetched that the Indians should be in contact with spirits of their own.

"Ha!" Soaring Hawk cried out jubilantly, hours after the Kansan's meditation on the American Indian. When Davy looked at his companion, he saw that the brave had reined in his pony and was pointing straight ahead.

A great cloud of dust rose in the east, a cloud whose size told the Kansan that it must have been stirred up by a multitude of hooves. He leaned forward in his saddle as he reined in his horse, squinting into the early-morning sun as he tried to make out the shapes of the creatures who had generated the vast dust cloud. And as he sat still and eager, Davy heard a sound like the rumble of distant thunder. Then, as he listened to the sound

41

which grew noticeably louder with each passing second, he felt the earth vibrate and tremble beneath the hooves of his mount.

"Buffalo!" the Pawnee cried exultantly, in a rare display of emotion. *"Buffalo herd come this way!"*

"Say, you ain't just whistlin' Dixie, ol' hoss," Davy Watson murmured as he made out the gleaming horns and dark, shaggy hide of the massive bull buffalo that ran at the head of the great herd.

The sound of thunder grew ever louder, and the earth shook to the beat of thousands of hooves. Dust arose behind the oncoming herd in great voluminous clouds, billowing up into the blue sky over the plains, causing the Kansan to imagine the oncoming buffaloes as some sort of Heavenly Host, a legion of angels in fur coats.

Suddenly the Kansan frowned as he speculated upon the identity of the parties who might be running that herd. Was it Indians or white men? Buffalo hunters or the nomads of the Great Plains? Things began to get complicated.

If the hunters were Plains Indians, he and Soaring Hawk might well have to fight for their lives, unless those newcomers turned out to be Pawnees. There weren't that many friendly tribes in the area.

If it turned out that the herd was being run by white buffalo hunters, Davy also figured to have his hands full. He was willing to bet that Soaring Hawk would go for his big Sharps and start blasting away at them. His blood-brother had an impulsive streak and would surely do something rash about a situation which affected him so deeply. After all, he *had* freed Geronimo from the Phoenix jailhouse, hadn't he?

By now the plains were awash in the sounds of rolling thunder. The great mass of buffalos swept toward them like a bank of storm clouds, and the ground shuddered like the streets of San Francisco on the morning of an earthquake.

"Go there," Soaring Hawk told the Kansan, pointing southward as the great herd continued to advance upon them from the east. Then he pulled on the reins and wheeled his pony around in that direction. An instant later Davy followed suit, and they both proceeded to ride out of the herd's path.

Once they had reined in their horses and wheeled them around, Davy and Soaring Hawk sat back and watched the spectacle before them as the mighty herd thundered by.

The dust flew thick now, but the dark hides of the buffaloes—bulls, cows, and calves—stood out as clearly as if they had been figures in a lithograph. Davy was impressed by the speed and power of the herd, and his horse neighed, snorted and pawed the ground as the thundering mass flashed by. The sun gleamed on the points of their horns and lent a sheen to their hides. Powerful muscles rippled beneath those shaggy coats, and hard, cloven hooves beat out a deafening tattoo on the dry soil of the prairie.

It was a mighty and moving spectacle, and the Kansan finally understood, deep in his gut, the mystical feeing which the Plains Indian harbored for the buffalo. This was the sacrificial animal, dying to renew the life of the Indian, the holy beast

43

which the Great Spirit had created to provide for his children: the animal whose flesh would feed them, whose fat would grease their cooking pots, whose sinews would bind their tepees and travois, whose horns would provide their ornaments or serve as emblems and divining instruments for their medicine men.

Judas Priest! the Kansan swore to himself, as he saw what his blood-brother was about to do next.

Flushed in the face and smiling fiercely as the herd thundered past, Soaring Hawk suddenly leaned forward and pulled his big, heavy-caliber Sharps rifle out of its leather boot.

His mouth having gone suddenly dry, Davy Watson licked his lips and peered over the heads of the buffaloes, as he tried to make out just who it was that pursued the beasts.

Thank the Almighty it ain't white men, the Kansan thought with relief, noticing that the riders were Indians.

Then he scrutinized the feathers and beads the newcomers wore, as well as the weapons they carried and the way they sat to horse.

"Pawnee!" Soaring Hawk whooped jubilantly. "My people—my tribe! Now, I am home!"

"Well, what d'ya know," the Kansan sighed, turning to grin at his blood-brother. "I reckon you are home now, ol' hoss."

"Hoo-aw-w-www!   Hee-e-e-ee-yah!"   The Pawnee was whooping with joy now, expressing his elation in a series of bloodcurdling yells which far surpassed any that the Kansan had ever heard him utter. The brave's ungodly yowls raised Davy Watson's hackles and caused the flesh on the back

of his neck to break out in goose bumps.

"Hee-ee-eee-yaah-eee!" shrieked Soaring Hawk, as he recognized men with whom he had grown up and long hunted.

Davy Watson grinned at his blood-brother. "Yep, it sure feels good to see yer own people again, don't it?"

"There Plenty Bird," the sharp-eyed brave told him excitedly, displaying a higher degree of emotion than the Kansan had ever seen him register before, as he pointed to a figure whose lineaments Davy could barely make out. "Son of chief. You meet when we be here many moons ago."

"Yep. I remember now," Davy told him.

"That one Wolf Voice," Soaring Hawk went on, pointing at another distant rider. "I see Red-Armed Panther. And Sharp Knife. *Heee-ee-yaaah!"*

As he emitted this bloodcurdling shriek, the brave waved his Sharps in the air. Then, when he had exhausted himself, the Pawnee lowered his rifle and sat panting on his pony, as he scanned the buffalo herd which had begun to flash by.

A moment later he raised the rifle, sent a cartridge into its firing chamber, sighted down the length of its long barrel, and slowly squeezed the trigger. . . . *BOOM!"*

The loud report of the Pawnee's Sharps rent the air, making itself heard above the rumbling thunder of buffalo hooves. The Kansan's horse shied at the sound, and he turned in the saddle to look where Soaring Hawk's rifle was pointing.

A huge, fat bull at the outside of the herd tottered for an instant and then went down heavily, taking with it the two buffalos who had followed directly behind.

All three rose again, the two unharmed buffalos glaring about for a second before trotting off to rejoin the herd. But the bull who had taken the slug from Soaring Hawk's Sharps suddenly lowered its head, as if about to graze.

Staring in the direction of Soaring Hawk and Davy Watson, the bull began to walk toward the herd. After a few steps, the buffalo stopped and looked around once more, its eyes now glassy. The bull started to walk again, but stopped in its tracks as it was seized with a fit of trembling. Casting a brief, accusing look at Soaring Hawk and Davy Watson, it dropped its head. Then the beast's front knees gave out, sending the great head slamming down onto the ground. And in the next instant the bull rolled over on its side and hit the ground, dead as a doornail.

Soaring Hawk celebrated the kill with a fearsome screech. Once he had ejected the spent cartridge from the firing chamber of the rifle, he thrust the Sharps back into its boot.

Davy reckoned that one buffalo would be enough for Soaring Hawk, unless his blood-brother discovered that his tribe was especially needy. Unlike the white buffalo hunter, the Indian killed only enough buffalo to supply his needs. After the hunt, the Kansan knew that the Indians would perform a ritual of thanksgiving, followed by a great and joyous feast.

Soaring Hawk slid off the back of his pony and proceeded to tether it. The riders had seen and recognized the brave, and were now whooping back ferociously and waving their own rifles in the air.

"Welcome home, ol' buddy," Davy said, grinning down at his friend while he waved back at the Pawnees.

After he had tethered his mount, Soaring Hawk stood up and drew his scalping knife from the sheath which hung from his belt. It was the sharpest blade that Davy Watson had ever seen, and when the Pawnee had been attacked in San Francisco, he used that very knife to gut his attacker like a hog at a butchering.

The Plains Indian smiled up at the Kansan with a smile that was almost as bright as his keen blade. Then he trotted off toward the fallen bull buffalo.

Bam! Boom! Bow!

The crack of rifles rose above the diminishing thunder of buffalo hooves, as the Pawnee hunters began to fire into the herd. Buffaloes dropped to the ground, never to rise again, as the expert marksmen of Soaring Hawk's tribe claimed their victims.

Halfway to the bull's carcass, Soaring Hawk stopped and turned around. "Go hunt buffalo," he called out to the Kansan, pointing his finger in the direction of the departing herd. "You are Pawnee, now."

By Gad, he's right, Davy told himself, recalling his initiation into the tribe by none other than its chief, Running Buffalo, and its medicine man, White Wolf. *Y'know, I think I just might take a crack at bringin' one of them big sum'bitches down!*

He waved to the Pawnee and then leaned over,

drawing his rifle out of its boot. Then he waved it in the air and began to shriek like a banshee dancing barefoot on a hot stove, in imitation of the Pawnees. And by the time that the Kansan had ridden off in pursuit of the herd, Soaring Hawk was laughing so hard that he almost dropped his knife.

His horse was swift and strong, and it was not long before Davy Watson caught up with the herd. The sharp-eyed Pawnees had recognized Soaring Hawk's blood-brother, and they all waved to the Kansan as he sped by.

Davy's ears burnt as he waved back at the hunters. He knew that if he botched things, he would look like a damn fool to all the Pawnees. The first time he had visited Soaring Hawk's people, the Kansan had been welcomed as a hero; it would not do to return as a buffoon.

Behind him he heard the whoops of the Pawnees, as the hunters wished him well. As he reached the rear of the herd, Davy spurred his mount on. Then, as his horse shot past the hindmost buffaloes, the Kansan began to scan the herd.

It was not long before he spotted a bull that was so massive that it surely must have exceeded the size of the one brought down by Soaring Hawk. The beast was huge and powerful, its dark coat streaked with white, and a hump that seemed, in the Kansan's eyes, to be as big as an Indian lodge.

"That's the one fer me," Davy muttered as he gripped the reins in his teeth and began to shoulder his rifle. The dust was all around him now, since the wind had shifted in his direction, and it stung his eyes and made him blink, as well as penetrating his mouth and nostrils with its grit.

Sweat streaked down his face in rivulets, coursing over temples, eyebrows, eyesockets, and cheeks. This caused him to bat his eyes repeatedly and shake his head several times before sighting on the buffalo.

It was tough enough taking aim in the saddle when his horse was standing still, the Kansan realized; but when the creature was galloping full-tilt alongside a herd of bobbing buffaloes, in the midst of a cloud of dust which seemed to stretch up to the heavens and out to the far horizons, it was considerably more difficult.

Crack!

"Oh, shit!" he swore, as his first shot went wide of the mark.

Crack! Crack!

The next shot went over the bull's head, and the one after it hit the tip of the brute's left horn, taking off an inch or so of it.

"Judas Priest," the Kansan moaned, chewing on the reins as he worked the lever of his rifle. He was beginning to get annoyed by the difficulties involved in this form of hunting. But the next shot would do it, he told himself, for he had the feel of both his horse and the herd, and had compensated for windage and the up-and-down motion of the galloping animals.

Crack!

The next bullet entered the bull's body some-where in the vicinity of its short ribs, and the Kansan was dumbfounded to see that the buffalo, after shying to one side, had kept running right along with the rest of the herd.

Oh, hell, he swore to himself. *Of course! Fer a moment there I was thinkin' I had ol' Soaring Hawk's Sharps.* Davy nodded. *That's why that big ol' sum'bitch ain't dropped yet.*

His rifle, while a fine weapon in its own right, was a far cry from the heavy-caliber Sharps of the Pawnee, which also happened to be the preferred rifle of white buffalo hunters. Davy's was a Henry, of the M1860 series, the repeating rifle favored by the deadly marksmen of the Kentucky Volunteers during the Civil War. And while it was practically unequalled for firepower, its slugs were not heavy enough—unless one got in an extremely lucky shot —to bring down a buffalo on the hoof with one shot.

Well, if'n one shot won't bring down that big sum'bitch, the Kansan told himself, *le's see what a couple more'll do.*

Crack! Crack!

This time, both shots found their mark. The bull's legs suddenly gave out beneath it, and the huge animal fell sidewise onto the ground, rolling over twice before it came to rest in the dust.

Davy reined in his horse and then quickly sent another cartridge into the firing chamber of his Henry, as the remainder of the buffalo herd thundered by. He raised the weapon to his shoulder once more, ready to sight on the bull, as it rose from the ground. But the buffalo never rose again.

There was a smile on his face as Davy Watson lowered his rifle. He chuckled, feeling very pleased with himself, hoping that the Pawnee hunters had seen him bring down his prey.

One of his last two shots must have burst open

the bull's heart, he calculated, to bring the gigantic creature down so swiftly and surely. But the worst was yet to come, Davy realized, for he had never skinned a buffalo; and he was certain that it was going to be one hell of a messy business.

It was indeed, though not all that different from butchering a hog, something which the Kansan had done often enough at the Watson farm by Pottawatomie Creek. The buffalo hide was, of course, much thicker than the skin of a razorback, and the prime tools needed to skin the beast were an extremely sharp knife and a goodly supply of muscle.

The Kansan lacked for neither of these, being a powerful young man and the possessor of a Bowie knife which was almost as sharp as the fabulous scalping knife of his Pawnee blood-brother. And when Soaring Hawk and the Pawnee hunters had finished skinning their own game, they joined him and discovered that Davy Watson had progressed quite far with his bloody work.

"Very good for a white man," Soaring Hawk remarked to the braves who stood around him. "My blood-brother has learned many things. In some ways he is more like us than his own people."

"Can he track an enemy, or hunt the deer?" asked a brave named Feathered Arrow.

Soaring Hawk nodded. "I have taught him our ways."

"Can he throw the knife as well as my brother, Soaring Hawk?" This was asked by Plenty Bird, the son of the chief.

The brave nodded again. "He has an eye that is as sharp as the eagle's, and his aim is true."

A big, grinning buck spoke up. "Is he a man

who fares well with pretty young women?"

Soaring Hawk grinned back at the brave. "While my brother is good at most things, he is better at that than any man I have ever known."

"You do well yourself," the grinning brave told him.

Davy's blood-brother smiled a faint, Indian smile. "Tonight at the camp, I will tell you of the women we have seen and known." He pointed to his pubic region. "Even one with red hair there, as well as on top. Hair as red as the leaves of the forest in autumn."

"Hmm," grunted the big brave, an interested look on his face. The other Pawnees all nodded their heads. In the background, the Kansan puffed and grunted as he continued the laborious task of skinning and butchering the buffalo.

"I have made love with Cho-ko-le," Soaring Hawk went on in an unaccustomed burst of garrulity, "daughter of a big man of the Chiricahua Apaches. None of you has ever seen an Indian woman more beautiful than she. The woman of the Apaches are very beautiful when they are young."

The Pawnees began to nod once more.

"But their men work them like beasts of burden, and they soon lose their beauty. But sometimes, after they have been widowed, the women take up arms and ride beside their men, who are mighty warriors."

"Mightier than the Cheyenne?" asked Red-Armed Panther, referring to the great enemies of the Pawnees.

Soaring Hawk nodded emphatically. "They come and go like the wind itself. Even the horse soldiers of the Great White Father, in all their numbers, cannot control them. For they disappear into the desert canyons and mountains like the lizard and the scorpion."

"What is a scorpion?" asked one of the braves.

"It is a small creature of the desert, one which carries deadly poison in its tail."

"Are these Apaches the greatest warriors you have ever seen, then?" asked an older man known as Twelve Trees.

Soaring Hawk shook his head. "The greatest warriors I have ever seen were the Comanches. They are people of the plains, like ourselves, and they are the greatest horsemen in the world. They live far to the south, in the places called by the white man Texas, Oklahoma and New Mexico. Hammer Hand and I were taken prisoner by them one night. They all got drunk and made a big fire. Their chief, Pahanca, wanted to roast us in it, like pigs on a spit."

"And what happened?" asked Hawk Nose, a heavyset brave.

"We are here, are we not, Hammer Hand and I?"

Soaring Hawk had given that name to Davy Watson after the Kansan stood up for him against the sinister Ace Landry and his bully-boys in the Red Dog Saloon, in Hawkins Fork, Kansas.

The brave had been mobbed by the desperadoes in the street when he had not stood aside for them to pass, and was in the process of having liquor forced down his throat when Davy Watson, alone of all the men in the saloon, dared to stand up in his defense.

The Kansan looked up from the buffalo carcass when he heard his Pawnee name. And the image of the events of that fateful day rose up vividly in his mind's eye.

"Here's to redskin impertinence an' stupidity," Landry said as a second man roughly yanked the Indian's jaws apart. After that, Landry dashed the whiskey into the young brave's mouth.

"Hit 'im again, Fred," Ace Landry told the bartender as the Indian spluttered and coughed.

"But Ace," the bartender pleaded. *"If'n I git—"*

"Careful, Fred," Landry interrupted, shooting the bartender a rattlesnake look.

"Anything you say, Ace," Fred muttered, his face white as he refilled the two shot glasses with a trembling hand.

"I drink to the noble redskin," Landry jeered, an instant before he knocked back his drink.

The second man to grab the Indian pried the brave's jaws open once more as Ace Landry put his empty glass down on the bar.

"Now, hold on a minute," Davy Watson called out, fighting to master the quaver in his voice.

Everyone looked his way: the crowd at the bar, the desperadoes, Ace Landry, even the Indian, who stopped struggling after Davy had called out.

"Aw, shoot," the burly man who held open the Indian's jaws rumbled disappointedly. *"It's only some dumb kid. It ain't gonna be much fun bustin' him up."*

Davy's ears burned, and he could feel his knees wobble as he walked up to the man.

"Whyn't you let him go, mister?" he asked in a

54

hoarse voice, realizing that his throat had suddenly gone dry.

"Haw! Haw! Haw!" brayed the burly man, tightening his grip on the jaws of the struggling Indian. His coarse, flat-nosed face reddened as he continued his jackass laugh. "You must be drunk, boy," he said finally, after catching his breath. "This here's only a Injun. It ain't even human, like you an' me."

"You done had your fun now," Davy persisted. "So whyn't you let up on him?" He felt a chill as his eyes darted over to the bar, where Ace Landry gave him a smile as sharp as a skinner's knife.

"An' what if I wasn't to let up on this here red trash, boy?" the flat-nosed man asked. "What would ya do?"

Davy wiped his sweaty palms on his trousers and took a deep breath. "I'd, uh . . . be obliged to make you let up on him, mister," he croaked.

Considering this reply impertinent, the man cleared his throat, hawking up a mouthful of phlegm, which he promptly spat smack onto the breast of Davy Watson's new jacket.

"Haw! Haw! Haw!" guffawed the bully-boy who had spat upon Davy's coat, his ugly face now as red as the young sodbuster's.

At that precise instant, Davy decided what he must do. He pivoted on his left foot and came around with an overhand right, throwing behind it the full force of his one hundred and eighty pounds, and smashed his fist into the red, braying face before him.

"Hu-u-uk!" was all that the man said as Davy's fist drove his already flattened nose deeper into the

*mask of his face. The force of the blow caused him
to let go of the Indian, lurch backwards out of
control, and fall on top of a gambling table, which
promptly collapsed under his weight and sent him
crashing to the floor.*

*Shaking his stinging fist, Davy watched with
satisfaction as the man crashed to the floor in a
shower of playing cards and poker chips. Then,
cocking his right arm back and wheeling around,
he turned to the man who held the young Indian's
arms behind his back.*

*The man had already let go of the Indian, and
was about to lunge at Davy. But as he did, his
former victim leaned over and rammed an elbow
into the bully-boy's groin. With a piercing scream,
the man doubled up and pitched head-first to the
sawdust of the Red Dog Saloon.*

The Kansan smiled at the memory, clenching
and unclenching his fist as he did. The shot he had
landed on that bully-boy's red, ugly face had been,
perhaps, the best punch he'd ever thrown in his
entire life. And Soaring Hawk had been much
impressed by it, giving Davy Watson the name by
which he would henceforth be known among the
Indians of the Pawnee nation: Hammer Hand.

"But how did you and Hammer Hand escape
from these Comanches who wanted to roast you
like pigs in their big fire?" Hawk Nose asked
persistently, obviously anxious to hear the ending
of that particular story.

"You will learn of that tonight," Soaring Hawk
told the brave, "after we feast in the camp of our
people. We have much to tell."

The braves all nodded, and grunted in agreement
with this statement.

"We have been as far north as the great forests of I-da-ho," Davy's blood-brother solemnly told the hunters. "As far south as the land of the people who call themselves Me-hi-canos. And as far west as the great water that laps at the shore of this whole land." He raised his arms over his head and proceeded to spread them out in a sweeping gesture.

The Pawnees all looked impressed.

"We have done much, and seen even more," Soaring Hawk told the braves. "We have had many great adventures. Tonight, we will tell all."

It was twilight by the time that the hunting party returned to the Pawnee camp, and the last light of day imparted a soft glow to the ranks of teepees and made the smoke of the cooking fires rise in gentle spirals, as if they were painted in pastels. The glow was, in one sense, that of nostalgia, and the Kansan fully appreciated the sight, realizing that the scene could not have been rendered any more ideally in a painting or a lithograph. This was the way he would always remember the dwelling place of the Pawnees, his blood-brother's people . . . and his people, as well.

Once the riders drew near the camp, reality asserted itself. The ever-present camp dogs yelped and barked as they caught the scent of buffalo blood, and they ran alongside the horses, staring up at the riders with pleading, hungry eyes. Young boys ran up to the horsemen as well, calling out to their favorite warriors and yelling among themselves as they broadcast grossly exaggerated estimates of the day's hunt.

Some of the older boys recognized Soaring Hawk and Davy Watson, and news of the new arrivals spread through the camp of the Pawnees like a brush fire with a high ·wind behind it. Soon women were waving to the blood-brothers from the entrances to tepees or from the cooking fires which they tended. Old men rose stiffly and tottered over to the center of the camp, each of them nodding knowingly at the sight of Soaring Hawk and his white brother. The warriors who had remained at the camp called out loudly in the dusk, greeting their guests in hearty and excited voices.

"Soaring Hawk," one of the braves called out. "Where have you been for so many moons?"

"To the ends of the world," Davy's blood-brother replied without batting an eye, as he drew himself erect on his pony. "To the shores of the great Western Water, which no Pawnee before me has ever seen."

A great hubbub went up from the tribe.

"And did you see great wonders?" an old man called out in a thin, quavering voice.

Soaring Hawk nodded. "Yes, O Dark Cloud. We saw a mountain whose sides were gold, and the secret camp of the dreaded Chiricahua Apache Indians. We saw a vast canyon, one filled with trees and towering cliffs, and a river at its center that was as wild as an unbroken horse."

The crowd grew noisy once more.

Soaring Hawk held up his hand until the tribe was silent.

"We saw the great city of the white men, which is on the shore of the Western Water, a city bigger than a thousand Indian camps. A city rich and splendid; but at the same time, a place where the poor whites lived crowded together in filth, their lot even worse than that of the dogs of the Cheyenne.''

Again the crowd murmured excitedly.

"Did Soaring Hawk and Hammer Hand perform great deeds?'' a teenaged boy called out in a voice that broke, causing him to blush as the adults began to laugh.

Again Soaring Hawk nodded. "Many great deeds.'' He indicated the Kansan with a wave of his hand. "Hammer Hand fought a pistol duel with a big, fat white man who had killed many men that way. And my brother shot him dead.''

The tribe *oohed* and *ahhed* as the hunters continued to walk their horses through the camp.

"And my brother,'' Davy Watson called out, surprising the Pawnees with his knowledge of their tongue, "was attacked by a man who was as big as a tepee—a fierce giant.'' Here the Kansan paused for dramatic effect. "But Soaring Hawk made use of his keen scalping knife . . . and butchered the giant like a bull buffalo.''

The tribe cried out in delight at this.

"In the great, terrible canyon I spoke of before,'' Soaring Hawk called out, once the roars of the crowd had subsided, "Hammer Hand and I, and two more brave companions, fought sixteen of the deadliest white outlaws in the world. And they were led by the man who had killed my white brother's father.''

"And what happened?'' an excited old man called out from the edge of the crowd.

"We killed them all,'' the brave replied simply.

"And the murder of Hammer Hand's father has been avenged. Our two brave companions were killed, as well. But we did the Spirit Dance and laid their ghosts to rest."

"In a land far to the south," Davy Watson called out, now totally caught up in the spirit of the occasion, "Soaring Hawk freed the war chief of the Apaches, after that man had been betrayed into the hands of a bounty hunter by a corrupt Indian agent." Davy suddenly reined in his horse, having seen that he was before the chief's tent.

The crowd *oohed* and *aahed* again.

"And we faced a thousand Cheyenne, Sioux, and Arapaho at Arikaree Creek," Soaring Hawk proudly told his people, "with only fifty white men—scouts, hunters and traders—led by the great white chief, Colonel Forsyth."

"And what happened?" a number of voices cried, almost in unison.

"They charged on horseback—a thousand strong. We dismounted and made our stand on a small island in the center of the dry creek bed. We held, and even killed the Cheyenne war chief, Roman Nose, who was said to be invincible."

Cheers went up from the tribe at the news of the death of a chief of their great enemy.

"We turned back their charge," cried Soaring Hawk. "But they came again, and again. But still we held. For eight days we held, until the white horse soldiers came for us."

The cheering continued. Soaring Hawk turned to the Kansan, permitting himself the luxury of a small, proud smile.

"You see, we are big men now," he told Davy, speaking in English.

"I reckon so, ol' hoss," Davy replied. "You sure done got 'em worked up."

"There will be big feast tonight," the smiling brave told him. "With much good food. And young women will dance. It will be good night."

"I wonder where Bright Water is," Davy said, scanning the crowd as he did. But it had grown dark, and it was impossible to tell whether or not the young Pawnee woman with whom he had once made love was present.

"Tonight, you will see," was Soaring Hawk's reply.

There was indeed a great celebration that night, one which lasted into the small hours of the morning. Buffalo was the main dish, with venison and dog served alongside it. There were corn cakes, and a mush that Davy Watson identified as a relative of hominy grits. Corn, sweet potatoes, and squash were the vegetables.

These last were provided by barter with some of the other Pawnee tribes. Soaring Hawk's people were nomadic hunters, but many of the other Pawnees were sedentary, having settled in one place and taken up the life of the farmer. And it was from these that the tribe got its vegetables and grains, trading skins and game for them whenever their wanderings brought them near the settlements of their brothers.

Davy and Soaring Hawk sat and dined at the fire of Chief Running Buffalo. And after the abundant meal, the pipe was passed around. The scene reminded Davy Watson of his visit to the Pawnee camp two years earlier.

"White Wolf was right," he told the tribe's medicine man, who had predicted that the man who had gunned down the Kansan's father would himself be killed.

"The man we set out after is dead. And the spirit of my father is at peace."

"It is well, Hammer Hand," said White Wolf, handing the smoking pipe to Davy Watson. "When a man learns the language of the spirits," the shaman continued, "he discovers that they never lie. The spirits told me that bad man would die a hard death, and so I knew it would come to pass."

Davy coughed and handed the pipe to Plenty Bird. "That took only a short time. The rest of the two years we spent trying to come home."

"The paths of our lives are rarely laid out in straight lines," the shaman commented. "There are many forces over which man has little or no control."

The Kansan sighed. "We sure found *that* out." Then he smiled. "Ol' Soaring Hawk here sure missed the plains an' the buffalo."

The shaman nodded. "Our lives and the lives of the buffalo and the life of the land," he clasped his hands and held them out together, "are all one."

Soaring Hawk nodded, as did all the other Indians. "I saw the buffalo many times in my dreams," he said.

"It is good," White Wolf told him. "The buffalo will always be with you." He took the pipe from Plenty Bird. "They were sent to us by the Great Spirit. And in one way or another, they will always be with us, for we are the people of the buffalo."

The Indians at the campfire all nodded and

murmured their agreement with this statement.

Davy nudged Soaring Hawk. "What about Bright Water?" he asked out of the side of his mouth.

"Soon you will know," was the brave's reply.

The spring moon sat high above the plains, yellow and round as a pumpkin squash. The night was cool and still, its heavy silence broken only occasionally by the howl of a distant wolf or coyote. Springtime perfumed the air, and a gentle breeze sighed through the Pawnee camp. It was a perfect night for sleeping . . . or making love.

Bright Water was standing outside her tepee as Soaring Hawk led Davy Watson to it. The lissome, raven-haired beauty stood gazing up at the full moon, her back to the two men who approached her.

Tall an' trim as I remember her, the Kansan told himself. *An' I see that she still likes to stand all quietlike an' gander at the moon.*

"Soaring Hawk comes to Bright Water's tepee in the company of an old friend of hers," the brave said softly, breaking the heavy silence of the night.

Slowly Bright Water turned to face the two men, and Davy Watson caught his breath when he looked into her doe's eyes. And then his glance traveled down the handsome oval face which was framed by black hair that gleamed with the reflected light of the moon.

She was smiling, and for an instant her dark, lovely eyes met his. Then she lowered them and shyly looked down at the ground by her feet.

"I greet my dear old friend," Davy told Bright Water.

"Davee Wasson has come this way once more," she whispered. "I did not know if he would ever return again."

"It is good to see Bright Water again," the Kansan said in a husky voice, surprising her with his knowledge of the Pawnee tongue.

"And it is good to see you," she told him, relieved that he could speak her language, for the last time they were together, they communicated only through look and touch. Bright Water stole a quick glance at Davy Watson, and then lowered her eyes once more.

"Now that I see you do not forget each other," Soaring Hawk told Davy, "I will go." And as he left, the Indian had the faintest trace of a smile upon his lips.

"Well, uh," Davy called out as the Indian disappeared into the shadows behind the teepee, "thanks fer ev'rythin', ol' son. I'll see you in the mornin'."

Davy turned to Bright Water. "It has been a long time," he said in Pawnee, "since I have looked upon the tall and beautiful daughter of Dull Knife, brother to Running Buffalo."

"After a time," she whispered, "I did not think you would ever come back. I wondered if you were even alive."

"I'm alive, all right," he told her, taking several steps forward until he stood at Bright Water's side. "It has been a long, hard ride, but Soaring Hawk has come home. And I will return to my people in a little while."

The tall, graceful young woman sighed.

"What's the matter?" Davy asked. "Is Bright Water sad?"

She nodded and turned away from him.

"Aren't you glad to see me?" the Kansan asked, taking Bright Water's hand.

"When you go home," she said, speaking in a halting manner, "will another woman be waiting for you?"

It was Davy Watson's turn to sigh. He didn't want to answer her question, but he was not a man who lied to women.

"Yes," he said, clearing his throat an instant later.

"When will you leave this place?" Bright Water asked, her eyes still downcast.

"In a few days," the Kansan whispered, squeezing her hand gently. "Then I must go back to my people."

"And Bright Water will never see Davee Wasson again," she said in a sad, small voice.

"Aw, don't say that," he told her, squeezing the young beauty's hand once more. "I'll be by from time to time."

"With your woman," Bright Water added accusingly.

Davy cleared his throat again. "You want me to go now?" he asked quietly.

Bright Water squeezed his hand fiercely and spun around to face him. The Kansan saw that there were tears in the corners of her eyes.

"No," she told him emphatically. "Stay with me tonight . . . and each night until you leave."

He smiled and nodded his head. Then Davy took

Bright Water in his arms and held her close to him. He could feel her slender body heave as it was wracked by sobs.

"It's all right, honey," he whispered, rocking her back and forth as they stood together. "We're together now, an' I'm right glad to see ya. You know that. Now, don't ya?"

He put his fingers under Bright Water's chin and raised her head. Tears were streaming down the young squaw's cheeks as she looked at the Kansan.

"You *know* I'm glad to see ya."

She sniffled and began to nod her head, breaking into a smile a moment later, just before they entered her tepee.

A short while after that, Davy and Bright Water stood by the small fire in the tepee, stepping out of the last of their clothing.

Bright Water's bronze flesh gleamed softly with the reflected light of the fire. The Kansan admired her lean, dancer's body, with its long legs, tight buttocks and pert, dark-nippled breasts. And then, as she turned to face him, Davy noticed that her long, night-black hair had its echo in the small black patch between the lovely Pawnee's trim thighs.

Davy Watson cleared his throat and reached out a hand, as he began to stroke the young Indian's shoulder.

"Bright Water is very beautiful," he murmured. "I have seen the young women of many tribes, and none has ever been more beautiful to me than Bright Water."

She looked up at him with sad, loving eyes. "But that is not enough for Davee Wasson," she whispered.

He sighed. "Davy Watson's heart had been pledged long before he met Bright Water. The Great Spirit caused it to be that way."

It was her turn to sigh. Then she flashed him a mischievous smile. "Stay for a week," she told him, reaching out at the same time to stroke his erect sex.

"Well," he said, trembling as her touch inflamed his senses. "I was only going to stay for a couple of days."

"Stay a week. I wish it."

Davy smiled at Bright Water, as his hand traveled over her smooth flesh and came to rest when it cupped her stiff-nippled breast.

"All right," he whispered. "A week it is."

Then they embraced and went down on Bright Water's blanket. Her lean, smooth body quivered as the Kansan's big hands gently caressed its length. And when he touched any of the young Pawnee's sensitive areas, she would gasp and moan and make low, growling sounds deep in her throat, as if she were a lynx in heat.

For her part, Bright Water alternately hugged Davy Watson close to her bosom or explored his body with her own deft and eager hands. She was fascinated with the Kansan's hairy chest, and often stroked or ran her fingers over it, cooing in wonder all the while. And when she grabbed his cock and began to stroke it, the young squaw would remark how fine and hard was her warrior's lance.

After a time, Davy transferred his attention to Bright Water's small, firm breasts, circling their dark areolae with his darting tongue or pausing to suck and nibble at her erect nipples. And she began to utter a series of bird and animal sounds, which indicated to the Kansan that Bright Water was now highly aroused.

His lips and tongue left her breasts and followed a course due south, until they came to the musky, black-thatched grotto of delight between Bright Water's thighs. The scent of her arousal was like a perfume to Davy Watson, and he kissed the Pawnee's nether lips. A second later, he ran his tongue up between them, causing Bright Water to shudder and gasp.

Then he went to work in earnest, running his tongue over the slick, pink insides of her outer lips, pausing at times to graze her perineum or to skim the throbbing nub of her clitoris.

She was making canine sounds as her pelvis began to twitch involuntarily, and Bright Water's long, plaintive moans made the Kansan think of coyotes under the moon on the open prairie. Then, when it was over, her body relaxed, and the young Pawnee sighed and was still.

Minutes later, after she had recovered from the effects of her intense orgasmic convulsions, Bright Water gestured for Davy Watson to lie down. Like many Indian women, she was conditioned never to initiate oral sex, but once her male partner had, she was free to join in with ardor and skill.

She lapped and licked and sucked, in what the Kansan imagined to be the manner of an amorous she-wolf. And it was not long before he came, grunting like a downed bull buffalo, as his orgasm shook him to the depths of his being.

After that they lay together, holding one another and exchanging whispered endearments by the flickering light of the small fire. And Davy could see that Bright Water was very happy; and he had to admit that he was far from disappointed himself.

A while later they made love again. This time Davy mounted Bright Water, entering her sopping pussy with a squish, catching his breath as he felt the snug clutch of her sex. She proceeded to wrap her long legs around the small of his back and thrust her pelvis toward the Kansan, urging him on, whispering and cooing like a dove in his ear or speaking in a mindless, ecstatic gibberish that had as much to do with the Pawnee tongue as did Eskimo with English.

She gasped and cried out at her climax, which Davy Watson shortly joined, moaning like a man about to expire. They lay together after that, watching the dancing flames of the fire, until each drifted into a deep, contented sleep.

THREE

The Kansan Comes Home

Davy Watson spent seven days in the company of the Pawnees, and seven nights in the tepee of Bright Water, the quiet, graceful young Pawnee squaw who loved him. And they were both very happy in that time, even though the Kansan was anxious to depart, and return to his home by Pottawatomie Creek, and thence to the nearby town of Hawkins Fork, to Deanna MacPartland, the woman who waited for him at the end of the trail. But he was so warmed and touched by the love which Bright Water lavished upon him, that the week was one of the happiest in his entire life.

At the same time it was the stuff of adventure, for if he sat beneath the countless stars of the prairie sky or made love with the lovely young Pawnee at night, he was out buffalo hunting with the warriors during the day, and dining in the evening at the fire of Running Buffalo, in the company of the elders of the tribe.

"It's gonna be hard leavin' here tomorrow," Davy Watson told Soaring Hawk, as they walked through the Pawnee camp on their way to the chief's tent. "I mean, sayin' goodbye to Bright Water." He shot the brave a pained look. "We done got to be purty close, these last few days."

Soaring Hawk nodded.

"Well, ain't you gonna say nothin'?" the Kansan asked, irritation suddenly coloring the tone of his voice.

His blood-brother darted a quick glance at the anxious Kansan. Soaring Hawk was always amused by the white man's seemingly bottomless capacity for making himself nervous and upset about things. And yet, this capacity for self-inflicted guilt and suffering—the whites called it conscience— never seemed to prevent them from perpetrating further heinous crimes or ignoble deeds.

He had discussed this once with Davy, and the Kansan had quoted him a line from the works of a great wise man of the whites, one "Shake Spear." "*Conscience makes cowards of us all*," the man had said, long ago. And then Davy had told Soaring Hawk the story of Macbeth, the warrior of the tribes of Scotland, who, with the help of his squaw, had murdered his own chief, while the latter was a guest in his lodge and slept in his bed.

Later, after the murderer Macbeth had become chief of his tribe, the spirit of his murdered chief came back to haunt him. Soaring Hawk saw that as perfectly natural, the logical consequence of spilling the blood of one's own tribal leader. Conscience then gave the murderer great pain and fear as he reflected obsessively upon his terrible deed, and it even drove Macbeth's squaw (whom Soaring Hawk always referred to as Bloody Hands) mad.

All was as it should be, the Pawnee had commented at the end of Davy's story, for the spirits of the dead which are not propitiated and put to rest will always haunt the world of the living, seeking redress for the wrongs that had been committed against them.

Any Indian knew that, Soaring Hawk told the Kansan. Except, perhaps, those who had been converted to Christianity. They tended, he told his white brother, to become stupid about these things, and consequently lost touch with the spirit world.

This conscience, the Pawnee had said to the Kansan, *what good is it, in reality? It may punish, as in the case of Macbeth and his squaw, but it did not prevent anything from happening. It would be much more practical if conscience were to make itself felt* before *the commission of some foul and awful deed, so as to deter the potential malefactor, instead of punishing him* after *the fact.*

No, Soaring Hawk had told him, *conscience was not a very practical thing, and he was glad that the Indian, as a rule, had none.*

Davy replied that he thought Christianity had given men their consciences.

The Pawnee's reply was that he now felt doubly thankful that he was not a Christian. The practice of that religion, he concluded, tended to make one both stupid and guilty. . . .

"What you want me to say?" Soaring Hawk asked Davy, curious to see in what particular fashion his white brother's conscience was now troubling him.

The Kansan cleared his throat. "Well, uh, it's like I feel I'm sorta runnin' out on Bright Water." He gestured helplessly. "Y'know what I mean?"

72

Stolid as ever on the surface, the brave hid his amusement and shook his head.

"I mean, she kinda. . .loves me, right?"

The Pawnee nodded.

"So, when I go. . .why, she's gonna be left behind. See?"

"See what?"

The Kansan shot Soaring Hawk a look of exasperation.

"Well, I mean, her bein' in love with me, an' all that." He sighed and made a face that looked as if he had just been sucking on a lemon. "Now, ain't it gonna break the gal's heart?"

"She not die."

Davy groaned. "Yeah, but ain't she gonna be all down-in-the-mouth an' miserable when I go?"

Soaring Hawk glanced at him. "Bright Water knows you have other woman. She loves you, but understand same time you go."

Davy sighed. "Well, I just feel kinda guilty, havin' to go today. Know what I mean?"

"That *your* conscience, not Bright Water's."

"Aw, I guess yer right. She knew what she was in fer."

The tantalizing aroma of roasting buffalo hump wafted over to them from the cooking fire before the chief's tent, as Davy and Soaring Hawk approached. A number of women tended the fires there, cooking the evening's meal in big kettles. Children played and laughed in the background, and the ever-present dogs of the Indian camp sniffed and prowled furtively in the vicinity of the cooking fires.

"Bright Water did what her heart told," Soaring

Hawk said to Davy Watson. "Our people say, 'Better to risk and lose than never to risk at all.'"

"I reckon you're right," Davy agreed with a sigh.

"She is woman. Smart woman. You did not trick her. You did not lie."

Davy nodded, his face suddenly brightening. "No, I didn't." He smiled. "I sure as hell didn't. Y'know, I feel better already, ol' hoss."

The Pawnee nodded. "When a man is honest, he does not have to feel bad about what he does."

"Soaring Hawk. Hammer Hand," someone called out in a deep, growling voice. "Over here."

The blood-brothers looked across the fire and saw the Pawnee chief gesturing for them to sit beside him. In attendance upon Running Buffalo were his son, Plenty Bird, the medicine man, White Wolf, Red-Armed Panther, Dull Knife, and a number of the tribe's elders.

"You have had many adventures and performed many great deeds," the chief told Davy Watson, once he and Soaring Hawk had seated themselves at his fire. "And now your long journey comes to an end. You will return to your people. It is good."

Davy smiled at the chief and nodded slowly.

"Eat now," the grizzled old warrior told him. "For it will be the last buffalo meat you have for a long time."

"Until you return to the camp of our people. . .your people," Soaring Hawk told the Kansan, looking deep into his eyes.

Davy placed his hand over his heart. "And my adopted people are always welcome at my home. If Running Buffalo should come to visit, there will be a big feast in his honor.''

The old chief smiled a wry smile. "Hammer Hand's neighbors would be very surprised if Running Buffalo and his friends rode up to visit.''

"My neighbors will mind their business, O Chief,'' the Kansan replied, smarting from the realization that he was about to move from one world to another, and that tolerance was in short supply in the other.

"But Hammer Hand must return to visit us often,'' Running Buffalo told him. "And he must bring his squaw.''

"And all his papooses,'' Plenty Bird added, grinning at the Kansan.

Davy held up his hands and grinned back at the chief's son. "My brother moves too swiftly. I have not yet married the woman I have come back to find.''

At this point, the Kansan noticed that White Wolf was staring at him in a peculiar manner, one which made him suddenly uneasy. The Pawnee shaman had predicted Ace Landry's death, and Davy Watson had great respect for the old man's clairvoyance and powers of divination.

"Has White Wolf anything to say to Hammer Hand?'' he asked the medicine man, suddenly anxious as he considered the possible significance of the latter's dark look.

The shaman turned away from the fire at this, ostentatiously pretending not to have heard the Kansan's words.

Suddenly uncomfortable, Davy looked to Soaring Hawk.

The brave merely shrugged and shook his head.

The Kansan wanted to pursue the issue, but realized that the Pawnees would have considered such behavior extremely ill-mannered.

Why did the old shaman choose to ignore him? What, if anything, did it mean?

"Do not pay any attention to White Wolf," Running Buffalo told the Kansan. "He is very cranky these days. He is getting old."

The medicine man chose to ignore this as well, and continued to stare off into the distance.

Davy nodded to the chief, and then picked up a piece of buffalo meat. He didn't know what was going on in White Wolf's head, but the medicine man's refusal to acknowledge his question left the Kansan with a cold, spooky feeling, a feeling of vague menace that lurked somewhere in the back of his mind, like a bushwhacker preparing an ambush.

It was, partaking as it did of the flavor of the occult, as uncomfortable a feeling as the Kansan had ever experienced, and it sent a chill throughout his entire body, one which managed to penetrate even to the very marrow of his bones. But it was gone the next morning, when Davy rose and prepared to take his leave of the Pawnee camp.

When he had first awakened, Bright Water was sitting by his side, staring down at the Kansan with sad, dark eyes.

"Hey," he whispered, sitting up and taking hold of her hand. "What's the matter?"

"You will leave this morning," she said flatly. "And I will never see you again."

"Oh no," he told her. "I will surely return from time to time."

"But you will bring your squaw with you," she said accusingly.

He smiled and shook his head. "Y'know, I ain't got home yet," he told Bright Water softly. "An' I ain't married yet, neither." He squeezed her hand gently. "So let's just take things one day at a time. All right?"

"I will miss you very much," she whispered.

Davy nodded. "And I will miss you, too, Bright Water. I will miss you a whole lot." Then he took her in his arms.

A moment later they were back down on the Kansan's blanket, making love with great intensity and emotion. The knowledge that Davy Watson would soon be gone from the tents of her people caused Bright Water to respond to her white lover with a passion that transcended anything she had experienced earlier.

The Kansan responded to this, and was swept along by the dark tide of longing and desperation which was the beautiful young squaw's final gift to him. He was moved by the revelation of the depth of her feelings. . .and his own. The lissome Pawnee had touched his heart with her quiet and graceful ways. Davy shared with her the sadness arising from the thought of his imminent departure, and he made love to Bright Water with all the passion and tenderness that he could muster.

When it was over she turned away from him, so that he would not see the tears which had come to her eyes. Outside the tent dogs barked and children called out to each other in high-pitched voices, as the tribe rose and began another day.

Davy sat up and leaned over Bright Water,

77

kissing her softly on the cheek.

"Goodbye, my sister," he whispered, beginning to rise from the blanket.

He heard her sniffle. Then Bright Water, still avoiding the Kansan's eyes, furtively wiped away her tears and whispered in a husky voice, in the language of the White Eyes, *"Goo-bye, Davee Wasson."*

He knelt beside her and kissed the lovely Pawnee's cheek once more. "I will always remember Bright Water," he whispered in the squaw's ear, before rising to his feet and leaving the tent.

Davy found Soaring Hawk outside the tent of the chief, where the Kansan was to have his farewell breakfast, in the company of Running Buffalo and the Pawnee elders and warriors.

Goat's milk, corn cakes, fried strips of buffalo meat, and wild blackberries were the fare that morning, and Davy ate heartily as he sat before the crackling fire of Running Buffalo. The meal was served by several of the married women, who went out of their way to heap the Kansan's plate with food. Hammer Hand was well-liked by Soaring Hawk's people, and they made it quite evident, in their quiet and understated way, that they would all miss him.

In addition to Soaring Hawk and Running Buffalo, many of the warriors and elders were already seated around the fire, among them Plenty Bird, Red-Armed Panther, Three Trees and Dull Knife, father of Bright Water and brother to the Pawnee chief. In fact, of the Indians whom Davy Watson had gotten to know well, only White Wolf was absent; but the Kansan had other things on his mind, and he never even noticed the old medicine man's absence.

"Now, you will go home to your people at last," Running Buffalo said, passing Davy the peace pipe at the end of the meal.

"Yes, O Chief," the Kansan replied in the Pawnee tongue as he took the finely carved pipe from the old man, "It will be good to see my loved ones again."

Running Buffalo nodded. "It is always good to come home to one's loved ones."

Davy nodded in turn, as he took a pull on the pipe. Then he passed it to Soaring Hawk.

The brave smoked it reflectively for a moment, after which he passed it to his left, to Plenty Bird. Then Soaring Hawk turned to the Kansan and began to chant, accompanying himself on the small drum he always carried in his blanket roll.

"You see, I am alive.
You see, I stand in good relation to the earth.
You see, I stand in good relation to the gods.
You see, I stand in good relation to all that is beautiful.
You see, I stand in good relation to you.
You see, I am alive. I am alive."

Then Soaring Hawk continued to beat his drum solemnly for several moments. And when he began to repeat the chant, all of the Pawnees present at the fire joined him.

Davy was moved by the beauty and simplicity of the chant, by the way it celebrated life and man's proper relationship to God, beauty, the earth and one's fellow man. There was much depth and meaning to be found in the Indian way of life, the Kansan reminded himself.

Then Davy put his hand on his heart and solemnly thanked all the Pawnees for the honor that they had done him. The pipe went around once more, and the men all smoked in silence.

"Goodbye, Running Buffalo," Davy said to the chief as he rose to his feet. "Goodbye, warriors and elders of the Pawnee tribe. Goodbye, my brothers."

He met their eyes, looking at each of them in turn. And when he had finished, Soaring Hawk rose and stood up beside him.

"Let us go to your horse, my brother," he told Davy. The Kansan nodded, and they began to walk through the camp.

"Goodbye, Hammer Hand!" a little boy named Dirty Knees called out.

The Kansan smiled and waved to the boy. And as they walked toward the outskirts of the camp, this farewell was repeated many times by women and children.

His horse was waiting at the edge of the Pawnee camp, saddled and ready. Davy turned to Soaring Hawk, and held out his hand.

"Well, I guess this is where we split up, ol' hoss," he told his blood-brother in a husky voice.

Soaring Hawk gripped the Kansan's hand fiercely. "We have done what we set out to do," he said in Pawnee. "We have satisfied our honor and laid the spirit of your father to rest."

Davy nodded. "We have done much, my brother."

It was the brave's turn to nod.

"Will you come to see me in the fall, after the planting is done?" the Kansan asked.

"After the *hunting* is done," Soaring Hawk corrected with a smile. "But I will come. Tell your mother that I honor her."

Davy smiled. "She'll be right glad to see you again."

"She tell me take care of her boy," the Pawnee said in English. "You no tell everything that happen. Or she faint."

The Kansan laughed. "Hell, no! I ain't tellin' everythin'. Leastways, not to my ma."

"You take wife soon?" Soaring Hawk asked.

Deanna MacPartland's beautiful, smiling face rose up before Davy's mind's eye. "I surely hope so, my brother," was his reply.

"Then I will bring presents for your squaw. You will have many sons."

"An' daughters, too," the Kansan added. "Where I come from, one's as good as the other." He turned and put his foot into the stirrup. Then he swung lightly into the saddle.

"Well, I'm off to Pottawatomie Creek," he said, smiling down at Soaring Hawk.

"May the Great Spirit protect you, my brother," were the Pawnee's last words to Davy Watson, as the Kansan wheeled his horse around and rode out of the camp of Running Buffalo.

It was a long ride back, and Davy Watson grew more eager to be home with each mile that passed, for at the end of the long trail which had stretched from the Sunflower State to the great western ocean, lay the Watson farm. There his mother, sister, and brother would be waiting to greet him. And just a few miles beyond that lay the town of Hawkins Fork, where the woman he loved waited for him in the bawdy house of Mrs. Lucretia Eaton, where she was, in effect, indentured to the madam, who posed as her benefactress. It was the Kansan's intention to buy Deanna MacPartland out of her servitude the moment he set foot in Hawkins Fork.

From the Pawnee camp, the Kansan rode southeast across the plains of eastern Colorado, heading in the direction of his home state. The vast level expanse of the prairie stretched endlessly in all directions around him, its monotonous flatness broken only by an occasional butte or sandhill.

When Davy came to the dry bed and grassy little islands which characterized Arikaree Creek, he remembered the great stand which he, Soaring Hawk, and fifty white men had made against a force of mounted Indians twenty times their size. And he remembered his old buddy, Jack Poole, the Indian scout, who would nevermore ride the plains.

Not long after crossing Arikaree Creek, the Kansan crossed the Smoky Hill River at its northern-most fork and rode into the state of Kansas. In the distance Davy could make out the shape of Mount Sunflower, the highest spot in all Kansas.

Then, riding back as he had ridden out over two years ago, Davy Watson passed through the towns of Sharon Springs, Wallace, Monument, and Oakley, as he covered the miles which lay before him. Back through Trego, Ellis, Lincoln and Riley

Counties, heading east now, past towns like Grainfield, Wakeeney, Natoma, and Tipton, crossing the Salmon and Republican Rivers, until he arrived at Pottawatomie Creek itself.

It was practically evening when the Kansan first caught sight of the Watson farm. Davy reined in his horse and took in the scene with blinking eyes and a heart full of longing.

"Home," he whispered. "I'm home. . .by the grace of Almighty God."

The sun had begun to set behind him, turning the water in Pottawatomie Creek to a ribbon of running gold. The grass was a deep green, like the surface of a billiard table, and the rich scent of the earth wafted by on the evening breeze, affecting the Kansan as if it had been a beautiful woman's perfume. As the colors of the sunset washed over the land, deep feelings of love stirred in Davy Watson's heart. He recalled what his father had said on an evening much like this one, more than two years before:

"*I like this country, boy,*" John Jacob Watson had told his eldest son. "*The air's sweet as a baby's breath, an' the soil's rich as a Beacon Hill widder.*"

The Kansan smiled at the memory, warmed by the love he carried within himself.

"*Y'know,*" the voice of love and memory went on, "*when I stand on top of the ridge that overlooks the creek, sometimes the wind comes up through the high grass an' sings to me with the voice of a woman.*

"*It's like the earth was a woman,*" Davy heard his dead father say, "*an' it's her voice I hear a-singin' an' a-whisperin' to me up on that ridge.*

*An' each time I hear her voice, she seems to be
tellin' me that if I treat her right, an' remain
faithful to her, she'll always do right by me. Do
you know what I mean, son?"*

At the time Davy was still a boy, too young and
inexperienced to understand fully what his father
had meant. But he had returned home a man, and
now he knew.

"Yessir," he said in a small, choked voice,
sitting all alone on his horse in the Kansas sunset,
with the wind soughing through the prairie grass
and singing him its sweet, plaintive song.

"Yessir," he told the ghost of John Jacob
Watson, blinking his eyes and smiling his love into
the gathering darkness. "Yessir, I sure do know
now."

Then he cleared his throat, flicked the reins, said
"Giddap!" and rode off toward the Watson farm.

His brother, Lucius Erasmus, was the first to
spot the Kansan. The lad was forking hay in front
of the barn and stopped suddenly as he heard the
distant hoofbeats of Davy's horse. He straightened
up and leaned on his pitchfork, straining his eyes to
make out the features of the rider who came
galloping toward him from the west.

"Hot damn!" Lucius Erasmus Watson swore in
an awed whisper. "I'll be a sum'bitch if'n that
ain't Davy." He squinted and leaned forward,
peering into the dusk as the sounds of hoofbeats
grew louder in the distance.

"Oh, shit, oh dear!" the boy cried suddenly,
straightening up and letting his pitchfork drop to
the ground. Then he spun on his heel and raced off
in the direction of the farmhouse.

"Ma! Ma!" the boy screamed, as he threw open the screen door and burst into the house. *"Davy's back! Davy's back!"*

Hearing this, Annabel Mullenax Watson looked up from the dough she was kneading on the kitchen table. And by the time that Lucius Erasmus had entered the kitchen, tears were forming in the corners of his mother's eyes.

"Ma, he's back!" the boy cried.

"Oh, thank the Lord," Annabel Watson whispered fervently, as she rubbed her hands with flour, sniffled and blinked her eyes.

"Davy's back," Amy Watson whispered in a voice thick with wonder as she stepped back from the butter churn. "Where is he, Lucius?"

"Outside," the fifteen-year-old told his sister in a voice crackling with excitement. "He's comin' up by the creek, ridin' like a sum'bitch—uh, 'scuse me, Maw." He flushed and cast a sheepish look at his mother. "He'll be here any second now."

A moment after he had said this, the screen door at the front of the house was heard slamming against the wall, followed by the thud of booted feet.

"David Lee," the Kansan's mother whispered. "It's David Lee."

Davy Watson stopped as he came to the kitchen. He straightened out his clothes, took off his hat, slicked his hair back with his hand, took a deep breath, and then proceeded to stroll casually into the kitchen.

"Hey Ma," he said, grinning from ear to ear, "what's fer supper?"

"David Lee," his mother whispered in a voice

that broke as the Kansan took her in his arms.

"That's right, Ma," he whispered, rocking her gently in his arms as she lay her head on his chest and began to sob. "I'm back."

He looked up and smiled at his sister Amy. "By Gad, you're even purtier than when I left. I bet I'm gonna have to ride herd on a heap of fellas, these days."

Amy Watson blinked her eyes and smiled back at her older brother. "It sure is good to see you again, Davy," she told the Kansan.

Davy nodded as he looked over to Lucius Erasmus. "Well, look at you," he said loudly, causing his younger brother to flush red as a raspberry. "You ain't no fat li'l prairie dog no more."

Lucius Erasmus Watson smiled shyly and looked down at his shoes.

"Yer a big galoot already," the Kansan said admiringly. "An' by the looks of ya, I'll bet ya could hoist a anvil into a Conestoga wagon with one hand. Well, I'll be dadblamed!"

Lucius Erasmus joined the Kansan's merry laughter. And when Davy let go of his beaming mother, he went over to kiss Amy, after which he proceeded to shake hands with his younger brother.

"Damn," he said. "You got you a grip like a blacksmith, boy. I reckon you's 'most growed up, by now."

The boy blushed again. "I do my share 'round here," he told Davy.

"Indeed he does," Annabel Watson proudly told her eldest son. "And so does Amy."

His younger sister ran to the Kansan, and he

swept her up in his arms.

"Davy, I can't believe it's you!" Amy Watson cried joyfully, as her brother hugged her tightly. Then, as he relaxed his grip and let her feet touch the boards of the floor, she began to sob loudly.

"Hey," he whispered, moved by her tears. "I'm back now, Amy. This is a time to be happy."

"I *am* happy, you big galoot," she said, chiding him affectionately. "Don't you know that it's proper to cry when the prodigal son comes home?"

"Praise the Lord," Annabel Watson intoned fervently. "He has come home, indeed. And now let us slaughter the fatted calf."

"Well now, I ain't been so prodigal," Davy told his mother with a smile. "I done run that damn Ace Landry to the ground." His face darkened as he scowled at the memory. "That rattlesnake ain't ever gonna spit out his poison again. You can count on that."

"*By Gad, you plugged that sum'bitch!*" cried Lucius Erasmus in a loud and exultant voice.

"Lucius!" his mother called out sharply, turning to the fifteen-year-old with a shocked expression on her face.

The Watson blush ran in the family, and in an instant Lucius Erasmus turned red as a beet, causing Davy and Amy to exchange grins and knowing looks.

"Sorry, Ma," the boy mumbled, looking down at the floor and shuffling his feet. "I, uh, was just tryin' to say that it was good that Ace Landry got punished fer what he done to Pa."

Annabel Watson gave her youngest child a stern look. " 'Vengeance is mine, saith the lord,' " she quoted. "And Almighty God will certainly punish that man more fittingly than any human agency ever could. I did not approve of your brother's quest for vengeance from the very beginning."

She turned to Davy, and there were tears in her eyes. "But my son is home now," she whispered, a smile coming to her lips. "And my heart is full. Let us give thanks to our Creator."

Annabel Watson held out her hands and closed her eyes. Davy took his mother's right hand, and Lucius Erasmus her left, with Amy linking the two brothers.

"God of our fathers," the Kansan heard his mother say reverently, "who has given us this green and bountiful land, this home where our family thrives and grows strong. . .bless this reunion, wherein you have restored to us David Lee, beloved son and brother."

Davy heard Amy sniffle.

"And since David Lee has been washed in the blood of the Lamb, please Lord, let there be no trace of blood on his hands, blood that has been shed unjustly. Please let my boy resume his life with a clear conscience and an open heart, as his father would have wished."

The Kansan thought of his beloved father, and then of the two-year odyssey throughout the West which had been the result of his quest for vengeance. So much had happened to him in just two years. He was a man now, and a very different person from the boy who had first set out on that long, hard trail.

"May the soul of John Jacob Watson, ever Your servant, Lord, be at rest," his mother went on.

"And if it be Your will, may his descendants flourish and prosper on the face of the earth."

Davy let all the love he felt for his family warm him like the summer sun of Kansas. He was home again, and his loved ones were well. His heart was full.

"Let the seed of John Jacob Watson bear fruit, if it be Your will, Lord. And bless David Lee, Amy Louise, and Lucius Erasmus, even unto the seventh generation."

The Kansan smiled. That was just like his mother, never asking anything for herself.

"*Bless this good woman, Lord,*" he prayed in his thoughts, gently squeezing Annabel Watson's hand. "*Bless her, and give unto her all the things she surely deserves, but is too humble to ask of You. And let all her days, right down to the very end of her life, be warmed by the love and devotion of her children, and the love and respect of all those who know her. Amen.*"

"And thank You for reuniting this family, Almighty God," concluded Annabel Mullenax Watson. "Let Your will, not ours, be done. Amen."

"Amen," echoed her children.

"What I was sayin' before, Ma," Davy told his mother, as he and the others let go of each other's hands, "was that I really ain't been all that prodigal."

He reached down to his gunbelt and began to untie the drawstring of the leather sack that was hanging from it.

"Y'see," he grunted as he fumbled with the knot, "whilst I was runnin' down Ace Landry, me'n my buddies was doin' a service for the miners of the Boise Basin at the same time, 'cause that varmint an' his gang done stole. . .''

At this point, the Kansan opened the sack and poured out a handful of gold nuggets into his palm.

"Sweet Jesus!" Lucius Erasmus whispered, earning him an immediate look of reproof from his mother.

"Oh, David Lee," whispered Amy Watson, wide-eyed and breathless as she stared at the shining nuggets in her older brother's broad palm.

Annabel Watson looked deep into the Kansan's eyes. "Now, tell me you come about this gold in an honest and Godfearing manner, son," she told him sternly.

The Kansan beamed down at his mother. "As God is my witness, Ma. Me'n Soaring Hawk done recovered most of the gold Ace Landry an' his vipers robbed from the Boise miners. This is my share of the reward—an' you can believe them fellas was grateful."

His mother smiled. "What remarkable fortune," she said. "Now I'm certain that the Lord has been looking after you, David Lee."

"What'cha gonna do with all that there gold, Davy?" Lucius Erasmus asked excitedly.

The Kansan handed the nuggets to his mother. "I reckon I'm gonna let Ma decide what to do with it," he told the boy, dumping most of the gold into his mother's open hands. "I'll just keep me a li'l bit of the stuff fer spendin' money, an' a few other things."

"How's ol' Soaring Hawk?" his kid brother

asked. The Plains Indian has been much loved by the Watsons, and postively idolized by Lucius Erasmus.

"Oh, he's right fine," Davy told him warmly. "Sends his best to all of ya. An' told me to say that he honors ya, Ma."

Annabel Watson beamed. "Now, there's a fine, courteous gentleman."

"I just come from a week of buffalo huntin' with Soaring Hawk's people. I stayed with 'em at the Pawnee camp."

"Hot damn," Lucius Erasmus whispered in a voice colored by awe and admiration, just low enough so that his mother did not hear him swear.

"You eat you some buffalo?" the boy asked in a louder voice.

Davy nodded. "More'n I care to recall. It was either that or dog."

"Dog!" exclaimed Amy Watson. "Land sakes, that's positively revolting."

"Not to an Injun," Davy Watson told his sister. "But ol' Soaring Hawk, he feels that way 'bout potato pancakes. Calls 'em 'pig food.' "

"Different folks have different customs," Annabel Watson told her children with a sigh, casting a motherly, compassionate glance at Rufus, the blind old hound sleeping by the stove.

"I allus thought dogs was man's best friend," Lucius Erasmus said to his big brother.

Davy cocked an eyebrow at the boy. "I reckon the Pawnees considers their ponies that way, Lucius. But they got a heap of dogs hangin' 'round their camp, an' sometimes when they have 'em a big celebration, a couple of them animals allus seems to find their way into the stew."

"Oh, yuk!" exclaimed Lucius Erasmus. "If'n that don't beat all. An' I'll bet that when the stew ain't been cooked good enough, it barks at ya when it's stuck with a fork."

The Watsons began to laugh, now sharing the joy which each of them felt individually.

"Well, you just be sure an' ask to see the menu when yer dinin' with the Plains Injuns, Lucius," the Kansan told his brother, calling forth another round of laughter.

"What other things are you going to do with that gold, Davy?" his sister asked him.

It was the Kansan's turn to blush. "Well, uh, I kinda figgered to ride into Hawkins Fork in a li'l bit. . .an' look up Deanna MacPartland. You, uh, remember her, don't ya?" he asked anxiously.

Amy beamed at him. "She's very sweet, David Lee. Deanna came to visit us each time she got a letter from you. She's just like family, now."

"How is she?" Davy asked, still anxious.

"She was always fine," his sister assured him. But we haven't seen her for a while, now."

This news brought a frown to the Kansan's face. "That's funny," he said slowly. " 'Cause I done sent her a letter not too long ago."

"She probably didn't receive it yet, son," Annabel Watson gently told Davy, moving close to him and stroking his hair. "You know how the mail from the West is. And besides, you'll be seeing her soon enough."

"She shore is purty," commented Lucius Erasmus, bringing a smile to his brother's lips.

"Yep. She is that," Davy agreed, warmed by the

thought of seeing his love once more.

"When are you going in to see her?" asked Amy.

"Well, I thought I'd spend the night with you folks first, an' then light out to see her 'round noontime tomorrow."

"That's fine, son," Annabel Watson told the Kansan. "Because we can all be together tonight, and talk about old times." She paused to clear her throat. "And your father."

The Kansan nodded. "Yep. I'd like to talk some 'bout Pa tonight."

"Well, we certainly will. You can count on it," his mother assured him, smiling warmly now as she took his hand. "And Amy and I are going to make you the best supper you've ever had in your entire life."

Davy grinned at his mother. "Judas Priest," he said. "It's good to be home."

His mother put a finger on the Kansan's lips. "David Lee, I *do* wish you wouldn't swear so. It's a terrible example for Lucius Erasmus."

Who prob'ly swears like a blacksmith, his own self, the Kansan thought merrily, keeping a poker face as he nodded solemnly at his mother. . . .

Dinner was magnificent, and called to mind Christmas, Thanksgiving, and all other special occasions—all the culinary glories of the past. Secure in the bosom of his family, and basking in the golden warmth of their love, the Kansan looked back upon his life, and recalled especially the strength, love, integrity, and quiet wisdom which had characterized his father, the late John Jacob Watson.

The Watson family stayed up far into the night, reminiscing about the past, calling up in memory loved ones distant and departed, living and dead. But there were no ghosts in the parlor that long night (which proved to be all too short for the celebrants), for all those whose memories had been evoked lived in the hearts of the Kansan and his family just as surely as if they had been sitting beside them in the room.

It was after two in the morning when Davy Watson finally eased his tired and saddle-weary body into the bed he had left more than two years before. He fell asleep instantly, entering the dark realm of his interior life, the theatre of dreams, desires, and powerful, basic drives.

That theatre came alive several times for the Kansan, its dark stage suddenly illuminated with visions of excitement and delight, as he dreamt of the woman he loved and desired, his lissome blonde angel of passion, Deanna MacPartland.

I'm ridin' out on the windswept plain,
Where only the buffalo goes,
And men will never see me again
'Til I find my prairie rose.

Bright and fine as spun gold, her hair brushed his chest as they embraced; and when he kissed her cheeks, he tasted the salt tang of her tears. His arms fit around her trim, quivering body as if they had been created expressly for that purpose; their groins were pressed together and they seemed to breathe in unison, as if animated by a single heart and mind.

Her feet were small and high-arched, and as delicately carved as those of a marble statue. Slender ankles led up to calves whose singing lines beckoned the eye up to trim thighs, the hollows of which Davy remembered with his senses as basins of salt and ivory.

Catching his breath once again, Davy ran his eyes over the girl's lovely form. His ardent glance traveled over the gentle, womanly swell of her hips and the graceful alder tree waist; over the beautiful hands with their long, tapering fingers, and further up, over the firm arms and delicately rounded shoulders. She suddenly turned her head away, and he watched the ivory column of her neck disappear behind a cascade of gold.

When she turned to face him again, he studied the exquisite oval of her face, within which he saw the full, pouting lips, a pert, slightly aquiline nose, and eyes of a penetrating blue which seemed to promise deep intimacy and delight.

Then he looked down, casting his eye over the lissome, glowing body. Looking past the delicate hollow of her neck, he beheld the beauty of her high, firm breasts and felt a desire to run his tongue down the gentle cleft between them, and then over the erect nipples and aerolae pink as ocean coral.

Below the dip of her ribcage, where her waist sloped down and then ran out in a gentle swell, Davy saw Deanna's navel, with its slight accent of shadow, and her belly, which was fetchingly adorned with a glinting, golden down. And slightly below that, the golden down became a thatch of darker blonde hair that covered the fleshy cupola of her mound of Venus and ran down the gently pouting lips of Deanna's sex, whose vibrant inner pink echoed with an amplified intensity the delicate tint of her cheeks.

As Davy stared at Deanna, her own glance traveled hungrily over the young Kansan's hard-muscled body.

Suddenly, Deanna startled Davy by kneeling before him and touching the old wound on his right side with her lips. He emitted a deep groan as her lips traveled down over his body, blazing a trail through the thicket of his pubic hair and coming to rest at the base of his erect and throbbing maleness.

Davy groaned again as Deanna's full, red lips browsed the length of his shaft. Then he gasped as her lips parted and she took him into the encircling warmth of her mouth. Looking down, he saw her head bob in long, even motions as she stroked his sex in that intimate oral caress.

"Oh, Sweet Jesus," he moaned as the drawing warmth spread over the head and neck of his cock. Somewhere in the back of his brain a light flashed, reminding him of the fire arrows of Arikaree Creek, and he felt the first throb in the pit of his groin, the first herald of the surging torrent that would flow, wild as the Snake River in Hells Canyon, at the culmination of his pleasure.

But Deanna was only beginning, and she drew back her head and released him, rising to stand on tiptoe and kiss him, cupping and gently squeezing his balls all the while.

Deanna came away from Davy once more, leaving him hotter than a branding iron in a fire. He took her in his arms. They turned toward the big brass bed, graceful as a couple dancing the waltz; and then he dipped, taking her down beneath him. "Ooooh, Davy," was all that she could say. And he could say nothing at all.

"Come inside me, Davy," Deanna urged in a voice like the rushing prairie wind. "Oh, I want you inside me now!"

Deanna reached down one of her hands; they were delicate hands, with a tracery of blue veins beneath their marble surface, and long tapering fingers: the hands of an artist. And the fingers of those hands encircled the shaft of his engorged organ and guided it into her wet and welcoming circle of delight.

He slid into her sheath, feeling the sudden warmth of that snug barrel as well as the squeeze of her sphincter muscle. And at that instant, Davy experienced an intense sensation, a feeling of completeness such as he had rarely experienced before.

"Now, don't you move, David Lee," she whispered in his ear. "Just lie there and be close to me. And let me do this for you."

He looked into her prairie flower-blue eyes and smiled, nodding his head as he did. Then, laying his head down on the pillow beside Deanna's, and breathing deeply of the fragrance of her hair and the musk of her sweet pussy, Davy gave himself over to his lover's passionate ministrations.

"Oh, I feel you so deep inside me," she whispered in a voice like the sweeping wind,

inflaming him incredibly. "Oh, you're filling me up."

Davy lay still on top of her, cushioning his weight with his elbows, his sex thrust deep within Deanna's, lost in the funnel of the whirlwind of his emotions and desires.

Deanna lay beneath him, with her eyes closed and small beads of sweat gleaming on her hairline like a band of diamonds, whispering passionate and incoherent endearments in her lover's ear. And even though her body was still, to all outward appearances, her vaginal sphincter communicated her longing and desire in a warm and gripping telegraphy of passion. Deanna worked the muscles of her pussy in the same inspired manner that Samuel F. B. Morse first worked the telegraph key.

Dit-dah-dit. Dah-dit-dah.

Davy's answer was non-verbal: the sum total of all his feeling and desire for the lissome blonde beauty who lay moaning in his arms. And a telegraphy of light, traveling in bursts behind his eyes, transmitted the encoded message of his combined delight, joy, and release into the field of his senses. And he came with a deep, wrenching groan; with a sound that issued forth from the deepest recesses of his being.

And then he awoke.

FOUR

The Bawdy House Of Mrs. Lucretia Eaton

When the Kansan awoke at nine o'clock, the other members of his family had already been up for hours and were tending to the daily chores of the Watson farm.

Davy had a breakfast of flapjacks, bacon, eggs, and coffee, which he ate sitting at the kitchen table while Amy and his mother filled him in on the events of the past two years.

He could not have returned at a better time, it turned out, for the last of the two hired hands which Davy had brought to the farm just before hitting the trail had recently packed his gear, declaring his intention to ride toward the wide open spaces west of the Rocky Mountains.

"Between you and Lucius Erasmus," his mother told him, "I don't reckon we'll have any further need for hired hands. You always were one for getting things done, and your little brother practically does the work of two men, himself."

Davy nodded. "Ol' Lucius growed up real fine, far as I can see. An' Amy," he smiled at his sister, "done got purtier than any gal's got a right to be."

His sister began to blush as she continued to shell peas.

"Yes, God has been good to us," Annabel Watson told her eldest son. "And you've come back a fine, handsome man yourself, David Lee. Why, you'll be twenty years old in less than half a year."

"I reckon," Davy replied, suddenly aware of the swift passage of time.

"Your father was twenty-one when we got married."

"And that's how old David Lee will be, when he gets married—at most," Amy said, looking up at last from her peas and smiling shyly at the Kansan.

"Now, hold on there, Amy," he cautioned. "I don't rightly know if Deanna will even have me."

"Oh, she'll have you, all right," his sister assured him. "She and me did us a heap of woman-to-woman talkin' whenever she stopped by. She loves you very much."

Davy felt his ears flush. "Well, that's, uh, right gratifyin' to hear. It kinda fortifies me fer my trip in to Hawkins Fork."

"She's such a lovely girl," his mother added. "You're right lucky to have a sweetheart like Deanna, son."

Wondering what Annabel Watson would think if she knew that Deanna MacPartland worked in a brothel, the Kansan nodded. "That's 'bout how I feel, Ma," he told her.

"I'd like you two to be married here on the farm, by the waters of Pottawatomie Creek, David Lee," Annabel Watson told her son. "That surely would have been your father's wish."

Amy nodded in agreement with Mrs. Watson's statement.

"Well, sure," the Kansan told them both. "If'n that's the way Pa would've wanted it, that's the way it'll be. I just ought to speak with Deanna 'bout it, but I'm sure there won't be no problem."

Amy sighed. "We'll have a lovely wedding."

His mother smiled, sniffled, and then dabbed at her eyes with a handkerchief.

"The first of my children to wed," she whispered in a husky voice. "My land, but that will be a day of rejoicing."

Watson-style, the Kansan began to blush.

"And Amy is being courted by Jack Hargreave," his mother went on. "You remember him, don't you, David Lee?"

"Ol' Jack Hargreave, whose people live down the other side of Possum Hollow?" he asked, eliciting a nod from Annabel Watson. "Well, he's a good ol' boy," the Kansan said approvingly, turning to his sister, whose blush was even redder than any of his.

"We used to run together when we was kids," Davy told Amy. "An' you couldn't find no more loyal or trustworthy friend than ol' Jack. He was allus a good man to have beside ya in a fight."

"I hope he won't be brawling after he's wed to your sister," Annabel Watson said disapprovingly.

"Ma, he's a perfect gentleman these days," Amy protested.

"Mebbe so," her brother told her, "but the boy's got a bit of the devil in 'im. So things ain't never gonna be dull fer ya."

"Thank God for that," Amy Watson muttered, casting a furtive glance at her mother.

"What was that, dear?" Mrs. Watson asked.

"I said, 'That godly Jack,' Ma," she told her mother with a straight face.

Davy rose from the table. "Well, once't I take a gander at the ol' place, an' see what needs fixin' or replacin'," he told the two women, "I think I'll just mosey into Hawkins Fork an' pay my respects to Deanna."

I'm ridin' out on the windswept plain,
Where only the buffalo goes,
And men will never see me again,
'Til I find my prairie rose. . . .

The words of that song, the song which the Kansan had initially heard after he'd first made love with Deanna MacPartland, kept running through his head as Davy Watson rode from the farm by Pottawatomie Creek to the nearby town of Hawkins Fork.

He had decided to stop first in the Red Dog Saloon, the place where Ace Landry had so drastically altered his life two years ago. A drink for luck, with Fred the barkeep, the first man ever to serve the Kansan a drink, would be in order. A drink for him and a drink for Fred. . .and maybe one more, if Fred insisted on buying back. Davy knew his bar etiquette and wished to observe the amenities.

Everything looked much the same to the Kansan as it had on the day he'd last visited Hawkins Fork. The town was the same ungainly jumble of rough frame buildings and log cabins bordered at the one end by the Calvary Baptist Church, and at the other by the Red Dog Saloon. In between those two landmarks were the Overland stagecoach depot, the blacksmith's shop, the combined barbershop and dentist's office, Doc Kincaid's office, the livery stable, the sheriff's office and town jail, the funeral parlor, and Mrs. Eaton's establishment, whose painted shutters stabbed the Kansan to the heart as he imagined Deanna Mac-Partland behind them, waiting for him.

Echoing memory, a jangly pianoforte was playing loudly as he entered the Red Dog Saloon, and the gravelly-voiced man who played it was singing a popular tune.

> *"Buf'lo gals, ain't'cha comin' out tonight,*
> *Comin' out tonight, comin' out tonight;*
> *Buf'lo gals, ain't'cha comin' out tonight,*
> *To dance by the light of the moon. . . ."*

The cut-glass lamps still shone with the flickering light of their kerosene-soaked wicks, and the big brass spitoons still sat by the bar rail, glowing with a dull sheen. The long and elaborately carved hardwood bar was the same as the Kansan remembered it, as was the huge oil painting of a blonde reclining nude which hung from the wall, over the shelves of bottles.

Only the bartender was different, a fat, red-faced man with white curly hair, whose features meant nothing at all to Davy Watson.

"Say, where's Fred?" he asked the barkeep.

"Fred who?" was the man's reply.

"Fred. Fella who used to tend bar here."

The fat, red-faced man nodded. "Oh, *that* Fred."

103

"Yep. That Fred."

"Well, sir," the man told him, scratching the stubble on his beefy jowls, "I guess you ain't been here for some time, now."

"A piece over two years, I reckon," the Kansan replied.

The barkeep nodded again. "That explains it," he said in that flat, low voice of his.

"Explains what?" asked Davy Watson.

"Explains why you don't know about ol' Fred."

Getting information from this man was like pulling the teeth of a bucking bronco. "What about ol' Fred?" he persisted.

The barkeep shook his head, a look of sadness on his face. "They was a bunch of trailhands in here, 'bout a year ago, all drunker'n skunks." He shook his head. "Real wild an' woolly them boys was. Well, all of a sudden, a couple of 'em started to shoot up the place." Here his expression grew somber.

"So what happened?" the Kansan asked.

The man paused to pour himself a hooker of rye.

"Well, what happened?" Davy asked anxiously.

The barkeep shook his head. "Oh, some no-good shit-faced saddle tramp done went an' put a bullet in ol' Fred's head. Said it was a accident. An' they wasn't a whole lot any of us could do just then, 'cause they was 'round forty of them boys here in the Red Dog." He sighed heavily. "So they rode out right after the shootin', takin' the fella what done it with 'em."

"What about Fred?" asked the Kansan once more.

The barkeep sighed again. " 'Twas a bullet from

a .44 that ol' Fred took at close range, mister. Blowed a real big piece out of his skull.''

"So he's dead?''

"Shit, yeah. Deader'n a ninety-year-old man's pecker. Fred was dead, we figger, afore he hit the floorboards.''

Davy shook his head and smiled a tight, bitter smile. "How d'ya like that shit?'' he muttered. Then he raised his glass. "Well, mister, here's to ol' Fred, wheresomever he might be. May his soul rest in peace.''

"Amen to that,'' the barkeep said, just before he knocked back his drink.

Their glasses clinked as they toasted.

Davy slammed his glass down on the bar and reached into his vest pocket. He came up with a fifty-cent piece, which he tossed onto the bar.

"Hey, mister,'' the barkeep called as Davy Watson spun on his heel and began to walk out of the Red Dog Saloon. "Have one on me.''

"Thank you kindly,'' the Kansan called back over his shoulder, never slackening his pace. "But I do believe I've had enough for tonight.''

"*Way down upon the Swanee River,*
Far, far away,
That's where my heart is yearning ever,
That's where the old folks stay.

"*All the world is sad and dreary,*
Ev'rywhere I go,
I hear the gentle voices calling
Old Black Joe.''

The pianoforte player sang one of Stephen Foster's poignant and immensely popular songs. This one, *Old Folks at Home*, was composed for Edwin P. Christy's minstrel show, and bore Christy's name on it rather than the composer's.

The Kansan knew a little about Stephen Foster (a great favorite of his knowledgeable Uncle Ethan), and the thought of the poor man's tragic end added to the pall of gloom which had enwrapped him since he heard the news of Fred the bartender's death.

Foster, whose avowed ambition was to become the best minstrel, or "Ethiopian," songwriter in the country, never realized a substantial profit on any of his vastly popular songs, and he had spent the last years of his life in a state of extreme alcoholism. He died, in debt, in 1864.

"Well, there's one thing left that's bound to cheer me up," the Kansan muttered to himself as he passed through the swinging doors of the saloon.

Looking diagonally across the street, he saw the bawdy house owned by Mrs. Lucretia Eaton. That was the place where Deanna was waiting for him; that was the spot where he would once more find his love.

"I reckon that's where I'm a-headin'," Davy muttered aloud once again, as he stepped off the boards of the sidewalk and began to cross the street with long, purposeful strides. "It's 'bout time I paid a call on Mrs. Eaton, an' got Deanna out'n there, once't an' fer all."

The Kansan was smiling confidently as he stepped onto the boards at the opposite side of the

106

street. He had waited a long, long time for this moment, and it had arrived at last. He was going to claim Deanna MacPartland, and take her home with him—once and for all.

He stepped up onto the porch, suddenly pausing to slick back his hair and adjust his clothing as he came to the front door of the establishment. Then he wiped his sweaty palms on his pants, took a deep breath, and tugged twice on the bell cord that hung on the doorpost.

What seemed to the anxious Kansan to be an inordinately long time passed before the door handle turned, and the front door of the bawdy house swung open. There before him stood a tall redhead, in a gown cut so low in the center that Davy was sure if he were to get close enough and look straight down, he would be able to see the woman's belly button.

She smiled a mechanical smile at him and opened the door wide.

"Well, come on in, handsome," she cooed in a voice whose syrupy accent located it somewhere in the deep south.

"Thank you, ma'am," the Kansan murmured, taking off his hat as he entered Mrs. Lucretia Eaton's establishment.

The reek of cigar smoke and the pungent, stinging smell of whiskey greeted Davy Watson's nostrils as he stepped into the foyer.

"Lemme take your coat, honey," the redhead with the mechanical smile murmured as she leaned toward him, rubbing her ample bosom against his back.

"No thank you, ma'am," he told her quietly.

The sounds of laughter suddenly arose from the parlor within, and the Kansan could hear the high, pealing laughter of women mixing with the deeper sounds of merriment made by the male guests. An upright piano could also be heard, playing a popular and sentimental ballad, one that Davy remembered hearing somewhere in his travels.

"Captain, Captain, stop that ship,
I see my sweetheart there.
O let me go to him and die,
Me and my orphan child."

"Gonna check your gun, cowboy?" the big redhead asked, holding out her hands to receive his gunbelt.

Davy shook his head. "No, ma'am. I'm not here fer the use of the facilities. I just mean to speak to Miz Eaton fer a minute."

The redhead's eyes widened slightly and her wind-up doll's smile softened over so slightly.

"Well, that's certainly a change," she murmured, looking the Kansan up and down with sudden curiosity. "There sho' 'nuff ain't too many gents who drops by *this* place with the intent of havin' a conversation. I do declare!"

Davy grinned at her. "Well," he said, "I 'spect there's exceptions to ev'ry rule."

"So it would seem," she purred in a low voice, suddenly interested in him.

"Do you, uh, s'pose you could fetch Miz Eaton?" he asked the redhead, who had come face to face with him and was now so close that her plunging neckline gaped before him.

"Won't I do, cowboy?" she asked, running the long, red nail of her forefinger down the nape of the Kansan's neck, causing him to shiver.

He cleared his throat and then took a deep breath, inhaling the magnolia fragrance of the red-head's perfume.

"Gal as good-lookin' as yerself'd certainly do in most instances, ma'am," Davy said gallantly, smiling at the redhead, who now had both arms twined around his neck and was busy rubbing herself up against his front. "But at the present time, I got me some business what needs to be discussed with Miz Eaton."

She pouted as he told her this. "It's always a good idea to loosen up some before talkin' business, Mister—"

"Watson," he said. "My name's Davy Watson."

"Mr. Watson. An' I'm just the woman to loosen you up." Suddenly she leaned forward, and brushed his cheek with her lips. And following that, she darted her tongue in the Kansan's ear and pressed her body full against his and began to writhe and grind her hips.

Davy cleared his throat again. "Uh, ma'am," he said awkwardly, feeling suddenly suffocated by the redhead's strong perfume.

"My name's Dale," she whispered, after running her tongue down the side of his neck. "Dale Wagstaff. From Savannah, Georgia. I haven't been with Miz Eaton long, but I aim to make my mark."

Saying this, she pressed her lips against Davy Watson's and thrust her long tongue deep into his

109

mouth. And at the same time, Dale Wagstaff reached down her left hand and began to stroke and gently squeeze the Kansan's genitals.

"Uh, listen," Davy grunted, once he freed his lips from the press of the redhead's and had drawn back far enough to remove himself from the range of her questing, insistent tongue. "I'm here to speak to yer employer, ma'am. An' I ain't got neither the time nor the inclination to pleasure myself right now, if'n you take my meanin'."

He grabbed her by the upper arms and gently thrust her back, until she stood at arm's length from him.

"I'd be right obliged if'n you'd jus' fetch Miz Eaton here, ma'am."

The redhead's mechanical smile began to crumble before the Kansan's eyes. A moment later, it was replaced by a sneer of contempt.

"Well, I declare," she snarled, jerking loose from his grip, her eyes narrowing as she stared at him haughtily. "You sure are one cold fish, mister. An' I reckon my services would only be wasted on a *man* such as yourself."

The Kansan's ears burned and he glared back at the redhead. "I'd be obliged if'n you'd git Miz Eaton to come on out here—*right now*."

She snorted like a lathered horse and spun on her heel, walking off with a toss of her head which sent her long locks dancing in the air.

"You just wait here and don't move," she called back over her shoulder. "Not that there's much chance of that," she added with asperity. "An' I'll see if Miz Eaton *cares* to receive you."

The Kansan shook his head. *Well, if'n this ain't*

the damnedest day, he thought. *Not a blessed thing seems to be comin' out right. Well, leastways that'll turn around once't I see Deanna, an' whisk her out'n this place.*

He reached into his jacket pocket and felt the sack containing the gold. There would undoubtedly be an indemnity due Lucretia Eaton for the loss of Deanna MacPartland's services. The madam was a businesswoman of no mean ability, and the Kansan was certain that she would ask a high price, once he had announced his intentions.

She would, the Kansan was sure, immediately go into great detail about all the care and attention which had been lavished upon the little blonde in the past two years, ever since the day when a man called John Hartung had brought her here, after finding the girl in the ruins of the log cabin where her family had been massacred by marauding Plains Indians. Mrs. Eaton had groomed and supported Deanna for over two years now, and the Kansan imagined that this act of "charity" would have a high price attached to it.

Davy shook his head as he recalled that Deanna had once told him that Mrs. Eaton was holding the bulk of her earnings in "safekeeping." The procuress must be making a fortune from the labors of the lovely little blonde.

Hell, he told himself, *I'll bet that ol' gal's got more money than Midas hisself. Mebbe I'll jus dicker with 'er a mite. She's made more'n enough off Deanna already.*

Just then, as he looked up, Davy made out the silhouetted figure of a large woman, coming toward him down the dimly lit passageway which connected the foyer to the parlor.

As the woman came into the brightly lighted foyer, the Kansan saw that it was none other than Lucretia Eaton.

The big, matronly woman looked much as he remembered. Her long, dark hair was still piled on top of her head, and she still sported a sparkling tiara. The procuress wore a tight-waisted gown of dark-green velvet, and her corseted midsection exaggerated the mighty swell of both her huge hips and pigeon-breasted front.

Well, at least ol' Miz Eaton's still here, an' lookin' much the same as when I last seen 'er, Davy told himself, his flagging spirits beginning to rise at the reassuring sight of the madam's familiar appearance. *I reckon ev'rythin's gonna be all right from here on out.*

The big woman smiled warmly as she came toward the Kansan. "Ah, it's so good to see you again," she purred. "I'm sorry to have kept you waiting, but this evening we're entertaining a number of grain buyers from the East. Now, what may I do for you, Mr. Weston?"

"Watson's my name, Miz Eaton. Davy Watson."

She blinked her eyes and smiled even more warmly than before. "Mr. Watson," she corrected herself. "Ah, yes. My girl, Dale, got your name wrong, sir." She gave him a little nod. "I do apologize, *Mister Watson.*"

He had been beaten, slashed, flogged, and shot several times over the course of the past two years. He had risked his life nearly a dozen times in that same period. He had known the enmity of many men, and the fast friendship of even more. And he had been the lover and intimate companion of a number of attractive and spirited women throughout the American West and Northwest. The Kansan suddenly realized that the woman did not have the slightest idea of who he was.

Davy Watson had been a boy when he last saw Lucretia Eaton, a youth who had just arrived at the threshold of maturity. And the person who now stood before the procuress was no boy, that was for sure. The Kansan was a man, and one whose incredible and perilous adventures had left their mark on him, etching those two years of intense living and experience indelibly into his features, bestowing upon him a maturity which was far in advance of his chronological age.

"Have we, ah, met before, Mr. Watson?" Lucretia Eaton asked, still smiling her gracious smile as she studied the Kansan's features.

"You don't remember me, do ya, ma'am?" he asked, grinning at her now.

Lucretia Eaton squinted and bit her lip. "You know," she told him after several moments of further scrutiny, "there *is* something definitely familiar about you, sir, and yet, I'm at a loss to place you." She drew herself up to her full, imposing height. "And *that* is not a thing which happens to me often, I can assure you."

"I'm John Jacob Watson's son, Miz Eaton," he told her in a low, quiet voice. Then he watched her eyes narrow in recognition.

"John Jacob Watson," she murmured, watching Davy like a hawk. "Then you must be—" Here her voice shook. "David. . .Lee."

He smiled at her. "That's right, ma'am. I'm back, at last. I been on the trail fer more'n two years. But now I'm back, an' I come fer Deanna MacPartland."

"Deanna MacPartland!" she said in a shrill, strangled voice.

A sudden, icy chill rippled up the Kansan's spine, and his hackles began to rise.

"I come to take Deanna home with me, Miz Eaton," Davy said, his voice hardening as he studied the madam's face.

"Ooohhh," the big woman sighed, producing a silk handkerchief, which she raised with trembling hand and used to dab at her forehead.

The Kansan watched as a trickle of perspiration ran down from Lucretia Eaton's hairline, streaking her powdered face as it coursed down her cheek. She was breathing heavily now, and trembling all over as if she'd been taken with chillblains.

Her anxiety transmitted itself to the Kansan, and Davy Watson felt his palms grow clammy. *Why was the woman reacting to him in such a peculiar fashion? Why had she become so upset?*

"Deanna. . .MacPartland," the procuress said in that curious, strangled tone of voice which had characterized her speech ever since Davy had spoken the name of his love.

"That's right, ma'am. Deanna MacPartland. I'm here to take her back with me."

Lucretia Eaton's face had turned as white as the skin of a three-day-old corpse. Her jaw was slack, and her big, red-lipped mouth hung open in the manner of a catfish hanging on the hook of a fish scale.

114

"Oh, Mr. Watson," she said in a quavering voice that was barely audible, taking a step backward at the same time.

The chill which had run up the Kansan's spine had now spread throughout his entire body. He clenched and unclenched his fists, feeling his circulation suddenly fail him.

"What is it, Miz Eaton?" he asked, taking a step toward the gasping, trembling woman.

He looked into her eyes, and saw the glittering fear in them. She continued to back away, but Davy lunged toward her and grabbed Lucretia Eaton by the shoulders, holding her fast.

"*What is it*?" he asked again, anger and urgency coloring his voice. "Where's Deanna? I want to see her."

"Aaah, aaah," was the only sound which issued from the stricken woman's mouth, in a voice which sounded as if someone were wringing her neck.

The Kansan shook the big woman, causing the string of pearls that she wore to clack and rattle.

"Oh, merciful God!" the procuress gasped, looking into Davy Watson's eyes with an expression on her face resembling those of men on the gallows who have just had their first sight of the executioner.

"Dammit, Miz Eaton," he growled. "Talk to me!"

The procuress merely continued to gape and gasp. Finally, after batting her eyes furiously, she began to cry, unleashing a flood of tears which further streaked her face powder.

Davy shook her again, harder than before. "Come on, now, I want to know what-all's goin'

115

on around here.''

Sobbing and gasping, the madam shook her head violently, indicating her desire for the Kansan to stop shaking her.

Davy stopped, and then released his grip on the woman's shoulders. She stood before him, fear glittering in her eyes, as she struggled to catch her breath.

"Hey, what the devil's goin' on in there?" a deep voice boomed from the passageway, causing the Kansan to look up and over the shoulder of Lucretia Eaton.

A hulking, big-bellied man lumbered into the foyer. His thinning hair was slicked down on his skull with a gleaming pomade, and his thick fingers were adorned with a number of expensive-looking rings. He held a big cigar clenched between his teeth, and glared at Davy Watson through narrowed pig-eyes.

Lucretia Eaton turned to the big man and cast him a look of mute appeal.

"What'sa matter, Lucretia?" the man growled in a voice which reminded the Kansan of a shovel digging into a pile of gravel.

The procuress batted her eyes and gasped, still unable to speak.

"This jasper givin' you a hard time?" the big man asked, casting an angry eye at Davy Watson. "Because if he is, I'll call the boys, and we'll give the bum the heave-ho any time you say."

Davy's hackles rose at this. "Whyn't you just mind yer own business an' go back inside," he growled, sizing the man up and realizing that the stranger spoke with an Eastern accent.

The man looked over to Lucretia Eaton, waiting for an answer to his question.

"Want me to get rid of him?" he asked, coming up behind the madam.

At that point Lucretia Eaton fainted, and collapsed onto the floor in a heap, with the sound of a side of beef hitting a slaughterhouse floor.

"Holy Hannah!" the big man exclaimed, shocked by the spectacle of the huge woman's thunderous collapse.

Davy Watson's nostrils flared in annoyance as he looked from the fallen woman to the intruding man.

"Jesus, look what you've done!" the big man exclaimed, taking the cigar out of his mouth as he started toward the Kansan.

Thwack! Davy threw a hard overhand right at the man, and it caught Lucretia Eaton's guest square on the point of the jaw, sending him backward to bounce off the foyer wall and crumple to his knees on the rug, where, an instant later, he fell, face-down and unconscious.

Shaking his stinging fist, the Kansan knelt down by the side of the fallen procuress, and proceeded to revive her.

"C'mon, Miz Eaton," Davy urged, lightly slapping the woman's face. "Wake up. We got things to talk about."

"Uh, wha-a-a," she gasped, wincing beneath the sting of his blows.

"Up ya go," he grunted, hoisting the big, fleshy woman to a sitting position.

She blinked her eyes like an owl suddenly thrust into sunlight, and looked around the room.

"What. . .happened to Mr. Patterson?" she asked in a feeble voice, recognizing the form of the big man sprawled out on the floor, his smoking cigar burning a hole in the rug.

"Never mind 'bout Mr. Patterson," the Kansan growled. "What you're gonna do now is tell me what's happenin' here."

"Oh, Mr. Watson," the madam wailed. "I'm afraid to tell you."

Fear clutched Davy's guts in its icy grip when he heard those words, and the Kansan's first reaction was to shake Lucretia Eaton the way a mastiff shakes a rat.

"*Stop! Stop!*" she screeched.

"Not until you tell me 'bout Deanna MacPartland, by gad!" he swore.

"*Oh, I will—I will!*" she squawked. "*Please stop!*"

"All right," he told her, bringing the woman's body to a sharp halt, and causing her head to jerk sharply.

For a few moments they were still, and the room silent except for the sounds of their labored breathing.

"Now, start talkin'," Davy ordered, once he had got his breath back.

Lucretia Eaton gulped, cleared her throat and nodded her head, her frightened eyes never leaving the Kansan's face.

"Well, what's goin' on?" Davy growled, scowling at the madam. "I want you to tell me straight—an' I want you to tell me now!"

She gulped and nodded again, mopping her brow with the silk handkerchief.

"Now, where's Deanna MacPartland?"

"Oh, Mr. Watson," sobbed Lucretia Eaton, peering at the Kansan's face with wide, frightened eyes. "She's. . .not. . .with us. . .any more."

Anger flared in his eyes. Davy reached out and grabbed the procuress by her upper arms.

"*Oh!*" she screamed. "*You're hurting me!*"

"Never mind that," he snarled, his cold eyes never leaving her face. "What the hell does that mean?" He shot the madam a look which made her blanch. "You ain't sayin' that she's . . .dead . . .now, are you?"

Lucretia Eaton gulped and frantically shook her head.

"Well, what then?" Davy asked gruffly, staring daggers at the petrified woman.

"She left here," the madam said in the feeblest of voices.

"What d'ya mean, 'she left here?' " the Kansan barked, squeezing her arms once more.

Lucretia Eaton screamed again. "Oh please," she whimpered. "Please, Mr. Watson. You're hurting me."

Breathing heavily, the Kansan relaxed his grip. "I'm sorry," he mumbled. Then he looked her straight in the eye. "Where did Deanna go?"

"To St. Louis," Lucretia Eaton gasped.

"By herself?"

The madam shook her head. "No. No. With the man who first brought her here. John Hartung."

"Did she go willingly, or did he force her?" he asked roughly, feeling a stab of jealousy in his gut.

"Hey, what's going on out there?" a man called from the far end of the passageway that connected

119

the room with the parlor.

The Kansan looked up and saw three men in business suits coming into the room.

"Hey, what the hell's goin' on in this joint?" the first, a burly, bearded fellow, called out in surprise as he saw the body of the man named Patterson on the floor of the foyer.

"Who is that fella?" the second, a lanky redhead asked, as the third, a short, stocky man with curly black hair and a handlebar mustache came up beside him.

The Kansan stood up at this, and he whipped out his big Walker Colt at the same time, leveling it at the newcomers.

"Now, go easy there, friend," the burly, bearded man cautioned in a voice that quavered. "We aren't armed."

"Git over there," Davy ordered, waving the three men to one side of the room. "An' move yer butts!"

Then, as the men shuffled hurriedly over to the place which had been indicated by the barrel of the Kansan's pistol, Davy stared down at Lucretia Eaton.

"Where'd Deanna an' this here John Hartung go, Miz Eaton?" he asked, turning an eye on the men again.

"To St. Louis," she gasped.

"Where in St. Louis, ma'am?"

The madam gulped, licked her lips, and took a deep breath. "To a place known as Gridley's, down by the river, where the steamboats put in. I can't remember the name of the street it's on, Mr. Watson," she shot him a fearful look. "But

Gridley's is owned by a man named Hoyt Altgelder. He's an old friend of John Hartung's. They used to—"

"What're they doin' there?" demanded the Kansan.

Lucretia Eaton gulped and shot him a frightened look. "He, ah, became infatuated with young Deanna. . .when he'd come back and seen how. . .beautiful. . .she's become," the madam said haltingly, raising her hands in a helpless gesture. "So he, ah. . .took her away from here, Mr. Watson."

Davy backed toward the door. "I'm goin' up St. Louis way now, Miz Eaton," he told the frightened madam. "So you better be levelin' with me. 'Cause I'll be comin' back this way."

Gagging with fear, she nodded her head vigorously.

"You gents just stay put," the Kansan told the three men, just before he backed through the bawdy house's front door, " 'less'n you want to stop a bullet."

In an instant, he was gone.

"Ooooh," moaned Lucretia Eaton, falling back onto the carpet.

The three men ran over to her, and proceeded to tend to the madam, rousing her from her second faint. She looked up at the lanky, mustachioed, redheaded man who was her associate in the skin trade.

"Warren," she whispered in a croaking voice. "You must leave instantly and warn John Hartung before that man reaches him."

The lanky man nodded. "You know what that's

121

gonna mean, Lucretia," he whispered, leaning toward her, so that the other men present would not hear him. "Hartung an' Altgelder don't fool around."

Closing her eyes as she took a deep breath, the procuress nodded as he helped her to sit up. Then, when she finally opened her eyes again, she said, "Yes, Warren. I know." She closed her eyes.

"All right, Lucretia," the lanky redhead told her as he rose to his feet. "I'll take care of it. That Watson fella won't be botherin' you no more—nor anybody else."

FIVE

In The Gateway City

After the Kansan had backed out of Lucretia
Eaton's establishment, the glint in his eyes as hard
and cold as the glint of moonlight on the barrel of
his drawn Walker Colt, he mounted his horse and
rode hell-for-leather back to the Watson farm.

Once there, he proceeded to pack his saddlebags
and blanket roll, taking as well his throwing knife
and Henry rifle. His mother was stunned when she
heard that Davy was going to St. Louis, and his
brother and sister just stared at him with wide and
unbelieving eyes.

"But you just got home," Annabel Watson told
her son as he rolled up his blanket.

"I know that, Ma," he replied between clenched
teeth. "But I got to go."

"When will you be coming back?" she asked in
a still voice, staring at her eldest son's face.

The Kansan shook his head. "Dunno, Ma. After
I've found out what's goin' on with Deanna, I
s'pose."

"She wasn't in Hawkins Fork, then?"

"Nope. Done lit out fer St. Louis with some
fella." He scowled and his face darkened.

"Deanna wouldn't do that!" Amy Watson
protested loudly.

Davy looked up as he finished tying the blanket roll, and shot a cold glance at his sister.

"I hope to hell yer right, Amy," he told her in a low, cold voice. "That's what I'm choosin' to believe. Way I see it, this fella done took her away forcible-like."

"That's absolutely the only way Deanna would leave without seeing you, Davy," Amy replied with a grave nod. "I'm sure of it."

"Well, I aim to git 'er back," the Kansan said in a voice which caused his mother to catch her breath and wring her hands.

"There's going to be trouble," she said accusingly.

The Kansan looked up from his packing. "Only if'n I don't git me no answers to my questions, Ma. I ain't a-lookin' fer trouble. . .but I'm sure as shootin' gonna be ready if'n any comes my way."

Annabel Watson's face was pale now. "I thought the shooting and killing was all over, David Lee," she said, her wide, frightened eyes boring holes in his brain.

"So did I, Ma," he told her, nodding solemnly as he did. "So did I. But I gotta find out why Deanna hightailed it out of Hawkins Fork without even botherin' to leave word fer me." He shook his head. "Somethin' ain't right there."

He was sure that Lucretia Eaton was mixed up in this business somehow, and Davy had half a mind to ride back to Hawkins Fork and interrogate the madam further. But that would turn out to be a dangerous business, he opined, especially since he had practically wrung her neck an hour before. He knew that the procuress was not without friends. . .dangerous friends.

It was enough, the Kansan decided, that he knew where John Hartung had gone. He would either confront the man in St. Louis, or track him down from that point. The Kansan had become extremely knowledgeable in the area of man-hunting, ever since he, Soaring Hawk, and the newspaperman, Marcus Haverstraw, had scoured both Virginia City and San Francisco in search of Harvey Yancey, the desperado who had abducted the three Mudree sisters.

"You gonna shoot somebody, Davy?" Lucius Erasmus asked eagerly.

Davy had to smile at this. "Not 'less'n I can't help it," he told the boy. "If'n I have my druthers, I'm fer straightenin' things out over a drink, whilst we discusses the details, amiable-like. That's how civilized folks settles their disputes. By talkin' 'em over an' comin' to some kind of agreement 'bout what they're gon' do."

"Be careful, David Lee," his mother cautioned. "For the love of God, be careful."

"I will, Ma," he reassured her. "I've learned a whole lot since I first rid away from here, an' there ain't no way I'm goin' off half-cocked this time. I'll be careful."

"We lost your father to senseless violence," she whispered in a voice that broke. "And we can't afford to lose you, too."

He reached out and took her hand in his. "Now, don't you worry none, Ma," Davy told her in a gentle voice. "I won't take no chances."

"Is Soaring Hawk going with you, son?" she asked, giving him a hopeful look.

He shook his head. "Ol' Soaring Hawk just got back his own self. An' besides, he's out somewhere on the plains of Kansas or Colorado, follyin' the buffalo herds." He smiled wistfully at the thought of his old companion. "No, this time I'll be goin' off all by my lonesome."

"Well, you be careful," his mother told him, giving Davy's hand a sudden, vigorous squeeze. "And I want you back here just as soon as humanly possible."

He grinned at her. "Yes, ma'am. I'll do my level best to settle up this here business just as soon's I can. You can count on that, Ma."

"Davy," Lucius Erasmus called out from the far side of the room, "will ya bring me back a steamboat cap'n's hat from St. Louis? An' a new steel huntin' knife?"

The Kansan smiled at his kid brother. "Sure thing, Lucius."

Amy came up to him and took his other hand. "I'm sure Deanna left against her will, Davy," she told him, an earnest expression on her pretty face. "For I know in my heart that she would never willingly leave you."

Davy Watson sighed, his shoulders slumping as if they bore a great, burdensome weight on them. "I sure hope you're right," he murmured, releasing the hands of both his mother and sister, and turning back to his packing. "I surely do."

The Kansan rode out of the gates of the farm by Pottawatomie Creek after wolfing down a hurried supper (for which he stayed only at his mother's insistence), and set out on the night of the same day in which he had discovered his love missing from the bawdy house of Mrs. Lucretia Eaton.

After days of hard and furious riding, sleeping only when he could no longer stay in the saddle, pausing to eat only when hunger's demands became imperious, pushing himself to the limits of his physical endurance, the Kansan reached the outskirts of the bustling river port of St. Louis, Missouri in record time.

The Gateway City, now a major port on the Mississippi River second only to New Orleans itself, had been founded as a French post in 1764, by one Pierre Laclede. Shortly thereafter, Laclede and his commercial associate, Maxent, were granted fur-trading privileges by D'Abbadie, the last French governor at New Orleans. In this manner, the city began its rise to prominence on the banks of the great river, and had become by 1870, when the Kansan rode into it, the premier port and trading city of the American Midwest.

Situated on the Mississippi just below the Missouri and Illinois Rivers, St. Louis was extremely fortunate in being the site where the great break in river traffic happened to occur. The big, heavy draft vessels which came upriver from New Orleans, and towns and plantations enroute, had to reload their cargoes at that point, transferring them onto the decks of the lighter boats required for the journey up from Saint Louis.

The city had first grown prosperous through the fur trade, which had its beginnings with Maxent, Laclede and Company. The Gateway City earned that name by further becoming the departure point for western exploration and settlement. Its greatest prosperity dated from 1817, when the *Zebulon M. Pike*, the first steamboat to navigate its waters, reached the docks of St. Louis.

After that, commerce increased rapidly, and the city's population grew in leaps and bounds. Prosperity reached boom proportions in the years before the Civil War, when the population of St. Louis, a mere sixteen thousand in 1840, exploded to a full ten times that number by 1860.

Only the panic of 1857, which foreshadowed the economic devastation of the approaching War Between the States, put a temporary halt to the burgeoning prosperity of the Gateway City. River traffic ceased shortly after the start of the war, and this wrought consequent havoc with the city's sources of trade. The sympathies of the many Germans in St. Louis swung the state of Missouri into the Union camp.

Packet-boat activity resumed on the Mississippi almost immediately after the war, and soon its tide surged and mounted until the waters of a fiscal flood inundated the Gateway City. By 1870, the city was enjoying a revival of its former prosperity, despite the fact that it was now engaged in a life-and-death struggle for Midwestern commercial dominance with the newly emerging city of Chicago, which had become the area's prime trans-shipment point for the railroads which had linked the continent from coast to coast only a year before.

The greater part of St. Louis was located on top of a bluff, leaving only the riverfront vulnerable to the occasional rampages of the Mississippi River. And while the warehouses which fronted on that great water were often hostage to the sometimes cruel whims of nature, it was fire rather than water which caused the Gateway City's greatest riverfront disaster.

In 1849, the steamboat *White Cloud* caught fire while lying at anchor in the crowded harbor and, fanned by a high wind, the resultant blaze soon spread among the neighboring vessels. Twenty-two other steamboats were consumed in the conflagration, and the fiery devastation extended for many blocks along the St. Louis waterfront.

Davy Watson was dog-tired by the time his horse had entered the city limits of St. Louis. He knew that the first things he needed were a hot dinner and a place to bunk. Even before he set out in search of Hoyt Altgelder's establishment, the Kansan wanted to rest and refr__ 1 himself, in order to prepare for whatever ordeal lay ahead, unseen in the darkness of the future, lurking hazardously in his path like a dangerous *sawyer*, one of the riverstream snags created by uprooted tree trunks whose root ends had become seated in the bed of the river.

Not caring to resume his search for Deanna Mac-Partland until he had replenished his energies, the Kansan rode down to the riverfront, and made for the first saloon which presented itself.

He found himself in an establishment called Hackenschmidt's, a big, noisy barn of a place where merchants and rivermen rubbed elbows. In the back of the saloon, a piano and a banjo played riverboat songs and barroom ballads, as well as the beautiful and moving songs of Stephen Foster. The smells of beer and whiskey, smoke and sawdust, filled the air, and the roiling energies of the sprawling port city's denizens seemed to discharge themselves in a crackling, electrical manner.

"Say, where would ya tell a fella to go, if'n he was to ask about a place to bunk fer the night?"

Davy asked one of the bartenders at Hacken-schmidt's, as the man served him a second schooner of beer.

The bartender studied him for a moment. "What kind of accommodations you lookin' for, stranger?" the barkeep asked in turn.

Davy felt inside his jacket and patted the sack containing the Boise nuggets.

"Somethin' purty good, I reckon," he told the man, feeling up to a little treat after the rigors of the trail.

"Oh well," the bartender grunted, walking a few steps down the bar, "in that case, I got just the place for ya."

The man stopped and leaned forward, reaching down under the bar. A moment later, he straightened up and began to walk back to Davy Watson. The Kansan saw that he held a big book which bore the title *The Shipping Guide and Directory*.

"I got just what ya need, stranger," the bartender told the Kansan, as he leafed through the worn and grease-spotted pages of the big book.

"Here y'are," the man grunted, slamming the book down on the bar and spinning it around to face Davy. "Right there," he told him, pointing to a hostelry advertisement with a thick finger. "That's the place to stay. They'll do right by ya there, Mister. You can bet yer boots on that."

Davy looked down at the book, squinting to read it in the gloom of the barroom.

SOUTHERN HOTEL, the advertisement pro-claimed in black and elegant block letters which filled a wide line across the page, under which there was a mezzotint of the establishment in question, a six-storied building with a capacity of 240 rooms and suites, at the very least.

St. Louis, Mo., it went on, immediately beneath the illustration of the hotel, *LAVEILLE, WARNER & CO. PROPRIETORS. On Walnut, Fourth and Fifth Streets.*

The only first-class hotel in St. Louis. This elegant House is second to no hotel in the country. Its elegant suites of parlors, wide corridors, and finely furnished apartments make it the most desirable house in the city for travelers and families. Its tables are always supplied in the most bountiful manner with the best the market affords. The proprietors and their assistants are attentive to the wants of the guests of the House, and spare no pains to render their stay at the house pleasant and agreeable.

N.B.—, the advertisement concluded, *This Hotel does not employ any runners, and the traveling public are cautioned against the representatives of runners sent out by other Houses.*

LAVEILLE, WARNER & CO.,

Proprietors.

"Looks right nice," the Kansan remarked as he looked up from the big book and reached for his schooner of beer. "How's the grub at that place?"

The bartender leaned toward him confidentially. "Better'n it is here, mister," he said in a low voice, darting furtive glances up and down the bar.

"Well, if'n that's the case, I'll just have my vittles over there tonight," Davy told the barkeep, reaching down into his vest pocket and coming up with a silver dollar, which he then plunked down on the bar.

"Thanks fer the tip," he told the man, just before he turned and strode away from the polished hardwood bar.

"And thanks for yours, mister," the grateful bartender called out as he picked up the Kansan's silver dollar and began to wipe the bar.

> *"Camptown racetrack's five mile long,*
> *Doodah, doodah,*
> *Camptown racetrack's five mile long*
> *O doodah-day.*
> *Gwine to run all night,*
> *Gwine to run all day,*
> *Bet my money on a bobtail nag,*
> *Somebody bet on a bay."*

The piano player sang out above the plunk of the banjo and the jangle of his own instrument in a strong and ringing voice as the Kansan traversed the beer-reeking, sawdust-covered length of Hackenschmidt's saloon. The customers all joined in the singing with great fervor, singing the words of Foster's song as if they were the congregation at a Saturday night tent-meeting.

It seemed to the Kansan as if he were the only unhappy person in the entire city of St. Louis. Davy sighed heavily as he went through the swinging doors and out into the Mississippi River night. A steamboat whistle sounded in the distance, its forlorn wail causing the Kansan to recall the Biblical image of a lost soul crying out in the wilderness.

Suddenly a great wave of apprehension broke

inside him, as Davy began to worry about Deanna MacPartland. *Why had she left him for this man, John Hartung?* he asked himself. *Why had she run out that way, leaving no word for him? Why had she deserted him?*

His anxiety mounted rapidly, and before long the Kansan's mood was blacker than the starless sky above St. Louis. But he realized that worry would do nothing to improve his situation, or bring him anything in the way of comfort or certainty. No, worry was a dog that chased its own tail, going round and round and round, never getting anywhere nor accomplishing a blessed thing in the course of its futile, circular journey.

All he could do was pray, the Kansan told himself; it was out of his hands. He would go over to Walnut Avenue, between Fourth and Fifth Streets, and register at the Southern Hotel. And then, after a hearty dinner and a nightcap, he would turn in and get a good night's sleep. He would take care of himself tonight. . .and deal with the possibilities of lost love or a life-and-death encounter when he awoke in the morning.

Then we'll see what happens, the Kansan told himself, *when I git to Hoyt Altgelder's place an' meet up with Deanna. An' this mysterious gent called John Hartung.*

Despite his anxieties, Davy Watson slept well, between clean sheets, on the mattress provided by the Southern Hotel. He slept long into the morning, unhurried in the knowledge that his search for Deanna MacPartland could not effectively begin until late the following afternoon.

The Kansan slept until nine in the morning, an hour which was considerably later than the sunrise which had awakened him on the trail. He bathed in a big tub which stood upon four brass lion's paws, and shaved in a mirror whose elegant frame was covered with gilded scrollwork. After dressing and packing his Walker Colt, holster, gun belt and cartridges in a kit bag (for Davy had learned that the bearing of arms by civilians was strictly forbidden by a St. Louis city ordinance) the Kansan left his room and made his way downstairs to the dining room of the Southern Hotel.

There he ordered a hearty breakfast of corn bread, wheatcakes, fried eggs, bacon and two tall glasses of milk. After this sizeable repast, the Kansan called for a pot of coffee, over which he began to make plans and prepare himself for the day's events, whatever they turned out to be.

One great disadvantage he labored under, to Davy Watson's way of thinking, was the fact that he knew next to nothing about John Hartung, other than the fact that he had left Deanna Mac-Partland to work in Lucretia Eaton's brothel, and that he probably maintained some sort of shady business connection with the madam and her backers.

Was the man bold and headstrong, Davy Watson asked himself, *ready to whip out his pistol at the slightest provocation? Or was he sly and crafty, the kind who would rather bushwhack an opponent than meet him face to face, or pay a band of ruffians to stab him to death in an alley?*

All Davy knew for sure was that Hartung had

found Deanna MacPartland lying dazed in the charred ruins of her family's cabin, the scalped bodies of her parents outside, when she had been barely sixteen years old. And then this man, ostensibly her benefactor, had taken the young beauty straight to the bawdy house of Mrs. Lucretia Eaton, where she had worked ever since, in what amounted to a state of indenture.

The Kansan frowned as he sipped his coffee, thinking sardonically of Deanna MacPartland's "benefactors." He recalled Deanna's innocent remarks to the effect that Mrs. Eaton was holding the bulk of her earnings "in safekeeping."

As he put down his coffee cup Davy Watson shook his head. *I ain't got no doubt now but them two is in cahoots*, he told himself, reaching reflexively down to the holstered Walker Colt which he no longer wore.

I'm startin' to see this whole business in a different light. This here Hartung fella is more'n likely tryin' to do with Deanna what that Harvey Yancey done with the three Mudree sisters, back in San Francisco. That sum'bitch prob'ly means to sell her off, an' turn a right big profit on the deal.

Suddenly he took a deep breath, and then felt a warm glow in the pit of his stomach.

By Gad! he exclaimed to himself, sitting up in his seat so abruptly that he nearly overturned the pot of coffee he had been reaching for. *That means Hartung prob'ly forced Deanna to go to St. Louis with him, that she didn't have no say in the matter.*

Pouring himself a second cup of the rich, steaming coffee of the Southern Hotel, the Kansan began to smile.

An' if that's the case, he thought, a joyful, expectant feeling now warming him like a bonfire made of burning corn husks on a frosty fall night in Kansas, *there's still a good chance that Deanna was a-waitin' fer me when Hartung lit off to St. Louis with her.*

His smile now flashed across the length of the dining room, cutting through the gloom of the gray morning like a steamboat light slicing through the river mists.

An' if that's the case, the Kansan went on exultantly, love and hope surging forth in his heart, leaping up like the flames of a newly kindled fire, *mebbe things is still like they was when I rid out of Hawkins Fork more'n two years back. Mebbe she still loves me!*

Davy took a sip from his coffee cup. While he was now reassured, and the chill mists of fear which enshrouded his heart ever since he had received the bad news at Lucretia Eaton's were dispelled by the bright flame of his rekindled hopes, the Kansan was sobered by the thought that he still had to get Deanna MacPartland away from John Hartung—a potential enemy about whom he knew less than nothing.

He wished that Soaring Hawk were by his side now, ready to stand up with him when the going got rough. It would be a good thing, he realized with a wry smile, to have a partner for the coming encounter, someone to cover his back and cover his tracks, someone he could trust with his life as he dealt with cutthroats and desperadoes.

The Kansan was not a man of the city, and in places as large and populous as San Francisco and

St. Louis, he was somewhat intimidated. At home in an Indian camp or on the open plains, Davy Watson had never felt truly comfortable within the crowded confines of cities.

He had, however, learned much in his travels and intended to put this knowledge to good use, trusting no one and keeping his own counsel until he felt safe and secure once more. His Walker Colt was in the kit bag he had brought to St. Louis, and he carried a throwing knife in a sheath which was strapped to his right ankle. The Henry rifle which had accompanied him back and forth across the American West remained beside his saddle and saddlebags, kept for safekeeping by the Southern Hotel.

Somewhat reassured by this inventory of his weapons, but wishing at the same time that he had something to make up for the absence of his Henry, the Kansan looked up and saw a familiar face.

There across the dining room, just crossing the threshold, was a man with whom he had ridden many months before, the man who had, in fact, been his companion and guide in the bustling red-light districts of Virginia City and San Francisco.

"Davy Watson, is that you?" the man called out in a clear tenor voice as the Kansan slowly rose from his seat. "My stars, it is!" he cried, throwing wide his arms and smiling warmly as he made for Davy's table.

"Judas Priest," Davy Watson murmured, overcome with surprise, his ears burning as he stood up. "Marcus Haverstraw, of all people!"

"How are you, Davy?" Haverstraw asked

excitedly, as he came up to the Kansan and began to clap him on the back. "How's the man who gave me my greatest story?"

The newspaperman beamed at the Kansan. His brown eyes gleamed merrily in the thin oval of his face, and his wide smile accentuated the man's long, pumphandle nose. And when he took off his hat, it was to reveal a full head of curly brown hair.

Davy took the reporter's hand and squeezed it, grinning broadly as he remembered the adventures wherein he, Soaring Hawk and Marcus Haverstraw had finally rescued the three Mudree sisters from white slavery on San Francisco's Barbary Coast.

"Did yer story git read by lots of folks?" he asked the newspaperman.

"Land sakes, yes!" Marcus Haverstraw replied enthusiastically. "I scooped all the San Francisco tabloids, and knocked 'em dead back in Virginia City. Why, the story was so sensational that offers for my services began to come in from all quarters—even from the *New York Herald* itself," he told the Kansan, referring to the newspaper which represented to him the pinnacle of American journalism.

"That's the nut you allus wanted to crack, wasn't it?" Davy asked, recalling the reporter's ambition.

Marcus nodded. "It certainly was," he replied with a wry grin. "But that wasn't to be the place for me, it turned out."

"You turned it down?" the Kansan asked incredulously.

"That's right," the other told him. "I took a job with a San Francisco paper. . .so I could hang around and pay court to Della Casson."

"Della Casson," Davy whispered, suddenly recalling the black courtesan who had once saved his life. "Hot damn."

The reporter grinned, reminding him of how attracted the man had been to the Louisiana beauty.

"How is ol' Della?" he asked.

"She, ah, was. . .fine. . .last time I saw her," Marcus told him haltingly.

Davy stared at him. "The gunshot wound in her shoulder healed up all right, didn't it?"

The newspaperman nodded. "Oh, yes. . .although I've yet to see it," he added wistfully.

"Did ya stop courtin' her?" Davy asked.

"Oh no," was Marcus' hasty reply. "It's just that she decided to go back to New Orleans. Got word that her mother was very ill." He sighed. "Just when we were beginning to get acquainted."

"That's too bad," consoled Davy. "What brings ya to St. Louis?"

The newspaperman's face suddenly brightened. "I'm on my way to New Orleans, my friend. Just accepted a position on the *Daily Picayune* there. And soon I'll be able to resume my courtship of the beautiful Della, my Black Rose."

"Well, that's right nice, Marcus," Davy told his friend. "I'm happy fer ya."

"And what brings *you* to the Gateway City?"

The Kansan's expression changed to one of solemnity as he told the reporter of his search for Deanna MacPartland.

"The woman you love," Marcus Haverstraw

whispered, his eyes suddenly glittering as he leaned toward the Kansan. "The woman you love—stolen from you, and in the power of an unscrupulous rogue and panderer."

"Uh, somethin' like that," Davy Watson grunted back, a bit overwhelmed by the newspaperman's extravagant language.

"Roast me in hell for a printer's devil," Marcus Haverstraw whispered in an awed voice as they sat down at the table, "but I smell a whopper of a story here."

The Kansan reached out and poured the reporter a cup of coffee. "Just like ol' times, huh?" he said, grinning at Marcus.

Haverstraw gave him a wolfish smile. "You appear to be a veritable mine of newspaper copy, old friend. The journalist's delight. There seems to be a story in everything you do."

Davy was still grinning as he shook his head. "You never spent no time at the Watson farm, Marcus. Things is purty quiet there most of the time. Howsomever, when I'm on the trail, life does tend to git a mite lively."

"Tell me what you've been up to," the newspaperman said eagerly, reaching for his cup as he settled back in his seat.

The Kansan raised his big hands and held them out above the table. "Oh, I've been in a bunch of places since I left you, Marcus, ol' boy. An' none of them been 'zactly what a body'd speak of as dull."

"I'm all ears," the reporter said as he raised the cup to his lips.

Davy reached into his vest pocket and took out

the gold watch which had belonged to his late father. He opened its lid and peered down at the black Roman numerals upon its face. The time was eight minutes to eleven.

"Reckon I got the time," the Kansan told his friend, as he snapped the lid shut and put the watch back in his vest pocket. "Now, lemme see. What happened to me'n ol' Soaring Hawk after we left you in San Francisco?"

"How is the illustrious Indian?" asked Haverstraw.

Davy grinned, suddenly warmed by the thought of his Pawnee blood-brother. "Oh, he's right fine. Out somewhere on the plains, a-huntin' the buffalo with his people. I just come from the Pawnee camp myself. Spent a week there."

"My stars, you *do* have an exciting life," the reporter exclaimed. "Let me order a fresh pot of coffee, and you can tell me everything. "

The Kansan recounted all the adventures which he and Soaring Hawk had shared since the time they parted company with the reporter, of the trail that had led them down the length of California and into the territories of Arizona and New Mexico, and thence through the state of Texas, where their latest scrape had occurred.

He told Haverstraw of the men and women he had met: Geronimo and Cochise; Major Forbes, the man who had ordered fifty lashes laid on his back; Hutzleman, the bounty hunter, and Darrell Duppa, the man who gave Phoenix its name; Don Solomon Mirabal, the New Mexican *rico*, and his enemy, Bill Fanshaw, the Texas cattle baron;

141

Captain Haggerty and his Hellions, the wild bunch that had terrorized West Texas and the area south of the Rio Grande; T.C. Pritchett and John B. Loudermilk, the former Texas Rangers who stood beside the Kansan and Soaring Hawk in that deadly showdown in a small, East Texas town; and Bart Braden, the hard-riding, straight-shooting Texas ramrod who had been one of the most unusual men he'd ever known, his rescuer as well as the man who'd gunned him down.

Women also figured prominently in the account of the Kansan's adventures, causing Marcus Haverstraw's eyes to glitter even more as Davy described his loves. He told his friend of Consuela Delgado, the beautiful *Mexicana* he'd met in the settlement of Phoenix; of Cho-ko-le, the young Apache squaw who had been Soaring Hawk's lover in the hidden camp of Cochise; of Samantha Fanshaw, the tall, proud daughter of the cattle baron; and Raquel Mirabal, the hot-blooded eighteen-year-old for whom Bart Braden had precipitated a bloody range war between the Texas cattlemen and the New Mexican sheepmen. And there were others, too—all the women of the saloons, bawdy houses, and honkytonks on the long, circuitous trail which had led from the western metropolis of San Francisco to the Kansas town of Hawkins Fork.

"Gad, we'd make a fortune writing for the penny-dreadfuls!" Marcus Haverstraw exclaimed at the end of the Kansan's narrative. "You've certainly been busy since I last saw you."

The Kansan nodded. "It ain't been dull, Marcus," he agreed. "A mite *too* lively fer my taste, howsomever."

142

"If I had the time," the reporter told him, "I'd write it all down. Why, I'm sure that I could do for you what this Ned Buntline fellow is starting to do for Buffalo Bill."

"Bill Cody?" Davy asked. "Is some fella writin' 'bout him?"

"I'll say!" Marcus told him, pouring the Kansan another cup of coffee. "Ned Buntline is in the process of turning Bill Cody into a folk hero. He's creating a legend out of the man's exploits."

"Ain't that somethin'!" the Kansan exclaimed.

"When I left San Francisco, everyone was reading those little books of Buntline's—dime novels, they call 'em. My stars, but the man must be making a fortune, to say nothing of Bill Cody's earnings. He's got a 'Wild West' show, now."

"So Buffalo Bill's a national hero," Davy said through a wide smile. "Just like Tecumseh Sherman an' ol' U.S. Grant, huh?"

"That's right, my friend," the reporter said. "He's in the process of becoming a figure of folklore, just like Paul Bunyan and Johnny Appleseed. Nothing less."

Davy's expression changed to one of extreme solemnity. "They ain't gonna be no more buff'lo in a few more years, Marcus," he told the reporter. "Bill's associates been slaughterin' 'em like there's no tomorrow." He shook his head. "It's greedy, an' it ain't right."

Marcus Haverstraw sighed. "Well, at least they'll live on in legend, in the hearts and minds of the American people."

"Bullcorn!" grunted the Kansan, scowling at his friend's rhetoric. "That ain't much comfort to the buffalo."

Marcus smiled wryly and nodded his head. "No, I don't suppose it is."

"There's big money in killin' buffalo these days," Davy told Marcus.

"Well, that's business for you—what Adam Smith called *laissez-faire* capitalism."

"Lessee what?" asked a puzzled Davy Watson.

"*Laissez-faire* capitalism," the newspaperman repeated. "*Laissez-faire* is a French term. What that means essentially, as I understand it, is a form of unrestricted free enterprise."

"Free enterprise bein' big business?" the Kansan asked.

"Yep. That's exactly what it is in this sense. And *laissez-faire* means that government, or any other agency, should not presume to interfere in the business of business."

"The business of business," Davy mused, his attention caught by the phrase.

"Oh, that's a saying," Marcus Haverstraw told him. " 'The business of business. . .is business.' "

"What the hell does *that* mean?"

"Well, another way of putting it is, 'The business of business is profit.' "

Davy Watson nodded. "I can understand that, right enough." He cast a sour look at Marcus Haverstraw. "But them greedy sum'bitches don't realize one thing."

"What's that?" the reporter asked.

"It's like a snake swallyin' its own tail," the Kansan told him. "Kill off all the buffalo, an' one day you're out of business. To make a dollar today, they're sellin' out the future."

Marcus nodded, a somber expression on his thin

face. "They have a responsibility to those who come after. . .and they're neglecting it."

The Kansan scowled and shook his head. "Them dumb suckers is cuttin' their own throats."

"And ours, as well, I'm afraid," added Marcus.

"They could learn from the Injuns, if they had a mind to," Davy informed him. "Them folks knows how to care for the things of nature. But the buff'lo killers is a-workin' to wipe them out as well, 'cause they git in the way."

"Whereas we do enjoy the manifold material benefits of capitalism," Marcus reflected. "I suspect what you have just told me is a revelation of its darker side."

Davy nodded.

"And there *is* a dark and cruel side to industrialism and capitalism," Marcus went on. "We see it in the poor working conditions of the factories, and in the degrading institution of child labor. The poet William Blake had a vision of industrialism consuming the people—in his poem, *Jerusalem*, I believe it was. His works are full of fearsome images of grinding turbines, hellish furnaces, and black, belching smokestacks. 'Dark, satanic mills,' that's what he wrote."

" 'Dark, satanic mills,' " the Kansan repeated. "That's sure a strong way of puttin' it."

"Blake felt strongly about things. He was a remarkable and visionary poet."

"Marcus," Davy said, reaching across the table to squeeze the reporter's forearm, "I could use another set of eyes an' ears, an' a good right arm when I go a-lookin' fer Deanna MacPartland in this here place called Gridley's. Are ya with me?"

The reporter's eyes met his. "You bet I am, friend," he said fervently. "Friendship, excitement, high adventure, and one hell of a good newspaper story. Who could ask for more than that?"

Davy Watson smiled at the man's limitless enthusiasm. "You happen to be packin' a pistol or a knife these days, Marcus?" he asked casually.

"Ah, no. I'm not," the reporter replied sheepishly.

"Well, then, le's take us a li'l stroll through St. Louis, 'til we come to a gunsmith's shop."

Marcus Haverstraw stared at the Kansan with wide eyes. "You're, ah, going to purchase a. . .weapon. . .for me?" he asked haltingly.

Davy grinned at the reporter, amused by the way that Marcus's face had suddenly been drained of all color.

"Reckon so," he replied casually. "Thought I'd pick us up a derringer apiece. Kind of a pistol we can keep concealed."

"This could really be dangerous, eh?" Marcus asked in a thin voice, raising his coffee cup with a hand that shook.

The Kansan fought to stifle a grin. "Mebbe so, mebbe no," he told the apprehensive journalist. "But think of the story you'll git, ol' hoss. How many pistol-packin' ree-porters is there, anyhow?"

Marcus Haverstraw gulped. "You have a point there," he answered in a faintly quavering voice. "Most newspapermen go forth armed only with pad, pencil, and their mother wit. And most of them—excepting those brave souls who report the course of a war from the front lines—risk their

146

lives only in the battle against demon rum. John Barleycorn is the newspaperman's prime adversary—editors excepted, of course."

"Well, here's a chance to distinguish yerself from yer fellow ree-porters," the Kansan told Marcus.

This elicited a sickly grin from him.

"Now, don't you worry none, Marcus," Davy told him. "You done distinguished yerself already, back in San Francisco, when ya plugged that there Bertram Brown fella, an' saved my life."

"Oh, *that*," Marcus said in a strangled whisper, going white in the face as he recalled shooting the gambler who had been slashing away like a maniac at a wounded Davy Watson with a broken champagne bottle.

"You ain't forgot, have ya?"

"Oh no," the reporter assured the Kansan, a sickly expression coming over his face. "That was my baptism by fire. I'll *never* forget that."

"So you ain't no virgin yer own self, when it comes to dangerous dealin's," Davy told his friend. "An' anyway, I'll do my level best to conduct this here business in a peaceable manner, I promise you that, ol' hoss."

The Kansan stood up. "Well, what d'ya say, Marcus? Are ya with me?"

Marcus Haverstraw stood up, took a deep breath, and held out his right hand. "All the way, old pal," he told Davy. "All the way."

"C'mon, le's take us a li'l stroll through this here Gateway City," Davy told the reporter, as he began to walk away from the table, "an' pick us up a brace of derringers."

The newspaperman cleared his throat loudly as he fell into step beside the Kansan. "Ah, yep. derringers it is."

Davy grinned.

"Set 'em up, bartender," Marcus Haverstraw said to him under his breath. "Pistols for two."

"The first slug's on me," the Kansan added gleefully, falling into the spirit of the moment.

"The subject seems to trigger a slew of associations, doesn't it?" Marcus punned back.

"Reckon we'll get served with shotglasses?" the Kansan went on.

"Not bad," the newspaperman told him admiringly. "Not bad for a cowboy."

"Say, how's Mark Twain doin' these days?" Davy asked. "What's the ol' scalawag up to?"

"Well," Marcus Haverstraw said as he and the Kansan stepped out of the dining room of the Southern Hotel, "I recently heard that he's writing a book about his travels in Europe. Calling it *Innocents Abroad*, or something like that.

"A book, huh?"

"Yep," the journalist replied, raising his eyebrows as he did. "But you know, writing a book is a whole different kettle of fish than writing for the newspapers." He shook his head emphatically. "I just hope old Sam Clemens has it in him to make a go of it."

"That there's your boy," said Warren, the mustachioed, curly-headed man with red hair whom Lucretia Eaton had sent to St. Louis in order to warn Hoyt Altgelder, the proprietor of the

148

establishment known as Gridley's. "I don't know who that skinny fella with him is," Warren went on, pointing a long finger out the window of the second-story office, "but that big young un's your man."

Hoyt Altgelder chomped on the expensive cigar between his teeth as he stared down at Davy Watson and Marcus Haverstraw. "So that's him, huh?" he grunted, sending a cloud of smoke out . the window.

He was a florid, beefy man of middle height, with full dark mustache and eyebrows, bald except for a fringe of hair that ran around the sides and back of his head. Dressed expensively, the man wore a small diamond ring on his little finger and sported a mouthful of gold fillings.

"Lucretia done warned John that jasper'd be trouble, if he ever came back." Warren raised his hands in the air as he said this. "Not that anybody ever thought he'd be back after two full years away. We figgered he was dead. Thought there wasn't a snowball's chance in hell of that boy's returnin'. John was sure of it too. Watson was just a kid, goin' out after a band of killers like the Landry Gang. Nobody thought he had a chance of comin' back to Kansas."

"Well, he come back," Hoyt Altgelder growled, mopping his forehead with a fine linen handkerchief. "An' he don't look like no kid to me. We got to deal with him."

"What you gonna do?" asked Warren, his face lighting up at this.

"Get rid of them two fellas as soon as possible. 'At's what I figger," Altgelder told him.

"How you gonna do it?" Warren asked eagerly.

Altgelder took the cigar out of his mouth. "I thought I'd let you figger that out," he told the other man.

"That's right kind of you, Hoyt," the lanky redhead said to Hoyt Altgelder, a smile on his thin lips and a glitter in his pale blue eyes. "I could use the exercise."

SIX

John Hartung And
The Butchers

"Mighty big place," Davy Watson remarked to Marcus Haverstraw, as the two men entered Gridley's and made their way to the long, hand-carved bar.

"Well, St. Louis is a big town, my friend," Marcus told him, smiling conspicuously as his eyes darted back and forth over the faces of the men in the huge room.

"Looks purty well-to-do," the Kansan went on as they drew near to the bar. "Folks seems to be drinkin' an' spendin' like they was no tomorrow."

"Well, it *is* Saturday night," the newspaperman reminded him. "And that's the night when everyone comes into town with an eye to whooping it up."

Davy nodded. "Yer right, Marcus. Why, I been on the trail so long that I plumb forgot what day it was." The Kansan smiled as he heard the labored sounds of an upright piano, and a fruity baritone voice singing the popular sentimental song, *Drunkard's Daughter*.

"Oh, I think I'm going to puke," Marcus Haverstraw said disgustedly as he saw the tearful crowd which had gathered reverently around the piano player.

> *"I'm alone, I'm alone,*
> *My friends have all fled;*
> *My father's a drunkard,*
> *My mother is dead.*
> *I'm a lone little child,*
> *I wander and weep*
> *For the voice of my mother*
> *To sing me to sleep."*

"Shit, I can't stand it!" growled Marcus, a man whose aversion to sentimental songs bordered on the pathological. And before the Kansan could stop him, he had made his way over to the piano.

Davy Watson reached him just after the song had ended, at which time the newspaperman had thrust a number of greenbacks into the piano player's hand, and then proceeded to plunk himself down on the stool, forcing the other man off.

Marcus tossed off a series of glissandos and smiled at the surrounding crowd like a man with lockjaw. The fiendish gleam in his eyes told Davy Watson that this would indeed be an unusual performance. And in a moment, when the newspaperman began to sing, the Kansan's suspicions were fully confirmed.

> *"What is this that I can see*
> *With icy hands taking hold of me?*
> *"I am Death and none can't tell,*
> *I open doors to Heaven and Hell."*

Haverstraw accompanied his piercing tenor and middling piano playing with a series of menacing gestures and ghastly facial expressions.

152

"I'll fix your feet so you can't walk,
I'll lock your jaws so you can't talk,
I'll close your eyes so you can't see,
This very hour come and go with me."

"Gawd, that's horrible!" growled an old riverman who stood to Davy Watson's right. "Sounds
like a Chinaman bein' tortured."

"Or a hawg gittin' its balls cut off," volunteered
a farmer behind the Kansan.

The listeners all winced as Marcus Haverstraw
sang the chorus of the eerie song, repeating it over
and over.

"Oh Death! O Death! O Death!
Please spare me over 'til another year."

"Somebody pop that fucker over the haid with a
spitoon!" roared a burly stevedore.

"O Death! O Death! O Death!
Please spare me over 'til another year."

"Git that varmint outta here!" some one else
roared, as a hardboiled egg crashed into the piano,
inches away from Marcus Haverstraw's head.

"Here, mister," quavered the terrified piano
player, handing the greenbacks to the newspaperman as he wriggled onto the stool. "Keep yer
money, an' git. They's gonna be a riot in here, if'n
you sing any more."

"C'mon, Marcus," Davy told his friend with a
grin. "The crowd in here's gittin' to resemble a
lynch mob."

153

"All right," Marcus Haverstraw sighed wearily, playing a last sombre chord as he stood up. "But anything's preferable to that mushy *Drunkard's Daughter*."

Boos and hisses accompanied Marcus back to the bar, where the Kansan ordered them a round of drinks.

"Our presence here ain't 'zactly no secret now, ol' hoss," the Kansan told him through a rueful smile.

"Sorry, Davy," Marcus apologized. "But those sentimental ballads make me want to puke."

The bartender came with their drinks.

"Say, fella," Marcus said cheerfully. "Where's Hoyt Altgelder? My name's Vince Dempsey, and I'm a friend of John Hartung's. He sent me to see Hoyt."

The bartender studied the two men before him for several moments before speaking. Then he said, "I'll go see if he's upstairs in his office."

"Well, I'll give you this, Marcus," Davy said before knocking back his hooker of rye. "You sure don't waste no time."

The reporter smiled grimly and hoisted his own glass. "We might as well get down to brass tacks, Cowboy." He turned to Davy and jerked a thumb in the direction of the piano. "Ah, now there's a good song."

"You can't never believe
What a young man tells you;
Unless he's on the gallows,
And wishing he was down."

"Your kinda song, huh?" Davy Watson asked as the bartender returned.

"Mister Altgelder'll see you gents now," the man told them, his eyes widening as Davy threw two silver dollars down onto the bar and ordered a second round of drinks.

"One for good luck, eh?" the newspaperman whispered nervously to the Kansan as the bartender made his way down the bar.

"Just keep yer wits about ya when we go into this fella's office, Marcus," Davy cautioned. "I don't expect no trouble hereabouts, but y'never can tell. 'Member what happened to us in San Francisco?"

Marcus Haverstraw shivered. "Oh God," he moaned, "that's something I'd rather forget. What a set-up that turned out to be—stalked by a bone-crushing ogre straight out of Grimm's Fairy Tales, and ambushed in bed by a sharpshooting gambler."

"Well, keep that in mind, an' you'll have a good appreciation of our present situation."

"For heaven's sake," protested the newspaperman. "I certainly hope that's not going to be the course of our relationship—that every time I meet up with you, I have to *shoot* someone!"

The Kansan was grinning broadly now. "I sure as hell hope not," he replied, lifting his hooker of rye off the bar.

"Well, here's to safety, compromise and the quiet life," Marcus toasted, raising his glass in the air.

155

Clink. The glasses came together with a sharp sound that sliced through the babel of the crowd in much the same way that the sound of a piccolo cuts through the deeper, massed voices of a full orchestra.

They drank, and then thumped their glasses down on the bar, after which they turned and began to make their way through the noisy, high-spirited crowd which populated Gridley's.

Hoyt Altgelder was smoking a thick black cigar and sitting back in a gilded chair behind a massive desk whose sides were covered with baroque carvings, as Davy Watson and Marcus Haverstraw entered the man's office on the second floor of the building which housed his establishment.

The beefy, balding man hooked a thumb in the pocket of his brocaded silk vest, took the cigar out of his mouth, and said, "What can I do for you, gents? You here on business?"

"Yep," the Kansan replied succinctly. "We're lookin' to palaver with John Hartung."

"I see," Altgelder grunted, thrusting the dark, damp end of the cigar back between his glittering, gold-filled teeth. "John ain't here now, but me'n him do some business ev'ry now and again, so I'm sure to see him before too long. How 'bout if I give him a message from you gents?"

"Sounds fine to me," sighed Marcus with obvious relief.

Davy Watson nodded. "I'd be obliged if'n you was to tell Mr. Hartung that I've got a deal fer him, one that would stand to make him a pile of gold."

The Kansan saw that Hoyt Altgelder's eyes were glittering as the man raised his bushy eyebrows and chomped down hard on his cigar, sending forth a dense cloud of smoke which momentarily veiled his features.

"Care to be more specific 'bout yer offer, Mister. . .?"

"Watson's my handle. An' my friend here's Mr. Dempsey,'" he told him, using the name which Marcus had assumed earlier.

He reached down into the pocket of his jacket and came up with the sack of Boise nuggets. It contained half the amount he had brought back to Kansas; the rest of the gold was in his mother's keeping.

The sack was still of a considerable size, and the Kansan hefted it in his hand, watching Hoyt Altgelder's eyes dance as they followed this action. Then he opened it and spilled some of the gleaming nuggets into his palm.

"This here's gold, come from the Boise Basin," Davy told Altgelder. "It's worth thousands of dollars. An' I'm willin' to give it all to John Hartung," here he paused and looked Hoyt Altgelder right in the eye, ". . .an' other interested parties, providin' he gives me one thing he's holdin'."

"And what might that be?" the beefy man asked, his voice gone suddenly hoarse.

"He's got a young woman name of Deanna MacPartland with 'im," Davy told the proprietor of Gridley's, still looking him straight in the eye. "An' if he lets me have 'er—*peaceable-like*," he went on, stressing the last two words, "this gold is all his. . .fair 'n clear."

Hoyt Altgelder took the cigar out of his mouth

and smiled his gold-toothed smile up at the Kansan. "Well, I'm sure John Hartung will be interested to hear yer offer, Mr. Watson. I'll convey it to him as soon as possible. Where are you and your friend staying, sir?"

"We're at the Southern Hotel," Davy told him as he put back the gold.

Altgelder nodded. "I'm sure John'll be in touch with me in the next few days. Care for a drink, gents?"

The Kansan shook his head. "No thank ya, Mr. Altgelder. Me'n Mr. Dempsey has got to skeedaddle. We got us a heap of things to do."

The Kansan and Marcus Haverstraw sat tight for the next few days, wandering through St. Louis by day, and sleeping with pistols beneath their pillows by night. It was Davy's hope that John Hartung would agree to his terms and hand Deanna over to him without a fight; but his common sense—abetted by that of the reporter—told him that Altgelder's and Lucretia Eaton's "business associate" would probably keep her and make a play for the gold, as well.

"I wisht I knew what this Hartung galoot looked like," Davy told Marcus as he turned off the gas lamp in their hotel room.

"Well, I expect you'll get to see him soon enough," the newspaperman groaned as he slid between the bedsheets.

"Yep, I reckon," agreed Davy Watson. "I'm right curious to see that ol' boy . . . An' I'm right eager to see Deanna again."

"I certainly know what you mean, old man," Marcus Haverstraw commiserated. "I'm, ah, somewhat anxious to gaze once more upon the beauteous form and visage of Della Casson."

Davy sat down on his own bed. "Damn, you're really stuck on that gal, ain't'cha, Marcus?"

The reporter made a face in the darkness like that of an amorous bloodhound. "That is a fact, my friend. I certainly am stuck on her. Do you blame me?"

Davy recalled the pantherine grace and beauty of the Louisiana courtesan. . .and her considerable amatory accomplishments. "No sir, I don't," he told Marcus. "Ol' Della's one hell of a woman."

Marcus sighed. "Well, she's back in New Orleans, and that's where I'm heading, once we conclude this business of yours, David Lee. We, ah, came close to being lovers while she was convalescing in San Francisco, y'know. And this time, I mean to press my suit and lay siege to the citadel of her heart."

"Well, I hope ya git together with Della, Marcus."

"Ah, yes," the newspaperman whispered back. " 'Tis a consummation devoutly to be wished, as the Bard of Avon has said."

"Y'know, me'n Soaring Hawk had us a big discussion 'bout Macbeth not so long ago," Davy told Marcus.

"My stars," the reporter exclaimed. "What were Mr. Hawk's views on the play?"

"He felt that ol' Macbeth done got just what he deserved. An' Lady Macbeth, too—he calls 'er Bloody Hands. Ain't no way, he told me, that a warrior can murder his own chief an' git away with it. He also called Lady Macbeth a real tough squaw. Said she was like an Apache woman.''

"You know," Marcus told him, "that would make a terribly interesting article for the Eastern tabloids. To tell Soaring Hawk the plots of Shakespeare's plays, and then—"

A knock on the door interrupted him.

"Who is it?" the Kansan called out, sitting up in his bed and whipping out the Walker Colt which lay beneath his pillow.

"Bellboy," a piping voice replied. "Got a message for Mister Watson."

"I think this what we been waitin' fer," Davy told Marcus as he got out of bed and tiptoed over to the door, Colt in hand.

The Kansan opened the door suddenly and stood to one side, holding his Walker Colt up against the inside of the doorpost. After several seconds he peered around the doorframe and saw a small, teenaged bellboy staring up at him with wide eyes.

"Here y'are, sir," the lad said nervously, handing the Kansan a letter.

"Thanks, son," he told the bellboy, reaching over to the chest of drawers and picking up two-bits for the lad's tip. Then he shut the door and made his way over to the bed, as Marcus Haverstraw struck a Lucifer and proceeded to light the gas lamp.

The Kansan opened the envelope and proceeded to read the note enclosed within it.

" 'Mr. Watson,' " he read. " 'Your terms are acceptable to me. Please be at the address given below at ten o'clock tomorrow night, and we will *be able to transact our business. Cordially yours, John Hartung.'* "

"Sounds good, Davy," Marcus Haverstraw told him. "But how do you feel about parting with all that gold?"

"Hell, Marcus. If'n it gits me Deanna back without no trouble, it's money well spent." He stared at the address below John Hartung's signature. "I'm goin' down to the desk an' find out just where this place is located."

When Davy returned to the room, his friend saw that the Kansan was no longer smiling.

"What is it?" Marcus asked anxiously.

"I ain't sure we're in the clear yet," he told the reporter. "This here place is called Dawson's warehouse, an' it's down by the docks in a real outta-the-way spot."

"Hmm. That *does* sound suspicious."

"I reckon. So keep yer powder dry, an' yer pistols loaded. It ain't over yet."

The newspaperman groaned. "I was afraid of that."

"Think of the story you'll git," Davy shot back.

"Damn the story," Marcus croaked. "I'm worried about my ass, right now!"

The moon above Dawson's warehouse was pale and anemic, smothered by fast-moving banks of storm clouds, a feeble moon which looked as if it would not last the night out.

Davy Watson and Marcus Haverstraw walked along the Mississippi dockside under this sickly, smothered moon, moving toward the warehouse

161

with slow and deliberate steps.

"My stars," Marcus whispered. "This is spookier than anything I've ever read in a Gothic novel. And when that poor excuse for a moon goes behind the clouds, it becomes darker than a murderer's thoughts."

"If'n that's the case," Davy told him softly, "use yer ears. Let 'em substitute fer yer eyes. That's how the Injuns does their stalkin'."

"I see," gulped the reporter.

"Here it is," the Kansan informed him.

The warehouse was now a big and menacing shape that loomed above them in the dim light. Davy had just made out the faded sign on its roof before the clouds obscured the moon once more, plunging all of St. Louis into darkness.

"Mr. Watson?" a voice called out from the entrance to the warehouse.

"It's me," Davy called back, his trail-sharpened eyes barely making out the form of a man standing in the doorway of the hulking building.

"Come in, sir," the voice called out once more. "I've been waiting for you."

"Who's there?" he called out into the darkness. "I can't see you," he lied.

"It's me, Mr. Watson. John Hartung."

"Coming," Davy called back. And then he whispered to Marcus. "Git ready, ol' hoss. This is it."

"Well," Marcus Haverstraw whispered back gamely. "If I'm still with you at the conclusion of this business, the drinks are on me."

"No, they're on me," the Kansan told him. "You bought 'em after the pistol duel at Virginia City. 'Member?"

162

"Oh yes," Marcus recalled. "When you downed Malcolm Shove."

Again the moon shone, and Davy Watson proceeded to look around and inspect the condition of the pier which housed Dawson's warehouse. Its beams, boards and pilings were dried and rotten, indicating to the Kansan that the place was not kept up, and therefore probably unused at present.

"I don't like the look of it," he murmured between clenched teeth. "Watch yerself, Marcus."

"Come straight ahead, Mr. Watson," John Hartung called out. As the Kansan crossed the threshold of Dawson's warehouse, he heard the nervous breathing of Marcus Haverstraw behind him.

The pale moon shone through a number of holes in the roof, casting a spotty light across the floor of the huge structure. When his eyes had become accustomed to the gloom, Davy saw that the building had been gutted by fire. And since he smelled no trace of that conflagration, he decided that the building burned down some time ago, and had probably been long deserted.

"Over here, sir," John Hartung called out from the shadows at the far side of the warehouse.

Well, it looks like I'm finally gonna get to take a gander at this fella, the Kansan told himself as he and Marcus drew near to the shadowy figure.

Taking a deep breath as he and Marcus Haverstraw came up to the man, the Kansan's heart began to beat faster as he realized that Deanna MacPartland must be near. . .waiting for him somewhere in the shadows.

"Forgive the secrecy, gentlemen," John

Hartung told his guests. "But it is necessary for me to keep my presence in St. Louis a secret. A temporary financial inconvenience."

Taking the man's measure, the Kansan nodded.

"Such precautions are, alas, for the moment necessary," Hartung went on in an apologetic tone of voice. He looked nervously from side to side. "Are you gentlemen armed?" he asked suddenly.

Davy and Marcus exchanged sidelong glances.

The Kansan shook his head. "Nope," he replied. "Didn't seem to be no need, whilst in St. Louis."

The man smiled a cold, cruel smile.

"Well, I am," Hartung told the two men, suddenly reaching down inside his swallow-tail coat and coming up with a sixshooter.

"Give me the gold," he ordered, leveling the gun at Davy's chest.

"I want to see Deanna MacPartland first," the Kansan told him angrily.

John Hartung sneered at Davy. "You dumb hick. You really expected her to be here, didn't you?"

"I resent his being called a hick," Marcus Haverstraw barked angrily at the man, causing him to turn his head.

"Shut yer trap, an' raise your hands, Mister," John Hartung growled. " 'Cause I ain't in a mood to waste time."

Then, as the Kansan gingerly lifted the sack of Boise gold out of his inside coat pocket, the man said something that made his blood run cold.

"Matter of fact," Hartung told him, "I'm in a real big hurry to get back to that pretty li'l filly."

He looked beyond Davy and Marcus. "So I'm just gonna let these here friends of mine take care of you two boys." He gestured impatiently with his big Smith and Wesson. "C'mon, hand over the gold."

Davy glanced at Marcus, who was in the process of raising his hands, inch by inch. Then the two companions slowly turned their heads.

Behind them, padding stealthily in the shadows, were the forms of six big men. And when the moon's deathly light shone once more, it was reflected on the blades of six long knives.

"Who are these men?" squawked Marcus.

Hartung smiled his cold, cruel smile again. "They're a bunch of local St. Louis boys, made a name for themselves on the waterfront. They call 'em the Butchers." Then he scowled at Davy Watson. "The gold. Give it to me."

Marcus Haverstraw's big hand came up as John Hartung said this, and the Kansan saw that there was a derringer concealed in its palm. Then Hartung began to glance at the reporter, while still holding his hand out for Davy's sack of gold.

"Hartung!" the Kansan whispered sharply, causing the man to turn back to him.

Crack!

Marcus's derringer flared briefly, and cracked with a sharp, ringing sound as the newspaperman fired pointblank into the face of John Hartung.

"Whuuuh!" was all that John Hartung said, his face scorched by gunpowder and a small dark hole in the space between his eyebrows.

By the time the body hit the floor of the warehouse, the Kansan had spun around, dropped to his knees, and was in the process of leveling his own derringer at the nearest of the knife-wielding bully-boys who advanced on them from the darkness.

Crack! Just as the man went into a crouch, his long knife held out before him, Davy Watson let him have the first of his derringer's two slugs smack in the forehead.

Crack! Gunpowder stung his face as Marcus Haverstraw fired off his second shot from the hip, causing one of the Butchers to scream and start backward. By this time, the man whom the Kansan had shot keeled over and thudded onto the boards of the floor.

"Git 'em!"

"Quick—git 'em now!" screamed the four remaining assassins, recovering from their initial shock and charging at Davy and Marcus while they brandished their long, sharp blades.

Crack! Davy's last shot caught the foremost Butcher in the neck, causing the man to spin around, clutch at his throat, and emit a shrill, gurgling scream. But the man had already thrown himself at the Kansan, and his body crashed clumsily into Davy, taking the Kansan to the ground beneath him.

"Judas Priest!" the Kansan swore, struggling to free himself from the thrashing, wounded man.

By the time he had rolled the assassin off, the other Butchers were upon him and Marcus. The one whom Marcus had shot was only winged in the arm, and had already recovered sufficiently to bend down and pick up the knife in his good hand. And once he had thrown himself back into the fray, Davy Watson and Marcus Haverstraw would be facing four big and desperate men, in a fight for their lives.

The Kansan was on his hands and knees now, reaching down to his right ankle and looking up at the same time. Suddenly he recoiled reflexively, as a booted foot came straight at his head.

"Unhhh!" he grunted, barely able to turn his head before the Butcher's kick landed.

Davy saw lights flash in the darkness and felt a stab of pain in his temple a moment later, as he fell backward heavily to the floorboards. Then the man who had kicked him gave out with a blood-curdling roar of triumph and hurled himself through the air, knife in hand, at the Kansan. . . .

Whi-i-i-shhh, went the assassin's blade, as it whistled past Marcus Haverstraw's chin, the reporter having thrown himself backward just in time to avoid having his throat cut. When he hit the ground, Marcus immediately began to propel himself backward in a desperate bid for time, as he scuttled and kicked to get away from the slasher. But a sudden obstacle stopped him cold, as Marcus bumped into the body of John Hartung, the man he had shot. And then, looking up in terror, Marcus Haverstraw gasped as he saw the Butcher coming at him, his long knife gleaming in the moonlight, a cold smile upon his lips and death in his eyes. . . .

"*YAAAH*!" screamed the desperado who had thrown himself upon Davy Watson. The Kansan had caught the wrist of the Butcher's knife hand, and surprised the man by having the point of his own knife ready for him. The man's kick had knocked Davy Watson on his back, but the Kansan had come up with the blade he kept sheathed at his right ankle, and had it waiting as the assassin flew through the air at him.

He thrust the man off immediately, before the Butcher was even able to react physically to the knife in his guts. As he rolled over, Davy suddenly wondered whether or not Marcus Haverstraw was still alive.

BOOM! BOOM!

Two thunderous roars split the air, and the Butcher who had come at the fallen reporter suddenly shot back and disappeared into the shadows, where the heavy thud of a falling body was to be heard a moment later.

Marcus had been stopped by the corpse of John Hartung, and at that point had rolled over and begun to scramble to his feet. And as he did, the newspaperman's hand came into contact with the Smith and Wesson .44 which Hartung had dropped as Marcus's slug tore into his brain.

Two of the Butchers remained standing, and both of them were about to converge upon the Kansan when the roar of the Smith and Wesson had stopped them in their tracks. But the Kansan did not stop, and his right arm swung round in a wide, backhanded arc, the keen blade of his knife slicing through the windpipe of the foremost assassin like a cutter through a piece of soft cheese.

The remaining Butcher, the one whom Marcus had winged earlier, screeched like a frightened owl, threw his knife up into the air and spun on his heel, fleeing the scene with all possible haste.

BOOM! BOOM! BOOM! Marcus fired off three

shots at the departing assassins.

"Oh, shit!" the reporter swore, when he saw that none of his shots had found their mark.

Pausing to catch his breath, the Kansan took his knife by the tip of its blade, and hefted it. A second later he squinted into the shadows, fixing his keen eyes on the back of the fleeing Butcher. Then he threw the knife.

The man uttered a short, grunting scream and tumbled face-down onto the boards, awkwardly clawing at the blade of the long knife which had lodged itself between his shoulder blades.

"Holy Hannah," whispered an awed Marcus Haverstraw. "Where on earth did you learn to do that?"

"From Soaring Hawk," the Kansan told him. "He's right good with a knife."

"Oh, yes," breathed the reporter, suddenly recalling what the Pawnee had done to Harvey Yancey, back in San Francisco. "Yes, indeed."

"Oh, damn," muttered Davy Watson, stricken by the sudden realization that John Hartung, the man he had come to St. Louis to find, lay dead on the floor before him. . .and he hadn't the slightest idea where Deanna MacPartland might be.

"Well, anyway," he said suddenly, starting toward the body of John Hartung, "lemme take a gander at this hombre."

As he drew near, the Kansan saw that the corpse smiled with the rictus of death, and stared up at the roof of Dawson's warehouse with glassy, sightless eyes. Those eyes were pale blue, and John Hartung had red curly hair and a riverboat gambler's pencil mustache.

"Judas Priest," the Kansan exclaimed in a whisper, suddenly casting a wide-eyed glance at Marcus Haverstraw's pale face. "This ain't the body of John Hartung!"

SEVEN

New Orleans Showdown

"Hey, you can't go up there!" warned the bouncer who blocked the staircase which led up to the second story of Gridley's, but the Kansan laid him out with one punch.

"Damn, but you've got a wicked right hand," Marcus Haverstraw said admiringly as they went upstairs. "That was a prizefighter's punch, Davy."

A moment later the companions stood before the door to Hoyt Altgelder's office, which the Kansan promptly proceeded to kick in.

"What the hell—" Altgelder bawled, looking up from the pile of greenbacks he had been counting at his desk. And at the sight of an angry Davy Watson, rapidly advancing upon him with drawn Walker Colt, the man's mouth hung open, and the ubiquitous cigar which he held in it fell onto the blotter of his desk.

It was replaced almost immediately by the long, cold barrel of the Kansan's Walker Colt. Hoyt Altgelder gagged as Davy Watson thrust the weapon's barrel deep into his mouth and cocked the trigger.

"I want some straight answers, Altgelder," Davy said in a low, cold voice. "An' if just one of 'em don't ring true, you're gon' be swallyin' some lead."

"Aa-aaak," was all that Altgelder was able to say by way of reply.

Davy slowly withdrew the gunbarrel from the man's mouth. Altgelder was sweating profusely now, and his face had gone white as a new bedsheet on a Dutch housewife's washline.

"Fella who posed as John Hartung was one of Lucretia Eaton's boys," the Kansan told him. "I done recognized the man." He stared hard into Hoyt Altgelder's eyes. "Even with a hole in his head." Altgelder began to cough. "You people's all in cahoots, ain't ya?" Davy asked when he had stopped.

The proprietor of Gridley's began to nod slowly, as the Kansan rested the end of the gunbarrel on the tip of his nose.

"An' them Butcher-Boy friends of yours have done their last piece of carvin', Altgelder. We're here to tell ya that, as well." The Kansan tapped the barrel of the Walker Colt against the tip of Altgelder's nose. "Yer just lucky I ain't in a killin' mood. Now, answer my questions."

"Anything you say, Mr. Watson," the man grunted in a voice that shook.

"Where's Deanna MacPartland? An' where's the real John Hartung?"

Just then heavy footfalls sounded outside the office, as a number of Gridley's bouncers and bartenders stormed up the stairs.

"It, ah, wouldn't be discreet to venture any farther, gentlemen," said Marcus Haverstraw, peering over the gaping maw of the late Warren's Smith and Wesson .44. "And don't bother to go back downstairs," the reporter added. "Just stand there, with your hands held high."

172

"Answer me, Altgelder!" Davy growled, as the men outside all raised their hands in the air.

The owner of Gridley's cleared his throat. "She's with John Hartung. . .in New Orleans."

"*New Orleans*!" the Kansan exploded. "How long they been there?"

"Just took the steamboat out yesterday," Hoyt Altgelder replied feebly.

Davy glowered at him. "What're they doin' in New Orleans? An' where can I find 'em?" He waggled the barrel of the gun impatiently under Altgelder's nose.

Choking with fear, the man gagged again.

"No tricks, Altgelder—or it's yer life. Answer me now!"

The Kansan heard a soft, pattering sound, and looked down to see drops of sweat hitting the surface of the green desk blotter. Altgelder was sweating like a pig and shaking like a man with St. Vitus' Dance.

"John's fixin' to sell her off to some Creole gent—fella name of Gaston Thibaudaux—fer big money," gasped Altgelder. "This Thibaudaux's got him a fancy pleasure palace on Royal Street. I reckon John's gonna dicker fer a real high price."

"All right," Davy said quietly, as he finally lowered the gun. "I believe you, Altgelder. An' I'm goin' down there now." His eyes narrowed as he stared down at John Hartung's associate. "But if'n you try one more trick, then you're a dead man." The Kansan leaned over the desk until his face was inches away from the corpse-white visage of Hoyt Altgelder. "An' that's a promise. Understand?"

"Aaak," gagged Altgelder, nodding vigorously

to the Kansan as he looked up with frightened eyes.

Davy Watson straightened up. "I'll be by this way when I come back," he told Altgelder. "An' you best not be here. Catch my drift?"

Still speechless, Hoyt Altgelder nodded again.

"All right," the Kansan said to Marcus Haverstraw, as he turned and made for the door. "Le's mosey on down to New Orleans."

Still holding his gun on the men outside, the reporter nodded. "That just happens to be my destination, old man," he told Davy Watson gleefully. "It seems that everything's working out just perfectly."

Davy and Marcus returned to the Southern Hotel, where they settled up and packed. And in less than two hours after the companions had left Hoyt Altgelder's office, they were down at the St. Louis dockside, ready to begin the Mississippi River voyage to the great port of New Orleans.

It so happened that the next steamboat bound for New Orleans was the *Great Republic*, a six-decked sidewheeler. The huge and majestic vessel had a hull which measured 335 feet, and a beam of 51 feet, with a hold depth of five and a half feet. Built at Pittsburgh in 1867, for the staggering sum of $235,000, the steamboat was one of the very largest on the Mississippi—or any other river, for that matter.

The appointments of the *Great Republic* were luxurious in the extreme, and the splendor of that floating palace rivaled that of the grand hotels of New York or Europe. "Steamboat gothic," the detailed jigsaw carpentry so popular on the vessels since the 1850s, abounded on the *Great Republic*, and the boat's cabins and passageways were elegant spaces with polished hardwood floors and furnishings worthy of the princes of Renaisance Italy.

According to custom, the boat's smokestacks were topped with vertical feathers of metal, and its wheelhouse was emblazoned with colorful paintings and intricate ornamental designs. The pilothouse woodwork was ornate, and lacy finials ran up to its ceiling; the room's delicate colors provided a contrast to the stark white of the steamboat's superstructure.

The main cabin of the *Great Republic* appeared acres long at first sight, and displayed opulent furnishings and Brussels carpet, as well as seemingly endless rows of intricately carved columns which led to arches whose graceful sweep was in stark contrast to the gleaming verticality of the many crystal chandeliers which enclosed the light of their gas lamps within finely cut globes of crystal.

Rows of stateroom doors stood at each side of the spacious main cabin, each opening out onto an individual cabin. The windows of these cabins were stained glass; and in the stern of those rooms, in the section devoted to the ladies, great mirrors stood, and gave the illusion of doubling the space.

Fine woods, such as walnut or rosewood, were used for the doors and trim of the cabins. Painting, sculpture, and upholstered furniture were to be found in the more expensive cabins, along with a private bar, a large and ornate silver water cooler, and even a grand piano.

This was true luxury, reserved traditionally for the aristocracy of the river. But in postbellum America, the aristocracy of money was respected far more than that of title and birth, and when the Kansan traded in one or two of his gold nuggets, the purser promptly escorted him and Marcus Haverstraw to the choicest of the *Great Republic's* most opulent staterooms.

Ironically, surrounded by all this richness, what the two companions did not know about the *Great Republic* was that the prohibitive cost of operating the sidewheeled behemoth was steering its owners on a sure and steady course toward the shoals of bankruptcy.

"By Gad, but the *magníficos* of Medici Florence couldn't have lorded it with any more spendor than we find here," Marcus told the Kansan.

"I never seen the like of this," Davy Watson remarked as they sat down to dinner in the main cabin and began to study the *Great Republic's* bill of fare.

The menu was extensive, consisting of a wide variety of meats, soups, and vegetables, with corn and potatoes most prominent among the latter. Also served in abundance were breads of many kinds, and pastries whose variety indicated the presence of a specialist on board. Milk and butter were missing, due to their perishability, the Kansan noticed; and wine or spirits were served with all meals, as the unfiltered drinking water was of an extremely dubious quality, coming as it did directly from the Mississippi.

The distance from St. Louis to New Orleans was

1,218 miles, and the *Great Republic* usually made the downstream voyage in three or four days. At this particular time, the entire river was a-buzz with talk about the forthcoming race between the *Natchez* and the *Robert E. Lee*.

Everyone seemed to be betting on what was shaping up to be a heroic contest between business rivals, Captain John W. Cannon of the *Lee*, and Captain Thomas P. Leathers of the *Natchez*.

While issuing vigorous denials in public (for steamboat racing was a very dangerous sport), the two skippers prepared in secret for the contest. The *Robert E. Lee* was stripped, and her captain had made provision for the boat to take on fuel from a series of coal barges strategically placed along the way. Both captains intended to burn pine knots, which were fed to the boilers along with pitch, turpentine, and sides of bacon, in order to produce a hotter fire. This was a hazardous move, as safety valves were either tied down in a race, or just ignored.

"Oh, that'll be a pip of a race," exclaimed Marcus Haverstraw, as he and the Kansan sat over coffee at the end of the sumptuous dinner served by the waiters of the *Great Republic*.

"Which one do ya like?" Davy Watson asked.

"Well, the *Natchez* is the bigger of the two, and has already set its share of records," Marcus told him. "But I think the *Lee's* got her for speed and maneuverability."

"I hear the cap'n of the *Natchez* is a real shitkicker," Davy said.

Marcus grinned. "Yes, indeed. Thomas P. Leathers is a first-class steamboat captain, and not the man to be trifled with. Why, I recall hearing that, one day when the *Natchez* was new, Tom Leathers came upon a passenger, some young fellow, who just happened to be whittling away with a big knife at the boat's railing."

"On the railing of the *Natchez?*"

"Yep. In all its glory." He signaled for the waiter to come and refill their coffee cups. "Seeing this, Captain Leathers goes down to the galley without a word, and comes back holding a big knife of his own."

He paused while the waiter refilled their cups.

"Then all of a sudden, he begins to slash away at the young man's expensive clothes.

" 'Hey! What're you doing?' cries the passenger, alarmed and outraged by this indignity. 'You're cutting my coat!'

" 'Yes, sir!' says old Tom Leathers, taking another slash for good measure. 'Yes, sir! Damn it, sir! You're cutting my boat!' "

Davy guffawed at this.

"*O Mark Four!*" a rich baritone voice called out eerily in the foggy night outside the main cabin.

"*O Mark Four!*" cried another voice, this one a sweet and melancholy tenor.

"What in the hell's that?" the Kansan asked.

"Those are the leadsmen," Marcus told him. "Black men who take the soundings—the measure of how deep the river is below the boat, at any particular point. The first man takes a weighted line, throws it over the bow, and then pulls it back, after which he takes a reading. This he promptly calls out to the second man, stationed on the Texas deck, who passes the information, in turn, to the pilothouse."

Davy nodded as the rich, eerie voices began to wail again, a few minutes later.

"*Quarter Less Three.*"

"*Quarter Less Three.*"

"Mark four means four fathoms, or twenty-four feet," Marcus said. "But I'm damned if I can remember what 'Quarter Less Three' works out to be."

"Sixteen and a half feet," volunteered a bewhiskered old gentleman who shared their table. He offered them both cigars, which Davy and Marcus gratefully accepted.

"*Half Twain,*" the first voice called out after a little while, its opposite number repeating the call a moment later.

The old gentleman introduced himself as Captain Andy Baker, a former Mississippi River pilot.

"*Mark Twain,*" was the next call, causing the Kansan to sit up in his seat and cast an inquiring look at Marcus.

"*Mark Twain,*" the second voice cried in the night.

"Well, how about that?" Davy said to the reporter.

"Sounds familiar, eh?" his friend replied. "That means a depth of two fathoms marked on the twine."

"Oh, Mark *Twine,*" Davy exclaimed, suddenly understanding the origin of Samuel L. Clemens's pen-name.

"You're thinkin' 'bout that Mark Twain fella, ain't you son?" Captain Andy asked.

"You hit it on the head, Cap'n," Davy told him.

"Well, that there young fella ain't the first to

call hisself Mark Twain," old Captain Andy told Davy and Marcus. "No sirree!"

"*Five feet!*" the voice cried suddenly.

"Oh, sweet Jesus!" exclaimed Captain Andy. "Hang onto yer hats, boys!"

Suddenly a bell was heard clanging below decks, as the pilot signaled the engine room. Then Davy heard the spumy churning of the paddlewheel, with its attendant rush of cascading water pouring off the great blades. Moments later, the *Great Republic's* timbers were shivered as the big steamboat came to a halt, its keel crunching harshly as it ground against the bottom of a shoal.

Captain Andy nervously chewed his cigar and listened to the sounds in the foggy night outside.

The Kansan listened too, and heard the smokestacks of the *Great Republic* sigh and wheeze. Then the strained churning of the paddle-wheel was heard. The boat began to tremble ever more violently, and then it suddenly leapt forward, as it freed itself.

"Close call, boys," Captain Andy told them, a solemn look on his face. "We almost run aground."

"*No-o-o-o-ooo Bottom!*" the first leadsman intoned triumphantly. "*There is No-o-o-o-ooo Bottom!*"

"*No-o-o-ooo Bottom!*" echoed the man on the Texas deck.

"Them boys sing real good," a smiling Captain Andy told Davy and Marcus, hailing a waiter at the same time. "This calls fer a drink."

"On us, Captain," Marcus told the old riverman. "In gratitude for your having the kind-ness to educate us."

"Thank you, kindly," the old man replied with a nod. "Where was I?" he muttered, biting his thumbnail. "Oh, yes. Gonna tell ya 'bout the name, Mark Twain."

"That's right," agreed Davy Watson.

"Well, the name's a river term, as you know," Captain Andy began. "But 'twas first used as a pseudonym by Cap'n Isaiah Sellers, one of the most highly regarded gentlemen ever to pilot the Mississippi.

"Cap'n Sellers passed away in 1864—he's buried in Bellefontaine Cemetery, back in St. Louis. They got 'em a real fine monument to the man up there. Well anyway, after the cap'n's passin', young Sam Clemens took the name fer his own. Did you know he used to be a pilot on the river right afore the Civil War? But it belonged to ol' Isaiah Sellers first, it did. He used 'Mark Twain' whenever he writ the river news fer the *New Orleans Picayune*."

"My friend here's gonna work for that very same paper," Davy told Captain Andy.

"Now, ain't that somethin'," the old man remarked. "Sam Clemens used to tell how Isaiah Sellers ordered his tombstone one day, and carried it with him ever after, on all his river trips, right up to the day he died."

"There exists no better teller of tall tales than Sam Clemens," commented Marcus Haverstraw.

"My pal here knows Mark Twain," Davy informed the old riverman. "They were newspapermen in Virginia City, durin' the war."

"So that's where that young scamp got to," Captain Andy said with a nod of his balding head.

The waiter came with their drinks.

"Well, here's to the glories of the river,

gentlemen," Captain Andy toasted, raising his glass aloft. "And to Old Al."

"Who in the world is Old Al?" asked Marcus Haverstraw.

"Old Al's the giant 'gator what watches over all the doin's in the Mississippi," the old skipper told them with a straight face, just before he knocked back his drink.

"To Old Al," toasted Marcus.

"To Old Al," repeated the Kansan, after the fashion of the man on the Texas deck.

"Captain, Captain, please change your mind,
Take the cotton, but leave the seeds behind."

Voices rose outside in a minor key, rich and low, as the black roustabouts on board the *Great Republic* began to sing.

"Captain, Captain, is your money come?
I jus' wants to know, 'cause
I wants to borrow some."

Again the steamboat's whistle sounded in the fog, sweet and deep and heartbreakingly sad.

Captain Andy sniffled and then wiped his red nose on a linen table napkin. "By Gad, I love this ol' river," he told Marcus and Davy in a voice that was thick with emotion.

Known as the Crescent City because it is situated on a sharp bend in the Mississippi, New Orleans sits 107 miles from the Gulf of Mexico. Founded by Jean Baptiste Le Moyne, Sieur de Bienville, in 1718, the city's present site was originally known as the "English Turn," because Bienville had met an English expedition there and forced them to turn back.

Named in honor of the Regent of France, New Orleans became the capital of French colonial Louisiana, superseding Biloxi, Mississippi. The *Vieux Carré,* or old square, was the site of the original settlement.

Due to the partition of Louisiana between Spain and England, New Orleans became the capital of Spanish Louisiana. Nearly destroyed twice by fire, in 1788 and 1794, the town was reconstructed with a definite Spanish flavor. France recovered Louisiana in 1800, and in order to thwart his archenemy, England, Napoleon Bonaparte sold it to the United States in 1803.

In 1812, when Louisiana was admitted to the Union, New Orleans became its capital. At the same time, the first steamboat reached the docks of the city, and New Orleans began its rise to prominence as the first of all Mississippi riverports. Two years later, the last battle of the War of 1812 was fought outside the Crescent City, and General Andrew Jackson's rag-tag army handed the British a crushing defeat.

Commerce boomed as river traffic increased, and the Crescent City was America's fourth largest municipality by 1840. This ushered in an era of peace and prosperity which was broken only occasionally by the floods and epidemics which ravaged that marshy section of the country.

New Orleans was a naval and military center of

considerable importance during the War Between the States, and Admiral Farragut's Union fleet took the city in April, 1862. Military rule was the order of the day until the end of the war. And then, under the corrupt carpetbag governments of the Reconstruction, there followed a period of racial and political unrest which had continued to the present day, in the spring of 1870, when the Kansan and Marcus Haverstraw stepped off the gangplank of the *Great Republic* and set foot on the docks of New Orleans.

Davy Watson looked upriver and saw the narrow banks where the Mississippi had eroded the soil of the levee, and the wide battures near the shore, where the water was shallow, the latter distinguished at points by strings on large, fifty-foot log rafts leading out from the levee.

New Orleans was a vital, bustling port, where powerfully muscled gangs of black roustabouts unloaded hogsheads of sugar, bales of cotton, barrels of pork, sacks of flour, and hundred-pound burlap bags full of aromatic coffee beans. And on other parts of the docks, the many fine products of the state of Louisiana were being loaded onto vessels.

> *"When the butcher went around to collect his bills,*
> *He took a brace of dogs and a double-barreled gun."*

The little black boys who seemed to be everywhere on the levees and docks chanted that popular jingle, and the hackmen yelled loudly as

184

the travelers disembarked from the *Great Republic*. The bells of pack mules, the clatter and racket of horse carts, the thunder of drays, the bass wail of boat horns and the soprano shriek of steamboat whistles contributed to the symphony of sounds which arose from the sprawling riverfront.

Since the Crescent City was a seaport as well as a riverport, evidences of marine activity were everywhere to be found.

Sailors from every nautical nation could be seen issuing from, or crowding into, grog shops and sailors' boarding houses; warehouses redolent of pitch and tar, salt-saturated garments and tobacco, stood like temples by the docks, piled high with jute, junk and all manner of sea-going gear; "one-piece stores" or slop-shops full of pea coats, seal-skin overalls, sou'wester hats and guernseys were also prominent on the riverfront.

Huge in length, the unpaved thoroughfare of the levee was the terminus for no less than 150 streets; and the port, housing great numbers of canvas sheds, depots and warehouses, berthed a variety of vessels which ranged from ocean steamers, brigantines and three-masted sailing ships to hundreds of the uniquely American Mississippi steamboats.

Davy Watson and Marcus Haverstraw boarded a hackney cab and left the teeming dockside. The horse-drawn vehicle proceeded along Canal Street, which was the social and business center of New Orleans. The Kansan was impressed by the width of the open boulevard, by its masses of nondescript architecture, by the crowded trolley cars, and the clouds of dust and hazy sky above the crowds which roamed Canal Street's arcades at a leisurely pace.

Marcus pointed out the various types who made their way along the thoroughfare. Commercial travelers, stevedores, country folk and Cajuns, sailors on a spree, jockeys, touts and bookmakers, as well as men of means on their way to enjoy an afternoon at the Pickwick or Boston clubs.

"Go down here," Marcus told the driver after a while, and the hackney entered the *Vieux Carré*, the old French Quarter of New Orleans. The reporter told the Kansan about the Creoles, who were recognized as either (there was some confusion) native-born New Orleaneans of white, Negro, or mixed blood, or just those white persons who had descended from the original French or Spanish settlers.

"And now, turn down Royal Street," Marcus directed. Then they made their way through the colorful and picturesque district until the hackney came to the house of Della Casson.

"Hallelujah," sighed the newspaperman, paying the driver while the Kansan stepped down onto the sidewalk. "I hope my angel is home," he said to Davy Watson, as the two men walked up the path which led to the front door.

"Yes, suh?" asked a pretty little mulatto maid, opening the door only moments after Marcus had released the brass door knocker.

"I've come to pay a call on Miss Casson," he told the maid. "My name is Marcus P. Haverstraw."

The maid invited them into the foyer, and then disappeared inside the house.

Moments later, as they were talking, Marcus stopped suddenly, going wide-eyed as he looked past the Kansan. And when Davy Watson turned around as well, he caught his breath.

Coming into the room, supple and graceful as a big cat, was Della Casson. The tall black beauty wore a low-cut dress of purple satin and a string of pearls around her neck, both of which colors were contrasted to good advantage against her smooth, chocolate-dusted-with-cinnamon-colored skin.

"The ravishing and radiant Della," Marcus called out after having cleared his throat nervously.

"Well, I declare," the black beauty said in her rich, drawling voice. "Providence has seen fit to bless me with the company of the two men I most enjoy in the entire world."

"Howdy, Della," the Kansan said in a husky voice. "It's good to see ya again."

She smiled incandescently and stared at Davy Watson through her dark, gazelle's eyes. Then Della held out her long, graceful hands and began to walk toward him. Her hair was done in the same manner as when the Kansan had last seen her in San Francisco, in oiled Greek curls, which showed off the fine planes of her long, oval face to perfect advantage. And when Davy looked at her long-legged, full-bodied figure, with its cinched and tiny waist, he caught his breath once more.

"Well, cowboy," Della Casson murmured, her full red lips parting in a smile, "you're one of the last persons I ever expected to see again."

They embraced, and he kissed her lightly on the cheek. And as she drew back, she gave him a searching look.

"Where you been, sugah?" Della asked him.

"You wouldn't believe it," volunteered Marcus Haverstraw. "Since he left San Francisco, he and Soaring Hawk have had enough adventures to fill several books."

Davy nodded. "You know a fella name of Gaston Thibaudaux?" he asked.

The black courtesan's eyes widened in surprise. "Do I know him?" she murmured. "Why, child, the man was my lover. . .before I met Bertram Brown."

Marcus Haverstraw winced at the mention of the first man he had ever shot. Then he and the Kansan exchanged uncomfortable glances. Della had taken one of Bertram Brown's bullets in order to save the Kansan's life.

"You miss Brown much?" Davy whispered.

The lovely black woman smiled. "Not so much any more," she told Davy, her eyes on the face of Marcus Haverstraw all the while. "I'm pretty much over it, now."

"Ah, how's your mother?" Marcus asked in a voice that was much too loud.

Della's smile grew brighter, its warmth palpably filling the room.

"Momma recovered almost as soon as I got to New Orleans," Della told him. "She's fine, thank you."

The reporter cleared his throat again. "I've come to take a job on the *Picayune*, Della. So I, uh. . .can be. . .near you." He flashed her a creaky smile.

Davy Watson was grinning as the Louisiana courtesan put her arms around the newspaperman's neck and said, "That's good, sugah. 'Cause I missed you a whole lot."

" 'Oh, 'twere paradise, enow,' " groaned Marcus Haverstraw, goggle-eyed as Della Casson leaned forward and kissed him on the cheek.

"Come again?" the Kansan asked.

"Oh, that's a line from a Persian poem. *The Rubaiyat,* written by a gentleman long dead, whose name was Omar Khayyam. It extolls worldly pleasures and—"

"Recite some more of it, Marcus," the black beauty urged in a sultry voice, her arms still around the reporter's neck.

Marcus cleared his throat for the third time. Then he looked Della Casson right in the eye, and began to declaim passionately.

" *'Come fill the cup, and in the fire*
of Spring,
Your Winter-garment of Repentance fling;
The Bird of Time has but a little way
To flutter—and the bird is on the wing.' "

"That's very hedonistic," murmured Della, lowering her eyes as she smiled enticingly at Marcus Haverstraw.

"Here comes the line I referred to before," he told her. "The word, 'enow' means enough." He began to declaim again.

" *'A book of Verses underneath the Bough,*
A Jug of Wine, a Loaf of Bread—and Thou
Beside me, singing in the Wilderness.
Oh, Wilderness were Paradise enow!' "

189

"Oh, I love it when you recite poetry," the Louisiana beauty purred.

Davy heard Marcus chuckling softly and happily beside him.

"Davy, sugah," Della drawled. "Now what was it you were about to ask me concerning Gaston Thibaudaux?"

"What's he up to these days?"

"Well, he's got lots of money," she told the Kansan, "but is always looking to make more. It's a great talent of Gaston's. Right now, he's got a deluxe bordello right here on Royal Street, which he's stocking with extremely beautiful women —'thoroughbreds,' as he calls them." She lowered her eyes. "He wanted me to be his madam."

"Well, someone named John Hartung's out to sell Deanna MacPartland to this here Creole fella," Davy told Della, shooting her a grim look.

"The woman you *love?*" she asked incredulously.

The Kansan nodded. "Yep. The one I told you 'bout in San Francisco."

"I declare," she muttered, shaking her head sadly. "That's awful. But there *is* something I can do for you, Davy."

"You'll put us in touch with Thibaudaux?" Marcus asked hopefully.

Della Casson smiled her incandescent smile. "Come inside with me. He's here at my *soirée.*" She stepped between the two men, and hooked her arms into theirs. "Come along, gentlemen."

They went inside, and Davy admired the opulence of the house, with its elegant furnishings and Persian carpets. In a great room, many people in gowns and evening clothes were gathered, the cream of New Orleans sporting society, Della told her two surprise guests. And she proceeded to identify well-to-do sportsmen, gamblers, financiers, merchant princes, and the mistresses of those men, who were all very beautiful mulatto or black women.

After a brief round of introductions, and an obligatory display of concern for her many guests, Della took Davy and Marcus over to meet the man whom they sought, Gaston Thibaudaux.

He was tall and slender, a man well into his fifties, physically well-preserved despite the dark circles under his eyes and other minor, but tell-tale, signs of dissipation. He had white, wavy hair and a small, trimmed mustache. Both Marcus and the Kansan realized that here was a man who had seen and done much in his lifetime.

Immediately after the introductions had been made, Della began to delicately broach the subject which was uppermost in the Kansan's mind.

"Gaston, my friend, Mr. Watson is rather curious about your current business endeavor."

"Yes?" Thibaudaux inquired politely. "In what way, sir?"

"I take it that you happen to be doin' some. . .negotiatin'," the Kansan began haltingly, "with a fella name of John Hartung? Now, is that right, sir?"

Gaston Thibaudaux nodded. "That is correct, sir."

"Is he askin' a lot of money?"

The Creole raised an eyebrow at this.

"You pay this Hartung anythin' yet?" persisted Davy.

"That is hardly your affair, sir," the New Orleanean told him coldly, darting a glance of annoyance at Della Casson.

"Well, save yer money, Mister Thibaudaux," the Kansan warned. " 'Cause there ain't gonna be no sale tomorrow."

"Monsieur presumes to give advice where his opinion has not been solicited," Thibaudaux shot back angrily.

"I ain't presumin', friend," Davy told him. "Deanna MacPartland ain't his to sell nor yours to buy."

By now, the two men were glaring at each other.

"You can't do that in the United States," warned Marcus Haverstraw. "That's white slavery!"

Thibaudaux recoiled at this, and turned to Della Casson. "*Qu'est-ce que c'est?*" he asked angrily. "What is this, Della? Am I being set-up for blackmail?"

"*Pas du tout, mon cher Gaston,*" the black beauty reassured him. "The young woman in question is betrothed to Mister Watson. She was duped by John Hartung—or so we believe—into accompanying him to New Orleans. And when Mister Watson attempted to recover her in St. Louis, Hartung's partner made an attempt upon his life."

"This is so, *vraiment?*" the Creole asked, turning to Davy Watson.

"It's the God's honest truth, Mr. Thibaudaux," Davy answered, looking him right in the eye. "An'

I aim to settle Hartung's hash tomorrow, an' then take Deanna back to Kansas with me."

The Creole entrepreneur looked thoughtful. "I did not know this. Hartung told me nothing."

"Where's he stayin', Mr. Thibaudaux?" Davy asked. " 'Cause when he gits up tomorrow, I want to be waitin' fer 'im."

Thibaudaux looked over to Della. "Perhaps we can settle this in a peaceable fashion?"

Della Casson turned to Davy Watson, as did both Marcus Haverstraw and Gaston Thibaudaux a moment later.

The Kansan's face looked as hard as granite. He shook his head. "It's too late fer that, now."

Thibaudaux made a Gallic gesture. "I do not wish to be a party to any violence."

"Fair enough," Davy told him. "Now, where's John Hartung stayin'?"

"At the Hotel Magnolia," was the Creole's reply. "On Canal Street."

"And Gaston," Della Casson said in Creole French, as she and the two men took their leave of Thibaudaux, "the last man who tried to double-cross these gentlemen now reposes in Bellefontaine Cemetery."

That night, after all the guests had gone, Davy and Marcus dined alone with Della Casson, eating with knives and forks of sterling silver and drinking wine out of crystal goblets. And at eleven o'clock the Kansan bade his friends good night, and followed the little mulatto maid to his room.

As Marcus Haverstraw poured himself another

glass of port wine, Della Casson playfully tossed him a small roll from the breadbasket.

"A loaf of bread, a jug of wine," she purred in her rich, musical voice, "and thou, sugah."

"Would you, ah, like another glass of port?" he asked.

"Yes," she murmured, "if you'll deliver it to my room."

His eyes met hers. "Of all the possible places to deliver it, you could have chosen none more to my liking."

"*T'es très gallant, mon cher Marcus*," she told him, praising the reporter's gallantry in French.

"*Moi, je suis ravi par ta beauté, ta grâce, mon ange*," Marcus declared passionately in the same language, praising Della in turn.

"*Viens avec moi*," she whispered, rising from her seat and beckoning for him to accompany her.

"*Avec grand plaisir*," the newspaperman replied eagerly, picking up the two glasses of port which he had just poured, as Della took a candelabra from the table and began to lead the way to her boudoir.

"I consider this a great honor," Marcus told her in a husky whisper.

The courtesan turned and smiled warmly at the reporter, taking his hand at the same time. "I missed you very much after I left San Francisco, Marcus," she confessed. "I would like to get to know you better. . .in every way."

Marcus Haverstraw cleared his throat as Della Casson opened the door to her bedroom. "Amen to that," he said. Then he followed Della inside, and once he had set the candelabra down on her night table, the reporter caught sight of her large, canopied bed.

194

" *'And I will make thee beds of roses,'* " he recited, " *'and a thousand fragrant posies.'* "

"Sit down there," she told him, pointing to the edge of the bed. And as Marcus did, the lovely black woman began to undress for him with such finesse and suggestiveness that she turned the simple act of disrobing into a performance of great skill and complexity.

"God, but you're beautiful," he whispered hoarsely as she stood naked before him.

The candlelight gleamed where it was reflected on her smooth, dark skin, and her tall, lithe form inflamed Marcus with desire. Della's waist was tiny, and it exaggerated the full swell of both her hips and bosom.

Her breasts were works of art, round and incredibly firm to the touch, he discovered as she came up to him and began to run her fingers through his hair; they were full, and had large black areolae and thick nipples. Then the scent of her perfume mingled with the scent of her arousal, as Marcus's kisses traveled down between her breasts and south of her small belly.

At the same time, he ran his hands lightly up and down the insides of the black beauty's thighs. Della started to moan as Marcus began to caress the prominent outer lips of her pussy and run his fingers through the thick and tight curls of the black fleece which covered her fleshy mount of Venus. "Oh, stand up, sugah," she whispered in a voice that shook with passion. "So I can undress you."

Marcus did as she said, and let the naked beauty undress him.

When they were both naked, Marcus put his

hands on Della Casson's beautiful breasts and gently squeezed them, marveling at their firmness and resiliency. Then he lowered his head and began to kiss and lick her nipples and areolae. And at the same time, her long fingers encircled his stiff and throbbing pole.

Sucking on her nipples, Marcus reached down his right hand and caressed the hollow of Della's thighs and her pouting lips. A moment later his thick middle finger entered her with a squish. Della gasped at this, and began to moan as he stirred up her juices.

After having withdrawn his finger, Marcus led his love over to the big bed and made her lie down. Then he proceeded to cover the front of her body with kisses. And after exploring that beautiful body from head to toe several times, his questing mouth found its way back to the dark grotto of delight between her thighs, and he began to work on her in earnest.

"Oh God, sugah!" Della moaned a few moments later, as her body began to stiffen and quiver. Then she bucked and heaved as spasm after spasm of a powerful multiple orgasm wracked her body.

"Oh, God!" she cried out into the darkness. "Oh, God!"

When it was over, and she had recuperated from the intense ecstatic experience, Della told Marcus to come inside her. This he did without any further urging on her part, groaning with delight as he felt the clutch of the black courtesan's sopping, musky pussy. And that sweet, snug hole seemed to have a life of its own, as it did things to his cock which

Marcus Haverstraw had never experienced before.

"Oh, my stars!" he exclaimed, feeling a sudden explosion deep in the pit of his groin and seeing fireworks in the darkness at the back of his brain. And then, as he came, the reporter moaned long and loud with the voice of a stud bull expelling its abundant semen into the vagina of a receptive cow.

When their lovemaking was over, and after Marcus's flaccid member had slid out of Della's sheath, they held each other, exchanging tender kisses and gentle hugs. And within five minutes' time, Marcus Haverstraw and Della Casson had fallen asleep in each other's arms.

The dining room of the Magnolia Hotel was a big, well-appointed place, and it was already crowded when John Hartung and Deanna MacPartland arrived for breakfast.

Judas Priest, the Kansan exclaimed in his thoughts, his eyes widening in recognition and his heart opening spontaneously as the woman he loved entered the room. *She's even more beautiful than I remembered.*

He wanted to jump up and run to her, to call out her name and sweep her up in his arms, but he knew that he could not, for Deanna's safety was his prime concern. And John Hartung, Davy Watson had learned, was a dangerous and deadly man, one whom he dared not underestimate.

Hartung himself was a big surprise to the Kansan, for the man's physical appearance was not at all what he had imagined. In his thoughts, Davy had conjured up the image of a big, broadshouldered man with great physical strength and the quick easy movements of a cat: someone much like the late Bart Braden, the Texas ramrod who had once gunned him down. But that was merely a product of the Kansan's imagination; and as truth is, as a rule, stranger than fiction, the truth of John Hartung's physical appearance was far stranger than Davy Watson's imaginings of it.

So that's what the sum'bitch looks like, Davy told himself, shaking his head in surprise as he watched Hartung and Deanna seat themselves at a table across the room.

Davy sat and waited as the couple ordered breakfast, casually sipping his coffee, but watching them like a hawk all the while, observing in its minutest detail the way in which Deanna MacPartland reacted to John Hartung, the man who had taken her from him. Instead of the square-jawed, steely-eyed desperado whom the Kansan had envisioned, the real John Hartung looked more like an accountant or a bank clerk than anything else. The man was slight of build, of no more than medium height, had thinning blond hair and a wispy little mustache, and looked about as dangerous as a glass of buttermilk.

Further, what was immensely gratifying, the Kansan soon realized after observing the behavior of his beloved for a time, was the fact that Deanna displayed absolutely none of her characteristic warmth and sweetness toward her "benefactor." In fact, the little blonde's coolness and reserve bordered on downright aversion, and Davy Watson knew for certain now that Deanna MacPartland did not leave Hawkins Fork for love of John Hartung. No there was another reason . . .and the Kansan would soon discover just what it was.

His chance came in a few minutes, when the old couple at a table adjoining Hartung's got up to leave. Making certain that he was not observed by his prey, Davy Watson made his roundabout way over to the newly vacated table. Pausing only to stuff a five-dollar bill into the hand of the surprised waiter who had come to clear the table, the Kansan slid noiselessly into a seat which was directly behind the man whom he had identified as John Hartung.

At that point, Deanna looked up from her plate. And when she looked past John Hartung, as was her custom, she caught sight of Davy Watson. Suddenly her mouth hung open and her eyes went wide; and an instant later, all the color had disappeared from her face.

Less than three feet behind John Hartung, the Kansan raised a finger to his lips and signaled for Deanna to be silent. Then, as she sat back in her chair, breathing heavily, her eyes never once leaving his face, Davy Watson silently mouthed the words which rose up from within his heart like an eagle taking flight into the eye of the sun.

I love you.

At this moment, John Hartung looked up from his ham and eggs.

"What's the matter?" he asked the pale and trembling Deanna. "You look like you've seen a ghost."

"She has, Hartung," the Kansan growled, leaning over and whispering into the man's ear.

"The ghost of the man you tried to have killed at Dawson's warehouse."

A sharp clatter punctuated Davy's chilling remarks, as John Hartung's knife and fork dropped from nerveless fingers and fell onto his plate.

Then, as Hartung sat bolt upright in his chair, trembling and in shock, the Kansan's eyes met those of his beloved.

"Why did you leave Hawkins Fork with this man, Deanna?" he asked gently, in a low voice that shook with suppressed emotion.

It was several moments before the girl could compose herself sufficiently to reply.

"They told me you were dead," she whispered finally. "John and Lucretia Eaton. They brought a man to see me, a man who said he had been on the trail with you and Soaring Hawk, and he told me that you'd both been killed in Texas."

Davy glared at the back of John Hartung's neck. The man still did not move a muscle.

"You let Lucretia Eaton read my letters, Deanna?" he asked softly.

She nodded. "I shared them with her, and all the girls."

The Kansan nodded back at her. "It's all right, honey. I'm alive, an' I'm back, now. By the grace of God."

"I reckon I owe you'n Lucretia Eaton some," he growled meanacingly in the frail-looking little man's ear. "I already done settled up with that boy, Warren, an' yer partner, Hoyt Altgelder."

"What do you propose to do, Mr. Watson?" croaked a frightened John Hartung.

"I ought to take you out back, an' shoot you like a dog, you sum'bitch," the Kansan growled fiercely. " 'Cause a stinkin' rattlesnake like you don't deserve no better'n that!"

"Oh no, David Lee," Deanna whispered in a voice that shook with emotion. "Don't kill him—please! Don't kill him. He saved my life once. . .and I'll never forget that."

Davy's voice shook as well, when he spoke again. "By gad, you're one lucky hombre, Hartung. 'Cause if'n Deanna hadn't've said that, I'd have taken you out back in jig-time an' put a bullet 'twixt yer eyes."

John Hartung shuddered.

"As it is," Davy Watson went on, "here's what I want you to do: I want you to git word to Lucretia Eaton, pronto—an' tell 'er to hightail it out'n Kansas afore I ride 'crosst the state line."

Pale and trembling, Hartung turned in his seat and beheld the Kansan for the first time.

"An' you," Davy said in a voice harder than the lead in his bullets. "I ain't gonna be satisfied 'til you're west of the Rockies, Hartung." His eyes narrowed and his nostrils flared as the Kansan looked the frightened man right in the eye. "An' if'n I ever hear you come east of 'em—no matter where or when—I'm gonna hunt you down an' finish off what I should've done today."

"Anything you say," John Hartung whispered in a feeble voice.

"We're gonna leave now, Hartung," Davy informed him. "An' I don't ever want to hear of you again. So you know what to do."

Breathing heavily, the man nodded as Davy and

Deanna got to their feet.

"Le's go, honey," the Kansan told his love, offering her his arm. "We got us a long trip back to Kansas."

Then they turned and walked away, leaving John Hartung alone at the table. The man sat watching them like a hawk, the color returning to his cheeks as he regained his composure. And just before Davy Watson and Deanna MacPartland had left the dining room of the Hotel Magnolia, John Hartung nodded his head. And as he did, two men suddenly rose from their seats at a table across the room.

One of the men was tall and powerfully built, with dark hair and a full beard. The other was short and wiry, with yellow mutton-chop whiskers and wall eyes.

The two men followed Davy and Deanna out into the street, while John Hartung picked up his cup and slowly sipped his cold coffee.

Out on the sidewalk, just as the Kansan stepped away from Deanna, intending to hail a passing hackney cab, the two men converged upon him from behind, crowding in on him as they drew stilettos from within their frock coats.

"Oh, no you don't!" growled Marcus Haverstraw, who had suddenly materialized behind John Hartung's two hired killers. Then, as the Kansan spun around, his hair-trigger reflexes activated by Marcus's warning cry, the newspaperman brought the butt of his big Smith and Wesson .44 down hard upon the base of the wall-eyed man's skull, sending the assassin unconscious to the sidewalk.

Quick as a cat, the big, bearded man spun

around, slashing with his knife as he did.

Marcus Haverstraw cried out in pain and dropped his pistol to the ground, stepping back as he clutched his right forearm.

Then the bearded man spun around again, and lunged at Davy Watson. But the Kansan was ready for him this time, and, whipping out his derringer, Davy proceeded to slam it down on the big man's knife hand in a continuation of that same motion.

Hartung's man grunted in pain and dropped his knife. But he was swifter and stronger than Davy had thought, and he reached out and grabbed his wrist, twisting it until the Kansan was forced to drop the derringer. And then, an instant later, the big man clubbed Davy to the ground with a vicious overhand right.

Seeing this, Marcus Haverstraw lowered his head and charged, hoping to catch the man in the midsection with his shoulder and knock the wind out of him. But the assassin moved quickly again, and planted a kick in the reporter's own midsection, causing him to double up and drop to his knees, retching and gasping for breath.

The man turned back to Davy Watson, his big hands balled into fists, expecting to see his victim lying prostrate upon the street in front of the Hotel Magnolia. But the Kansan was up and moving, with a speed which was fully the equal of his huge assailant's. Davy threw himself at the man, his shoulder catching him in the belly. The man gunted like a poled ox as they both went down, rolling off the sidewalk and into the busy street.

At the same time, John Hartung suddenly rushed out of the hotel and grabbed Deanna Mac-

Partland by the wrist, roughly dragging her over to a sleek new carriage which stood outside the Magnolia.

"Get us out of here fast, Jean-Pierre," he cried to the black driver, "and I'll give you a hundred-dollar gold piece!"

"Yassuh!" the man grunted, flicking the reins sharply once Hartung and Deanna were inside the carriage. The horse whinnied and took off like a shot, leaving a small cloud of dust in its wake.

"*Davy!*" screamed Deanna as the carriage moved out into the heavy flow of horse-drawn traffic. "*Davy!*"

Her screams pierced the Kansan to the heart, but he was powerless to come to Deanna's aid, for the big man was on top of him now, his ham-hands around Davy's windpipe as he proceeded to throttle the life out of him. The killer's knees were on his chest, effectively pinning the Kansan's arms down; and heave and thrash as he would, Davy Watson could not shake the huge man off. He fought desperately to breathe, his eyes bulging out of his head, his vision going dim.

Thunk! was the sound created by the contact of the toe of Marcus Haverstraw's boot with the side of the big man's head, as the reporter lashed out and kicked with all his strength. The assassin emitted a long, bass moan as he stiffened and then fell backward off Davy Watson, hitting the ground like a felled tree, already unconscious by the time he had landed on his broad back.

"That bastard cut me!" cried Marcus, he helped the dazed and gasping Kansan to his feet.

Davy shook his head when he saw the blood running down the reporter's arm.

"C'mon," he grunted, pulling Marcus out into the traffic with him.

A moment later he jumped into the path of the first hackney cab to come by.

" 'Scuse me, but I need this cab real bad," he said, yanking a fat young man out of the hackney, then climbing in and dragging the wounded Marcus Haverstraw after him.

"Follow that carriage—the one drawn by that chestnut horse up there!" he cried out to the driver, leaning forward and pointing into the distance, where John Hartung's departing carriage was little more than a rapidly diminishing flyspeck, a dot on the upper end of Canal Street. Then, before the hackman could protest, the Kansan pressed a gold nugget into his hand.

"*Sacré bleu*!" exclaimed the driver, once he saw what Davy Watson had handed him. "If dat cab, she can be catch," he told Davy in his Louisiana accent, tightening his grip on the reins as he did, "den Marcel Lacouste is de man to catch 'er!"

Off they flew in a cloud of dust, the hackman's Creole French cries spurring on his horse, as he deftly maneuvered his way through the heavy flow of morning traffic on Canal Street.

Davy turned to Marcus, pulled the handkerchief out of the reporter's breast pocket, and used it to bind up his wounded forearm.

"That's another time you saved my life, ol' hoss," Davy told him. "I owe you a lot, Marcus."

"The only thing I want right now isn't in your power to give, Davy," the newspaperman moaned.

"Peace and quiet. What are you going to do when we catch up with Hartung?" he asked anxiously.

"Once't I git Deanna out'n that viper's clutches," the Kansan told him through clenched teeth as he stood up and scanned the traffic ahead, "I'm gonna blow that sum'bitch's brains out—an' that's a promise!"

Davy saw Hartung's cab take a sharp, sudden turn off Canal Street. "Watch 'em!" he called out to the driver.

"I see dem, monsieur," the hackman told him. "*Je vous assure*. I no lose dem."

"Where d'ya s'pose they're goin'?" Davy asked a short while later, as their cab made the same wheeling turn.

"Look like dey go down to dock," the driver called out over his shoulder. "Dat what I t'ink."

"Well, keep after 'em!" Davy shot back.

"Oh, Judas Priest!" the Kansan groaned in dismay as the cab thundered onto the levee, looking around at the confusing jumbling of sheds, warehouses and other buildings. "We'll never find 'em now!"

"*Non, non, non!*" the driver called back emphatically, pointing down at the muddy soil of the levee. "I know de track of dat cab by now. She not get away, m'sieu."

And find it they did, after long minutes spent in the search.

"There it is, by gad!" the Kansan cried, suddenly vaulting out of the cab and sprinting toward the dock at whose entrance the abandoned carriage stood. Suddenly a boat horn sounded nearby, drowning out the rest of Davy Watson's words.

"Well done, *mon ami*!" said Marcus Haverstraw, praising the driver as he clambered out of the hackney.

"Dere ain't no cab be in New Orleans today what can get away from Marcel Lacouste," the black man proudly told him, as Marcus ran off after the Kansan.

The building at the near end of the dock was a customs shed, and the agent on duty there sat counting a wad of greenbacks as Davy Watson burst into it.

"What's goin' on here?" the man asked, jumping to his feet and hastily pocketing the money.

The Kansan came up to him, pausing to catch his breath. "You see a skinny li'l gent an' a purty blonde woman come this way, mister?" Davy asked as soon as he was able to speak.

The man shook his head. "Ain't nobody come through here recently," he told Davy, avoiding his eyes.

Just then, the boat horn sounded another blast.

"Git out my way," the Kansan told him quietly, moving forward as he did.

The man stood up straight and held out his arms. "Mister, they ain't nobody allowed onto that there pier at this time. Now, I'm a duly constituted Fed'ral official, so whyn't you just take my word for it. This here place is closed."

Then, as the boat horn sounded a third time, Davy hit the man with a right cross and dashed out before the agent (who had bounced off the wall) hit the floor.

Marcus Haverstraw burst into the shed and jumped over the body of the fallen man, as he

207

followed Davy Watson out onto the pier.

By the time that the Kansan had reached the end of the pier, the steamship's gangplank was up and the vessel was already a good distance away from the pier.

"*Stop this ship*!" he called out in desperation. "*Somebody up there tell the Captain to stop the ship—it's a matter of life and death*!" But the only two people on board who understood what the Kansan was screaming about were not about to lift a hand to help him.

John Hartung would not, as he stared down at Davy Watson from the afterdeck of the ocean-going vessel, standing in the shadows cast by the superstructure. The man smiled a vindictive smile of triumph as the big ship pulled away from the pier and the Kansan's voice was lost in the wind.

And Deanna MacPartland could not, as she watched the dwindling form of the man she loved, tears flowing from her prairie flower-blue eyes. She wanted to call out, to tell the Kansan that she would *always* love him. . .but John Hartung's hand was over her mouth, and it prevented her from doing so.

There were tears in the Kansan's eyes as well, as he watched the ship leave the port of New Orleans, tears of rage and frustration as he stood there on the dock, powerless to save the woman he loved, the woman for whom he had crossed a continent. And no words existed in all the languages of man, languages living or dead, to express the pain and sorrow of his loss.

the end